BEAR IN THE WOODS

BEAR
IN THE
WOODS

Robin DUVAL

Matador
5 Weir Road
Kibworth Beauchamp
Leicester LE8 0LQ, UK
Tel: (+44) 116 279 2299
Email: books@troubador.co.uk
Web: www.troubador.co.uk/matador

ISBN 978-1848763-449

A Cataloguing-in-Publication (CIP) catalogue record for this book
is available from the British Library.

Matador is an imprint of Troubador Publishing Ltd

to The Recorder Group

ONE

Chapter 1

Lay off, baby. Not now.

He was having real difficulty concentrating on the service. He could not fault the vicar who was bright and evangelical, and very hard-working. She had opened proceedings by announcing that this would be a time for tears and for laughter, which he thought promising. But the family's choice of hymns so far was from an earnestly modern volume called *The Gold Book*, and he'd recognized none of the tunes; and neither evidently had most of the congregation. He suspected that most were less familiar with the inside of a church than he was. He looked around. The largest single element was a group of middle-aged men, all wearing tiny round badges in their lapels. Probably members of Guy's local Rotary Club...

Are you sure?
Damn sure.

As the vicar embarked on her sermon, his thoughts drifted away again to that evening with Zelma and he wondered – not for the first time – where he had gone wrong. Was it a case of female propriety (the first date; the time of the month) or simply that his approaches were unwelcome? *Could* he have handled it more successfully?

The mortification rose again like dyspepsia and he tried to focus his attention on the Reverend Nicholls. Her faith, after all, was striking. Sometimes at funeral services the minister devoted the sermon to an encomium of the late departed. Not so on this occasion. Taking as her text Saint Paul's First Epistle to the Thessalonians

> For the Lord himself shall descend from
> heaven with a shout, with the voice of the
> archangel, and with the trump of God:
> and the dead in Christ shall rise first

the vicar's purpose was to persuade those of the congregation present who were not believers that death was a cause for great rejoicing not sorrow. Guy had not been a regular church-goer but was someone who, in the vicar's delicate phrase, "believed, however imperfectly" in the life hereafter. He was, she explained, even now "tangoing with Jesus".

Bryn thought he must have misheard. But no, Guy – she insisted – was "alive and kicking in Heaven" while surrounding angels were preparing to bear him back to earth to the sound of trumpets. This would be his old friend Guy then, the rational and pragmatic senior civil servant, descant recorder player and Reform Club and MCC member. That'd be the day…

Surely he could not have mistaken the signs? They had seemed to get on so well. Dinner at Marinello's in one of those dark private alcoves in the corner. Quite a lot of wine. A blossoming conviction that she really liked him, and no debate at all when he offered to take her back to her hotel in a taxi.

Even so, he had been prepared to believe when he deposited her that – for the moment – that was the end of it. But then:

Hey, how about a nightcap? Help me beat up the minibar?

As they rose alone together in the lift, he embraced her and she did not object. There was a more clumsy moment in the room when he intercepted her with two Courvoisier miniatures in her hands and they subsided onto the bed. She slipped a hand round the back of his head. There was a melting together. But when he started to move from the kisses and entwinement to the foothills of more serious business –

Lay off, baby. Not now...

At last: a hymn he could recognize.
> Lord of all Hopefulness, Lord of all Joy...
> Your hands swift to welcome,
> Your arms to embrace.

If only. The congregation rallied, and for the first time the vicar's amplified voice no longer dominated proceedings. The soaring cadences of the great old-fashioned tune engaged them like nothing previously and a new spirit of optimism seeped through the building.
> Be there at our sleeping
> and give us we pray,
> Your peace in our hearts, Lord,
> at the end of the day.

And now it was time for the recorder group. This was, in no fashion, a moment they had looked forward to. But Guy had asked for it a few days before he died. He wanted them to play their signature piece at the end of the service, the one they always did as an encore on the infrequent occasions when they performed to an audience. He had even made them promise to carry on as a quartet after his death.

The group was a central part of all their lives. It had started more than twenty years previously when the two eldest, Guy and Marshall, were singing together in the local Choral Society. They had discovered that both played the recorder and decided to look around for others to make up a larger group. Through the usual social networks, over a period of eighteen months or so, the others joined: Bill, Graeme and finally Bryn. Bryn was younger than the others and had joined the group fresh out of university. His unique appeal was that he was prepared to play the tenor recorder, the one essential instrument missing from their ensemble.

They were not so bad as musicians. For twenty years they had met monthly and practised their small repertoire of pieces, often for an hour or more before the evening disintegrated into gossip, wine and a meal together. Some were better musicians than others. Guy had perfect pitch, could have played clarinet professionally, and enforced such technical discipline as they had. Very occasionally, they put on a performance – in a local church, at a friend's wedding, or just for their wives and children.

But for the main part, the function of the group was social. A boys' evening like any other. Driven mostly by force of habit and affection. Over the years, it had become a forum for discussing individual problems, for mutual support and therapy. By contrast to their busy, sometimes high-flying, professional lives, the monthly gathering was as cosily suburban as a book group.

They had always said that, when the first one died, the group would split up. What they had not expected was that a death would happen so soon. Though Guy was the oldest, he had been as fit as any of them, an energetic gardener and a long-distance walker. Then one evening, as they sat and compared their various minor ailments together, he complained of a combination of back-ache and indigestion which he had been unable to shake off.

This hardly compared with the kidney stones that had toppled Bill groaning to the floor one evening ten years ago, still less the triple heart by-pass Marshall had undergone more recently. But within six weeks, Guy was dead from pancreatic cancer. It was a great shock to them all, not least because they had always felt that there were more obvious candidates, like Graeme with his hazardous life-style, or Marshall who everyone agreed still worked too hard.

So there was no question of winding up the group. Its continuation would be a memorial to Guy and a tribute to their enduring friendship. That was why also they had to play out the funeral today.

They formed a half circle of chairs facing the congregation, erected their flimsy metal music stands, and played their signature tune in the arrangement specially made for the five (now four) recorders by a local music teacher. After the formalities of all that had preceded them, it seemed to catch at last the essence of Guy: sociable, full of charm, light of foot, easy-going, affectionate, taking nothing too seriously.

They played it as well as they had ever played it, with the missing second descant recorder successfully covered by the other parts. For once in their lives, now that Guy was not able to make an issue of it, they did not overblow nor stray in pitch. The jaunty marching rhythms of the unforgettable little tune rose and fell. They had worried that members of the congregation who did not know the background might find the choice of music trivial, offensive even. Possibly a few did. But that was not their concern. This was what Guy had wanted. Perhaps the vicar was right after all, and maybe he was up there with the trumpeting angels, singing along with the missing words:

> If you go down to the woods today
> You're sure of a big surprise.
> If you go down to the woods today
> You'd better go in disguise…

Four black-clad undertaker's men advanced up the aisle to the coffin and hoisted it on their shoulders. As they processed back down the church, the family followed in twos: Guy's widow and their son and daughters, various elderly relatives and in-laws and finally, at the back, his grand-daughter – in tears and tenderly supported by her teenage boy-friend.

At the post-funeral reception, the four remaining members of the Ealing Recorder Consort stood together in a corner of Guy's sitting room, enjoying for the last time his generous hospitality, and modestly accepting the passing compliments of the other guests.

"Who would have thought it?" said Graeme.

"Thirty years of medicals at the public's expense, and then something they don't test for," said Bill the economist, who worked for the private sector, gazing into his empty glass.

"Seize the day," said Marshall the lawyer, brutally. "Do it now. You could be dead before they put you in prison."

They contemplated this for a while. The same reflection was in each of their minds. Guy, who had never been in hospital in his life, or had not – so far as any of them knew – ever taken a day off work.

"If *he* could drop off, just like that, then we're all buggered," said Graeme the actor indistinctly, unhelpfully putting their thoughts in a nutshell.

One of Guy's daughters was circulating with a bottle in each hand. They refilled their glasses a fourth or fifth time.

"My money's on Bryn. According to him, he's the next candidate," said Graeme, more cheerfully.

"Any particular reason?" said Bill.

They all brightened up.

So Bryn narrated, as he had earlier to Graeme, the story of his two recent near-death accidents. For him, repeating a tale just told never quite worked. The second recital added a significance he had not intended and he became too conscious of the story's flaws. What had happened, he explained, was that a couple of weeks ago he had been crossing the road near his office and a big German car had turned out of a side street and missed him by a hair's breadth. If he had not heard the squeal of the tyres as it accelerated towards him, and if he had not jumped back in instant reflex, he was certain he would have been killed. He would have been dog's meat.

"Really?" said Marshall. "In central London? How fast was it travelling then?"

And because Marshall was the sharpest of the group, Bryn, as he always did, began at once to doubt his own judgement.

"Who can say?" he said defensively. "It was frightening enough at the time. Besides which… that's only half the point."

He proceeded to explain about the *second* near-accident,

every commuter's nightmare. He had been standing on the platform at Oxford Circus, waiting for the Central Line to Ealing Broadway. As he had done for fifteen years, every working day, he took up a position at the extreme western end, his toes on the yellow safety line, perfectly placed for the first set of carriage doors to open. There was a bustle of rush hour passengers passing through from the platform entrance behind him, and he turned himself slightly to the side, again as he always did, in a token gesture of bracing himself against anyone who might accidentally bump into him.

It was the wrong train coming in. Not the Ealing Broadway service signalled on the unreliable overhead platform display. The little illuminated window above the driver indicated instead a West Ruislip train. He stepped back a pace to let other commuters through and, just as he did so, a man in a smart black overcoat and a trilby cannoned heavily into him, spinning him round on the spot. If Bryn had not had the benefit of his own backward impetus, and if he had made his movement even a half second earlier or later, he would surely have toppled in front of the train cab. It would have been hopelessly too late for the driver to brake.

Then he had watched as the trilby man tottered in slow motion along the edge of the platform, wind-milling his arms in a frantic attempt to restore his balance. The frozen faces of the incoming passengers could be seen gaping through carriage windows while – as if in a dream – the trilby lurched and careered past them, flailing wildly at the sides of the train. At last, though probably after no more than three or four seconds, normal time reasserted itself. The horror was over. Quite suddenly, the man regained his footing and his balance, and scuttled away into the passing crowds and was gone.

"He thinks someone tried to kill him. Twice," said Graeme, helpfully.

The other two looked at him in silence, respectfully for once, he thought.

"That's a very good story," said Marshall, "As well as another good reason for not taking the tube."

"Or a good reason for having barriers along the edge of the platform like they do in other countries," said Bill, sagely.

"Did you see the trilby hat man again?" asked Graeme.

By now Bryn's wife, Marion, had joined the group, sent over by some of the other women to break the men up and get them to circulate.

"*Not* Bryn's near-death experience again," she sighed. "Boys, this is not the time. Janet says she wants you to have your next recorder group here. So you can talk about it all then. I suggest your topic for discussion should be why these amazing things seem to happen to the most accident-prone man in West London."

And so, dutifully, they moved on and around. The laughter flowed as it frequently does at such events. Indeed, it was as lively and as relaxed a party as there had ever been in Guy and Janet's house. People who had not seen each other for thirty years, or since school or university, became best friends again. Memories were revisited, connections and email addresses renewed, lunch dates fixed, rude gossip and old jokes exchanged. There was no question of any *lack* of respect or affectionate regret for the departed. Of course not. No doubt, if Janet and her daughters had been less relaxed and hospitable, the hubbub and hilarity would have been the more subdued. But funerals are as much about moving on as looking back. Guy's name came up, though not frequently and usually in relation to the shock of so unexpected a death. Only when, after an hour or two, the guests started to depart and had their final conversations at the door, did Janet allow a few tears to rise unresisted to the surface.

Chapter 2

The incident at Oxford Circus, as well as the encounter with the German car, had been more or less successfully relegated to the back of Bryn's mind – until the funeral. His friends' unexpectedly serious reaction had shaken him. He was still turning it over when he went into work two days later and found an email from Zelma awaiting him on his computer.

It would be possible, many months after the event, to recognize this as the moment when Bryn had his chance to escape the nightmare that lay ahead of him. On this particular morning, however, the action of opening Zelma's email and responding to it held only slightly greater significance than any other of his daily decisions.

She was inviting him to give a lecture at the University of Michigan in Ann Arbor. He had not been in his tiny office off Gordon Square for a while, partly because of Guy's funeral, partly because he had no lectures or tutorials that week. So a reply to the email was already overdue.

Bryn was a Reader (or Senior Lecturer) in American History at University College London, specializing – perhaps too narrowly – in the American Civil War. At all events, his efforts to get a full professorship over several years now had been fruitless. He might have managed it at one of the newer universities and he had been tempted. At one time he even contemplated an offer to set up an entire department at Wye Valley University in Hereford, but he knew that administration was not his strong suit and he could not imagine life in so unfamiliar a part of the country.

A pre-existing professorship at a major British university, into which he might slip seamlessly, would have been ideal. But the right posts were few and far between and, when they came up, over-subscribed. His mind, now that his children had left home, had begun to turn to America. Other colleagues had taken up posts at places like Syracuse and Tulane, at more substantial salaries than the UK offered, and appeared to prosper. Maybe he should do the same.

As a consequence and in order, as it were, to stimulate the market place, he had started publishing occasional pieces in academic journals that circulated in America. A recent short monograph about American Civil War generals seemed to have gone down particularly well.

He had also been engaging more closely with stateside colleagues in similar disciplines. Four months previously in October, a group of them had come to London to talk about possible exchange arrangements for students or even lecturers. Bryn met them with his departmental head, Professor Kenneth Burns, and a few representatives from other college faculties. Among the American party was a blonde, buxom, lively person around thirty called Zelma Weiskopf, an Assistant Professor in Contemporary Studies at the University of Michigan.

Bryn and she hit it off from the start. She was the kind of extrovert, uncomplicated woman who made it easy for him to relax. With Zelma he never had to search for things to say, still less work at keeping the conversation going. Yet it was noticeable that she was not entirely at ease with her American colleagues. Maybe she was too dominant for them and they too blandly academic for her. He caught her standing by herself at the faculty's post-discussion welcoming party.

"I don't suppose you guys have anything like a Gin and Tonic?" she asked, when he came alongside.

"Wouldn't you rather have a Martini?"

"Oh baby. A Martini. A Presbyterian. A Manhattan. A straight Gin. Is there anything here except South American merlot and chardonnay?"

"No," he said.

Faculty "cocktails" – Ken Burns really did call them that – were always red and white wine, orange juice, and bottled water. Now and again, some basic canapés also circulated, tiny, dry and not many. Their main effect upon Bryn was to make him more hungry.

"Do you fancy a meal?" he said to her impulsively, and to his own surprise.

"You bet."

They spent the remainder of the evening in Marinello's. It was the most affordable restaurant he could think of within striking distance of Gower Street, without seeming cheapskate. It was not a bad investment. Zelma loved the place, had no difficulty this time with the wine, and drank furiously to no obvious ill effect. Her warmth was infectious. From time to time she reached out and touched his hand for emphasis as she spoke; he made sure his hand remained there on the table.

He told her about his academic work, about his half-finished book on the Civil War generals, and, in case she should think him as desiccated as her colleagues, about his other passions, music and food – though whether the enthusiasm he expressed for symphony concerts and French cooking made him appear more attractive to her was unclear. He did not mention Marion or his life in West London. And neither, he noticed, did Zelma refer to a husband or a partner or anything else that might disturb his developing interest.

When it came to pay the bill, she startled him by offering to pay *all* of it, because she was on expenses and she was damn sure he was not. He demurred and they finally settled for a halfway split. But so relieved was he at this unexpected economy that he insisted on calling a taxi and escorting her back to her hotel. At the entrance, he gave her a farewell peck on the cheek. Her response was brisk, unromantically so, and threw him off his stroke for a moment.

"Hey, how about a nightcap? Help me beat up the minibar?"

"Now? Yes? I'd be delighted."

Damn sure he would.

And now the memory of that lost opportunity haunted him. The embrace in the lift. The grappling on the bed. His pathetic attempt at sexual intimacy and the instant veto. The frail effort to behave as though he did not really mind. What a clumsy prat he had been.

They parted cordially enough, with the appropriate pleasantries.

"Maybe we can hook up again, sometime."

"Of course," he said.

"No. Really," she said.

"Of course. Really. Me too."

He knew she had to fly back the same day and that it was hardly likely they would ever renew their brief acquaintance. They exchanged a polite kiss and he left.

Where *had* he gone wrong?

The absence of any further communication from Zelma seemed to confirm the deadness of the end. He had been too embarrassed at his own behaviour to follow up himself.

And now her email.

She was inviting him, on behalf of the Department of History, to give a lecture at Michigan. She suggested that he might wish to address students on the subject of British Attitudes to the American Civil War. Her liveliness and irreverence were as engaging as before. Do not assume too much, she wrote. We have mid-Western sophomores here who think Robert E Lee was a Mississippi paddle steamer.

What *did* it mean? Was it possible that Zelma fancied him after all? He would never know of course unless he accepted the invitation – and he could combine it (and justify it better) with a similar one that he had on the back-burner from an old friend in Utah. It was all fairly short notice and everything depended on the acquiescence of his departmental head. But if he could fit it in, he might even enjoy a few days' extra vacation at the same time.

It was easier than he had anticipated. Zelma's own boss, who had led the American delegation the previous autumn, had already emailed Ken Burns and Ken was delighted by the idea. He saw it as the first fruit of his great new project for cross Anglo-American fertilisation. Although the department had some history of exchange arrangements, he envied the more 'global' and lucrative achievements of his colleagues in other disciplines, such as languages. Bryn would be (Ken congratulated himself on his witty use of an American Civil War expression) the first 'skirmisher'.

"But don't get into any military manoeuvres with Professor Weiskopf" he said, giving Bryn what used to be called an old-fashioned look.

Bryn affected not to understand. He was irritated that Ken was concerned at all about his private behaviour. Part of the problem was that Ken knew his family, and was a close friend of one of his cousins and not above passing on gossip. He was also irritated that his interest in Zelma at the departmental cocktails had been so obvious.

The university was content to pick up his travel expenses but he would have to arrange it all himself, at the least possible cost. Once he had established that Marion was content, eager even, for him to take the trip, he needed only three days to set the whole thing up. His friend in Utah, who was Dean of Studies at Brigham Young University there, was happy for him to come any time. Yes of course a lecture on British Attitudes to the Civil War would be fine, but don't expect our students to be familiar with all the detail. And we'll put you up and look after you whilst you are here.

He hit the internet. He scoured the airline websites and assembled a package which allowed him to fly direct to Chicago, with a couple of internal flights and a return from Salt Lake City. Ken did not flinch. In his euphoria at the ease of it all, Bryn then searched a few more websites to test his personal theory that there is no venue in the world that cannot sell you – however short the notice or popular the evening – a *singleton* ticket at the end of a row, somewhere.

A few clicks and, slightly to his alarm, he had bought – though for much less than he would have paid in London – a perch on the extreme left of the front balcony, for a performance of *Cosi Fan Tutte* at the Chicago Lyric Opera. As he gazed at the ticket print-out, he wondered if there was any way of swinging this one too on the faculty.

A month or so later, in March, he was on the plane to Chicago, with his lecture on the American Civil War in his pocket. He intended to visit the city for a couple of days of music, exploration and good food before travelling back eastward to the University of Michigan and then south to Utah.

The arrivals hall at O'Hare airport was a refugee camp. He had known waits at other international airports but this was always the worst. Hundreds of passengers edged imperceptibly forward through a series of maze-like pens that eventually, an hour or more later, debouched before a line of booths stretching across the width of the vast building.

Most of the booths – for, notwithstanding the seething mass, not all were occupied – contained a uniformed officer whose job it was to ensure that no enemy alien, criminal or otherwise unacceptable person was permitted entry into the country. The deeply unwelcoming demeanour of these surly apparatchiks admitted no recognition that only the *tiniest* proportion of their clients was likely to have impeachable credentials or bring anything but economic benefit to the American nation. Their only eye contact was to check the passport photograph. Words and physical gestures were peremptory to the point – and some way beyond it – of offensiveness.

It was a reasonable assumption that things had become worse in the years since the destruction of the World Trade Center and the wars and paranoia that followed. But that had not been Bryn's experience. The truth was that it had been every bit as unpleasant at O'Hare the first time he came through the airport, way back in the 1990s on a family holiday. He always wished someone – anyone but him of course – would protest and demand a minimum level of courtesy. But of course no one ever did.

When he at last arrived at the head of his particular chain of incomers, a woman officer directed him to a booth occupied by a crew-cut individual who took his passport without comment. The man gazed expressionlessly for what seemed like minutes at his computer screen.

"You here on business?" he said suddenly, without looking up.

Bryn did not know how to respond. Once before, when he had replied with a yes to a similar question, he had wound up in a side room for an hour being quizzed about his commercial intentions. So, after a moment's thought, he decided discretion was probably the better part of honesty.

"No," he said. "Ah... pleasure. Vacation."

The officer pursed his lips and tapped his keyboard. Another minute or two passed. Bryn began to be concerned, absurdly, about the people behind him in the endless queue, whom he was now responsible for holding up even longer. The man spoke briefly on his telephone and seconds later an evidently more senior officer materialized who began to gaze at the computer screen with him. Bryn considered edging round to get a view of it himself, but thought better of it. The senior officer looked up.

"Come with me."

"What?"

"We need to check a couple of things. This way, buddy."

His mind swam. Was it a problem with his current passport? He had used it before in America. Maybe it was not now up to new security requirements. But it had been checked twice by airline and by security staff at Heathrow. Did they then suspect his business intentions? Did they have secret lie-detection machines now?

He followed the senior officer down a side corridor and into a small room with a table and two chairs either side of it, much like the criminal interviewing rooms he had seen in Hollywood police films. He looked around for any evidence of a two-way mirror overlooking them. It seemed a normal office room. Of course, with modern technology, you might never tell.

The officer did not interview him. And neither did anyone else. After a few minutes, a woman opened the door and asked him if he would like a coffee. Since he had no idea how long he was going to be here, he said yes. But the coffee never came either. Instead, and after probably another fifteen minutes, the senior officer returned, handed back his passport and told him he was free to go.

Something in Bryn finally turned.

"I'm sorry," he said. "Was there a problem?"

"No problem, sir. You're free to go."

"No there must have been *some* kind of a problem," he insisted stubbornly. "I really don't want to have to go through all this again, do I?"

"Just something came up on the computer, which we had to check," said the man blandly. "Just routine. Nothing for you to worry about. You can leave now, sir."

The conversation was unlikely to go anywhere very interesting. Except that, as Bryn suddenly realized, the man had now addressed him twice as 'sir'. This was a word he had thought never to hear from any Chicago immigration official. Perhaps he should be grateful for such small mercies and cut his losses. He picked up his bag and followed the official back into the heaving arrivals hall, where the man vanished as suddenly as he had first appeared.

Even after the incomer cleared immigration, Chicago had never been a welcoming city. Wise travellers learned to avoid unpleasantness by driving into town in a hire car or a taxi. Or, if they could, they arranged for someone to pick them up. Bryn had rented a car in the past but, since this part of his visit was not on college expenses, he had decided to rely on the city's celebrated public transport system.

He should have known better. On paper the Chicago Transit Authority might look impressive: a dainty bouquet of variously coloured lines snaking out from the centre of the city to the suburbs and the airports and beyond. But years of depression and neglect had long ago turned the system into a ghetto for the city's poorest travellers.

Bryn, accustomed to the London Underground, brought no high expectations to his journey. But what he had not anticipated was how unwelcoming the CTA had become. He pitied anyone who was neither familiar with Chicago nor spoke American English – though this was perhaps not the only city burdened by the assumption that what was good enough for its inhabitants was good enough for everyone else. He also suspected that the infrequency of signs and directions, and their monolingual character when they did appear, reflected a hostility to the foreign incomer which was not confined to proverbial small-town America.

He was grateful at least for the tongue in which he was mainly fluent. Thank God also for the internet and his uncharacteristic foresight in plotting his way from the terminal to the public transport systems *in advance*. And there it was indeed: the Blue Line train, waiting to take him into the city.

It was the economic depression on wheels. Filthy, over-crowded, rubbish strewn; people struggling to get on before the doors closed; harsh imprecations from the driver. It might have reminded him of the Piccadilly Line from Heathrow on an exceptionally bad day. Were it not that every single one of the carriage's occupants was male.

He clambered over a pile of rucksacks and found a space to lean into by the window, where he could study his fellow passengers. They were a mix of young travellers in small groups, possibly students, and a number of other more solitary individuals, many of them black or latino, who seemed to carry no baggage at all. He guessed he was the oldest as well as the least indigent person in the carriage.

The train travelled on through the outer suburbs. Very few people got off or on. There was almost no conversation. It was obvious that some of his companions – those without earplugs, uncocooned in their private music – were very poor indeed, with the absent stares that suggested a drug or alcohol addiction, or maybe pure exhaustion. They gazed at the floor or out of the window; never at each other. Except for one man, who had entered the carriage at O'Hare with him. He was white with a bristly two-week growth of beard, a light grey hood and dark mirrored glasses. He stood at the far end of the carriage. After some time, Bryn became aware that the man was watching him.

At first it seemed like one of those embarrassing occasions when you find yourself locking gazes with someone who happens to look up at precisely the moment you are looking at him. Bryn turned away to the concrete and low-rise landscape peeling past the window. After a minute or so he glanced back. The man was still watching him. But this time it was the other who turned aside. His pale, rather puffy face withdrew into the folds of its hood, invisible except for the reflected gleam of his glasses.

Bryn's heart began to pound.

This was very silly. He could only explain it to himself on the basis of his two near-accidents in London: he was evidently more sensitive and easily spooked than he had believed. He forced himself to look away. He sought out the man's reflection in the smudged and greasy window glass, and watched that instead.

It was a long journey. As the train approached the city, the carriage at last started to empty. The hooded man stayed where he was. Bryn was conscious of a small knot of anxiety building again within him. His hand closed round the bunch of keys he always carried in his pocket: not much of a knuckle-duster but *something*. Slowly, and with all the nonchalance he could muster, he manoeuvred his travelling bag until it covered the front of his body and held it there with his free arm.

The train arrived at his station.

As he made his way out of the carriage, he kept the man, as discreetly as he could, on the edge of his peripheral vision. He saw him begin to move to the door.

Bryn walked sharply past a knot of people clustered on the platform, up a flight of steps and out onto the street. He flipped his bag over his shoulder and marched on rapidly through the crowds, weaving and side-stepping between them. He did not stop until he reached the Paris Court Hotel, two hundred yards away.

Chapter 3

At the hotel lobby entrance he looked back. There was no sign of a pursuer. He wondered if he had really followed him. Or if the man's interest in him was after all nothing more than innocent curiosity. He felt nonetheless a tiny shudder of relief.

He had chosen the Paris Court because it looked good on the website and was relatively cheap. It was also conveniently placed in the centre of Chicago. The hotel, though, had known greater days. A short flight of steps took him to an over-decorated lobby area the size of an aircraft hanger. Colossal crystal chandeliers and other ageing mementos of the early twentieth century hinted at what might, in its time, have been the last word in Grand Hotel living. It had evidently been compelled since then to reach a long way down-market for the larger and less refined clientele that now filled its thousands of rooms.

There were other indications of a more glorious past in photographs on the walls from the 1920s which spoke of the largest hotel in the world, with a roof top golf course and its own hospital and theatre. The aircraft hanger lobby – "decorated in the French Renaissance style" – had been the grand ballroom, until in more straitened times during the Second World War it became, aptly, a mess hall for the American air force.

It was as crowded now as it ever was then, but with squadrons of Japanese tourists and young people with back-packs and plastic water bottles. The reception desk was a counter wider than the longest saloon bar, with a dozen O'Hare-style queues snaking back across the lobby. Bryn checked in and then followed the clerk's directions to a bank of lifts somewhere beyond the pulsing scrum of young people. Eventually, and after many twists and turns down narrow corridors, he arrived at his room.

By the bedside telephone, there was an envelope with a name written on it. Not his surname but the single and intimate word 'Baby'. It could only be from one person.

In his last email he had suggested to Zelma that he meet her before his lecture (which it was her duty to introduce) at the theatre in Ann Arbor where he was due to deliver it. He had given her his itinerary for the whole trip – just in case she might want to get in touch with him. He had had no special expectations, given the circumstances of their last meeting. But if she needed to advise him of a change of plan, or venue or starting time for the lecture, then at least she knew where to contact him.

He assumed the message had been dictated down the telephone to a hotel clerk. It conveyed nothing about any change of plan or arrangements. Instead it read, quite briefly: "I will pick you up at the motel at 6pm. Zelma." Nothing else. Rather official and cool in fact. Only the single word on the envelope gave the remotest hint that she might – *might* – have other plans.

He tried to put her out his mind. He had his seat at the opera this evening and before that he meant also to indulge another private passion at the *Cordelia* Restaurant on the other side of the Chicago River. In the euphoria of instant internet access and easy commitment, he had – a month previously and four thousand miles away at his desk in Gower Street – booked a table for one.

He snoozed fitfully on the bed, showered, changed, and set off towards West Randolph Street, with his street map in his hand. The *Cordelia* – according to his internet researches – was one of the city's very best restaurants.

He loved reading the reviews and the food books; loved to do so more than he enjoyed the food. But this was a real opportunity. The word was that Chicago was now the foodie capital of America and a sight cheaper to eat in than the great coastal cities. What was even more appealing, the dollar was going through one of its periodic devaluations against the pound, he only had himself to pay for, and the opera did not start till 8pm.

He had when he was younger developed some very set views about America and food. One was that no serious eater should look for satisfaction in the big city, where the best you could hope for were bland impersonations of other nations' cuisine. Away from the crowds, a thousand miles from Chicago or New York or Los Angeles, you *might* by contrast have found a country cook offering a no-choice dinner hardly different from what her pioneer grandmother had served up, and just as delicious. Like the sublime pot roast of buffalo and beans he had once enjoyed with his wife in a tiny hamlet north of Monument Valley.

On the other hand again, one of the things he increasingly admired about Americans was their capacity to reinvent themselves. And to adapt the ideas and practices of other nations and make them their own: a form of conquest, beyond impersonation, of which he now approved. Californian wines were outstripping Bordeaux and Burgundy in international blind tastings. A few high-profile restaurants on the east and west coasts were competing for critical honours with the Europeans. Micro-breweries modelled on British and German standards were spreading like a rash across the continent. But the one thing Americans could *never* do, of course, was cheese.

The journey to the restaurant was more difficult than he expected. For a start, and not for the first time in an American city, it took him much longer to walk there than the map appeared to suggest. There were fewer and fewer people on the sidewalks as he travelled west, and by the time he had crossed the Chicago River, hardly any cars on the streets. The landscape had changed. One minute he seemed to be passing under the monstrous, glassy,

Willis Tower, glistening red and gold in the evening sun. The very next he was walking by low rise brownstone buildings similar to those he had seen through the train window on his journey through the depressed suburbs.

It was still a couple of blocks to go before he reached the restaurant. He turned north up a dingy side street, and pulled out his map to check his bearings. As he did so a puffy-faced white man in mirrored sunglasses and a light grey coat and with his hands in his pockets materialized out of a doorway. There were no other people on the street.

The man's voice was cold and mocking, with what sounded like a Southern accent.

"Got change for a dollar, feller?" he said.

One of his hands began to emerge from its pocket.

Bryn's half-swallowed response was the only one he could think of – "I'm fine, thank you" – and he strode on, unbreathing, with what he devoutly hoped was a confident and muscular gait. He glanced back as he turned the corner. The man was following at a half-block's distance. When he saw Bryn looking at him, he deliberately returned his gaze. This time there was no looking away. Bryn watched like a rabbit in headlights while the man brought his empty hand up to his face and slowly removed his sunglasses, revealing deep-set, cold, blue eyes. Then he nodded, pulled his light grey hood over his lank, greasy hair and turned away. He was gone.

The *Cordelia* was barely thirty yards further on. It was 6 o'clock and he was the first customer. He took a seat at a table. Without thinking, he ordered a large "G and T" and watched while the barman poured a huge shot of a very superior English gin and unscrewed a bottle of the world's most famous tonic water. He was shocked to discover that he was shivering from his jaw to his knees, as if he had a fever.

He needed to think this through.

The difficulty was that none of it made sense. Why should anyone want to trail him around Chicago? Because that is what it had to amount to. And if it was the same hooded man trailing him, he must have deliberately picked him up at the airport. Which meant that he must have been waiting for him there. Was the man put onto him by the security people at O'Hare? Why on earth should they want to do that? In any case, one thing seemed clear: the man was entirely unbothered that Bryn now knew he was trailing him. But that must in turn, surely, imply a threat. What kind of threat? Or warning? Was he in serious danger? And why should anyone want to threaten him or kill him? Would he not expect to have been told first?

He laughed out aloud. He was being ridiculous. And he would get nowhere with this questionnaire. Plus the gin and tonic was huge and excellent and just what he needed: so he might as well enjoy the moment. The man had taken himself off somewhere else and if he, Bryn, had a problem, it was one he could defer. *Carpe Diem*, as Marshall might have said. The shivering had ebbed away. He felt as content as he had for weeks. He turned to study the menu and his new surroundings.

The dining room was bistro style with banquettes against the long wall, and a bar on the other side. The staff were young, handsome, charming and well informed. They avoided the characteristic unctuousness of so many American restaurants. He opted for veal sweetbreads, some lamb chops and a silky, lemony mousse. With each course he had a glass or two of a Californian wine recommended by the sommelier. It was – his ultimate compliment – European-class presentation. And he was wrong about the cheese.

He had ordered a platter of American produce, something he would probably never have done if he had been less drunk, happy or reckless. It all came from tiny farms in Indiana, Vermont or Colorado, in the business for not more than five or ten years: a soft French-style goats' cheese, a salty Roquefort clone, a cheddar, a hard Pecorino. Meantime, a junior waiter placed alongside each small slice an accompaniment: candied kumquats, smoked almonds, caramelized onions. It seemed a defensive gesture, as if the restaurant was worried that diners would not take the home-grown product seriously without the decorative additions. He ordered a large glass of port and polished them all off. No longer *Das Land ohne Käse...*

The Lyric Opera, fortuitously, was halfway between the *Cordelia* and his hotel. Far enough for Bryn to get some fresh air before the performance. Not too far for his waning stamina. He sauntered back across the River and turned up the main street towards the theatre. As he did so, a familiar figure in a light grey coat emerged from a shop doorway on the other side of the road and walked along in parallel with him. Bryn watched him out of the side of his eye but this time made no attempt to catch his gaze.

Maybe because he had had his fright earlier and got over it or – which may come to the same thing – because he was swaddled in his post-prandial contentment, he really no longer cared. He strolled into the theatre and settled into his very comfortable seat in the balcony.

And fell asleep.

He slept peacefully through most of the first act of the opera. After that, he awoke refreshed and alert and directed his attention to a well sung if rather dull performance. Part of the problem was that the production was economical not to say cheap, which seemed surprising in such a wealthy city. He had seen more money on stage at the chronically underfunded English National Opera. The ostentatiously displayed boards in the Lyric Opera's grand lobby suggested a long list of wealthy sponsors and he wondered where their riches went. To pay the stars perhaps.

It was the usual mix of travelling international names to draw the crowds and relative unknowns to balance the budget. One who for the moment fell into the latter category was a young American near the beginning of his career. He was tall and big with a clumsy college boy presence but a clear and flexible voice. He was more like a Wagner than a Mozart hero. Perhaps, in twenty years' time, when he was fat and paunchy and no longer looked the part, he would be making his debut at Bayreuth.

His attention strayed to the programme. There were a

scattering of British names, always billed as "Sir Thomas Allen", or "Sir Andrew Davis" as they never would be in London. Even a "CBE" was appended to another singer's name in the cast list. It was extraordinary how Americans were besotted by other nations' titles. Maybe, Bryn reflected, they needed a *Légion d'Honneur* all of their own, with lapel badges or ribbons so that they could at last feel on equal terms with the British and the French.

As the performance drew towards its close, and the alcohol seeped out of his system, and his thoughts took on more focus, his mind turned back to the bizarre business of the man in the light grey hoody. It was barely possible that he was out there. But the idea that he *might* be, nonetheless, was still alarming. It was already late in the evening and he could not be sure that the walk back to the Paris Court would be well-lit or that many people would be on the street. He dared not guess how many opportunities there might be to intercept him as he hurried past a dark doorway or a side street.

His seat at the extreme left of the front row of the balcony suggested a simple strategy. As the house rose to applaud the final curtain, he slipped away alone, down the carpeted stairs, through the great lobby, and out to the rank of waiting taxis.

"Paris Court Hotel," he commanded.

The driver looked at him briefly, as if he had expected someone more appropriately dressed in a shiny lounge suit or furs.

"Anyone else to come, mister?" said the driver.

"No. Just me."

"You from New York?"

"British. Can we go now please."

The cab pulled out and was on its way. The sidewalks were empty and there was no sign of Bryn's nemesis. They took a route which seemed to him about as unlikely (and expensive) a way of getting to the hotel as might be devised. And once again, he really did not care.

Chapter 4

This City now doth, like a garment, wear
The beauty of the morning; silent, bare,
Ships, towers, domes, theatres, and temples lie
Open unto the fields, and to the sky;
All bright and glittering in the smokeless air...

There is something quite shocking about an early winter morning in Chicago. The city sparkles. It is ablaze with light. Above the glittering steel and glass skyscrapers which crowd the roads to the horizon, the cloudless sky is an eye-achingly brilliant powder blue.

And in March it is *cold*. Incredibly cold. It is easy for an incomer to be fooled because if he walks briskly on the sunlit side of the street he is liable to build up a sticky underwear sweat. But simultaneously his ears are beginning to crystallize and his fingers are losing all feeling.

Chicagoans wear woolly hats, fur ear-muffs, buttoned up heavy coats and 'thinsulate' ski gloves. You can tell who the tourists, the others, are. They are the ones in baseball hats with a scarf inadequately pulled up to cover the bottom half of their face. In general, though, they do not come out till after breakfast.

After their blueberry pancakes and cream, rashers of streaky bacon dry-fried to a crisp, eggs over-easy, hash browns and as much coffee as you can drink. They are wise to take their time. For most of them it is still the best meal they will eat in America.

Chicago is a more spectacularly modern city than New York. From any distance, the skyscrapers are closer and newer with more steel and glass and less time-weathered brick and stone. They rise up startlingly along the very edge of Lake Michigan, a body of water which seems from here as vast as the Atlantic Ocean, with waves rolling in from the horizon and smashing against the concrete shoreline as far as the eye can see. The city seems neat and contained in a way that New York, sprawling either side of the Hudson and the East River, is not. Chicago is the City of Oz, rising abruptly out of the mid-Western plains.

It is only when you move away from the waterfronts and the grand highways that you begin to see another picture. In the dark canyons deep within is the celebrated "L" – the elevated tramway – a marvel no doubt when it was built in the late nineteenth century and still an effective means of getting around on the cheap. The rails run twenty feet above the middle of the streets, excluding light and creating a kind of underworld where the middle and upper classes do not go. The buildings either side of these streets tend *not* to be glass and steel and there has been less recent development. You can see why.

Bryn was sitting in the hotel restaurant, gazing at his quarter-finished plate of Belgian waffles and maple syrup. This was his day for fun. The big question was whether he was going to allow it to be spoiled by an obsession with a man who – so far at least – had shown no actual sign of wishing to do him harm. It was perfectly possible that he had shaken him off. The man had not followed him to his hotel either from the Blue Line from O'Hare or after the opera, and quite probably had no idea where he now was.

The worrying curiosity, though, was how he had been able to intercept him on the way to the *Cordelia*. How could he possibly have known he was going there? Could it have been a coincidence? The more he thought about it, the less likely any alternative explanation seemed.

A new and, it seemed to him, sensible strategy began to form in his mind. He had less than two days left in Chicago before he had to fly to Detroit and travel by road from there to Ann Arbor. He would spend this particular day as much indoors as possible. Then, if at the end of it, there had been no sign of the light grey hood, he might begin to relax.

He might start by checking the internet again for details of shows and exhibitions in Chicago. Previously, he had been accustomed to the free web access provided by the motel chains. Frustratingly, this did not appear to extend to 'grand' hotels like the crowded Paris Court. There was on the fifth floor a business suite, attached to a conference centre, which charged a dollar a minute for a seat in front of a personal computer, but he thought this exorbitant, particularly since he expected to spend anything up to a leisurely hour browsing.

His alarm at the cost was no surprise to the hotel clerk who briskly suggested to him instead that he might like to cross the road to the Fed-Ex Kinko shop – where much cheaper access was available. This made even more sense when he realized that the Fed-Ex Kinko was opposite the back entrance of the hotel. He stood for a while in the shadows under the exit canopy, looking up and down the street. No sign of his nemesis. He crossed the road and entered the shop.

The place was full of students, which was usually an indication that the price was right. He found a keyboard in the corner, where he could keep half an eye on the shop door and on the street the other side of the big glass windows. There was no difficulty finding websites for his list of local attractions most likely to interest him, and within less than half an hour he had not only sorted out an itinerary for the day but had also managed to locate a seat (that unsellable singleton at the end of the row again) for a concert the same evening at Symphony Center. He put in his credit card details and printed off an email with his ticket number and instructions.

There was a drugstore next door, so he popped in to replace the shaving cream that airport security at Heathrow had confiscated because in some obscure way it breached their latest carry-on constraints. He found on the shelves, clearly labelled for the purpose, a small can suitable for taking onto airplanes. A dinky little two ounce number, about the size of a rape alarm which looked as if it would barely survive the first week, and which cost pro rata about three times what he normally paid. He wondered how large a slice the airlines were getting of the toiletry industry's fabulous profit margin.

Then, leaning against the nose-biting wind, he made his way to his first safe haven of the day: the Art Institute of Chicago. He liked the way he was required to put his bag and coat into the cloakroom. And he appreciated the stern appraisal of the Institute's security guards as he passed through the gates into the galleries.

He concentrated on the roomfuls of European art. Just as through the centuries the rich north European nations had plundered the stock of the poorer nations of the world, so the Americans, when their time came to be the rich ones, had plundered the heritage of Europe. There it was on their walls: the Italian Renaissance, the French Impressionists, even the British Raeburn, Reynolds and Gainsborough. It seemed foolish to complain. But it was a long way to travel to see something that memorialized the place you had originally set out from.

He dawdled through the huge rooms, spinning the time away, occasionally and absent-mindedly scanning the crowds for an unwelcome face. He was irritated by his inability to put his silly fears aside, by his feeble irrationality. Was he going to be like this the whole time he was in America? And *here* – surrounded by security staff in every room? He looked around for something instead that might provoke the grumpy traveller within him. It was a sound diversionary strategy that he had successfully deployed in the past.

He noticed that everything in the Institute seemed restored to an inch of its life, glowing and brilliant. He had felt the same irritation in other galleries. In Chicago, possibly because it was so brightly lit, the pigments, particularly in the oldest pictures, seemed to blaze out – and the comparison came irresistibly to mind – like Hollywood *technicolor*.

Was he seeing the real thing at all? Though these were 'original' paintings, maybe the only thing left of them that had not been remade and transformed was the canvas upon which they sat. But then, as he read the Institute's guide, he discovered that some paintings had even been lifted from the decaying original cloth and re-sited on a more permanent fabric – before the army of restorers had set about them yet again, cleaning off layers, replacing pigments, impersonating the master's brush strokes.

What a wonderful metaphor for the American Way. The colonisation, improvement and final replacement of historic civilisations by Uncle Sam's bright and homogenized new world.

And were these paintings and sculptures more than trophies hanging there, like so many sets of antlers? As he sat and gazed at a favourite picture, young people passed through, took a quick photograph with their mobile phones and passed on. Occasionally a group of people entered the room and gathered around one of the more famous canvasses while their guide explained its virtues to them. Some of the group seemed to be paying attention; most were disengaged and chatted quietly together or wandered away and checked their text messages. Only when the guide touched on the cost of an acquisition and its rocketing value over the centuries did a wave of more evident interest ripple through the crowd.

"That's far enough – step back please!"

He wheeled around. There was no-one approaching him and no-one behind him. No-one in the room except half a dozen bored Japanese students gazing at a wall-full of Late Impressionists. Then a couple of students moved on and he saw beyond them, sitting on a stool in the corner and staring at him, a small, furious official.

"Stand away from the picture, sir!"

33

He backed away and sat on a bench in the centre of the room. The painting he seemed to have threatened was *Sunday Afternoon on the Island of La Grande Jatte* by the French Neo-Impressionist Georges Seurat (a snip at $22,000 in 1924), so huge that it hung on an end wall all by itself and so unprotected and vulnerable that he had been able to advance right up to the canvas, close enough – if he had been so minded – to poke his finger through it.

He sat for a while, intermittently conscious of the beady eye of his welcome new friend in the corner. The furious little functionary could stay and watch over him as long as he liked. There were after all poorer ways of passing time than contemplating a picture so imitated, so iconic, and now so American that it had even been the subject of a successful Broadway musical.

It was late afternoon and he felt jet-lagged and exhausted.

Back in his hotel room he scanned the room service menu and ordered a chicken and parmesan sandwich. It was an act whose consequence brought him back to earth with a bump. And how ironic. The previous evening he had enjoyed one of the best meals of his life, and a proof that America was learning to out-do Europe at its own gastronomic game. But here, in the *fons et origo* of fast food, the land which brought the rest of the world McDonalds and KFC, there shortly arrived on his plate a confection so vile and flavourless as to drive away even the last sensation of appetite.

Of course part of the problem was that he had misunderstood the word 'sandwich'. As a Briton, he thought it meant sliced bread, perhaps white, perhaps brown. What actually lay before him were two halves of a giant ivory-white bap the texture and taste of polyurethane, distributed either side of a dried lump of white meat supporting a green crust of something that may once have been cheese.

There was enough here to feed the proverbial family of four, or one normally overweight American matron. He nibbled round the edges a little before he consoled himself with some variously labelled small cans of beer that he found in the mini-bar, each indistinguishable from the last. The room service menu was not entirely a lost cause though. He had happily ordered also a dessert of cookie dough ice-cream. The portion was massive, and delicious, and about this he had no reservations at all.

He turned on the television set and flicked through twenty or more channels, all news or drama serials, until the potent mix of jetlag, alcohol and a hard day on his feet all became too much for him. He guessed there was time before the concert for a catnap and closed his eyelids for sleep.

That evening the Chicago Symphony Orchestra played Bach and Mozart with Mitsuko Uchida. The great Japanese pianist's entrance onto the orchestra platform was more exotic than ever, with flying long black hair and filmy over-garments trailing horizontally behind her. At the keyboard she was almost boneless. She sank and drifted over the instrument like melting ice-cream. Now and again she raised a long arm and waved imperiously at the orchestra accompanying her.

He found it increasingly difficult to see her. In the row in front of him was his usual *bête noire*, a young couple more interested in each other than the music, who were entirely occluding his view unless he leaned out into the stairway aisle alongside. Beyond *them* though was a woman – he could not believe it – who was actually wearing a wide, flower-decked hat. Only in America.

He gave up the unequal battle and sank deep into his seat until the piece – a popular Mozart piano concerto – ended. Long before Uchida had raised her hands for the last time from the piano, indeed before the final chords had even been struck, the audience rose to its feet with a mighty howl of pleasure. It was the Frank Sinatra concert approach to classical music, he reflected gloomily. The ovation went on and on and on while he stayed stubbornly in his seat. An old man standing alongside turned and glared at him.

His resolve waned and he began to struggle to his feet. As he did so, a young man on his other side, applauding too enthusiastically, nudged him off balance and he found himself spinning and falling towards the young couple in front of him. Hands grabbed at his coat. The old man shouted for help. He saw Uchida's aghast face gazing directly up at him. A figure in a light grey hooded coat was advancing up the aisle.

He awoke with a jolt.

Light was coming through the window. The television set was still on, tuned to a local news channel. The clock in the corner of the picture clicked through to 06:00. He had slept infuriatingly through the whole concert and most of the night following.

The main overnight story was the previous day's Presidential primaries – for both main political parties – in Illinois and Michigan. No outgoing President or Vice President was involved this time and the main candidates were barely known to him. The successful front-runners in both states were a former mid-Western governor for one party and a black woman senator for the other.

His attention was riveted, however, by the second item on the news channel. A man had died the previous evening in Symphony Center. The story was confused. It had been initially assumed that he had had a heart attack at the end of the concert and later that he had somehow been suffocated. Now the young reporter standing in front of the Center was able to report that the Chicago police had been called in, and the building sealed off, though she could not explain why. There was "no further news at this hour".

All fairly disturbing, but – Bryn reminded himself – hardly likely to have anything to do with him.

Chapter 5

At breakfast he remembered his instruction to himself the previous morning to relax: there had after all been no sign of the hooded man since his visit to the opera. Even so, the incident on the news, however irrationally, continued to nag at him and – as a sort of sop to his inner coward – he resolved to keep taking a few basic precautions during what remained of his final day in Chicago.

Accordingly, he left the hotel again by the back entrance and passed briskly through the Fed-Ex Kinko shop and out the other side. In front of him was the "L": the elevated railway riding on its century old iron struts, above the great streets and avenues of the downtown business precinct known as The Loop, until it crossed the river and came down at last to ground level. He climbed up a stairway in the middle of the street and caught the Green Line to Oak Park, sharing a carriage with a scattering of young black men, huddling from the bitter cold.

Riding the Green Line high above the surrounding suburbs was a little like one of those American theme park trips through history. Except that the images reeling past the enclosed carriage windows were those of a bleak and economically depressed modern wasteland. Acreages of derelict, concreted areas, second hand cars, Black and Hispanic inhabitants. Here and there knots of young men chatted, smoked, engaged in obscure transactions. There were very few older people on the streets, no buses or other evidence of public facilities and – so far as Bryn could see – no police. It was a decayed and alien country populated by the excluded and other-coloured poor. He was in the same moment relieved and ashamed to be insulated from it within his steel and glass bubble, moving constantly onwards and beyond.

The approach to Oak Park was foreshadowed by a gradual lifting of the quality of life further from the railway line. West of Laramie, Illinois, the houses began to rise from their dour two-storey norm, and playgrounds appeared amongst grassy public areas, with tree-lined streets, churches and fine looking high schools. He was the only person to alight at Oak Park station, which was in a more run-down part of the suburb, depressed by the downmarket presence of the Green Line itself. But then, as he walked north from the station, ancient trees began to line the road, the buildings fell back behind their defensive lawns, and expensive space opened up all around.

He had come here because this was Frank Lloyd Wright country. This was where, a hundred or so years previously, the Great American Architect had changed the face of middle and upper class American living for all time. This was the cradle of an aspirational phenomenon which, if he could grasp it, would help him a little more to understand this peculiar land.

So what was so special about it all? The older houses Bryn passed first, put up before Wright arrived, were classic new rich homes of a kind broadly familiar all over America. They were an American version of nineteenth century Europe, multi-storey, probably with cellars, with wide front windows and sharply upward-thrusting gables, clawing at the sky like churches. They were also – being American – made largely of wood, with external white weatherboarding, and a single core of brick for the massive fireplaces within.

About half a mile north of the station, he passed one of the first houses Wright had built in Oak Park, an extraordinary mad fusion of Jacobean Revival and Plains Indian tepee. There were plenty of dominant verticals still. But the balconies which ran the width of the south face gave the first indication of a new emphasis on wide, confident horizontal lines in natural browns instead of white, which echoed the vast flat surrounding landscapes of the new country and shook off the remembered confinements of the old world and the city. What Wright called his 'Prairie Style'.

He wandered around Oak Park, happily alone on the street with his thoughts, spellbound by the unflagging reinvention and surprise. The buildings seemed to have the linear inevitability of simple melodies; and he remembered that Wright was an enthusiastic amateur pianist who played Beethoven to himself for hours as he mulled over his architectural problems.

He reached the architect's own home, at the top of Forest Avenue. It had been built on the edge of town, when nothing lay beyond the house except forest and the great prairie; but it had long since been consumed by the sprawling roll-out of Chicago's suburbs. Wright had created it as a shop-window for potential clients as well as a home and an office. This was where he worked and lived for twenty years with his wife and six children until the scandal of one of his many affairs – this time most indiscreetly with a colleague's wife – prompted him to leave for the east, and national and international fame.

There was a small gift shop attached to the house. Bryn browsed through the tea-cloths, post-cards and glass tumblers and other Arts and Crafts mementos of Wright and his contemporaries. He bought two bronze door numbers designed by the great man, as a coming-home present for Marion. They were characteristically eccentric but he hoped not too impenetrable for West London postmen. Better than a t-shirt at least. Then, as he was signing his credit card, an unnerving presentiment caused him to glance across the shop towards the pictures section.

There, half-obscured by a hanging display of architectural drawings but unmistakeable nonetheless, was a white man in mirrored sunglasses wearing a hooded, light grey coat.

For the moment at least, the man did not appear to be watching him. A group of elderly Americans was leaving for a guided tour of the house, and Bryn quickly slipped in among them. A door from the gift shop was unlocked; they passed through; and the guide locked it again behind her.

It was only now, when he felt briefly secure, that his mind engaged more objectively with the vision from which he had fled. It dawned on him that there had been something unusual this time about the hooded man. He had been carrying a black bag slung over one shoulder, the kind of canvas freebie that came with the documentation and hand-outs at conferences and conventions. This particular bag, however, bore an image of a rifle superimposed over a beehive and some printed words.

He struggled to focus his limited powers of recall upon them. Two words formed: *CITY* and, he thought, *RAPID*. He pulled out his diary and made a note. If this was a clue to his opponent's identity, then he needed to follow it up. The only Rapid City he knew of was in South Dakota. Was that where the man came from? The beehive reference also puzzled him. A bear-hunting gun club possibly? He added a couple of large question marks to his note, tore off the edge of the page to help remind himself to revisit it later, and redirected his attention back towards the Wright family home.

The interior of the house was surprisingly Japanese in style, with sliding partitions between a sequence of interlocking domestic rooms. At the centre of the building, by contrast, like a reminder of traditional European values, was an inglenook fireplace, as old-fashioned and cosy as a Little English pub. The uncluttered, oriental neatness of the house no doubt reflected the requirements of present-day tourism rather than those of Wright's growing family. Every internal fitting and piece of furniture had been designed by Wright. But he wondered how much of this display had passed unregarded as Wright ushered those first tourists – his hoped-for clients – through clusters of children and toys towards his office at the end of the building.

The guide – an architecture student, probably – moved

amongst the group, describing the history of the house and collecting the tour tickets. He thought it wise to absent himself for a while and slipped away up a flight of stairs. He was now at the end of a long dark corridor leading to a door which might provide some possible means of escape. But when he reached it and passed through, he emerged into another room, blazing with sudden light from the clerestories all around the ceiling.

It was as if he had tumbled through a rabbit hole into a sun-drenched Wonderland. It was the children's playroom. And more than that: there, tucked away in the corner with most of its body lost in a secret alcove was Father Wright's grand piano. The most important room in the house.

He felt the pressure of a hand lightly on his sleeve.

"I don't think I've got your ticket," said the guide.

He debated for a second whether he might argue that he had given it her earlier. But he was never an effective liar. The rest of the group was beginning to fill the room around him. He had better cut his losses.

"I didn't think you needed one," he suggested.

The young woman looked at him scornfully.

"You'll have to get one from the gift shop. It's too late for this tour. You'll have to join the next one. It's at eleven."

He nodded obediently and she escorted him back along the corridor and down the stairs to a door which opened onto the street.

He was in no doubt about what he had to do. He walked away as fast as he could, down Oak Park Avenue towards the station. He passed the tall Victorian house where Oak Park's other famous resident, Ernest Hemingway, was born and raised, while around him his neighbourhood was being transformed by a young man about twenty years older. A hundred yards or so further on, as he approached the station and the property values fell away again, he passed a down at heel saloon misspelled "Hemmingway's Bar", its frontage partly obscured by election posters for the handsome, square-jawed Presidential candidate from the Mid-West. He crossed the road and ran up the stairs to the platform.

41

There was no sign of a pursuer. While he was travelling back towards the city, it occurred to him that it might be sensible now to lose himself in the crowds until it was time to return to O'Hare and catch his plane to Detroit. So, when he reached the Loop, he transferred onto the Red Line of the "L" and took the train up to the northern end of the busiest stretch of the city, the so-called Magnificent Mile, the great boulevard which runs from the Chicago River up to the shore of Lake Michigan.

He stood briefly at the edge of the Great Lake, gazing at the skyscrapers shouldering each other along the shoreline with the breakers crashing in below them. Then he turned south into the safety of the throng.

He supposed The Mile was crowded at the best of times. But this day, he soon realized, was St Patrick's Day. As he approached the Loop, the heavier and greener the crowds became. There were people of all ages wearing huge floppy leprechaun hats and carrying plastic beakers of Guinness. Green coats, long green socks, green and white scarves. Some were carrying green helium balloons and giant green plastic shamrocks. When he reached the river, and started to cross on the road bridge, he looked down and the water was emerald green all the way to the Great Lake. A nasty, chemical colour that glistened lividly in the sunlight.

There was one final thing he needed to do before he left Chicago. About half a mile to the south lay the site of the last serious battle of any size on American soil. He had paid professional visits to most of the battlefields of America, but not to this one. He walked on until the buildings to his left, between the highway and the Great Lake, fell away, and the ground became flat, bleak and open. He had arrived at Grant Park.

At this place, during the Democratic Presidential Convention of 1968, police sent in by the city's Democrat mayor had launched an infamous assault upon a large crowd of young people protesting against the war in Vietnam. It was one of the political turning points of American history.

He stopped at the huge Baroque-effect fountain around which many of the protesters had gathered on that hot late August day.

Today, because it was winter, the water was turned off, though a few small crusts of ice had formed in its basin. A quarter of a mile away, he could see the Field Museum on whose roof National Guards riflemen had been posted with instructions to fire on the demonstrators if the police did not prevail. The great irony of it all was that Mayor Daley's brutal reaction fatally undermined his party's chosen candidate, and allowed the Republican, a serial loser called Richard Nixon, to win the Election; and in due time, with even greater irony, to proceed to bring the Vietnam War to an end.

Now, like all old battlefields, Grant Park – named after the Illinois general who led Lincoln's armies in the Civil War – was serenely peaceful, as if innocent of its own history. It was wide, bare and almost devoid of life. At this time of the year there was little reason for normal folk to go there; it was far too cold to lie around on the brown grass. Lake Michigan lapped at its eastern flank, the grand South Michigan Avenue ran down the other side. It seemed to be parked to the side of Chicago, on the way to nowhere in particular, and forgotten. Unlike other American battlefields, there were no official guided tours and no Visitor Centre to celebrate it.

He walked back to the hotel and picked up his bags. This time he ordered a taxi.

As he crossed the Chicago River, he took a last look at the towering cityscape beneath its dazzling sky. He recalled fragments of a poem he had learned when he was barely twelve; lines written while crossing another bridge in a different city, long before Chicago was born.

The flight from O'Hare to Detroit was in a smaller, more low-ceilinged and thin-bodied plane than he was used to. It seemed quite unsuited to the usual contingent of huge Americans who were able neither to stand up to their full six or so feet, nor fit into their seats. While they might hope to ease the second difficulty by flipping the elbow rests up, it could only be to the discomfort of the thinner people sitting alongside them, one of whom inevitably this day was Bryn.

He was grumpy in any case about the unexpected surcharge he had had to pay for carrying on his two bags. Not for the first time he wondered if it would not be fairer to weigh the whole consignment – each passenger *with* his/her luggage – and charge only if the aggregate exceeded an overall limit. At 5'9" and 150 lbs that might suit him very well.

But small planes sometimes provided their own solutions. There was the usual problem with the trim and the pilot asked a few of the passengers to change their seats before take-off so that the plane would be better balanced. Bryn watched contentedly as his giant companion moved back to the rear, shedding pounds of sweat as he squeezed down the corridor.

On arrival at Detroit, he hired a car from the National desk. The clerk was an expressionless black man. Bryn tried to soften him up with some mild pleasantries about the weather being better than London at least, but he might have been talking to a wall. Maybe the man had long since exhausted his tolerance of wise guy clients; and no doubt particularly white ones. However, it turned out that the entry level car Bryn had ordered was unobtainable and the clerk gave him a free upgrade of two classes so that he wound up in a large shiny sports coupé with walnut fascia. He felt even more nervous than usual as he pulled out of the airport. He reminded himself twice as he turned right that in America you must always – always – drive on the wrong side of the road.

He crawled down the motorway through the slow, drizzling rain, west towards Ann Arbor. Lorries the size of country mansions overtook him amid clouds of spray, hoovering him towards a blind and early death beneath their vast wheels. It was not until he was passing Belleville and the rain cleared that he felt able to relax and turn his mind to his hopes for the evening. And it was late in the afternoon before he turned off the motorway, into the car-park of a motel on the western outskirts of Ann Arbor, where he checked in.

He had a few hours before Zelma was due.

Chapter 6

It was an opportunity to get the remaining jet-lag out of his system. He booked a wake-up call for 5.45pm, showered and put himself to bed.

He was roused from a deep sleep by the bedside telephone.

"Hi," said a familiar voice. "This is your personal wake-up call. I'm a tad early, baby, but I guess they didn't think you'd mind."

He met her in the lobby. She looked gorgeous. When he had last seen her – the only time he had seen her – she must have been tightly wrapped in academic beige. Certainly the off-duty Zelma was a different creature: thick blonde hair shaken out, hippy, ethnic, in rich earth colours and contrasting fabrics. She wore a wide skirt and boots, a deep magenta blouse unbuttoned to her cleavage and a loose shawl across her shoulders.

"Aren't you freezing?" was all he could say.

"Thermal underwear, dude…" she replied. "I'm kidding. I just don't plan to be anywhere tonight without American central heating. Speaking of which, would you care to share *your* plans with me?"

The question was direct and challenging, the way (he imagined) she addressed her students. And also, almost imperceptibly, coquettish. He had vaguely intended to take her out to dinner; but he could think of nothing now that could possibly be more interesting than letting *her* take the initiative. He grinned at her helplessly.

"OK," she said, pre-empting him. "Did you eat on the plane? Sorry. You haven't eaten. No problem. I'm gonna take you to my favourite pizza restaurant. It's not Soho, London, but then you don't get haute cuisine in the mid-West. And I'm paying this time, dude. If you don't mind."

He was not about to argue. He climbed into Zelma's bright yellow VW Beetle and she drove into town, talking all the while. She had been voluble in London, refreshingly so, but this evening she dominated the conversation. She talked as if she was on a mission. It occurred to him that he had met or worked with many successful women in his time but never any quite so forthright as Zelma. Could it be an American woman thing? Or a Jewish one? He remembered a childhood friend whose mother was, or so he had come to believe, the matriarchal archetype – embracing, loquacious, commanding, and a great deal too powerful for him. Was this what Zelma was destined to be?

He had no sense that their gender roles had been reversed; or that his surrender of the initiative to her was, God forbid, emasculating. There was, after all, no loss on her part of warmth or femininity. And yet, perhaps, it was a little excessive. He began to wonder whether she was always like this, or whether her flamboyance concealed some welcome insecurity that he had not yet identified. It was possible – of course – that she felt, as others had before her, that she needed to make up for his own conversational deficiencies. Best, he thought on consideration, to go with the flow.

When he had the opportunity, he told her about his time in Chicago. He had thought to share some of his worries – tell her about his hooded stalker – but at the last minute he decided to keep the atmosphere as light as she had set it. Then, as he was animatedly describing his night at the opera, her smile started to fade.

"You're really into classical music, aren't you, that kind of stuff? That recorder group of yours… all this opera…"

"No. No," he said, sensing a chasm about to open up between them. "I like anything really. My tastes are… eclectic."

"*Eclectic?*" she exclaimed, with sardonic relish. "Now who would use a word like that if they were really up for anything? Let's see then, here's an acid test. Are you, for example… into tap?"

"Tap?"

"Yup," she said. "Have you ever been to a tap concert? I have two tickets tonight for Claudel's Creole Tap. But if that's not your bag," she added rapidly, "that's perfectly OK with me."

He took a few seconds out to get his bearings. Beyond all the energy and force he thought he caught a glimpse of the vulnerability he was hoping for. But why on earth should she want to take him to a *tap* concert?

"I got them," she explained, " because I guessed you'd be at a loose end and they were the only thing on tonight. Believe me, there's not a great choice of entertainment in Ann Arbor. But," she continued, a little too emphatically, "you don't have to come."

"Please," he said.

Yes, he liked the tiny suggestion of concern. He took hold of her hand.

"I'd love to come," he said.

The theatre was packed. It was difficult to know whether this was because, as Zelma had claimed, it was the only show in town, or whether the mysterious Claudel had a large and enthusiastic following in the rural mid-West. The fact that Bryn had never heard of the star of course meant nothing. But he had to admire him. A small, wiry man from Guadeloupe, he was on stage throughout, thrashing his limbs with unflagging vigour to a relentless, percussive beat. With the best will in the world, though, a little tap went a very long way.

The entertainment, which had no interval, lasted mercifully no more than an hour. There was no story to the show that he could detect. More a random sequence of athletic dance numbers exotically costumed and broodingly underlit. The high stage and unramped theatre prevented most people seeing the stage floor, so that they could only react to the *sound* of the tap; and that was so unrealistically loud that he concluded that the whole programme had been pre-recorded and what they were watching was a shadow-play of the real thing. This was a modern phenomenon he would never understand. It was like going to the opera to watch singers miming to their CDs. But he kept his heretical thoughts to himself. The Ann Arbor audience adored it. He was in a very small minority.

"What did you think?" said Zelma challengingly, as they left.

"Really, really… interesting," he replied, nodding his head, he hoped, gnomically.

"You hated it."

He saw that she was laughing at him.

"Even *eclectics* are allowed to hate stuff now and again," she said. "I think we need a drink."

They drove back to his motel. Zelma, unstoppably, set up a tab of her own and they sat at the bar drinking Margueritas and subsequently, because Bryn found it on the cocktails list, Golden Cadillacs, a confection which turned out to be a mixture of an Italian liqueur, Cointreau and cream. They were delicious. And treacherously easy to drink. They tasted like a not especially alcoholic smoothie.

"I can't drive," said Zelma after an hour or more of this regime.

"Shall I get you a taxi?"

"In Ann Arbor? At this time? We're not in New York City, baby."

"Why don't I get you a jug of water or some coffee?"

"Why don't I lie down in your room for a while."

It was not a question he felt he needed to answer. She paid off her tab with some effort of concentration, took his key from him, and marched off.

Bryn's room lay on the other side of the motel atrium from the bar. He walked, a little self-consciously, across the floor with her. None of the other guests or the staff showed any interest in their promenade. And Zelma, once she was on her feet, seemed to regain her natural command. If she was drunk, it was impossible to tell. He flicked on the room light, and followed her in.

Up to this point, it may be fair to say that all Bryn had in mind was the usual optimistic male availability to whatever fortune might bring. This had been the case when he had first met Zelma in London, and it was just as true now. He did not regard himself as a philanderer or a womanizer. Indeed, as he might regretfully acknowledge to himself, his record fell a long way short of that. He was also sufficiently detached to know that anything that happened now with Zelma was likely, and for a second time, to be regretted later. Of course, as a mature and sensible person, he expected to be able to withdraw from a compromising situation at any point. Though whether he would do so, should the opportunity present itself, was another matter entirely.

There were the customary two queen-size beds in the room. Zelma kicked off her shoes and lay, still fully-dressed, on the nearer one. She closed her eyes and was soon sound asleep. Bryn turned off all the lights except for a strip above the bathroom mirror. He left the door open so that its glow might provide some gentle background illumination to the main room in case she should wake up. He settled down for the night in the other bed.

He could not sleep. He imagined himself crossing that narrow Rubicon to Zelma and slipping gently in. He wondered if he would ever forgive himself if he did not now seize the opportunity. He looked across at her shape but all he could see was fabric. She had rolled slightly on one side and was cocooned within the folds of her duvet, her shawl, skirt and – as likely as not – her thermal underwear. She was snoring peacefully and he could see the white of her teeth through the gape of her open mouth. His resolve began to ebb. His eyes fluttered and closed. Perhaps, he reflected, she would let herself out quietly…

He awoke after an hour or so. It cannot have been too long

because he was aware of distant laughter still from the bar. There was no sign of Zelma and his first assumption was that she had recovered sufficiently to slip out without disturbing him, and had driven home. But he was wrong. The bathroom light clicked off and he heard her soft footsteps as she crossed the bedroom floor. She did not, however, go back to her own bed. She gently eased his duvet away and slipped in alongside him. It was at once obvious to him that she was naked.

As he rolled over towards her, she grasped him immediately and with some power, and pressed her lips against his. He tried to kiss her more lightly but this was not what she required. Her tongue flicked out between her teeth and into his mouth. A hand slipped down his belly towards his groin. His first and most vivid impression was of a great, unexpected energy that he had not known since he was a younger man. It was almost more than he could cope with. When he entered her, guided by her hand and earlier than he might have wished, it was she – not he – who controlled the pace and rhythm of their love-making, arching herself up against him till he felt close to pain. He was shocked, even as they clung to each other, by how youthfully vigorous she seemed and how large the gulf between them in intensity. They came to a climax together, and he fell away to the side of the bed, shuddering and exhausted.

After a while, she curled back towards him and slid an arm over his body and one leg across his. In that position she fell once more asleep. For some time he stared at the ceiling and listened to the distant noises of the motel, the departing cars as late night carousers finally released the bar staff to their homes and beds, and the hum of the central heating. Was this what he had wanted? It was no comfort to recognize that his needling sense of regret was exactly what he could have predicted. Or that, in similar circumstances, he would probably do the same again…

He drifted away into unconsciousness.

When he awoke, it was clearly morning. The brightness of the atrium had filled his room with an eerie, filtered light and he could hear, not very far away, the clatter of the breakfast area which last night had served as the bar. More gradually he became aware that Zelma was not with him. On the small table between the two beds he could see her watch, lying where she must have placed it before she had come to him in the darkness. It was a curiously down-to-earth and practical memento of their night together. It was the only evidence indeed that she had ever been there. She herself, and all her clothes, were gone.

He rose, showered, shaved, dressed and went out for his complementary breakfast of orange juice, doughnuts and coffee. A couple of aspirin capsules helped to dispel his headache.

Beyond the glass doors to the motel, everything was white. Ann Arbor and the flat countryside beyond, as far as the eye could see, lay under a six inch blanket of snow. Several cars parked outside the motel had disappeared entirely into the tsunami-like drifts. Where Zelma had parked the previous night there was a black, snowless space, crisply and sharply delineated as if very recently vacated.

Bryn went out through the motel doors and looked up and down the car park in case she might still be there. There was nothing but the dead, echo-less silence of the snow-muffled landscape. When he came nearer the empty space, his attention was caught by what looked like tiny drill holes in the snow alongside where the car had been. He fumbled for his spectacles in his pocket and held them in front of his eyes so that he could inspect them more closely.

The holes were a centimetre or so deep. Within them, and scattered across the nearest part of the snowless black space, were drops of blood. He slid his hand across a couple of them and looked at the red smear on his fingers. There was no possibility of confusion.

He pondered the situation. He could think of as many reasons why he should not be alarmed as he could for taking action. It did not seem likely, for example, that whatever took place here had been missed by the clerks in reception the other side of the glass doors. He went back in and enquired if anyone had seen a lady this morning in a magenta blouse and shawl. Or her yellow Volkswagen car leaving. But it appeared that no-one had.

"Was she a resident, sir?" enquired the smooth-looking man at the desk.

"No," he replied, beginning to recognize the difficulty he might be in.

The sensible course might be to wait until, as arranged, he met her before his lecture. If there had been a problem, he would find out soon enough. He went back to his room and packed his bag. Her watch, large and unfashionable, still lay on the bedside table. He picked it up and turned it over. On the back had been engraved a sequence of numerals, presumably a telephone number. He slipped it into his jacket pocket and left.

The lecture was to take place in the Lydia Mendelssohn Theater. He had looked it up earlier on the University of Michigan website and believed he had memorized its position on the central campus. But when he got there, the location was occupied by a complex called the Michigan Union. He wandered through its empty shops, offices, lounges, study rooms and dining areas, bereft of students at this unsocial time of day. He eventually discovered two young women, composing on a laptop together at a coffee table and asked them where the theatre was. They did not know.

At last, at the end of a long corridor, he passed through some heavy oak doors and found himself outside an old-fashioned theatre Box Office. On the floor in front of it was a trestle-supported noticeboard and pinned to the board a computer-generated document announcing that "*Professor Bryn Williams will be lecturing here at 10:00 hours on the subject of 'The Civil War – the Second American Revolution? A View From Across the Water'. He will be introduced by Professor Zelma Weiskopf. All are welcome.*"

He pushed though another door and then another and found himself abruptly on the bare stage of the theatre itself. It was a museum piece. He guessed it went back a century or more and was possibly the oldest unrestored building on campus. It was easy to see how other more modern constructions would have arisen around it, sealing it in like buried treasure, a memorial to the thespian achievements of some earlier generation.

A notice indicated that it had recently been 'renovated' but there was little evidence of that unless its previous condition had been even more spectacularly drab and rundown than it appeared now. He gazed at the small wooden balcony at the back of the narrow auditorium, at the rows of hard, uncomfortable seats, the tiny, deep and dangerous orchestra pit. It was not what he had expected. But no worse than many venues in which he had lectured in London and elsewhere. No-one expected an academic's life to be glamorous.

A door at the back of the auditorium opened and a tall, bespectacled man came in. He stopped in surprise.

"You're not Professor Williams?"

"Well... uhh... thank you for the 'Professor' bit... yuh."

"Oh we're all professors here, Professor Williams, you know that," said the man, smiling warmly. He came down to the orchestra pit.

"I'm Arnie Kendall," he said, and held out a hand.

Bryn leaned cautiously across the gaping crevasse and lightly shook it.

"I'm afraid *I* have to introduce you now. Professor Weiskopf called in sick this morning. Did you meet Zelma?"

"Not today..." said Bryn, uncertainly.

"No, in London, of course. Anyhow, she sends her best. She's really sorry she can't make it. Not feeling too good, I fear. So... I hope you like the theatre. Believe me, this is where we have our *special* lectures. It's a mite quaint and..." here he made an italicizing gesture with the two fingers of each hand "...'oldy worldy'. But, what the hell, we love it."

Perhaps that explained Zelma's absence and her early departure this morning. Maybe she was suffering from nothing more serious than a raging hangover. Or a nose bleed – though of course he should recognize that the blood spots might have had nothing to do with her. But even as he rationalized his concerns away, he felt uneasy. Maybe he employed arguments like these too frequently…

Arnie took him down to an old dressing room below the stage. He suggested that he might leave his briefcase here, have a coffee, take a short power-nap if he wanted.

"Or you could put your make-up on!" said Arnie and laughed uproariously.

They had made some effort to accommodate him. There was a deeply upholstered modern armchair, a coffee machine and Dixie cups in the corner, even a bowl with a fresh bunch of flowers. The dressing room certainly needed uplifting. Its white tiles looked as though they co-dated the original structure. A strip light and an old mirror with peeled silvering ran the length of the wall. There was a white plastic veneered working surface below, whose edge still bore the brown scars of a hundred neglected cigarettes of an earlier age. He thought he could even detect the stale whiff of old Leichner sticks. It was wonderful. He could have been back in his student thespian days a quarter of a century ago. Nothing seemed to have changed. And he wondered how familiar it would still be to actors the world over.

He poured himself a cup of coffee and carried it out. He found himself in the actors' Green Room. There were armchairs generations more ancient than the one that had been set out for him, and so badly stuffed that he could see the outlines of the springs in the seats. On every wall there were pin-up boards, a few of which were enclosed behind glass. These contained programmes going back for fifty or more years, and memories of performances in this theatre by Hume Cronin, Ellis Rabb, John Macunovich, Ed Roosevelt…

When the hour came to deliver his lecture, Arnie rematerialized with his unfading smile and a half-drunk cup of coffee in his hand. They went up to the auditorium together, where a disappointing turn-out of perhaps twenty students was waiting. Bryn glanced around in case Zelma had come after all, but there was no sign of her. As he waited for his new friend to complete the introduction, his hand felt for the chunky watch in his jacket pocket. He turned it over and his finger tips explored the rough inscription that Zelma, he supposed, had had cut into its back.

And then it was his time.

"This is a great privilege," he said. "You may wonder why I, a Brit – indeed, a Welshman – should be speaking to you about such a very American subject, your Civil War. But knowledge of course is the unique province of no-one. Just as in your studies you lay claim to our history, not to mention our culture, so do we – occasionally – claim yours. As a matter of interest, this university and my own alma mater, University College London, have many *other* things in common also. We can be proud that we are both listed among the top ten or a dozen universities in the world. We were both leaders in our respective countries in offering an alternative to the so-called élite universities – what you call the Ivy League and what we call Oxbridge. Not coincidentally, our foundations were less then ten years apart: you in 1817, UCL in 1826. We have, together, so much to be proud of..."

He had lost them already.

When it was all over, he walked back across the central campus to his car. Fat grey American squirrels, twice the size of their English cousins, sat on their haunches, munching the winter hoard of nuts. The giant university flagpole, with its mandatory national flag, towered like a pine tree at the centre of the field of snow. A number of posters for the presidential primary candidates had been pasted on the concrete flank of a lecture hall. Most were for the black woman senator. There was just a single poster for the former mid-Western governor, and that had already been half torn away.

About five miles east of Ann Arbor, as he was driving past Ypsilanti on his way to the airport, he became aware of a Ford Explorer following him in the slow lane. Most of the other vehicles on the motorway were, as usual, overtaking him but this one seemed happy to fall in behind his cautiously moderate speed. He recognized it as the kind of widely available, relatively cheap SUV that had given gas-guzzling in America a bad name. And sure enough, the Explorer – with its three rows of seats and capacity for at least eight adults – was carrying only one person. He caught a glimpse of the driver in his mirror. With the slightest twinge of relief, he made out a totally bald, tanned, thin faced, respectable-looking older man, probably in his fifties. He had an intent and focussed expression on his face. He was not, possibly, a very confident driver. The one mildly curious thing about him was that he seemed to be talking to himself. Then Bryn noticed that he had a wire running down from a plug in his ear, probably to a mobile phone in his jacket pocket.

The SUV continued to follow along behind him as he turned off towards the airport. Later, however, as Bryn negotiated his way uncertainly back to the rental company car-park, the vehicle turned away to the south. He watched it as it swept down the curving exit avenue and accelerated towards the motorway.

He returned his car, and caught a Frontier Airlines flight to Denver and then onwards to Salt Lake City. As he emerged into the hot sunlight of Utah in late March, he was met by his old friend, colleague and Mormon, Dan Buchanan.

Chapter 7

Dan had been a lecturer at UCL years previously, when Bryn was starting up professionally. Indeed, he had occupied the post that Bryn now held. His background was University of Utah, Rhodes scholarship, Oxford, UCL and now Dean of Studies at Brigham Young University in the town of Provo, Utah. He was a handsome man who wore his Mormonism lightly, certainly discreetly, and at UCL the only characteristic that had marked him out from other academics was a disinclination to smoke or drink alcohol or coffee. He made nothing of his beliefs in conversation and Bryn had always found him tolerantly uncritical of his own shortcomings, which at that time embraced a fair amount of tobacco and a great deal of alcohol. He was, you might say and quite accurately, a Christian gentleman. Indeed, Bryn had always been a little in awe of his remarkable lack both of doubt and arrogance.

BYU was the flagship university of Mormonism, or – as the believers preferred it to be called – of the Church of Jesus Christ of Latter Day Saints. Nearly all the students were of the faith and famously well-behaved. A condition of their enrolment was that they did not drink, fornicate, smoke or take drugs. A condition to which, uniquely in Bryn's experience of students, a large number actually seemed able to adhere.

Dan at this time was both an eminent Utah academic and a Mormon bishop. Bryn found that, also, slightly intimidating. He had never quite overcome the childhood memories of his first Sherlock Holmes story, *A Study in Scarlet*, and its highly-coloured and conventionally hostile portrayal of the Mormon leadership as fanatical and ruthless – a sort of nineteenth century Taliban. In reality, it was several years since Dan had served as a bishop, which was a spare time function of strictly limited duration. As with old American Presidents, though, the title did not desert the holder after he had ceased to perform its duties.

"Have you ever thought again about moving to America?" said Dan suddenly, as they drove down the main highway from Salt Lake City that dives south towards Las Vegas.

"It has been in my mind," he replied. Cautiously.

"Is it still a problem for Marion?"

"No."

He knew perfectly well what Dan was getting at, with his usual discretion. Marion's refusal to travel to America had always puzzled his friend, who was accustomed to a less discriminating level of spousal support. Years previously, an outside chance of a post at an east coast university had gone begging at least partly because of Marion, and Dan had probably thought Bryn's reluctance to pursue it unprofessional. If Bryn was now less than honest with his monosyllabic response, it was because this was still not a subject that the two of them could discuss freely.

He turned away from the conversation and watched the road markers speeding by. He noticed that each one was topped with an image of the beehive; it was, his friend explained, the symbol of the Mormon community.

He had been invited to stay at Dan's family home. This was a massively baronial structure in the Utah desert below Salt Lake City, surrounded by its own sprinkler-nourished oasis of green lawns, vegetable gardens and lavish flower beds. It had been built fairly recently in cream brick, with gables and dormer windows sprouting at the flanks. The presence of the Church within was inescapable. The Book of Mormon lay on small tables all around the house. Photographs of Brigham Young and other leaders up to the present day were framed on the walls. In Bryn's own bedroom hung one of the Victorian illustrations from the great Book itself: a painting of a white-robed Jesus Christ, glowing with inner light and communing with a group of sturdy young men in skirts. He recognized them as 'Nephites': the pre-Columbian, Jewish-descended Native Americans, belief in whose historical existence is central to the Mormon faith.

That evening, Bryn was guest of honour at a dinner in a restaurant in nearby Sundance Village. Half a dozen faculty members had been invited to keep him company and it became evident quite early on that *their* devotion to the Church might not always match Dan's or that of his charming and equally committed wife Martha. While these two stuck to orange juice and water, others less devoutly indulged the wine list. Most of them at the end of the meal also took coffee; one or two a Bourbon or a Scotch.

Bryn's immediate neighbour round the table was a lively forty-ish female academic who answered his more direct questions about current Mormon politics with a startling frankness. He began to suspect that, though something like ninety per cent of the population of Utah was still formally Mormon, their relationship with their faith might cover as wide a spectrum of relative commitment as the millions of his fellow countrymen who, in public opinion polls, still claimed affiliation to the Church of England.

He was conscious though of one other, unifying, factor, which was their history. There was a palpable common pride in what they had achieved since Brigham Young's great trek across America in the middle of the nineteenth century to found their community here in the salt desert.

"You will still find," said his neighbour, "a very powerful sense of family. In the literal sense, because children are so much at the centre of our lives. Also because the founding families that colonized the State one hundred and fifty or so years ago are still here and many continue to be influential. Also because we feel, even those of us who are imperfect believers, *chosen*. We are a tribe not so unlike the Jews. If you were to read the Book of Mormon you would know what I mean by that. And unfortunately we evoke the same kinds of passion in others."

Somehow – though Bryn suspected he might have helped to steer it in that direction – the conversation turned to crime and the likelihood of being robbed, assaulted or murdered in such a God-fearing community. He told his story about being followed in Chicago and his brush with a potential mugger on a side street on his way to a restaurant. An older man sitting opposite, to whom his colleagues deferred in these matters, assured Bryn that Utah had one of the lowest rates for violent crime in the United States.

"Statistically, you have a zero point zero zero two per cent chance of being murdered in Utah," he said authoritatively. "You were approximately ten times as likely to be murdered in Chicago as you are in Utah."

"The Saints are a peaceful community," said Martha kindly, and patted his hand. "I do not think you should worry yourself here."

"Do you not allow guns then?" asked Bryn.

It was a disingenuousness thing to say. And not a topic he should have raised with Martha. She sat for while in uncomfortable silence until Dan intervened.

"Bryn, dear friend," he said quietly from across the table. "This is a frontier community. Do not ask too much. But we do have gun control laws, even if they might seem a little permissive from your civilized European perspective."

"And you have gun fairs too, I think," said Bryn.

Maybe he had drunk too much good Californian wine to register the warning in Dan's tone. He did not mean to be rude. But this was a subject that had become very interesting to him.

Dan meanwhile did not respond. He gazed at him quizzically. It was Bryn's lively neighbour who stepped into the breach.

"Sure we do," she said briskly. "Our very own *Crossroads of the West* Gun Show which I'm proud to say is the biggest in

America, several times a year. You should check it out, Dan. Anybody can go and pick up a hand-piece there, anybody. Or two or three."

"Is there a Rapids gun show?" asked Bryn.

There was another moment of silence before the older academic opposite him spoke.

"Well there's the *RAPID Show*," he said. "But that's altogether a different matter. It's a once a year at the Expo Center in Salt Lake City and it's only for dealers and insiders. 'Rapid'," he added, "as in Rifles And Pistols for Internal Defense. That's a serious affair. They don't let the good ole boys into that show. Or you and me. No sir."

"He means it's only for the really big guys. Like security companies and arms salesmen. And the Mafia," said Bryn's neighbour, grinning at him.

As they left, Bryn noticed that Dan hung back to have a conversation with a short, grey-blonde man at a neighbouring table. His face struck a chord. The man rose and shook Dan's hand warmly.

"Who is that?" said Bryn to his new friend.

"He's called Robert Redford," she said. "He owns the place."

Next morning, Dan drove him in to the university and he gave his lecture, with laptop illustrations, just as he had at the University of Michigan. The auditorium this time was packed. Not only were there students but also many senior members of the faculty in attendance. It was a considerable contrast to the twenty or so reluctant spectators in Ann Arbor. They listened in attentive silence as he talked about the Civil War, its effect upon the British economy, the disastrous assumption of the South from the outset that Britain would support them against Lincoln, and the great numbers of immigrant soldiers from the British Isles and Europe who fought on both sides.

In Ann Arbor, when he had finished, and Arnie Kendall had been thanking him on all their behalves, the students were already drifting out, checking for text messages on their cell-phones and chatting amongst themselves. Here, they stayed in their seats and there were questions from all parts of the house. A number even indicated some prior research into his topic and he found himself fairly hard-pressed to answer them.

The most taxing question though – albeit politely enough couched – came from an elderly academic into whose territory he suspected he may have strayed. But the old scholar seemed pleased by Bryn's answer and nodded to him afterwards in approval. Finally, as if on a pre-arranged cue, one of the students stood up and proposed a vote of thanks to 'Professor Williams for coming all this way to share his great knowledge so generously with us.' There was a long round of applause. It had been a thoroughly pleasant – and quite unreal – experience.

He was sorry to leave Dan and his community, though he had never really understood Mormonism and had never wanted to. He was confounded by the movement's bizarre origins, based as they were on scriptures apparently inscribed on gold plates buried by a Jewish Indian in a mountainside in upstate new York in the fifth century AD; and which had then mysteriously disappeared after the movement's founder, Joseph Smith, had rendered them into English in 1828.

It was never difficult to draw up a charge sheet of unacceptable practice, from the extreme prejudice shown early on to Negroes (in contrast to their faith-led admiration for Native Americans) to the rampant polygamy of the energetically founding fathers. And though all this had long since been formally expunged from mainstream Mormonism, he thought he could still see traces of ancient attitudes. Such as the contented subservience of women like Martha to the all-absorbing needs of husband and family. Or the discomfort within parts of the Church about private behaviour – homosexuality, for example – that was perceived to challenge their natural order of things.

And yet.

It might have been no more than the normal hospitality extended by a frontier people to a stranger, but Bryn sensed in this modern version of Mormonism an unusual generosity of spirit. In Dan and his friends he glimpsed something close to what he imagined was the essence of Christianity, which he took to be the inclusive tolerance of Christ rather than the unforgiving and partisan God of the Old Testament.

He had of course met people of similar disposition within other Christian communities. Nevertheless, it did appear to him that the Mormon commitment to charity, to serving others, and to family was a deeper, more all-embracing and more institutionalized phenomenon. He recognized in Dan the iron certainties of a Scottish presbyter; but he also saw a practical willingness to co-exist with other people's foibles. In this, his friend did not seem untypical. Bryn could not avoid contrasting the mixture of commitment and tolerance with so much of the rest of America; or, if it came to that, with his own country. Neither America nor Europe. This was a land where he might – one day – be very comfortable.

He had given himself three free days in Utah before he had to fly back to London. He rented a car and set out to explore some of the canyons to the south of Salt Lake City. The weather was perfect. Warm, dry, cloudless. He drove off down Route 15, past Salem, Nephi, Scipio, Fillmore and Parowan until he reached Cedar City, where he turned into the car park of a Denny's restaurant for lunch.

After he had eaten, he returned to his car and spread an old map across the bonnet. He had borrowed it from his recorder-playing friend, Bill, who had used it on a family tour of the American West ten or so years previously. The map showed what it called the 'Indian Country' of Utah and Arizona – which meant that it highlighted helpful alternative routes to the main tourist highways. Bryn hoped that it would allow him to cut across country and save time in his ambitious schedule. Today he hoped to get to both Zion and Bryce Canyons and tomorrow drive down to Monument Valley.

It looked feasible. The main road for tourists skirted the mountains by going due east and then turning ninety degrees to the north. On the map though there was an 'Indian road' which cut out half the distance by going directly and diagonally from

Zion Canyon to the turn-off for Bryce, using a mountain pass. It seemed a straightforward and unexceptional route, the obvious short cut to take, if only you knew about it. He decided to spend no more than a couple of hours in Zion so that he could travel on and enjoy the evening sun on the famously pastel-shaded columns of Bryce Canyon, weathered like stalagmites and melting ice-cream.

As he folded up the map and put on his sunglasses, a very thin, bald man came out of the restaurant, climbed into a Ford Explorer and drove away to the south. Bryn registered the South Carolina number plates but attached no greater significance to it.

It was now satisfyingly hot. He stripped off his jacket, rolled up his sleeves and drove on.

At this time of the year there were few tourists. The car park at Zion was almost empty except for a couple of saloon cars. He wandered off down the trail into the Canyon itself. He felt utterly at ease in this wonderful land with its azure sky and almost total absence of evidence of present-day human intervention. He revelled in the primitive power of the place: the great stone monoliths towering over him and the spectacular mountain waterfalls. As he wandered deeper in, the valley opened out and he came upon some ancient Indian hieroglyphs scratched on a cliff face. How remote and lonely and perfect. He screwed up his eyes as he struggled to make sense of them, and the sweat trickled into his brows.

He really wished he had been sensible enough to buy a hat.

He gave himself an extra thirty minutes or so in the silent paradise. Not a soul passed him. He found a rock to sit on, shaded by the cliff face, and thought about Zelma and how, or whether, he would see her again. There would have to be other visits to America, other lectures to contrive. Perhaps she might find it easier to come to London.

Or perhaps not.

Time was passing. He walked, quite briskly now, back to the car park.

As he rounded the final corner on the path approaching it, a loud crack, as of a rifle shot, rang out.

His initial response was one of confusion. The sound was at first more puzzling than alarming. He pondered for a second or two whether his ears, or his brain, were interpreting correctly. Then, unmistakably this time, there was another loud shot, re-echoing and ricocheting around the canyon. Halfway up the cliff opposite, he glimpsed – just for a fraction of a moment – the reflection of sunlight on glass and something dark and thin which might have been a rifle barrel. He flung himself abruptly to the ground. He began to scrabble his way frantically on his belly to the shelter of a large, fallen rock.

There was a third shot followed instantly by a fourth. A large fragment of his rocky shelter burst over him and he heard the bullet whine away down the canyon. He tore away at the hard red earth with his fingers in a fruitless effort to make some kind of shallow trench.

And then he waited.

It seemed to him that he had two courses. He might stay here, cowering in the shadow, until it was possible that his assailant had given up and gone or until – it occurred to him – the man decided to come up the track, found him in his pathetic foxhole and put a bullet through his temple.

That was the first course. On balance, he preferred the second. But this would require him to make a sprint for his car, which was probably three or four hundred yards away. There were other rocks on the route that he might be able to dive behind if – as he surely would – he came under fire. The immediate problem, though, was screwing up enough courage to break from his fragile cover.

He strained his ears for any assisting clues to guide him. For several long minutes there was total silence. Not even a breeze in the scrubby trees scattered down the valley. And then – at last – he heard the revving engine of a vehicle, by the sound of it a fairly large one. It was not – as he had hoped – leaving, but arriving. He heard tyres scrunching to a halt on the gravel, doors opening and closing, and some distant voices. The voices approached and faded away. He waited.

And waited.

Total silence still. He really had to make a move. He peered around the edge of his rock and saw, about a quarter of a mile away, a group of youngsters clustered around a Park Ranger who seemed about to take them on a tour up the adjacent valley. He began to feel bolder. Keeping still within the shadow of the cliff face, he lifted his head to scan the surrounding terrain, and in particular the rocks and the precipice in front of him. Nothing. No sign at all of the rifle. No glimmer or suggestion of a sighting glass.

Time at last for action.

He burst from his rock, bent low like a sprinter in the blocks, driving his thighs forward with every ounce of power a sedentary, middle-aged, academic could muster. Then a hundred or so yards further on, as the lactic acid built in his muscles and the pain began to fill his legs and lungs, he hurled himself behind the largest stone on the track and lay in the dirt gasping. There was still no sign or sound. He waited until his energy seeped back, and then burst out again. On he careered, dodging and lurching left and right like a drunken rugby player, until he reached the car park. He half collapsed, half threw himself into the shadow of the biggest vehicle he could find.

He slowly regathered his strength and wits. Next to his left cheek was a South Carolina number plate, almost certainly the same one he had seen in Cedar City. The Ford Explorer was empty. Parked next to it was the Park Ranger's truck, with three rows of seats inside it. Beyond that was his own car.

He fished out his keys and aimed the electronic beam at the doors. They clicked and flashed; and he was off again. Into the driver's seat. No time for the seat belt. A roar of the engine as he crashed it into *DRIVE*. And away. A group of the children were returning to the car park, led by the Park Ranger, and he swerved wildly round them. Somewhere behind him he heard the Ranger's outraged "Hey!!" and a few mild squeals from the children as he sped away. But he had no time for that. He was out of the park, and driving as fast as the car allowed, east towards Bryce Canyon.

He found the short cut immediately. Without the map he would certainly have missed it. It was about a hundred yards beyond an Indian trading post set alongside the main highway and decorated with displays of moccasins and head-dresses to lure in the tourists coming from the National Park. At the turn-off for the Indian road, there was a small sign saying *Impassable When Wet.*

It was now eighty degrees or more and the sky was cloudless and blue. There had been no rain in the west for weeks. He turned back in his seat to check the main road behind him. There was not a car, or SUV, to be seen.

"Wet, it ain't" murmured Bryn to himself as he turned off the highway and accelerated past the sign.

For some time, the new road was no worse than many he had travelled on in America. At first it was tarmacked. Then after a few miles it became the familiar hard dusty surface of so many American backcountry by-ways. As he had expected, it began gradually to rise as it got deeper into the mountain pass. Early on he passed the occasional dwelling: a log cabin or even a single storey brick house set back in a clearing amongst the trees. After that the only sign of human occupation was a rare glimpse of a corral or of a small wooden building way up on the mountainside.

His car for this trip was the kind of robust, small General Motors saloon popular with the rental companies, who knew how badly their clients could treat it. Since there has never been much compunction in the rural states about driving any vehicle off the road, such cars had been routinely manufactured to give passengers what might euphemistically be described as a firm ride. As the surface of Bryn's Indian short cut began to deteriorate, the little saloon came into its own, bouncing along uncompromisingly on its tough Detroit City springs.

After forty-five minutes or so, high up on the mountain pass, some snow appeared on the side of the road. This was something he had not expected at all. He was tempted to stop the car and take a shutter-delayed photograph of himself against the blazing sky and the melting snow, to amaze his friends back home.

As he drove on, the snow on both sides of the track began to bank up. But because the air was still very warm, the road became progressively more wet and slippery. Every so often the car slid on a small patch of mud. When a patch was serious enough to set the wheels for a split second spinning freely, he began to be concerned that he might lose traction altogether. His solution was to press on harder so that the car's impetus would take him clear of all hazards. It was a challenge to his driving skills; and very satisfying.

The pools of mud became more frequent. He developed a technique which involved driving slightly above or below anything that might be a rut or a hole in the road, and giving a little touch on the accelerator just as the car reached the muddy hazard, sufficient to ensure safe passage to the other side. He found this worked very well, though it needed an unusual amount of concentration.

After a while, as the road continued to rise higher, the mud and slipperiness began to subside and the surface improved. Good driving, he reflected, was its own reward. There were higher banks of snow on either side of the track, but the snow was harder now and crisper. It was possible to drive with more confidence and even, with the right skill, a little faster.

He had been travelling in this way for quite some time, when the car swept round a bend at about thirty miles an hour and rammed straight into a tumbled pile of snow. The rock face from which it had slipped glistened above him. The car had driven deep into the fall and was stuck firm. The wheels spun. The snow beneath them gradually turned into a churning, muddy liquid. The vehicle over-revved hysterically and sank deeper and ever so slowly into the enveloping whiteness.

He climbed out to look for damage. The car seemed fine; but all four wheels were hub-high in slush. He tried to drive out forwards and then in reverse. He unloaded his bags, the spare wheel, and anything else that could be detached and stacked by the wayside. Fallen branches and stones from the forest were squeezed under the wheels to give them some purchase on the ground. He even got out and pushed himself, with the car in first gear. The wheels spun uselessly in the creamy mud.

The struggle lasted nearly an hour until he was utterly exhausted. The light was beginning to fade and with it his last shreds of optimism that the car could be shifted. It was even further embedded in the snow than when he had started. He leaned against the boot in despair.

A wave of nausea welled up within him and he trudged away into the trees to retch. By his own reckoning, he was at least thirty miles from civilization. The day was closing in. The temperature was dropping like a stone. Up here on the mountain under the cloudless sky it seemed certain to fall well below zero by nightfall. He cursed his failure to bring a mobile phone to call for help; but then doubted that reception would in any case have been possible in such a remote location. As he stood there, bent over amongst the trees and with his hands on his knees, he began to wonder if he would even survive.

He pulled himself back upright and started to collect his thoughts. He searched the surrounding landscape for clues and assistance, but found himself instead marvelling at its sheer, stark, unforgiving beauty.

There were pine trees everywhere, scattered in groups across the fading white mountainside. As the country rose to the north, the blanket of snow became thicker until it overwhelmed the trees and the edges of the mountain softened to the horizon. Towards the south, the road that had brought him curved out of sight under the tumbled drift. There was no question of driving back.

He went back to the car and looked again at Bill's Indian map. He calculated that he was nearer to the end of the pass than to its beginning. It was possible that the road would start descending again beyond the rise just ahead. He repacked the car, switched to his toughest shoes (unfortunately his smartest pair), put on several more layers of clothes and struck north.

When he reached the next ridge, it was only to see another snowbound ridge a mile or so ahead. It was becoming impossible now to tell whether the going underfoot was likely to be a reasonable dirt road, or a broken track, or worse. Here and there were traces of a snowmobile which had passed through perhaps weeks before. The only other sign of human existence was a single animal shed set well back from the path, which he passed after about three hours of walking.

The snow was thicker and thicker on the ground and the effort of trudging first ankle and then shin deep was taking its toll. Yet it seemed perfectly clear from the map that he should very soon reach the final ridge from which he would see the main road below and perhaps some habitation. So he pressed on again.

A further hour later, when he breasted what he fervently hoped was the last ridge, the sun had long since fallen below the western mountains. And all he could see ahead in the gathering gloom was snow. He had no choice. He turned round and trudged back the way he had come until he reached the solitary animal shed. He had hoped that he could retrace his footsteps to the car and sleep there, but it was already too dark and too late. He turned off the track and climbed up the hillside to the little wooden building.

It was in surprisingly good condition and appeared to be weatherproof. There was a small door and even a latch of sorts which he had no difficulty prising open. Inside was a wooden plank floor raised a couple of feet above the ground and in the corner was a large blue tarpaulin sheet.

He rolled himself up within the tarpaulin and tried to sleep. The cold was very near to unbearable. Only by wrapping himself within the tightest cocoon, with as many concentric layers as possible, was he able to achieve some degree of tolerable warmth and persuade his juddering shivers finally to subside and fade away.

Initially, the silence outside was more absolute than he had ever in his life known. Then gradually he became aware of the faint sounds of animals moving through the snow – and an occasional low bass grunting and scrabbling of something larger nearby. Some of the noises were very close indeed. At one point he thought he could hear movement under the floor of the shack itself. He did not sleep that night.

Chapter 8

The sky next day was once more a brilliant, cloudless blue and the mountain whiter and more featureless than ever. The ridge he had been aiming for seemed very remote indeed. After two hours of walking, the snow had become so thick that he was sinking knee-deep into it with every step. He remembered also that this part of Southern Utah was exceptionally high, possibly as much as twelve thousand feet above sea level, with some danger of altitude sickness as well as all the fatigue and hunger.

He carried on for a mile or more until he felt barely able to move forward. He was now ploughing waist deep through the snow. Yet he could imagine no alternative to struggling onward. The escape route had to lie ahead. The map said so, and he had travelled so far that it could only be a matter of time, surely an hour at maximum, before he broke through to the main road. It was inconceivable that he could abandon his plan.

And then, as he reached the brow of another bend and gazed at the unfolding whiteness ahead, he could see that the ridge before him merely heralded another ridge and another beyond that, stretching away to the north under an unbroken shroud of snow. There was no sign of any civilization and no possibility whatever of breaking out in that direction. He had to go back.

His only chance now lay with the car, with the prospect of another night on the mountain, wrapped up inside it – if he had the strength left to reach it. And then? He *had* to be able to walk out to the south, even if it meant a forced march of thirty or more miles the following day.

At least the going improved once he had, for the second time, passed the animal shack. Because it was quite early, the ground was colder and less muddy than it had been before. Even though he was tired he began to make good progress and his morale to improve. Eventually he reached an old trailer parked in the trees, which he had missed in the twilight of the previous day. It looked as if it had been left there years previously. A pine sapling had grown up through the tow-bar and the tyre-less hubs were badly rusted and supported on bricks and chunks of pine trunk. He decided to climb in through a window in the hope perhaps of finding supplies of food or drinkables that he might annex.

It was a reasonable guess by now that no human being had stayed overnight on this pass since, at the latest, the previous autumn. The chances of there being anything edible were risibly slight. But optimism and slight chances were all he had to cling to. In this surreal landscape, as far beyond his experience as the country at the top of Jack's beanstalk, anything after all might happen.

It turned out that the trailer was not difficult to break into. Though the door appeared to be locked – or rusted or frozen in – it was possible to prise open a poorly-fitted window and squeeze and scramble through.

The inside was adrift with dead flies, and filthy. There were a few shredded rags of curtain on the windows and a bulgy grey mattress on a built-in bench. Two hundred or more insects lay in the bottom of the sink, in what might have been the trailer's kitchen. But there were no food cupboards, no cooking arrangements and no fridge. Above the sink, though, was a small cabinet with a wire front and inside it was a single open box about a quarter full of the little multi-coloured corn rings popular with children as a breakfast cereal. He emptied them all into his pocket and scrambled out the way he had entered.

He carried on down the track, crunching the corn rings as he walked, washing them down from time to time with a little water manufactured from handfuls of snow. He had started to feel so buoyant that he sang to himself as he walked and the echo of his music came back to him encouragingly from the distance.

> *If you go down to the woods today*
> *You're sure of a big surprise.*

It was not beyond possibility that the sound might carry a few miles across the silent landscape and be heard by some passing snowmobiler. Might there indeed be skiers beyond the surrounding ridges who would hear his voice and raise an alarm? What a splendidly iconic British image he would present, filing through the white wilderness like a heroic marriage of *Scott of the Antarctic* and *The Bridge Over the River Kwai...*

As time passed, the distances between landmarks began to seem greater than he had remembered. After the euphoria of finding something to eat, and the sugar rush that followed, his mood was replaced by one of mounting pessimism. Even if he reached the car, was he sure he could endure another night as cold as the last? How could he manage a thirty mile march without better sustenance?

He had slowed his pace considerably. The important thing, it seemed to him now, was to conserve what little energy he had so that he could be sure to reach the car. He sat down on a bare rock, mockingly warm and dry in the sunshine, and raised his head to look around him.

He could see a building through the trees away to the right. It was impossible to tell whether it was more substantial than the rusty trailer. But it might be worth another deed of burglary. The track divided ahead of him and he turned off down a fork towards the west side of the valley.

The way went unexpectedly downhill. There were stones underfoot and a trickle of melt water now where the snow had been washed away. A hundred yards further on, the route vanished into a fast-flowing river sweeping past at right angles.

No doubt in the summer months this would have presented no obstacle to a high axle four-wheel-drive truck intending to cross it. In the spring, though, swollen as it was by the run-off from the mountain snow, the torrent looked impassable. He stood in the middle of the track at the edge of the rushing waters, gazing at this latest cruel and beautiful phenomenon. When he looked up again, he could make out the top of a cabin above the pine trees ahead. But he could see no way of reaching it.

He had, however, long since parted company with old-fashioned commonsense. Just as hours earlier he could not intelligently accept, until physically compelled to, that it was impossible to walk out of the mountain to the north, so now it became a case of pressing stubbornly forward until there was no remaining scintilla of doubt that the attempt was yet one more hopeless folly. He took what encouragement he could from the fact that, though the river was wide and running alarmingly fast, it did not appear – at this point in the terrain – to be very deep. He could at least test the possibility of wading across it.

He took off his shoes and socks and trousers and tied them all together in a rough bundle around his neck.

The water was colder than he would have thought physically possible. He had to lean into it at an angle of about sixty degrees to stay upright. There was a scattering of boulders strewn across the riverbed, swept down from the mountain above, and he elected to use them as stepping-stones to reduce the volume of rushing water pressing upon him. Progress became a hazardous sequence of jumps and stretches from rock to rock, with some of them further below the turbulent surface than others. The water, though, was so crystalline that it was possible to plot a path ahead all the way to the other side. The trick, if he could only manage it, was to keep his nerve and not think of the dangers of slipping in too deep and being swept away downstream.

He had never had a sportsman's balance. There were several moments when he found himself fighting with all his energy to stay upright. The stones, though large enough, were treacherous. Some lurched unpredictably when he stepped on them, or revealed themselves too late to be highly polished and slippery. At one point, as he teetered uncertainly in mid-river, it seemed as if it was going to be a re-run in microcosm of the whole experience on the mountain, unable to go forward and too fearful to retreat.

But in the end he got there. He exhaled the lungful of air he had been holding for the best part of two minutes. He put on his socks, trousers and shoes and looked again around him.

On this side of the river, the path curved sharply to the left and through a little cleft in the hillside towards a six-barred iron gate. When he reached the gate, he found it heavily padlocked and bound with barbed wire. He clambered very carefully over it and carried on up the hill along an avenue lined with dense bushes and pine trees. After a hundred yards or more he emerged quite suddenly into a clearing. He was at the top of a rise from which he could survey the valley in all directions. In another part of the world and another time, he reflected, it might have been the perfect location for an Iron Age fort or a medieval hill town.

In front of him now, on the very peak of the hill, were not one but three cabins. All were raised a couple of feet above the ground, with steps up to the doors. Their setting was austere and windswept and forbidding. Even in the bright sunlight, it was a location for a frightening children's story. It was obvious again that no-one had been here for many months.

The nearest cabin was the one he had spotted through the trees. It looked at first the most promising. It had a verandah and appeared to contain two or three rooms. It was also very securely locked up. The windows were shuttered and bolted and the door was thick and impregnable. He debated smashing his way through a window with the aid of one of the logs of wood that lay in a neat pile alongside the cabin, but an inappropriate aversion to such violence persuaded him – this time – to try the other cabins first.

The second building was even more substantially made, with thick logs for walls instead of weatherboarding. There was a main door under a small porch at the front and a smaller door at the back. Both were, if possible, more impregnable than before. The windows were high and difficult to reach. But he found one at the rear of the building which was accessible and which – if he was prepared to break glass – could be unlatched and forced open.

Very tentatively, he fractured one of the panes with a stone and levered the shards away until it was possible to reach inside and open the latch, and hoisted and wriggled himself through. He found himself in a tiny, dark room with a single bed hard against a wall. A door led to a short corridor and to another door beyond that into the large main room. There he found a settee, a dining table and chairs, a built-in scullery and cupboards with glass doors through which tins and packets could be seen.

Unfurled fly paper hung from the exposed ceiling rafters and flies again lay dead in their hundreds in the sink and in drifts on all the windowsills. He puzzled why this should be so. Maybe their entire life cycle had been run within this house, and their final collective act had been to batter themselves to death against the window glass images of the world outside.

But he was not the only one to have broken into this cabin. A hawk plunged across the room in panic and flew again and again at the huge stone fireplace in the opposite wall. It could only have entered down the chimney and he guessed it had been trapped in the cabin for several days. It was not a large creature, perhaps about the size of an English Peregrine, an undistinguished brown and white except for some reddish feathers around the tail.

After a while the bird stopped its wild flapping and clung to the top of a dresser with its beak open, panting and watching him with a staring yellow eye while he looked over the provisions in the scullery cupboards. There was nothing he particularly recognized but there seemed to be food supplies of some kind. He picked up a large tin jug from a shelf, unbolted the main door, propped it open with a piece of wood and left.

The cabin had changed the picture entirely. He knew at once what he had to do. There was now no question of attempting to walk off the mountain today, or of huddling in the car or a mountain shack. He did not know what the packets and tins in the cabin contained but he was confident he could contrive some kind of meal. He had already decided to spend the rest of the day and all the night in the cabin, sleeping as much as possible, and gathering strength for the following morning. He would start out by dawn at the latest to give him the best possible chance of reaching the road to the south before nightfall.

He took the jug back down to the river, washed it thoroughly and filled it with water. He climbed upstream to an overlook from which he could see the main track curving away to the south. Far away, just before the road disappeared around a rock face, the car could be seen, half-submerged within the snow. As the road came nearer, and descended to the valley junction where he had just turned off, he noticed that the snow had melted away and the track had become clear and dry.

The hawk had gone by the time he returned to the cabin. Within the recesses of the food cupboard he found a packet of desiccated instant mashed potato, some tins of corned beef, more dry breakfast cereal, and a bottle of concentrated cola flavouring.

It was the box of matches in one of the scullery drawers that made the final difference. He had not been looking for anything like this, and it was a gift from heaven. Not for the first time he found his mood swinging back from grim determination to euphoria. It seemed obvious that things were beginning to turn in his direction. He could begin to enjoy himself once more.

He carried in some of the logs and kindling that were stacked outside and made a great fire which soon transformed the cabin into his own little nirvana of cosiness. He poured all the river water into a heavy pot and placed it in the centre of the flames. He had probably read too much history about the dangers of the fast-water born bugs characteristic of that part of the country, and which had so debilitated Brigham Young when he was leading the great Mormon trek through the Wasatch Mountains to the Utah desert. Very likely the iciness of the winter water would have prevented them this time of the year. But he decided not to take the risk.

While he waited for the water to boil, he went exploring. The cabin was rather well appointed. Attached to the main sitting room with its scullery was a suite of very much smaller rooms: the tiny bedroom he had first passed through and two other little bedrooms, plus a bathroom. The back door had been locked and was evidently the normal means of final exit, though he could find no key for it. There was a layer of perhaps six months' dust over everything but otherwise all was neat and tidy. It had an economic and practical feel about it with no books or games or other means of entertainment.

A more interesting and disturbing find, though, was the cabin's attic. It was accessed by a flight of wooden steps directly from the sitting room, and through a trap door. The only light reaching it was from below or leaking through the eaves. When his eyes became accustomed to the gloom, he could see that the floor was littered with large packing boxes, and a couple of dusty beds. There were also pieces of agricultural equipment and horse bridles and saddles; and two long-barrelled rifles wrapped in coarse blankets. Other less explicable materials lay at the far end of the space but he did not explore further. There might be secrets here which he preferred not to probe. He was glad to scramble back down the steps and close the trap door securely behind him. He went outside.

The snow had melted almost entirely from the bare, rocky ground on which he now stood. Outside the cabin the ground fell away on all sides into pine forest. A few hundred yards to the west log fencing marked out a huge clearing which he took to be a corral. Way beyond that, it was possible to see a low-lying greener valley stretching into the far distance. The white mountains to the north, though, gleamed as fiercely as before. How foolish even to have contemplated taking them on.

The sense of remoteness was magnificent. He felt newly secure, not threatened now but protected by his environment. He had made the right decision at last.

When the water had boiled, he mixed up a hash from the dry potato and the contents of two of the corned beef tins and cooked it over the fire. It was as fine a meal as he had ever known. To say he wolfed it down would be to malign wolves. He flavoured a pint of the remaining warm water with a little of the very sweet, sickly cola essence, and drank it all. He had derived less pleasure from a fine claret.

There were blankets in a large chest of drawers and he made up a bed on the settee by the fireplace. He banked up the fire with ashes from the grate until it was an almost smokeless glow and settled down for the night. It was barely six in the evening. He intended a very early start.

He was asleep within seconds.

He did not wake at all until about five in the morning. The light was just beginning to creep over the mountains to the east. The fire was still alive and warm and circles of red glowed deep within the grate. He lay for a while examining the memory of a dream.

It had been another of those perfectly rational, fully narrated, dreams which are so difficult at first to separate from waking reality. He had dreamt that a black Ford Explorer with South Carolina number plates and chains around its wheels had driven slowly up the main track from the south. It had stopped at the junction with the path down to the river. Then it had driven to the north and returned and stopped again. And there it had waited. And was still waiting when the dream ended.

He brooded on this narrative for some while.

Then he felt compelled, however absurdly, to confirm that it had only been in his imagination. So he pulled on his clothes and walked down to the river and went upstream again to his earlier overlook. There was the main track still curving away to the south. The dawn light glowed faintly on the windows of his stranded car far in the distance. The road climbing up to it was clear and dry. And of the black Ford Explorer, there was no sign.

Back at the cabin, he used the last of the water to make himself breakfast with some dry cereal from a package, and coffee without milk. He found a large piece of brown wrapping paper and a pencil stub and – like Goldilocks apologizing for the porridge – wrote out a letter to the cabin owners. He set down his proper regrets for the broken glass and for the supplies he had consumed. He provided his address in England and urged the owners to let him know the costs of repair so that he could in due time reimburse them. He provided a brief but suitably vivid description of what had happened to him on the mountain. He did not suppose they would ever follow up – but they would at least have the comfort of an explanation for the assault on their property.

He placed the wrapping paper letter as ostentatiously as he could in the middle of the table. He slid the bolts of the front door back into place and climbed out again through the broken window. He hoped the piece of board he jammed into the space where the pane had been would make it secure against the elements.

It was still very early morning.

The deep frozen night had, for the time being, moderated the snow melt and the river was raging a great deal less fiercely. It was barely more than a brook and some of the stepping-stone rocks stood proud of the surface of the water. He crossed quickly and walked back up the path, now icy and slippery, and turned right at the fork. As he approached the stranded car, the sun edged above the mountain horizon and the eggshell sky began to take on some brighter colours.

The snow crunched again under his feet. He slipped in a small trough of black ice and almost lost balance.

And then he stopped.

In front of him, in the snow, and away up the road beyond the car, were two sets of tyre tracks. They were wide, as of a heavy vehicle, and the contours of wheel chains were precisely etched in the frozen snow.

He held his breath. Absolute silence.

After a few moments he walked slowly up to the car. He moved as quietly as he could, keenly listening for any sound that might suggest that he was not alone. He knelt down to examine his vehicle.

It was still deep within its white sepulchre, just as he had left it nearly two days previously. But in other respects the situation was transformed. Where before the car had been sunk in snow up to and beyond its axles, its tyres now rested on iron hard ridges of ice. Some of the entombing snow had fallen back, and downhill from the drift the road was clear and brown. He worked round to the front of the car and, quite gently, pushed the bonnet. It slipped a few inches across the ice. He pushed again, harder, and the whole vehicle slid suddenly away till the rear tyres reached the brown ground at the edge of the snow, where it halted.

It *had* to be worth a try. He climbed in and turned the ignition key: the engine fired immediately. He slipped it into reverse gear and applied the most cautious and gradual pressure to the accelerator to give the front-driven tyres every chance to bite. Almost at once the car eased out of the drift and onto dry land.

He could barely believe it. Again, the mountain had overthrown his expectations. After the shocks of the first two days, its tricks had – at least for the moment – turned more generous. But it was obvious that he needed to move quickly now, before the sun rose higher above the mountain skyline and the snow and ice began to melt and less welcome developments supervened. And there was now also another, and more troubling, reason for him to get out as rapidly as possible.

As he drove, he became aware that the road had deteriorated markedly since he had last travelled on it. Already – and increasingly as he descended (and the temperature began to rise) – melted snow was covering stretches of the track in pools of water. Ice was no longer the problem. The greatest danger was again of becoming stranded, with wheels spinning in the mud. He *had* to keep going to clear it all. He only hoped he would have enough wit, awareness and skill this time to negotiate everything safely.

He did not see much of the landscape. The sheer concentration on getting out and off the mountain consumed him. On a few occasions, as the car slid close to the edge of the track, he had the briefest glimpse of a steep gradient falling away to the right and forest or rock beyond. At other moments, as he wrenched the steering wheel to avoid pools and ruts or bounced against the earthen bank on the safer, left-hand side of the road, he felt for all the world as if he was in some terrifying, devil-driven go-kart race.

At last, after half an hour or more, the track became firmer. The tarmac he remembered from two days previously returned. He eased off the accelerator and, as he looked around, recognized the houses and clearings he had passed, it seemed, a lifetime ago.

He arrived at the main road. It was silent and empty in both directions. He turned right and parked alongside the 24-hour Indian Trading Post.

There was a solitary Navajo man behind the counter.

"Good morning, sir" said Bryn.

The man glanced at him and made no comment. Bryn took four Doctor Peppers from the cool cabinet, and some chocolate Hershey bars and placed them on the counter.

"Am I your first customer of the day?" he asked.

The man said nothing. He took the ten-dollar note, examined it against the light, and started counting out Bryn's change.

"I've been two nights on that mountain," burbled his customer. "I was stranded, you know. Only just escaped. Car got stuck in a snowdrift. I guess I'm lucky to survive. Spent a night in a cowshed wrapped up in a tarpaulin. Bloody cold, I can tell you. There were animals snuffling around. *Big* ones. What do you think? Grizzlies?"

The Navajo stared at him. He placed the Doctor Peppers and the Hershey bars in a large brown paper bag and pushed it across the counter towards him.

"No bears here, mister" he said at last. "Too far south."

Then he brightened slightly.

"Mountain lions though."

Chapter 9

He drove straight back to Salt Lake City and checked into a Travelodge on the southern outskirts. He left his car carefully parked around the back of the motel where it would be invisible to anyone passing up the main road.

He debated for some time what he should do next. Normally when someone has tried to kill a person, he reasoned, that person goes to the police and provides a full account. But it seemed to him that there were a few problems with this.

First of all, it was now two days – possibly three – since he had been attacked, and the trail was very likely to have gone cold. And he was not sure that he had *any* evidence to offer. Perhaps a broken rock fragment at the scene of the crime. He had not even had the wit to note down the South Carolina number-plate. But then of course it would have been false. And how could he expect the police to take his improbable tale of being stranded for two nights on the mountainside and escaping unscathed? Not to mention the dangerous driving as he left the Zion car-park, which might already have been reported by the Park Ranger. Plus the breaking and entry, and the theft of private property...

The clinching argument though was the near certainty that, if he reported the attack, he would miss his plane the next day. He was now simply anxious to escape the nightmare as rapidly as possible, and fly home to the – albeit relative – safety of the United Kingdom. He had no idea, none at all, why anyone should wish to kill him. But if they were determined to track him down in Chicago and follow him all the way to southern Utah, then only a fool would hang around to tell tales. Best to put it all behind him and get the hell out of here.

He stayed in his room for much of the day, dozing and watching television. Late in the evening, when it was dark, he went out and found a *Ruby Tuesday* restaurant where he filled up on spare ribs and – surprisingly good – micro-brewed ale. There were few people in the restaurant and none of them, he was careful to confirm, were thin and bald or wearing a light grey hooded coat.

Next morning was Sunday. His flight was early afternoon and he did not intend to leave until he had to. He slipped down to the motel breakfast bar and brought up a couple of doughnuts and some orange juice and coffee, and settled down to watch the early morning channels.

The news was dominated by the fall-out from the recent Presidential primaries. It seemed that the former governor from the mid-West and the black woman senator were both beginning to establish sizeable leads over the other candidates in their respective parties. An interesting contest was developing between a return to the 'traditional values' of family, enterprise and low taxes (on the one hand) and the 'liberal values' and intervention-ism current in Washington (on the other).

But Bryn was not in the mood for serious politics. He moved on to an early morning chat-show, hosted by the usual middle-aged comedian, but even he was having a discussion about the shifting demographics of modern America with his guest – an unsuccessful vice-presidential candidate of a few years' past.

He flicked on through three or four worship broadcasts until he arrived at a station he had never seen before. The main preacher had not yet arrived. The warm-up act was a middle-aged woman in a theatrically extravagant cocktail gown and a great quantity of make-up. She was singing a modern gospel song in front of a set that would not have looked out of place in Disneyland. The stage was decorated with artificial waterfalls and a giant revolving globe. Above it all flew an enormous American flag, its stars and stripes spreading across the scene like a giant cyclorama.

There were no seats in the vast auditorium. A packed crowd of perhaps ten thousand – he could only guess – stood together with their arms raised towards the *chanteuse*. The camera swooped over them, emphasizing their numbers and uniformity; and then cut to closer shots of small groups of shiny-eyed people, many very young, swaying and whooping with the music.

There was a commercial break. During it, the chanteuse appeared again, this time sitting at a table with a couple of small stars and stripes flags planted on it, like a cocktail decoration. She exhorted the viewers to send their donations to the *GodWorks* organization, to help spread the Christian message worldwide and to support their effort at home. She turned to a shiny-faced, middle-aged man sitting beside her and asked him what *he* had done for God. He also turned to camera, as if she was no longer there, took a deep breath, and explained how he had found God through the 'organization', had put behind him Satan, alcohol and loose behaviour, and now gave a tenth of his income. His reward, he already knew, was eternal happiness.

"And I believe you have made provision for *GodWorks* after your death?" prompted the chanteuse.

"I have so," said the man.

Back in the auditorium, an invisible electronic orchestra was winding up to a huge climax. Doors at the back of the stage opened upon a flood of light, through which emerged a tall figure in a shining lounge suit. He advanced downstage.

"God is good!" he bawled, and his voice echoed around the auditorium through a hundred loudspeakers. "God is good! And he loves ya!! God bless America!!!"

There followed a period of what a more ironic onlooker than Bryn might have called *pandemonium*. The crowd screamed. The cameras swooped. Men and women burst into tears. A number fell to their knees and held up their clasped hands as if praying to a holy icon.

The camera cut close to the man in the lounge suit. He was handsome, middle-aged and with a fine, glossy head of wavy brown hair. He was talking now to the greater audience the other side of their television sets. He became quieter and more intense.

"My fellow Americans," he said, in a gentle Southern accent. "We... *you*... are Almighty God's best hope. He is smiling down on each one of you today. We are all, all of us, called... *called*... to his presence. We are made in his image. This nation of ours, which was brought into existence *by* God, is *made* in his image. Just as our forefathers set out the way to God in our Great American Constitution, so must we bend all our thoughts, all our energies, all our resources, to making this land *again* a Christian land, bound to God and pledged to *His Works*!"

By now, his voice was mounting the rising curve of a huge crescendo. The camera pulled away and further away, forced back by the power of his oratory. Then he threw wide his arms as if about to embrace the throng within the auditorium and the millions beyond it.

" God," he cried, "is a good God! God *loves* America! God is smiling down on each one of you not just today but every day! Come to God! Let Him fill you with love, hope... *charity*! Be *changed* by God!! Let us *change* this nation, with God!!!"

In the front of the auditorium, below the stage, twenty or thirty young women appeared, all in cocktail gowns similar to that worn by the chanteuse, and carrying trays like cinema usherettes. Every tray had attached to it a credit card reader. The multitude surged forward, competing to be the first to slip their Amex, Visa or Mastercard into the anointed slot. The electronic orchestra burst into the American National Anthem, and an all-surrounding celestial choir thundered out the words.

Bryn sat on the edge of his bed, mouth agape.

"My God..." he murmured. "My God... I did not expect this..."

His mind had turned to an event a few months previously, long before Zelma emailed him or he had any thought of this visit to America. To a meeting in London. A bungled chance of a life-changing career move. Weeks of regret. And a narrow escape...

"Thank you," he said, "Oh thank you..." He chuckled with relief.

He left the television on while he strolled into the bathroom to brush his teeth and start repacking for the journey home. When he came out, the entire auditorium crowd was singing along to a gospel tune which he recognized as the first hymn they had sung six weeks ago at Guy's funeral. But this American congregation was singing it with an energy and enjoyment an ocean and a continent distant from that diffident West London gathering.

The camera was searching out the faces of the faithful, dwelling occasionally on the most starry-eyed and devoted. It paused on a middle-aged lady with dyed-blonde bouffant hair. Just beyond her stood a man who – uniquely in that auditorium – was *not* gazing ecstatically at the stage. Instead he stood slightly apart, relaxed and unsinging, silently looking about him.

He was thin, tanned, in his middle-fifties, and entirely bald. It was the face Bryn had seen on the motorway outside Detroit airport. The same face he had seen climbing into the Ford Explorer in Denny's car park in Cedar City. The camera moved on and away.

Bryn stood, waiting, for another fifteen minutes. But the camera did not return to the bald man.

It was time to pick up his bags and check out. He found his car and drove straight to Salt Lake City airport.

The security arrangements were more elaborate than at Chicago or Detroit. Though, by O'Hare proportions, it was more like a local airport, and the queues were a fraction of what he had experienced before, the process was considerably more protracted. At first he assumed the difference was that this time he was booked onto an international flight. But the requirements appeared to be the same for passengers with internal destinations. Possibly the Salt Lake City Mormons, with fewer people to process, had time to be more punctilious. Or maybe they were simply a more conscientious people.

As instructed, he stripped down to his socks, shirt and trousers (removing everything metallic from their pockets) while the rest of his belongings went through the X-ray machine. Even after passing soundlessly under the arch of the magnetometer, he was required to stand with legs apart while a metal wand was waved over his person and up between his thighs. A swab was taken from his hands and analysed in a machine. His bag was opened and comprehensively searched, and a plastic corkscrew in his washbag, which had survived a dozen flights, confiscated. Finally, the bag too was swabbed. He could not help but be impressed.

Nevertheless, as he sat beyond the security area, pulling on his shoes and watching later passengers passing through, he wondered how many people were being as elaborately screened as he had been. Was it just his impression or was the wand waving more cursory and the bag searching (and only about one in every dozen or so) briefer? And there seemed, even here, to be a separate fast-track process for the privileged. As if to prove the point, a well-dressed, slightly overweight man in a grey-striped business suit passed unhindered through a magnetometer arch further down the hall, picking up a small black leather case from the conveyor belt without breaking stride.

Bryn put his jacket back on and hoisted his carry-on bag to his shoulder. An official in an ordinary suit but with a security ID hanging on a ribbon round his neck, came up to him.

"Don't forget this, sir," he said and handed Bryn his passport.

He put his hand to his inside pocket, where the passport had most certainly been when he had placed his jacket on the conveyor belt. It was, of course, empty.

"Thank you," he said blankly.

The official nodded politely at him and walked away.

En route towards the airport terminals, he passed a shop

selling books and newspapers. There was, he supposed, an outside chance that after so long away he might find a copy here of an English newspaper. He discovered a cache of out of date European newspapers including a single Guardian International, five days old but a Godsend nonetheless.

A man bent over next to him and picked up a copy of the Wall Street Journal. Bryn recognized him as the privileged fast-tracker in the grey-striped business suit.

"You flying home today?" the man said quietly.

He had a Southern accent, Texan perhaps. Bryn was struck by the cool blue eyes behind the expensive rimless glasses. The face seemed friendly, familiar even.

"London," said Bryn after a pause. "You?"

"Washington," said the Texan. "I expect you'll be glad to get back to your family."

"Well…" said Bryn, considering this. "It's been an interesting trip."

"You bet!" said the Texan. "Have a good flight."

And he turned away, paid for his paper and strolled off, carrying his black shoulder bag, towards Terminal Two. Bryn last glimpsed him passing through the glass doors into the Delta Executive Class lounge.

An hour later, Bryn was in his seat on his United Airlines flight to Heathrow. As the plane taxied down the runway and turned for take-off, and he recalled the bizarre adventure he had passed through and survived, his mind filled with faces. Faces, by and large, he hoped and trusted never to see again. The evangelist on his television this morning, focussed and intent and dangerous. The thin, tanned bald man he had seen in the worshipping crowd. Him above all.

As the aircraft accelerated across the tarmac and climbed into the sky towards the safety of England, he brooded on the inexplicability of it all. The further the ground receded, the less possible it seemed that a complete stranger, for no apparent reason, might have intended to kill him down there in the canyons of Utah. Mistaken identity perhaps? He could think of no better or more rational explanation. He could only hope the man would have subsequently discovered his error.

More faces. He thought about Zelma asleep, hair spread on the pillow. He wondered whether – since he doubted, all considered, that he would be visiting this country again for a long while – whether he would ever see *her* again.

Finally, he thought of the pale-faced character who had dogged him in Chicago. It seemed obvious now that he had been in some way an accomplice of the older, bald man. It had probably been his job to trail him and report back. A particularly vivid face: bristly two-week growth of beard, light grey hood, dark mirrored glasses. And when he took them off on that street by the *Cordelia*, deep-set, cold, blue eyes.

The face dissolved into another. A slightly overweight businessman, crew-cut and clean-shaven and with rimless spectacles instead of mirrored shades. Carrying a black canvas bag with, almost certainly, an image of a beehive with a rifle across it.

Of course. It was the same man.

TWO

Chapter 10

The April meeting of the Ealing Recorder Consort started uncomfortably.

As agreed, they met at Guy's house. The problem was that Janet had installed a borrowed electronic keyboard, with a tinkly harpsichord programme, so that she could play along with the group. They had permitted this in the past on a couple of occasions when they were exploring the well-forgotten continuo and recorder repertory of Pepusch, Bertali and Samuel Scheidt. But the men, including Guy, had never found the arrangement satisfactory.

For one thing, Janet was dishearteningly proficient and not always tactful enough to avoid comment on their own technical shortcomings. For another, her female presence disturbed the group dynamic. They could not gossip so freely or on quite the same range of topics. They felt that they had, in all kinds of ways, to be on their best behaviour.

Janet was not unaware of this. But the group had been an important part of Guy's life and she was anxious to maintain a relationship with it. She hoped that in time they might even accept her as a normal part of the mix. She was, however, sensitive enough to take it in easy stages and so, after half an hour of music and polite and rather stilted conversation, excused herself and went off into the kitchen to prepare their meal.

There was a lot to discuss. Initially the group was most concerned about Bill who had recently set up his own economic consultancy and needed to share with them the stress of management, something he had never really had to cope with before. Notwithstanding the fact that none of the others had ever run his own company, there was plenty of advice. Marshall as usual was the most vocal. He held a couple of non-executive board appointments where his legal acumen and political contacts were thought to be useful to the companies he, nominally, helped to oversee. Like most lawyers, he did not allow practical inexperience to get in the way of his opinions.

But essentially what they had to offer on this, as on other occasions, was empathy. This was quite different from what they might expect from their partners. It was a robust and laddish exchange in which judgments were sometimes sharp and as often rejected, and where they found comic potential even in disaster. They trusted each other's frankness, confidentiality and good will. The group provided an opportunity to let off steam, share out frustrations and put an individual's problems firmly back into perspective. It was an important reason why, in spite of the large differences between them in background, ability and achievement, the group had survived for so long.

Just as they performed on different instruments, so they all had different (though analogous) roles in their discussions. Graeme, who as first descant recorder played the top line in their music, was the most likely to be in need of the group's support. He was the only gay amongst them and his domestic problems, which were usually exotic and complicated, never failed to fascinate the others. As an actor, he had always needed regular reassurance. However, more recently he seemed to have diversified into producing short films, about which he was uncharacteristically discreet – except to say that they were 'fictional' rather than 'factual'. His friends were still awaiting the long-promised invitation to a premiere of one.

Marshall, whose treble instrument was usually buried within one of the inner parts, was the least likely to bring his problems to the group. As the most obviously successful among them, he liked to take a detached position. Here, as in most other environments, he recognized himself as the cleverest person in the room. But he enjoyed the exchange of views as much as any of them and sometimes provided the most sensitive and thoughtful advice. He, most of all of them, relished the gossip about mutual friends and often brought the tastiest nuggets – about politicians and other well-known people of his professional acquaintance – to the table.

As this particular evening wore on, the group's main focus settled upon Bryn's recent adventures in America. America was a topic they often discussed. It was a country about which all of them had quite complex, not to say confused, feelings.

But Bryn was less frank than usual. He was still too disturbed by his experiences in Chicago and Zion Canyon to bring them to the group at this time. Instead he told them about his adventure on the mountain, in dramatic and lurid detail, so that they might the better appreciate his Scott-like heroism. He described his fearless trek into deepening snow, his terrible night in the animal shed at the mercy of circling pumas, his life-saving discovery of the log cabin, and his death-defying, break-neck drive out of the pass. But he made no reference to the wheel tracks he had discovered in the morning. And he did not mention the gun attack.

They were nonetheless impressed.

"The trouble with America," said Marshall, in one of his typically *ex cathedra* statements, "is that it is like England and yet completely different. You think, because the language and the cars and the food and the people are more or less like us, that everything else will be too. Here is Bryn treating Utah like he was in the Lake District."

"What Bryn may overlook, because he is such an amiable cove," offered Bill, "is that England is – by and large – a tranquil country and America is a hostile country."

"Hostile as in…?" queried Marshall.

"As in trackless deserts, dangerous mountains, tornados, hurricanes, floods. And, since you ask, yes, quite a lot of dangerous people."

"I suppose we are talking about gun deaths," said Marshall.

"Ah," said Bill, who was now on semi-professional territory. "Did you know that if you aggregate in a single figure all the murders in America with all their serious *non-fatal* assaults, and do the same for Britain, there is actually – once you have adjusted for overall population size – very little difference in the totals?"

"So the Americans are no worse than us…" suggested Graeme.

"The difference is, *they* have guns. And what all that proves is that violence in general does not vary greatly between our two communities. And also that, to coin a phrase, it's guns that kill, not people."

"I'd quite like to hear you give that speech to the National Rifle Association," said Marshall.

It was time for dinner.

Like the other group partners, Janet had always been uneasy about her role as backstage provider and cook, while the lads sat in the front room tootling, gossiping and drinking the wine. This time, however, she had decided to close the book on her reservations and put on a serious spread. No longer the usual, slightly grudging, spaghetti bolognese and no dessert. She had laid on a starter of mozzarella and tomato, a steaming straight-out-of-the oven tray of beef lasagne with plenty of scope for seconds; and jelly – the Boy's Own special favourite.

They sat round the table still in high conversation.

"Why are we talking about America *again*?" asked Bill suddenly. "Don't we have any other subjects?"

"You do talk about it a lot," said Janet.

They thought about this for a while.

"I like this wine," offered Bryn.

"Waitrose Californian, let's see, discounted to £6.99… and a lot better than the group usually gets," said Graeme, who liked to study these things.

"Darling… you are *so* clever," said Janet affectionately, and pushed the bottle up the table to him.

"I'll tell you why we talk about it so much," continued Marshall. "It's because America is the way we would have been if we hadn't lost an empire."

"You mean if we hadn't lost America?" suggested Bill.

"In fact if America was poor," said Marshall, "it would probably look like Blackpool."

He sounded pretty pleased with his conceit.

Graeme as usual rose to the bait.

"I wish it *was* more like Blackpool," he said, with emphasis. "What's wrong with Blackpool? I'll tell you what's wrong with *America*. It's too rich, too powerful and too bloody arrogant."

"What's wrong with America," persisted Marshall, "is that it is everything we really want to be. And because they speak English and are full of families related to us and are ruled – most of the time – by people with the same names as us, and because they win our wars for us and love our literature and theatre and our Queen more than we do, and generally do everything we want to do more successfully than us… we hate them. Some of us anyway."

"So if you hate them, why do you keep going there?" said Janet after a pause. "You and Bill and Bryn. And Graeme. All of you."

"I'm not saying I subscribe to this view," said Marshall, sulkily.

"I don't go often," said Bryn.

"I'll tell you why," said Bill, gently. "And I think Marshall and Graeme are *both* right. It's because it's our special fantasyland. Where do most British people go for their American holidays? They go to Florida of course which *is* the American version of Blackpool. Or anyway the *fairy story* version of it, like the land at the top of the beanstalk, all endless beaches and eternal sunshine and as much comfort food as you can get down…"

"Isn't there supposed to be a giant at the top of this beanstalk?" said Graeme.

"Oh come on," said Bill. "It's a *giant's* land. The Grand Canyon. The Great Lakes. Niagara. Built for giants. Skyscrapers. All those national parks as big as a European country."

"That figures," said Graeme. "So your actual giants themselves, the ones that are going to gobble up the rest of us, they'll be the conglomerates and the bankers. The insatiable maw of Business and Wall Street that the rest of us have to keep feeding. Fee-fo-fi-fum, I smell the blood of a taxpayer."

Bill refilled his glass.

"If you insist, Graeme," said Marshall with a theatrical sigh.

"But I'm not sure that's right," said Bryn.

The others looked at him in some surprise. He did not usually enter this kind of argument, which was more natural territory for Graeme and Bill.

"You talk about national parks," he continued. "In America they are sacrosanct. South of Alaska anyway. Think of all the oil and natural resources they're not allowed to touch. Are we sure we are as dedicated in Europe? It's a paradox. The most single-mindedly entrepreneurial economy in the world and also the one which most aggressively protects its physical heritage from even modest economic encroachment."

"I'm not sure I ever said they didn't do things better," said Bill vaguely.

"Poverty, for example," said Graeme suddenly.

"They do poverty better?" queried Marshall.

"If you want. I read an article in the Guardian that said that nearly one in five children in America now lives in poverty and that even today there are so many millionaires they've stopped counting them. Instead, there are something like a thousand billionaires."

"This is probably true," said Bill. "Even if you did read it in the Guardian."

"I would like to suggest," interrupted Marshall, "that Americans are among the most generous people in the world. And that goes across the spectrum from poor people to the billionaires. I remember when I went there as a student and I was always being invited to stay for weekends, Christmas, Thanksgiving – any opportunity to show hospitality. I remember one New Jersey family I was sharing pumpkin pie and turkey with at Thanksgiving that year, and who were certainly never going to be rich, asking *me* when I expected to make my first million. It was a perfectly natural, straightforward question directed at someone they took as destined for greater things than them. There was not a shred of envy in it. I don't think that attitude of generosity has ever changed."

"Meantime," said Graeme, "I believe it is a fact that the richest and most powerful Americans make sure they pay a lower proportion of their income in taxes than anyone else. Not much generosity there."

"I don't think you should be surprised by that," replied Bill. "In the UK poor people also pay a bigger slice of their income in tax than the richest. It's the way things are. But in America you have a tradition of incredible philanthropy from Andrew Carnegie, Rockefeller and Getty to Bill Gates and Warren Buffett – paying for schools, libraries, healthcare. And overseas aid. That's pretty generous."

"So what these plutocrats are actually doing," retorted Graeme, "is putting their money into things you would expect any respectable government to pay for out of taxes. It is a sad day when a country's collective responsibility for its poorest and most vulnerable citizens is left to the whim of some unaccountable, unelected, super-rich oligarchy."

"Nevertheless," Bill persisted, "it is also a fact that charitable giving in the States as a proportion of national wealth is greater than *any* other country in the world. Actually it is – pro rata – anything up to ten times what many European countries give. Now *that's* generous."

"Can I ask a question?" said Bryn quietly. "How much of that charitable giving goes to religious organizations? Just as a matter of interest..."

"About a third of it."

"Which would be?" asked Graeme.

"Oh… about 100 billion dollars. Or more," said Bill with a shrug.

Graeme gaped at him.

"You're not really defending this, are you Bill?"

"You're very hostile, Graeme," responded Bill.

He looked to the others for support.

"After all, Graeme, what have the Americans ever done for you except save you from Hitler, invest massively in your country, and raise your standard of living?"

The two of them stared at each other.

Bryn spoke again.

"I remember the day after 9/11, when I went into a lecture and suggested, before I started, that we had a minute's silence for the thousands of victims. One of my students stood up and made a speech about how she couldn't in all honesty join in unless we first had a minute's silence for all the people in occupied Palestine. And then someone else said they were very sorry for all those dead Americans too, but when did I ever ask them to have a minute's silence for Kissinger and Pinochet's victims in Chile or the Sioux Nation dying in poverty and disease on their Dakota reservation? In the end of course we had no silence at all. Not for anybody."

There was a collective inhalation as the other three prepared simultaneously to launch their right of reply. But it was Janet's quiet voice which prevailed.

"I think that's enough politics," she said firmly. "Are you ready for jelly, boys?"

"You bet," said Graeme.

Later, when it was time to break up, there was no ill-feeling. They had known each other and each other's views too long for their friendship to be disturbed. The truth was they enjoyed the *craic*. They thanked Janet for the wonderful feast and each gave her a kiss as he prepared to leave. Their last act, almost as an after-thought, was to huddle together in the hallway, comparing diaries and fixing a date for their next meeting.

It was raining heavily. None of them had far to go, not even

Marshall, who lived only two blocks away but had a taxi waiting and was in such a hurry to jump into it that he left his music behind. Bill prepared to cycle home through the downpour and would not be persuaded to wait until it eased. Bryn had, like a wise virgin, remembered to bring his golf-sized Cardiff City Bluebirds umbrella with him. He had not long left the house when Graeme caught up with him. They shared the umbrella until their routes diverged.

When they reached the top of Bryn's road, however, with Graeme a quarter of a mile or so from his destination, it was still pitching down. A car passed by too close to the pavement and sent a wave of water over their feet. Bryn gave Graeme his umbrella and sent him on his way while he sprinted the remaining thirty yards to his own house.

He never saw his friend again.

Chapter 11

It was around 7.30 next morning when the call came. Bryn's wife, Marion, had already left for work.

Marshall was on the line and clearly agitated. He came straight to the point without preamble.

"I have terrible news. Graeme is dead."

"What?"

"He was killed last night."

"How do you know this?"

"The police called me. He probably had an address book on him. The police recognized my name. The thing is, he's dead, Bryn. Some kind of gay assignation that went wrong."

"Graeme was going home. He had my umbrella. He wasn't going to an assignation."

"Look. I've got to go to work. I should think the police are with Dieter at the moment. Maybe you should ring them there. Let's keep in touch."

And he rang off.

Bryn sat for a moment to allow this to sink in. His last image of Graeme hovered in front of him, as if he was viewing it on a screen in the cinema. The ridiculous football umbrella with its pattern of little black and yellow shields and bluebirds, bobbing away through the driving rain. It was inconceivable that Graeme had had sex on his mind. He was going home to Dieter as fast as he could, to his nice, cosy, suburban set-up – a couple of respectable gentlemen well past their cottaging prime, settled and comfortable with each other for the last ten years or more. To herbal teas, some gossip about their day, television and bed.

He rang Bill but could only get an answering service. So he left a message to call back. Then, after some thought, he rang Janet. He could not quite come to the point as Marshall had, and started by thanking her for their splendid evening.

"Is there something else?" she said after a pause in the conversation.

"Marshall called me."

"This morning."

"This morning... I'm afraid it's very bad news. Graeme's dead."

"What?"

"An accident. Some time last night apparently. The police are at his house. They think it was a gay assignation that went wrong."

Janet burst into tears. He had not expected this. But all the female partners had been fond of Graeme, who had always made the greatest effort to embrace them within the group. He was the one who usually stayed on to gossip after the other men had left. He was the one who sent a thank-you card the next day.

"I don't know the circumstances. I'm going to call the house. Would you like me to call you later?"

"Yes. Yes please, Bryn. Oh, this is awful. Awful."

Dieter answered the phone. His voice was dull, probably sedated, and he thanked Bryn formally for his condolences. Yes, the police were here. An officer's voice came on the line. He took down Bryn's name and address and then confirmed that, yes, we have your details here in his diary, sir. He asked Bryn to stay where he was and an officer would be round in due course. When? Difficult to say, sir, but some time this morning.

A single plain clothes policeman arrived shortly before noon.

He accepted a cup of coffee and made himself comfortable in Bryn's sitting room. He seemed reluctant at first to divulge any of the circumstances of Graeme's death.

"Could you just tell me when you last saw him, sir?"

Bryn described what little he could remember of the walk home; his last sight of Graeme trudging off through the rain.

"It's not much to go on," he apologized.

"No, sir. Was there anyone else around?"

"It was very wet. Just a bit of traffic."

"Any cars? Any particular car?"

"No. I don't think so. There was a car that drove by us just before we split up which I remember because it was too close to the pavement and splashed us. That's all."

"Driving quite slowly."

"Well. Yes. Otherwise we would have been drenched."

"Can you remember anything about it? Make? I don't suppose you noticed the number plate."

"No!" He laughed, inappropriately. "No, I didn't see the number plate. I think it might have been obscured. I don't think it was lit up."

The policeman waited.

"A big car. Black or maroon, difficult to say at that time of night. Mercedes perhaps."

"A Mercedes?"

"No, no, no. I can't say. Something like that. Is that significant?"

The policeman made a note in his small pocketbook and closed it. He gave a sigh and slipped it back into his jacket. He finished his coffee.

"Could you possibly tell me what happened?" said Bryn.

"We don't know what happened, sir. We have two witnesses. A neighbour of the deceased saw him getting into a car probably very soon after you left him."

"A Mercedes?"

"Possibly. A similar car was seen by the caretaker at Gurnell Leisure Centre leaving about half an hour later. It was the caretaker who reported the body."

"Where was that?"

"In the Gurnell car park. I'm afraid your friend was killed there."

"How?"

"I can't tell you that, sir. There's a way to go yet. But it looks as though he may have been suffocated during a…"

He seemed reluctant to go further. He gazed at Bryn unblinkingly.

"How well did you know your friend, sir?"

"Twenty years."

The policeman waited again.

"I knew he was gay if that's what you mean."

"Is that right?"

He took out his pocketbook again and made another note.

He got up from his armchair. But there was something else Bryn needed to say.

"What about the umbrella? And his valise, with his recorder and all the music in it?"

"We've got his case. And the instrument. We have to hold onto that, sir. But no, I don't know anything about an umbrella."

"A big blue umbrella with Cardiff City Football Club colours. I lent it to him. I'm a supporter."

"Are you, sir? No, we have nothing of that kind."

He seemed entirely uninterested.

After the officer had left, a new fear began to gather in Bryn's mind, like a multiplying virus. He tried to busy himself with other thoughts.

He puzzled at what might have happened. But the more he turned it over the less he could believe that Graeme had accepted a lift from some gay pick-up. That might have been possible years ago, but he was surely too old and settled for that now, like the rest of the friends. And if the police were suggesting some very rough and abusive trade which had gone disastrously wrong then that in any case, he felt sure, was never Graeme's style.

No, the fear that was forcing itself up through his thoughts and into the forefront of his mind was that it was not Graeme's at all whose death had been intended, but his *own*. If anyone had been following *him*, they would have seen him emerge from Guy and Janet's house with his signature umbrella, seen Graeme catch up with him further down the street, and seen them part. But it was Graeme who continued to carry the damned thing, not him. Had the Mercedes, or whatever it was, targeted the wrong man?

The more he thought about it, the more alarmed he became. He decided to ring Marshall. His usual number did not answer, so he called his chambers. A man answered, possibly his clerk, and undertook to pass on a message to call back. He made himself another coffee and waited.

He did not have to wait long. Marshall was clearly on his mobile and probably – judging from the background noise – in the Royal Courts of Justice in the Strand. He could imagine him in his well-worn QC's gown, standing alongside a pillar while his profession and its sad clients flowed around him.

"You called?" said Marshall, in his rather harsh professional voice.

He did not need to signal further to Bryn that he was busy and had little time to spare for any unnecessary conversation.

"I've had the police round."

"Yes."

"Graeme was picked up by a Mercedes probably and taken to Gurnell and killed there. They think it was some rough sex that went too far."

"I know that." But he had caught Bryn's tone. "Is there any reason to doubt it?"

"When they picked him up, he had my umbrella. I think it may be mistaken identity."

There was a long pause. He could hear Marshall exhaling very slowly.

"Why on earth should you think that, Bryn?" he said at last. "This is nonsense, isn't it?"

"When I was in America, somebody tried to kill me."

He waited again for a reply. The acoustic changed, as if Marshall had walked out of the Law Courts building and onto the pavement outside. He still said nothing, so Bryn explained as briefly as he could what had happened in Utah. Then eventually Marshall spoke.

"Let me get this right, Bryn. Someone – possibly – tried to shoot you in Zion Canyon but you did not report this because you did not think you would be believed. You did not mention this to the recorder group because, presumably, you didn't think we would believe you either. Now you think that the same unknown, unexplained person has followed you to Ealing, and confused you with Graeme and killed him during an act of homosexual sex...

"Are you proposing to report your suspicions to the police?"

He had never been exposed so directly to Marshall's practised forensic manner, and he began to feel foolish. Put like that, his fears seemed not far short of paranoid. He decided to cut his losses.

"That's helpful, Marshall," he said, in his own most professional and detached tones. "It's been useful to talk to you."

"So are you going to the police?"

"No. I don't think I will."

"Let me say I think that's wise."

He rang off.

Bryn spent the rest of the afternoon, a little abstractedly, marking tutorial essays. Not until he had finished did he realize that he had given every one of his students a straight *Beta*. It was while he was contemplating whether he should add in a few plus or minus signs that his wife unexpectedly returned from her teaching job at a local primary school. He had not attempted to ring her at work with the news about Graeme. But she had heard about it anyway from Janet and had decided to come home earlier than usual in case he needed comfort.

They had a middle-aged kind of marriage. Marion never hid her deep frustrations with him in public – his vagueness, his obsessions, his reluctance to commit himself energetically to the opportunities that came his way. As a consequence, she had some reputation among his acquaintances as a sharp-tongued wife or, as his less reconstructed male friends might put it, bossy and a bit of a shrew. He never argued back when she got after him in front of friends, and she was infuriated by the way he withdrew into his shell at home – 'sulked' as she put it – whenever she tried to engineer a confrontation.

Throughout their married life he had been, for her, work in progress. In the early days his deficiencies had not mattered so much. They had started a family early and the process of bringing the children up had deflected her from the great project of making him better. Now that the family had left home, it was as if her irritation had free rein. The trouble was that it had no satisfactory outlet. She had missed her chance. Maybe when he was younger she could have changed him. Maybe if they had not had children she might have left him for somebody more dynamic. He appeared now chronically unable to improve or even – so much worse – *accept* that he needed to be more ambitious, aggressive, productive, argumentative, all the things he was not. Once when she had challenged him to have professional therapy, he had even had the gall to laugh.

And so, in the last few years, her frustrations had found other outlets. Her criticism of him in public had become more noticeable. She spent more time away, weekending with girl-friends, leading school trips, evenings out with colleagues. She was a fine looking woman and had always had her admirers. She began to take an occasional lover – just as she had suspected of *him*, indeed from early on in their life together. This had less to do with sexual necessity than with a complex of other compulsions – a sense of time passing, a need for reassurance, *fury*. At first she was half-determined to confront him with her infidelity, in some last-ditch attempt to shake him out of his complacency. Then she became fearful of the consequences. She realized that, with all his deficiencies, she could never leave him.

So she kept these secrets from him. Though it irritated her to acknowledge it, she knew that she was committed, and for life. She found herself forced to recognize that, in her own fashion, she loved him.

This afternoon, she had decided to make the kind of dinner they usually had only on Friday nights and then only if she was in a more affectionate mood. It was her way today of expressing sympathy. But she also hoped that it would help him to talk more freely about the day's events and his feelings. She sent him down the road to the off-licence to get a couple of bottles of something South American and red, while she set to with the sirloin steaks she had bought a couple of days earlier for another occasion.

She was perhaps less fond of Graeme than Janet had been, and had fewer illusions than Bryn about his extra-mural activities. The possibility that he had accepted a pick-up from a passing stranger did not strike her as exceptional. It had been typical of Graeme that he could be more revealing about the disreputable side of his life to his female than to his (heterosexual) male friends. She knew, for example, which Bryn did not, that Graeme's video work had included male pornography for the licensed sex shop market. And that Graeme, certainly until quite recently, had not been above cruising the streets looking for likely talent for his productions. It was seamy stuff, but his confidential tales of the disastrous misjudgments which had ensued were delivered with a self-deflating wit which charmed and delighted his female audience.

Now, though, she was more concerned about Bryn. The dinner and the wine did not seem to be having their usual effect. He talked about the day's events, and they examined together their feelings about Graeme, but there was a veil between them. She felt partly to blame for this because, out of a kind of deference to the so recently deceased, she felt unable yet to be frank about everything she knew about him. But Bryn seemed disengaged and pre-occupied. There were periods when he lapsed into silences while she waited for him to share whatever was troubling him. Perhaps he would talk more freely later.

In bed they made love, as they generally did on Friday nights, with the routines and tricks built up in their younger days together, but now by rote rather than inspiration. They came to a climax more or less together, as they usually did, and fell away more or less satisfied. When they were younger, they had used to enjoy a post-coital cigarette or a final glass of wine, and chat for perhaps half an hour until their eyes closed. This evening, Marion gave him the usual light kiss on his cheek, turned over onto her side, and opened her latest Book Club novel to read herself to sleep.

Bryn lay awake. He began to talk about America. He had provided a bowdlerized account on his return, omitting all the details that might have alarmed her. Now he felt compelled to share at least some of his anxieties with her. He started by describing his trip from the airport to Chicago and the man who seemed to be following him. His experience on the way to the *Cordelia* restaurant. The man who trailed him down the motorway to Detroit. Marion stirred beside him.

"I never knew you led such an exciting life," she yawned. "People trying to run you over in Gower Street, gangsters following you in Chicago. And I thought I married a boring academic. It's definitely an improvement, darling."

Why would she not take him seriously? His thoughts drifted to Zelma, whom he had very deliberately edited out of these reminiscences, with no reference to her even in her professional capacity. His attempts to make contact since he returned had been fruitless. She appeared to have covered her tracks. The emails he had sent had all resulted in delivery failure notices, and the University of Michigan was unable or unwilling to provide any new address. He would find some way of getting in touch with her again. Even if it meant returning to America.

"Do you think you are having a middle-age crisis?"

"No, I don't think so," he said.

"Well... you're very restless recently. Looking for a new job outside London in spite of all the disruption it would cause us, especially me. That head-hunting business, for instance, out of the blue. And you never used to go to America. You never used to go on overseas lectures and conferences or swans of any kind."

"David Lodge made them unfashionable," he said.

"Whatever happened to the head-hunters, by the way?

Weren't they supposed to get in touch with you? I thought you were going to be a professor..."

She did not wait for an answer. Her light clicked off and she pulled the duvet over her shoulder. She settled into her usual, comfortable position, with her back pressed up against his side for warmth. A few seconds later, her book fell to the floor. With its usual thud.

He lay there in the dark, waiting for her snores to begin, and trying to puzzle things out. She was right of course. However unwittingly, she had hit the nail squarely on the head. It *had* all started when the head-hunters approached him. With a telephone call to his home, though, not to his office.

Chapter 12

It would have been September the previous year. It seemed so long ago now. A lady describing herself as an 'executive searcher' telephoned him and asked him if he would be interested in a professorship at an American university. She would not say where and she was vague about the academic requirements. He explained to her that his speciality was American history and particularly the Civil War period and she said that was fine, would he be able to come and see her?

Two days later, he turned up at her offices in Curzon Street in the centre of Mayfair. The marble floors and oak panelling greatly impressed him. It was not quite the first time he had been approached by a head-hunter but it wasn't something he expected in his profession. And he was certainly not accustomed to this level of grandeur.

The lady head-hunter was young – barely out of her twenties – and distractingly good-looking. A secretary brought in a silver tray with a bone china tea service and they sat opposite each other in huge and deeply upholstered armchairs. It would be a full professorship, she explained briskly, with departmental responsibility. She could not yet give a figure for the salary, but she suspected it would considerably outstrip his present one. She had done her homework and knew that he was a Reader in

American Studies, or one down from a professorship. No doubt she was familiar also with the London university scales.

Was he still interested?

"Well," he said, rather boldly, "that would depend on the university."

"OK," she said. "Obviously everything I tell you must be treated in strict confidence."

"Of course," he said. "Rely on me."

"It's Nathan Bedford Forrest University in Davisville, South Carolina. Shall I continue?"

This was not what he had expected. Harvard or even University of Michigan would have been too much to hope for. Something like Syracuse or Columbia would have been very acceptable. He knew a little about Nathan Bedford Forrest. It was a private university dedicated, like Brigham Young University or Notre Dame in Indiana, to fulfilling a specific Christian mission. In NBFU's case, this was a species of southern evangelism broadly similar to that promoted in Bob Jones University or Oral Roberts University.

And it was not as if offers like this came up every day. The name of the university had a particular attraction for him. Nathan Bedford Forrest had been the most heroic and brilliant of the cavalry generals of the Civil War, a Southern hero whose military prowess he admired and had written about in learned publications. And he knew that NBFU had amassed a mouth-watering archive of diaries, letters, military records and other primary sources about the Civil War.

On the other hand… there was no denying that Forrest, from whom the university derived more perhaps than just his name, remained a controversial figure. There was a part of him of which Bryn was aware but which he had never felt the need to explore professionally: his racism. He had been a slave trader before the Civil War. When, as an army general, he encountered black Union troops, he had massacred them – notoriously at the Battle of Fort Pillow in 1864. Then in 1867, when the War was over, he had become the first Grand Wizard of the Ku Klux Klan.

Correspondingly, he was aware of a controversial side to the university's activities. Its academic publications, in line with its general purpose, tended to be highly selective. One of its professors was a vehement spokesman for the 'intelligent design' argument which sought to restore God to the centre of evolutionist theory. The professor who led its media studies department was well known for regular presentations to Congress demonstrating with similar certainty the malign influence upon social standards of cinema, television, video games, the internet and – broadly speaking – all modern forms of entertainment.

Since Bryn regarded himself as politically unengaged (when he voted, it was always for the Green Party or the Liberal Democrats), none of this seemed to him to pose a serious problem. At this stage he was flattered to have been recognized and pleased that his reputation in the field appeared to have been its own recommendation. So it was a slight shock when his interviewer turned to the question of other candidates.

"Who would be the front-runners for this job, would you say?" she enquired silkily, with her silver ballpoint pen poised over her notebook.

The previous time a head-hunter had asked him this question – indeed the only previous time he had had dealings with a head-hunter – he had answered the question so helpfully that the post he coveted actually went to someone he had recommended. He had not even been short-listed. So he was not about to make that mistake again. He offered two names of London-based candidates who were, he was confident, not simply unsuitable but also – just in case – locked into relationships which were likely to prevent them leaving the country anyway.

That accomplished, the pretty, blonde lady executive searcher laid down her pen and embarked upon the most penetrating and sharply focussed grilling he had ever endured. Not that he found it unflattering to be pressed to talk about himself for the best part of an hour and by an attractive female. He enjoyed the tasty competitive edge. He found himself warming and flowering under her pressure to explain how he might handle a department of his own given his signal lack of front-line management experience. And he was confident he had convinced her that, in spite of his supposed years ("I'm only in my early 40s," he demurred, charmingly) he still had the youthful energy for combat. By the end of it, he had persuaded himself that he actually wanted this job more than anything else in the world.

And that was the last he heard from her.

Months passed, and Bryn had quite given up any hope of a further interview, still less a job offer. Then, very early in the New Year, as he sat at his computer at home working on the third draft of the now almost book-length monograph about the Confederate generals of the Civil War which he hoped might significantly enhance his academic reputation, he received a telephone call. It was from "the office of the President of Nathan Bedford Forrest". The President was in London on business and would Professor Williams be free to meet him in two days time..?

Of *course*.

He went directly to NBFU's own website on the internet. The President – the peculiar English equivalent would probably be University Vice Chancellor – was Jack Carroll Smith III. His official biography proudly proclaimed his descent from a famous signatory of the 1776 Declaration of Independence – one Charles Carroll of Carollton who had signed for the State of Maryland. It also revealed that the university had been started in 1920 by the first Jack Carroll Smith, the current president's grandfather. Its foundation followed in a fine Southern tradition of naming educational institutions after their lost leaders.

The website home page was dominated by the Bible Reading of the day (several bible extracts in fact) and photographs of good-looking and well-showered white undergraduates. There were fewer Departments – or 'Schools' – than any British university he knew, but the list included two Schools of Religion (one for Graduates). After a little difficulty, he located the History Department embedded within the School of Cultural Studies. Two or three of the professors there were known to him by name and he looked up and read the few of their publications that were available on the net.

He Googled in Jack Smith's full name and found nearly a million entries. He clicked on one website and discovered that he was also Congressman Jack C Smith for the 7th District of South Carolina, already serving a third term. Clearly a busy man. He noticed that his campaign slogan was, without any apparent hint of irony, '*Vote for Jacksy*'. Either Mr Smith had a highly developed sense of humour or none at all. He looked forward to finding out.

In the couple of days remaining before the appointment, he devoted all his spare time to setting down on paper the questions the head-hunter had asked him, and then writing out in longhand every point of reply he could think of. He practised them as he walked to the shops and as he travelled on the underground. Finally, he printed off from his computer three copies of his monograph about the Confederacy generals – Lee, Jackson, Hill, Stuart, Forrest, Pickett, Longstreet and the rest – which he had now provisionally entitled *America's Trojans*. He packed them in the handsome black *Trevor Pickett* attaché case with its characteristic little round key locks that Marion had, rather wittily (and with an apology for its slightly shop-soiled appearance – without which it would have been unaffordable), given him for his last birthday.

He intended to drop one copy off with his literary agent and leave another with Jack Smith at the end of his interview. He was beginning to relish the thought of a transfer to sunny South Carolina, the opportunity – on site as it were – to kick start his studies to another level. How satisfying it would be, at last, to have the right to call himself 'Professor' in any country.

And so it was that, one cold January morning, he took the underground to Oxford Circus and set off, first to his agent's office in Poland Street, and then to Claridge's Hotel in Mayfair.

The meeting with the agent was, as it always seemed to be, brief. Bryn's had never been a profitable engagement. He had been taken on years previously on the enthusiastic recommendation of another client, a successful screenwriter excessively grateful to Bryn for the historical background he had provided for a film script; and the agent – albeit a tough self-made lady from Islington who had been in the business for years – had regretted it ever since. There was absolutely no money in Bryn's academic publications. She had been on the verge of removing him finally from her books when the idea of expanding the Civil War monograph had come up. So, when he dropped in that morning, she accepted the latest draft and undertook to scout out the possible market in schools, America or even – who knows – a movie. She knew of at least one publishing house in New York that *might* be interested.

He marched onwards down Great Marlborough Street, past St George's Church in Hanover Square to Brook Street and, buzzing now with determination to make a good showing, pushed through the rotating door of the hotel and crossed the gleaming black and white marble atrium to the main desk beyond. A smartly dressed clerk was studying a computer screen behind a sign announcing that, in line with the requirements of the Health Act, smoking was not permitted in any public area of the building.

"I have an appointment with Mr Smith," he said.

The clerk looked at him. It occurred to Bryn that 'Smith' might not be a name well known to Claridge's.

"Congressman Jack C Smith. Of Nathan Bedford Forrest University."

The clerk looked at his computer screen again.

"And you are... sir?"

"Mr Williams. Professor Bryn Williams."

The clerk looked a bit more. Then he clicked his fingers and a uniformed young man materialized by Bryn's side.

"Please take Professor Williams up to The Royal Suite," he said. And, almost as an after-thought, "Thank you, sir."

The lift rose up several floors and opened onto a corridor. The young man escorted Bryn to a door and ushered him in. A middle-aged white lady was standing there with hand extended.

"Professor Williams, it is so great to see you. I am Gloria Teasdale, Mr Smith's Personal Assistant. I hope you had a safe journey. There is so much traffic in the big cities today."

"I came by tube, Miss Teasdale."

She considered this for a moment.

"Well. The President is not available just at this time. You're not early," she said, as if to pre-empt any concern. "Mr Smith is a very busy man. But you know that. I'm sure he'll only be five or ten minutes. Please make yourself comfortable here."

She smiled again and left through an inner door.

Bryn studied his surroundings. It was exactly the kind of thing he would have expected a rich American to enjoy. He was in a kind of eighteenth century vestibule with pillars (very South Carolina, he thought) and matching furniture. He sat down in an armchair which he assumed was a modern reproduction but might, for all he knew, be a genuine Sheraton or Chippendale.

Ten minutes passed. His case sat on his knee, its first outing since Marion gave it to him months previously. He took out his key and opened it. He wished now he had printed out *America's Trojans* on single sheets instead of economically double-sided. It did look rather thin. He took out one of the copies and flicked through to the chapter on Nathan Bedford Forrest.

The inside door opened and the Personal Assistant came through.

"He's ready to see you now, Professor," she beamed.

Bryn had expected some degree of opulence but the reality startled him. A chandelier hung from the centre of the ceiling. Crimson sofas lined the walls and a grand piano was parked in space at the far end of the room. The walls and ceiling had been painted a light mushroom colour and inlaid with more delicate white plaster work in the eighteenth century style. Velvet-curtained French windows opened onto the street below. In a giant red armchair, with a faint trail of smoke rising from the thick cigar wedged in the side of his mouth, sat Jack C Smith. He did not rise to his feet or offer to shake Bryn's hand, but waved him towards one of the matching sofas.

He was about fifty, good-looking in a craggy, Gary Cooper kind of way, with a full, virile and impeccably barbered head of hair. He was wearing an open-necked button collar shirt, long slim trousers and brogues – every item looking as if it had been fresh bought that morning. He did not appear to have much time.

"OK Professor Williams. You come with good recommendations. Why would you want to work for us?"

He spoke in a light southern accent and from time to time emphasized his words by pointing the unlit end of his cigar at Bryn.

"Mr President... "

"I like that. But call me Jack."

"Mr... Jack, I believe I have gone as far as I can in the UK in my specialty of American History..."

"Are you the best in the UK then?"

"Well. No. Well. Possibly."

"You're not sure about that, Professor?"

"Ah... then I guess I am. In my particular specialty. But of course everyone likes a challenge and I think Nathan Bedford Forrest would provide me with that opportunity. I admire your... style, I admire your... archives, frankly I would love to do a lot with them... and, well, I admire the great man from whom you take your name."

"Nathan Bedford?"

"Very much."

"That's good. So why exactly do you admire him?"

Bryn took a deep breath. This was a line of questioning he should have anticipated and he was irritated with himself for having marched so recklessly into this particular minefield.

But then sometimes the disingenuous response was the most effective.

"Well, clearly," he replied, "because he was a great general. As you probably know, the late Shelby Foote – I think your best recent historian of the Civil War – described him as one of its two authentic geniuses."

Smith removed the cigar from his mouth and knocked half an inch of ash into a china bowl on the arm of his chair.

"The *War*, sir."

"I beg your pardon, sir" said Bryn.

"Where I come from, we call it The War. We don't need a defining adjective to remind us what we're talking about. And I believe the other authentic genius – according to your friend Mr Foote – was Abraham Lincoln."

Smith pursed his lips.

"That's right," Bryn agreed. "And William Tecumseh Sherman had a similar view. Said he was the most remarkable man produced on either side. Nathan Bedford Forrest, that is."

"Sherman? You're quoting Sherman now...?" said Smith incredulously, almost in a whisper.

Bryn decided to move on.

"The greatness of Forrest of course has to do with his tactics and the single-mindedness with which he effected them. I would claim that he actually invented modern guerrilla warfare. He used his cavalry much as a modern general might use motorized infantry, riding as fast as he could to the point of vulnerability, then dismounting and fighting like infantry. We forget that cavalry in those days were more often employed as scouts and as a general's means of communication with the world surrounding him."

"That's fascinating, Professor. Now why don't you give me your opinion of Fort Pillow and after that of Nathan Bedford's career in the post-War period?"

He was now backed up and in a place he did not want to be. It was a fair guess that Smith's views about Forrest the white supremacist and founder of the Ku Klux Klan differed substantially from his own. He cleared his throat.

"There are historians who believe that Forrest has been traduced. It seems, for example, that the order to burn the black Fort Pillow soldiers in their barracks may in truth have been given by a Union officer. It is very difficult in the aftermath of battle to be sure of anything."

He might as well take the bull by the horns.

"And great military leaders always make enemies" he

continued, with emphasis. "Think of our General Montgomery and his relationships with your American generals. I believe we should also bear in mind that Forrest was the product of his age and many generals on the other side – Sherman and Grant for instance – went into the War with similar views about slavery. They just happened to come from the North and so, like Forrest, gave allegiance to their homeland. I think the involvement with the Klan is understandable from that perspective."

God forgive him. He took a deep breath.

"That's clever, Professor," said Smith, and sucked on his cigar.

Bryn now sensed an opportunity.

"I have actually brought along with me my – so far unpublished – monograph on the leading Confederate generals. I would be very happy for you to read it at your leisure. There is a chapter about Nathan Bedford Forrest which I hope you might enjoy."

He wished the chapter had been longer. He offered the copy to Smith who took it and placed it, unlooked at, on the coffee table beside him.

"Now let me tell you what my view of the War is," said Smith quietly.

A hazy ring of blue smoke spread from his mouth.

"It is a Northern and European myth that the War was about freeing slaves. The War was *nothing to do* with slavery. It was, or should have been, the Second American Revolution. It was about the desire of the southern states – the exact same people and families incidentally as those who led the First Revolution against you British – to resist the encroachment of central government on the God-given freedoms enshrined in the United States Constitution. That model is as relevant today as it was then. In other words, the Confederacy was a heroic precursor of our modern commitment to cutting back on taxes, anti-social legislation, gun control and *all* the other anti-democratic impositions of central government on the rights of individual states to determine their own salvation..."

The moist tip of the cigar hovered in the air between them. Smith returned it very deliberately to the side of his mouth.

"Do you have any difficulty with that as a statement of fact, Professor?"

He certainly did. It was not a proposition that he could possibly share, not least because – as he now recalled – he had expressly addressed it in the monograph that now lay beside the President's chair. In an introductory chapter about the present state of Civil War historiography, he had addressed Smith's familiar argument head on. In an uncharacteristic attempt – which he now regretted – to spice up his masterwork with a little controversy, he had described this particular view as an 'unreconstructed and self-serving obsession of southern right-wing historians'. His own, fairly conventional, view was that the Civil War was essentially about an old, rich and highly privileged order being challenged and overthrown by a democratically-elected government.

"I understand your view, sir," he said finally. "And as a professional historian, I have to say that that is all it can be. A view."

The other man glared at him. The first few bars of *My Country 'Tis Of Thee* rang out tinnily in the room. Smith put down his cigar in its china bowl and pulled a cell-phone from his inside pocket.

"Yup," he said and listened for a while to the other voice. Then, without so much as a glance at Bryn, he got up and left the room. The cigar lay smouldering in its receptacle.

Bryn waited in silence. Somewhere, far beyond the double-glazed windows and the oak doors, he could just about hear the hum of the London traffic. He began to feel as if he was caught in a time-capsule. The barely audible sounds were of a distant conflict while he sat marooned in the sumptuously over-furnished room of a great house on the outskirts of a Virginian battlefield.

He stood up and strained an ear for something closer at hand. Nothing. He crossed the room to the door through which Smith had departed and cautiously opened it. There was a dining room beyond, used currently as an office, with two sets of computers, a printer and a large photo-copying machine. A television set in the corner was tuned to the Fox News Channel with the sound turned off. On the dining table, directly in front of him, lay his leather Pickett attaché case, which he had left behind in the outer lobby and all too easily forgotten. What a relief. He picked it up and returned to his seat.

It took him perhaps a further ten minutes to conclude, beyond reasonable doubt, that the interview was over. He debated whether he should reclaim the copy of his monograph which still lay on the coffee table. But who knows, he reflected, at the very least it might remind President Smith that I was here. He might even read it. Who knows.

He left. Rather than catch the bus, he walked all the way back to his small office behind Gower Street the better to clear his head of the disappointment and frustration. He seemed to have set more store by this interview than he had realized.

He threw his beautiful case into the glory-hole that was his academic locker.

And resolved to forget about the whole affair.

That had been in January, three months ago now.

Then there had been Guy's death and the funeral. And the invitation from Zelma which had led to the whole American nightmare.

And one other thing. Marcus. That strange meeting around the middle of February, just before he went to America. He had almost forgotten about that too.

Marcus was Bryn's clever cousin. As a child he was small, skinny, hopeless at sport, arrogant; and nothing had changed since. He was a classics scholar at Cambridge where he had struck up a life-long friendship with Ken Burns, then a history exhibitioner and now Bryn's boss at UCL. The best thing about Marcus was that he had – or affected to have – a high opinion of Bryn's talents, with a tendency to introduce him as the 'real brain-box in the family'. The worst thing was that his friendship with

Ken meant that Bryn was never quite sure how much Marcus really knew about him, or what family information Bryn would have preferred to remain confidential was fed back to Ken.

Because Marcus was a gossip. His father and Bryn's mother had been siblings, within an extended family from that part of west Shropshire where all names are Welsh. Cousins had moved to Chester, Newcastle-under-Lyme and Telford; and Marcus had kept in touch with them all. He made it his business to know their business.

There seemed to Bryn to be a self-congratulatory element in all this. So far as he knew, none of the family, through generations beyond recorded time, had ever managed to take more than a few modest steps from their humble origins; *except* Marcus and to an extent himself. Marcus, naturally, was greatly admired within the family. He was the Cambridge Scholar who had gone into the Diplomatic Service and had enjoyed an illustrious, if slightly opaque, career. Marcus liked to preserve an air of discreet superiority about his success, but he had evidently had senior postings of some kind in Washington, Geneva and Moscow. It was, as Bryn saw it, typical of Marcus that he gave little of himself away so that others might assume the best, while busily patronizing his less fortunate relatives with detailed enquiries about *their* health, career and family.

Nonetheless, Marcus did seem to rate him. And Bryn enjoyed their regular lunches at the Travellers Club and the opportunities they afforded for good food and wine at Marcus's (or the government's) expense and for self-indulgent monologues about his own latest exploits. Marcus was always fascinated, for example, by the recorder group and gossip about its individual members.

It was not so very different when they had met at the Club this February. Over the potted shrimps, lamb cutlets and club claret, Bryn had talked about his bizarre meeting at Claridge's with Jack C Smith, which was still quite fresh in his mind. It turned out that Marcus knew a little about Smith from his earlier American posting.

"Very interesting character," he mused, as he spread mint sauce over his cutlets and all the vegetables on his plate. "I once met him at an Embassy Reception even before he got into Congress. Pretty well a self-made man."

"I don't think so," said Bryn, pleased to capitalize on one of those rare occasions when Marcus's know-all certainty might have to yield to his superior knowledge. "He's actually Jack C Smith the Third and he inherited the university from his grandfather."

Another of Marcus's irritating characteristics was that, even when he was scoring points, he remained impeccably almost unctuously polite.

"Well of course you are quite right about that, old boy."

He refilled their claret glasses.

"But I think you'll find that the little college he inherited was nothing like the enterprise it is now. And it is not, in any case, the main source of Jack's income."

"Oh really?"

"Yes really… did your researches, for instance, reveal that Jack also runs an international evangelical business called *GodWorks*?"

This was sudden and unwelcome news.

The approach from the head-hunter, the summons to Claridge's, the interview with Smith – all began to fall into place. Of course Bryn had heard about the *GodWorks* organization. It operated in the British Isles as a religious pressure group dedicated to raising what it called 'standards'. This meant for example supporting legislative initiatives for tighter restrictions on abortion or television, cinema and internet content. The reason he knew all this was because its chief legal advisor and professional representative in the court actions it took in furtherance of its causes was none other than his old friend, Marshall.

There now seemed little doubt that it was Marshall who had recommended him to Smith. No doubt he had also thought it inappropriate to encourage any false expectations by telling him so. It would be typical of Marshall to be both patronizing and discreet at the same time. Bryn's academic reputation evidently had a great deal less to do with it than he had believed. He was profoundly depressed.

"Actually Smith's main source of income," Marcus continued, "is a five thousand acre theme park owned by *GodWorks* outside Charleston. It's a sort of biblical version of Disneyland. I've never been there but I believe it's very popular with the churches and takes ten million or so visitors a year. They can go for a sail in Noah's Ark, get to climb inside the Whale like Jonah, and I'm sure there's a parting of the Red Sea just like at Universal Studios in Los Angeles. But I believe the most popular attraction is the opportunity to be photographed hanging from the thieves' Crosses either side of Jesus. Oh, and I remember. They call it '*Bibleland*'."

"I'm glad I didn't get it," said Bryn.

"The university job? You're well out of it, I should think," said Marcus. "Anti-gay, anti-black, pro-life, creationist. Not your liberal cup-of-tea, old boy. Surprised you even considered it."

The pudding arrived. Sticky Toffee for Marcus, Eton Mess for Bryn. The waiter poured two glasses of port from a decanter. Bryn's depression lifted a few notches and, to change the subject, he started to tell Marcus about his two recent scares with the speeding car and on the Underground. It was only a few days since Guy's funeral and he thought it might be worth repeating a story that had gone down so well on that occasion. Marcus, as always, listened politely. Then, when Bryn had finished, he paused and stared at him intently.

"Do you think the car and the man who pushed you on the platform were a coincidence?" he said.

"Of course," said Bryn.

"OK… did you see the man's face at all? The one at Oxford Circus?"

"No. It was all over in a flash. And he was always going away from me, up the platform. All I saw was his trilby hat."

"Did you wonder why he was wearing a trilby?"

"Of *course* not," said Bryn.

Marcus's incessant interest in detail did sometimes get a bit tedious.

"Do you think he might have been bald?" asked Marcus mildly.

Even at the time, Bryn remembered, he had thought this a most curious remark. It was not even really a question – more of a statement for him to agree with. He had gazed at Marcus uncomprehendingly, waiting for him to explain what – if anything – was in his mind. But Marcus changed the subject.

"I hear you're going to the States."

How on earth did he know that? Oh. Ken Burns of course.

"I was invited by old friend Professor Dan in Utah, and a Professor Weiskopf in Ann Arbor. The same lecture twice," he replied. "The Civil War as usual."

"Well," said Marcus, "be careful. I'm sure you're right about your two little scrapes. But I think you should treat them as a kindly warning from providence. To be vigilant."

He signalled to the waiter for the bill.

"Oh and if you're there on a Sunday, do tune into the *GodWorks* channel if you want to see your friend in action. He's quite something, I believe, Mr Smith."

Chapter 13

Marion was still snoring.

Bryn lay pondering his cousin's remarks. Marcus did like to give an impression of all-knowingness and it might be that his observations about Smith and *GodWorks* at their February lunch had been the full extent of his information on that subject. All the same, there had been a few passing comments here and there which were now beginning to worry him. The bald man on Smith's television show and Marcus's strange suggestion that the man at Oxford Circus had been bald. And then Marshall's association with Smith's organization in England. He needed to do some more research. He might start with another lunch with Marcus, if necessary at his own expense.

He was still thinking about this in the morning when the telephone rang. It was, incredibly, Marcus's office. Was he free for lunch that day and if so could they meet at 1pm at Merryweather's in Baker Street?

Marcus, he reflected, was full of surprises. And he had never, ever, known him to lunch out in a public restaurant. Always at the Travellers. Except for the one time they had met round the corner at the Athenaeum when the Travellers was closed for refurbishments.

He arrived early. Even so, Marcus was already in place at a table by the window, his thin, small form neatly clad in its usual three-piece pinstripe, a very dry Kir alongside him. He continued to study the menu as Bryn sat down and, for once, made no opening enquiries about Bryn's mother or his wife or the family. As soon as the waiter had been sent away with their menu decisions, he came straight to the point. He sounded as if he was preparing an indictment.

"I believe you know a woman called Zelma Weiskopf" he said.

Bryn's first instinct was to deny. He was not sure it was any business of Marcus's anyway. He composed himself.

"Why do you ask?" he said, coolly.

"I have an interest in your welfare, Bryn," Marcus replied, "as I think you know."

Even by Marcus's standards, this was pompous in spades. The information came from Ken, he was sure of it. In which case he need divulge no more than Ken would have guessed or might have been told by a University of Michigan contact, which was unlikely to be a great deal. If Marcus thought he had a rôle to play in protecting Marion from some imagined shenanigans, then he would be disappointed.

"Yes I know Professor Weiskopf," he said. "I met her in London, once I think, at an academic function. And then briefly when I was lecturing a few weeks ago in Ann Arbor. Why do you ask?"

"Well I also know something about Ms Weiskopf. Apparently, she has some history. She's a lady from a very leftist background. Her parents met at the University of Michigan during the big period of student unrest in the 60s. They worked with Tom Hayden and other government-bothering radicals. Students for a Democratic Society, and the Yippies, and some association with the Black Panthers. Sit-ins, clashes with police, even a spell or two in gaol. They were the leading trouble-makers at the Grant Park riots in 1968. Zelma herself is believed now to be part of a new and highly illegal group which even you may have read about. It's had quite a lot of coverage. They specialize in trashing the offices of radio presenters."

Bryn did have some recall of this.

"Fighting back against the extreme right, the shock-jock channels? 'The only way to reduce nuclear weapons is to use them.' She's opposed to people like that, is she?"

His cousin gazed back at him impassively.

"'Feminism is for ugly women' – or was that Rush Limbaugh?" Bryn continued. "Or some similar shock-jock they've raided?"

"I really wouldn't know," Marcus said. "I understand, however, that she also contributes to a website which defends Islamist terrorists."

"Or maybe it's one of those websites which explore the reasons why Arabs and Afghans are anti-American, so that they can be intelligently addressed?"

Marcus sighed. They had had conversations like this before. He was not accustomed in his normal working environment to have these – to him – perfectly conventional views challenged, and he only accepted it from Bryn because he was his cousin. Bryn, for his part, always found himself more left-wing with Marcus than he was with anyone else, even within the recorder group. They had known each other since early boyhood, and it had always been thus.

"I'll say no more," said Marcus. "Or maybe just one thing. Ms Weiskopf, I am told, is by way of a man-eater. A sort of *La Pasionaria* of the Midwest. I really would advise you – as a married man – to have no further dealings with her."

He avoided Bryn's gaze and began studiously to tear his bread roll into small pieces, and butter them.

It took a moment or two for Bryn to recover from this extraordinary pronouncement. And then he put the two questions he suspected a more forthright person might have asked at an altogether earlier stage of this conversation.

"What *possible* justification have you got for bringing all this up, Marcus?" he said. "And for a second thing, what *fucking* business is it of yours anyway?"

His cousin appeared to recognize that he may have strayed too far. He did not reply. A waiter appeared and cleared away their plates. Marcus delayed again until the man had left and then spoke so quietly that Bryn had to strain to hear him.

"I know about your connection with Zelma Weiskopf through a mutual acquaintance. Please don't ask me more about that. And, though you may not remember it, you did mention her yourself at our last lunch. That struck a bell and I checked her out. The internet, you know, that kind of thing. You might like to do the same yourself. I think you'll find a deal of quite alarming information about her. Depending on your personal view of course. Incidentally, the University of Michigan website billed your lecture so I knew anyway she was with you and that she introduced you on the day."

He drained his wine glass and refilled it from the bottle.

"I do have a duty to you as your cousin," he continued. "And, if you'll allow me, I have a duty to Marion too. I know you think I interfere. However, you are one of my few really close relations and… well OK then… I am concerned about you. I hope you can accept that."

Bryn was not mollified.

"I'm sorry, Marcus. I think you go too far. I hear what you say, but I really… don't… believe… this is any of your business."

Then, as an afterthought:

"And perhaps you ought not to put so much faith in websites. The U of M one you were relying on was obviously written before the lecture because Professor Weiskopf never turned up. And – as it happens – I have heard absolutely nothing from her since."

Marcus stared at him.

"You haven't seen her at all?"

Bryn was gratified that this news had such an effect.

"She didn't turn up at the lecture and I have had no contact with her subsequently," he said, with punctilious accuracy.

So much for Ken or whomever Marcus's source was. And possibly a lesson well-learned for Marcus.

The lunch ended early, and as frostily as it had begun. Marcus rang for a taxi but did not offer Bryn a lift. They parted at the entrance to the restaurant. As they did so, a large maroon car drifted slowly alongside the kerb towards them and fell into line behind the taxi as it drove away towards Oxford Street.

Bryn resolved that the meeting would be their last, at least for some while. It was not until he was on the tube and riding back to Ealing that he realized that he had raised none of the questions with Marcus that had troubled him after their previous meeting. What he knew about *GodWorks*, for example. And if there had been any significance in his remark about the trilby man being bald. It was too late now. It might be sensible, however, to follow up Marcus's suggestion that he spend some time on the internet.

He knew before he reached his front door that he had been burgled. The frame alongside the lock had been splintered and two or three small shards of wood were rearing up at him like cries of alarm. His key would not turn the lock and he was obliged to force the door open to get in. Though it was Marion's day off, there was no sign of her. A quick tour of the house revealed some clear signs of disturbance in several rooms but he could not at first glance be sure what was missing.

He rang Marion at once on her mobile and was relieved when she answered promptly. She was surprised to hear his voice and – it seemed to him – not especially pleased. He explained what had happened.

"I'll come right back," she said. "I have been meeting Janet for lunch. I'm sorry I didn't tell you."

His second call was to the police. While he waited for them to arrive, he went through the rooms more carefully to see what the burglars had taken. A few chairs had been turned over and cupboards opened. A pile of his students' essays had been scattered across the floor and a box of books up-ended. And yet, so far as he could tell, nothing had actually been removed. The most serious damage, apart from the door, was to the old bureau in which he kept his domestic papers. It now hung open with its drawers emptied and the fractured lock lying a few feet away on the floor. A roll of three hundred euros, unspent since a holiday a year ago in France, had been tossed into the fire grate. When he went upstairs and checked the small drawer by the bedside where Marion kept her jewellery, its contents also seemed intact. It was not even apparent that the thieves had opened it.

He returned to the kitchen, bemused. There was a piece of brown paper on the table. At first he imagined it was something that Marion had left. A message for him, perhaps, in case he came home early. And indeed it was a message, or part of one. It took a while for it to sink in. It was not from Marion. Or anyone else. It was in pencil, in his own hand-writing and torn off from a rather larger sheet of what had once been wrapping paper. On the paper was his own address, as he had written it down four weeks ago in the mountain cabin in Utah.

He was still considering this, when the police arrived. He folded the piece of brown paper and slipped it into his jacket pocket.

This time it was a uniformed officer, in a car. He walked around the house, not very carefully, and took a few notes. When he came back he asked Bryn if he had a list of what had been taken.

"No," said Bryn.

"We'll *need* a list, sir," said the policeman, with emphasis.

"I don't think I can give you one," replied Bryn.

The policeman looked at him sideways as if he doubted his intelligence.

"I'm afraid nothing's been taken," said Bryn.

"Ah. You're quite sure of that?"

"I think so."

The policeman closed his notebook.

"Well, sir, do call us if eventually you find something's missing. I'm sure your insurance company will want to know about any claims."

He looked at Bryn and waited for his response. He sighed. There was no helping some people.

"And I'd get the lock fixed right away if I were you. OK, sir?"

135

And he left, attempting briefly to close the broken door behind him.

Marion arrived soon afterwards and found Bryn in the process of restoring the furniture to its previous state and tidying up. She gave him an uncharacteristically warm hug and, something else she rarely did these days, kissed him on the lips. She persuaded him to sit down while she made a pot of tea. As it was brewing, she strolled around the house to see any damage for herself. After a while, she came back.

"Where is your laptop?" she said.

She was right as usual. Bryn always stowed it when not in use alongside his armchair in the sitting room. He had returned the overturned chair to its normal position but omitted to check for the laptop. He searched in some other possible places until there was no doubt about it: it was gone. He would have to phone the police and tell them; and he might then tell them also about the brown paper address.

But not just yet. He was, of course, in a state of shock. Marion must have guessed it too because she was specially considerate and insisted he take it, for the while, very easily. He heard her on the telephone in the next room talking to someone quietly. The doctor, perhaps.

The loss of the laptop concerned him, as any loss might have, though he was less worried about its actual contents. It had his current work-in-progress on it, including the last draft of the monograph about the Confederacy generals. Fortunately, he had backed all that up on a couple of CDs which were secure in his office at UCL. But he would not particularly want anyone to see his abortive emails to Zelma. On reflection, he was pretty sure he had deleted them twice. That is to say, once to the Delete folder, and then, terminally, from that folder too.

Marion rang the police to report the loss. She did not mention the brown paper address; but then Bryn had still not told her about it. Her telephone conversation with the case officer – the same policeman who had visited the house – puzzled her. When she asked for a case reference number so that she could give it to the insurance company, he asked her whether there was anything else she wanted to add to the list, an iPhone perhaps or a TomTom.

Graeme's funeral took place in late April, after a delay while the police completed their forensic investigations. It was difficult to know how thorough they were, because no member of the recorder group heard much from them after the initial interviews. It was also difficult to avoid the impression that they had begun to lose interest as soon as they had established, to their own satisfaction, that Graeme had been suffocated – most likely accidentally – during an act which involved a degree of asphyxiation to enhance the sexual pleasure.

A few things were reported at the inquest or emerged informally. The police believed Graeme had accepted a random pick-up from someone unknown to him and that was why the trail had gone cold so quickly. It also appeared – to most of his friends' surprise – that Graeme's main source of income, once his acting career had begun to dry up, had been soft porn videos for the gay trade. Initially he had performed in them, later directed them, for an organization called Dark Productions. The police were puzzled by the discrepancy over the years between what he earned and what his bank accounts held. One suggestion was that the difference might be accounted for by a little blackmailing income on the side, but it was doubted if this would shed any useful light on the present enquiry.

The funeral was arranged as soon as the body was officially released. Graeme's German partner, Dieter, was very much in charge, which meant that the ceremony became a celebration of their life together; which in turn meant a great deal of Wagner. Dieter had not forgotten the recorder group and asked them to play in the guests as they arrived at the crematorium. He requested that they do their recorder setting of the *Siegfried Idyll*. It conveniently included a part for Janet on a portable Yamaha which could double for the two missing descants.

The three surviving members of the group, treble, tenor and bass, plus keyboard player, arrived early. As soon as the mourners from the outgoing shift had left, they slipped in and set up their music stands. There were only wide bench pews for the congregation, and no single chairs. So the four of them, including Janet, stood to play, like an elderly folk-rock group.

The mourners had gathered in a waiting room nearby, and there was a short interval before they were ushered through, during which the group started their music alone. The first arrivals came into the chapel almost reluctantly, as if unwilling to disturb the performance. In the cold, dry acoustic, the noise they made seemed to Bryn and his fellow players inappropriately small and remote. They played on until they saw the long black Volvo hearse draw up beyond the open chapel doors. Then they folded up their stands and withdrew.

Dieter had managed to persuade the funeral director to allow him to replace the professional coffin bearers with six of his closest gay friends. All were dressed in a respectful silky black, as chic and exquisite as a funeral team could possibly be. All but one had gleaming bald heads. All but two wore a stud in one, or both, ears. They paced together in flawless unison through the doors and up the length of the building, to a recording of the funeral march from the last act of *Götterdämmerung*. It was the grandest and certainly the loudest entrance of a deceased person any West London funeral chapel had ever known.

The six men carried the coffin to the rolling platform in front of the congregation and stood in a line alongside it, heads bowed and hands modestly clasped over their Reiss belt buckles. There was no minister to lead the service. Instead, one of the bearers detached himself from the rest and took up a position behind a lectern, stage left.

"I have been asked to speak by Dieter," he said.

He had that rather precise, rather prissy accent of the educated German speaking English.

"My name is Claus and I have known Dieter and, so sadly, until now Graeme, since their beginning. As you probably know, they met in Bayreuth, at the Wagner Festival where Dieter was working in the box office and Graeme was queueing for returns for *The Ring of the Nibelungs*. As we all know, it was love at first sight. There were no seats left of course – there never are – but somehow Dieter produced a couple for the whole Cycle and they sat together. Then I met them in line for cushions for those hard seats in the *festspielhaus*. I remember my first question to Graeme was 'How on earth did you get your tickets?' "

There was a knowing ripple of laughter in the congregation.

"My second was 'When on earth will the Wagner family hand over the reins?' In those days, always the same questions."

The congregation, or at least its gay contingent, laughed again appreciatively and two or three applauded. Claus reminisced briefly about the operas they had all attended, their travels together to North Africa and to the new eastern European states. Finally he asked Dieter, very gently, if he felt able to speak. But Dieter, supported on both sides by friends, bowed his head with a little shuddering shake.

"Then we must say now goodbye to our dear, dear friend, Graeme," said Claus, after a respectful pause.

He moved at a stately slow pace across the stage and pressed a concealed button. Simultaneously, the coffin started to roll towards the doors at the top of the chapel, the velvet curtains began to encircle it, and the voice of Kirsten Flagstad singing Brunnhilde's Immolation scene from the end of *The Ring of the Nibelungs* welled up and filled the chapel. The curtains closed, and the rumble of the disappearing coffin ceased. On the words "*Ruhe, Ruhe, du Gott!*" Dieter collapsed into the arms of his two acolytes and was led gently from the chapel.

Chapter 14

The reception was held in the exquisitely decorated and punctiliously tidy house that Dieter and Graeme had shared. A recent photograph of Graeme, expensively framed in polished wood, sat on the mantelpiece. Other photographs of the two together were tastefully scattered around the sitting room. The bald-headed coffin-bearers circulated smilingly with trays of crustless cucumber sandwiches, home-made sausage rolls, bridge rolls and tiny triangles of pizza. In a corner of the room, another friend was dispensing Louis Roederer champagne in cut-glass flutes. "This is to celebrate him not to mourn him," he said several times whenever he sensed any element of surprise.

Bryn fell in with Janet. As with the other recorder group wives, she had never been to Graeme's house before and was enchanted by it.

"It is a bit... well, feminine," said Bryn.

"Nonsense," retorted Janet briskly. "No woman would dare to be as romantic and old-fashioned as this. And no woman I know would be allowed to spend so much on it."

"It hardly looks to me as if it has been lived in at all," said Bryn.

Janet looked at him over her champagne flute. She sighed.

"I miss him," she said suddenly. "He was the nicest of the lot of you."

"Yup," said Bryn. Out of the side of his eye, he could see Marion talking animatedly to Marshall. One of the nice things about the recorder group, he reflected, was the ease with which all the partners as well as the males had always got on with each other. It would be a great pity if those bonds now began to loosen.

He realized Janet was still talking.

"I'm really sorry about the burglary. I only heard about it today. I hope they didn't do too much damage."

Now it was his turn to look at her. There was something not quite right here.

"I'm sorry," he said. "When did you hear about the burglary?"

"Today. Marion told me."

"I though you were having lunch with Marion when I called her about it. The day it happened."

"What? No, no. I haven't had lunch with Marion since before Guy died."

She laughed and shook her head. One of the bald friends eased alongside her and gracefully refilled her flute. She asked the friend how long he had known Graeme and they started chattering vigorously. Bryn drifted away.

A chill feeling settled on him. A sensation he had rarely known before. And even as it did, he was conscious of an irony, a sort of hubris, that *he* should be the one to feel this. She was still talking to Marshall. She had, so far as he could tell, been talking to him all evening. And there was a warmth between them, perhaps even a physical closeness, that he had not perceived before. He watched, out of the side of his eye so that he might not be suspected of watching, for any more blatant signs of a closer than normal recorder group friendship. He recalled her reaction when he had rung her that day. Her unexpected affection when she returned. The discreet phone call which he had thought might be to his doctor.

141

"Bryn! We have not spoken all day!"

It was Dieter, high on champagne or perhaps other substances. He grasped Bryn fervently by the shoulder and began to steer him away to a gorgeously chintzy sofa at the far end of the room. As they passed Marshall and Marion, she looked up at Bryn as though startled by his presence. He caught her gaze very, very briefly before Dieter moved him relentlessly on. In that tiny moment, it was clear to him that she recognized that he had guessed her secret.

"We need to talk," said Dieter.

He put his champagne glass beside him on a small occasional table, and turned his full face upon Bryn. The gaiety and the artifice drained away. This was a serious, intent Dieter he had not often seen.

"First of all, Bryn, I have to thank you – as I must thank all the others – for everything you have done through all this. You do not know how important the recorder group was to Graeme and how grateful I am for the pleasure you have given him. I do not know how I could have survived the last few weeks without this circle of friends. Not just the group of course. Janet, Marion, all the wives who have been so generous and supportive. I hope so much that these friendships will survive."

Bryn squeezed Dieter's hand and smiled in what he believed was an appropriately supportive way.

"But there is one other thing, which is just for you."

Dieter paused and glanced fleetingly around the room.

"There is a matter arising from Graeme's Will. I need to speak to you separately."

"To do with the recorder group?"

"No. To do with you."

"Could we talk about it now?"

"No," said Dieter, emphatically. "We must meet separately. Are you free tomorrow?"

They agreed to meet over coffee at a shop on the Pitshanger Lane, at 11 o'clock the next morning.

Later, as he rejoined the party, Bryn noticed that Marion and

Marshall were no longer together. Marshall appeared to be absorbed in Dieter and Graeme's huge CD collection, shelved with alphabetical precision across the two longest walls of the room. Meanwhile Marion was in animated conversation with one of Dieter's inaccessibly gay friends. What kind of signal was this, he pondered. That he should not be concerned about Marshall or any other particular male she happened to be with today? He drifted across to talk to Janet and was conscious of Marion's eye following him all the way.

The next morning, Dieter was already in the coffee shop when Bryn arrived. He looked ill and miserable. It might have been a reaction to the excesses of the previous day, from which Bryn was also suffering; or a more deep-seated hangover as he began to come to terms with his new life alone. Bryn could not tell. In fact, as their conversation developed, it seemed more to do with another matter entirely.

At first, Dieter was reluctant to come to the point. He talked about the funeral and the reception afterwards, rather like a stage director reviewing his own production, soliciting Bryn's compliments for the performance and complaining about imaginary shortcomings of the support staff. Bryn provided the required, effusive responses and they were received with extravagant relief. But none of this brave show appeared more than briefly to alleviate Dieter's over-arching cast of misery.

In the end it was Bryn who broached the subject.

"Do you want to talk about the Will?"

It was as if Dieter had not heard him. He stared out of the coffee shop window at the week-day shoppers passing up and down Pitshanger Lane, and then at his coffee cup. Two or three minutes elapsed. Finally, he leaned over and pulled out a bag from under his chair. He extracted a large, sealed, manila envelope which he pushed across the table towards Bryn.

"I am not interested in the contents," he said quietly.

"Do you know what it is?" said Bryn.

143

"I am not *interested*," said Dieter, with a sudden flare of aggression.

"I cannot receive this if it is money or something like that. That is yours."

Bryn was surprised at his own firmness.

There was another long pause.

"There is no money or anything like that... well, possibly I suppose, that's up to you. This is nothing I would ever want."

"Did the Will say anything? Why I should have this?"

"Graeme has asked that you take this into safe-keeping. No-one else. You. That is all."

"Well, whatever it is, thank you. I'm sure you could have junked it if you had wanted. I will do whatever Graeme wanted."

Dieter said nothing. He made a sharp, dismissive gesture, pushing the envelope off the table into Bryn's lap. His eyes welled with tears and he stood up. He placed a note and some coins on the table, picked up his bag, flashed a wintry smile and left.

Bryn opened the envelope in his study. Inside was a large photograph, nothing else. It looked as if it had been taken professionally. It was deep-focussed, well lit, and, he guessed, an original print. It showed two men, both naked, kissing each other. As pornography, it was very small beer – members barely visible at all; and the only evident sexual contact on the lips. Their faces were lit softly from the front, while a bedside table light behind threw their profiles into sharp relief.

The photograph had clearly been taken many years previously, because one of the men, the one taking the less dominant position, was – beyond any doubt – a much younger Marshall. Perhaps thirty years younger. Two stone slimmer than now, with longer, glossier hair. But unquestionably Marshall. The other man's face was also familiar and Bryn struggled for a while to place it. Not someone he knew personally, he was sure of that. A face he may have seen on television or in a film. He turned the picture over to see if there was any information on the other side. Nothing – save for a small ink rubber stamp with the legend 'Dark Productions'.

But *Marshall*... how bewildering was this? He sat back in his chair and contemplated the situation. He knew any number of card-carryingly heterosexual men of whom he could just about imagine a gay fling or two some time in their younger, prettier past. He might indeed have fallen into that category himself. But not Marshall. Marshall was without doubt the least camp, least feminine, least experimental alpha male he knew. He wondered if the photograph could be a fake, a magical digital contrivance of some kind. It looked too natural, however, with shadows and light too realistically graduated to be the product of somebody's computer. It was the genuine article all right.

How then had it fallen into Graeme's hands? And what was Graeme's purpose in bequeathing it to *him*? (And when on earth, and why, had Graeme decided to write it into his Will, given that he presumably had no expectation of early death?)

It was easier to speculate about the first question. He knew Graeme had been involved in pornography. Either he had taken the photograph himself or – and this seemed more likely, given its age – he had acquired it from someone else in the trade. He thought he knew Graeme well enough to guess what he then did with it. There had always been a tough streak in him – the product, Bryn now suspected, of his involvement in the harsh world of pornographic films.

He could easily imagine him using the photograph, probably quite discreetly, to blackmail Marshall. Probably not for large sums either, but just enough to tide him over difficult professional periods. That might explain the needling edginess between the two of them which all the other recorder group members had detected. It might also help to explain why Marshall, the least likely stayer in the group, had nonetheless persisted with it: to keep an eye on Graeme. He recalled the number of times, for example, the pair of them used to leave their recorder group meetings together. He remembered also the recent police comment about "a little blackmailing" being the possible explanation for the healthy state of Graeme's bank account. It all seemed very plausible.

Of course, if the police had been less convinced that Graeme was the victim of a random pick-up, they might have looked deeper into his finances and discovered the Marshall connection. Discovered indeed this very photograph.

Did that mean then that Marshall had killed him? It was a terrifying thought.

He scoured his memory of that night. Marshall had left before the rest of them, in a taxi, and might therefore – he supposed – have had the opportunity. But then – to murder Graeme in the course of an act of S & M gay sex, that was surely inconceivable. Not even this extraordinary photograph could persuade him that that could be Marshall's style. And then there was the phone call next morning. For all his talents, Marshall was no actor. His distress had been evident and genuine.

But he still came back to the photograph. Which Graeme had wanted him to have. Was this his way of ensuring retribution in the event that Marshall did somehow contrive his death? But that had to be nonsense. And the surest way of effecting that would have been to make sure the photograph was delivered to the police, with an appropriate commentary. Not, and quite without instruction, to a friend.

He gazed at the image. It began to dawn on him that whatever secret it held might have more to do with the other, dominant, character in the photograph, than with Marshall. Graeme's failure to pass the photograph to the police could suggest that he did not want it to fall into the hands of officialdom, to be lost perhaps or buried, or misused. Bryn was touched that he should have chosen him. Perhaps he trusted him more than others of his friends to treat the matter responsibly. It would be nice – and flattering – to think so…

He had thought the second face was familiar. As he studied it more closely he became less certain. The other man in the photograph had the conventionally handsome looks of a thousand actors or models. But what he looked like now, a possible thirty years later, might be beyond recognition. He tried to imagine the young man's sharply-etched profile softened and

146

coarsened by age, with a receding hairline, bald even, maybe with some facial hair as well. Who could guess what he might have come to? He placed the photograph face-down on his desk, and turned away.

It was difficult to know what to do next. He had a fleeting compulsion simply to return it to Marshall. But if Graeme had intended that, he would not have bequeathed it to *him*. And so long as Marshall's role in Graeme's death remained obscure, it made little sense to over-rule Graeme's intentions. Whatever they were. And if he did not want the picture to be delivered to the police, then what *did* he expect of him? That he, Bryn, might use it for further blackmailing purposes? In that case, his ghost would be disappointed. It was true that the unpleasant thought had occurred, tempting for only a second or two, that he might reveal the photograph to Marion to discourage her depressing interest in Marshall. But that, on the briefest reflection, was an even worse idea. One that was likely neither to leave him with credit nor even, reliably, to achieve its purpose.

The photo after all belonged to a much earlier period in Marshall's life, and nothing he knew of Marshall suggested that it was relevant to the person he was now. After some further reflection, he decided to put it away permanently in the safe custody envelope he kept at his bank in the Tottenham Court Road for his aged mother's old share and unit trust certificates. Out of sight, he thought, but not – he did not doubt – out of mind. Perhaps one day, when its true significance became clearer, he would retrieve it.

He could not remember the last time he had visited his bank. For years he had conducted all his business on the internet, with the occasional cheque when he could not avoid it, and perhaps a phone call or two a year when he needed to talk directly about a problem on his current account. And the bank had changed too. It had started as a small local branch opposite Warren Street Station, then grown up and been amalgamated with others in a steel and glass monster further up the Tottenham Court Road near the Dominion Theatre. He had never met his current bank manager. He was not even sure people like that existed anymore.

He took the precaution of ringing the bank and arranging a formal appointment to visit his safe custody envelope. When he arrived, he found the bank had been transformed into a great atrium stretching the width of the building frontage. There were two or three customer access windows tucked away to the right, with a handful of unreconstructed walk-in clients meekly standing in line. The entire rest of the perimeter was taken up with open-plan offices and doors to more private parts of the building. He presented himself at a small reception point halfway along and waited till a female clerk emerged from an office to speak to him.

The process of accessing his mother's envelope, however, had not changed. It seemed to be the last visible redoubt of Dickensian banking practice left. The clerk ushered him into a private room with a wooden table in the centre and a couple of chairs. No open plan, no windows. She returned with his envelope and a second one, pristine and unused; and also a bank ballpoint pen in lieu of the quill he had half-expected. He slit open the original envelope and, out of force of habit, checked that everything was still in order. He made an addition to the list of contents he kept with it, slipped the photograph in with the rest, and sealed everything up in the new envelope. Finally, as he had been instructed, he wrote his signature several times across the sealing points. He pinged the old-fashioned bell on the table and waited for his release. The whole enchanting ceremony had taken perhaps thirty minutes.

On the way out, he was intercepted by a young man in a city suit.

"Do you have a moment, Mr Williams? My name is Patel," he said.

He was, it turned out, not his mythical bank manager nor the deputy, but an apparatchik who identified himself as his 'account manager'. He wanted to discuss Bryn's overdraft arrangements.

They withdrew to one of the open plan offices in the atrium, with low glass partitions so that a customer could watch the queuing public and the public could watch him. Mr Patel snapped open a laptop and made a couple of passes across the keys.

"We were intending to write to you, sir, but I hope you don't mind me taking advantage of this opportunity to talk to you face to face."

He smiled wanly. Bryn knew perfectly well what this would be about. He had an overdraft arrangement with an understanding that he would progressively reduce the amount owing. A rather contrary-wise process was his reality and had been so for a long time.

"It's your overdraft, Mr Williams," said Mr Patel.

"Ah," said Bryn.

He reckoned he might as well get his retaliation in first.

"I would like to increase my limit, if you don't mind."

The other man made a show of running over what Bryn took to be his account details for the last few years. He looked up from his laptop.

"That would be fine, Mr Williams, if your income over time was likely to exceed your outgoings. With respect, this has not been the situation for three years now. I have not checked further back but I believe this may be a long-term issue."

"I think you will find I would have done better if I had not had to pay all those exorbitant overdraft charges. And that's the reason I need to raise the limit," said Bryn with as much effrontery as he could muster.

A tiny moue of irritation hinted that Mr Patel might have been over this ground before with his clients.

Bryn tried to lighten the atmosphere.

"In any case, I doubt *I'm* the real threat to the bank's profitability," he said, with a smile.

Mr Patel was not amused. The facetious remark seemed to trigger the frustrated anorak within him. Without taking his eyes for a moment off his computer screen, he embarked upon a rapid exegesis of the banking system. The retail sector on which ordinary customers depended was, he emphasized, *sustained* by the investment business to which Bryn, he assumed, had alluded.

If a customer believed the bank was making an unreasonable profit on his current account, then he could assure him that, if anything, the reverse was the case. All the banks were facing new challenges, all the time. One example of the newer problems they shared was the need to future-proof against the costly downsides of modern technology. For example, internet and credit card fraud. And by and large, it was the banks – and not the customer – who paid the price.

Bryn enjoyed a good academic argument. Mr Patel reminded him of one of his more intense students. And, though he recognized that on this occasion he knew far less about the subject than his adversary, he could not resist the temptation to plunge further in.

"Of course," he responded, "the reason the banks tolerate – encourage – the greater use of cards and the internet is that it removes the need for paperwork and handling cheques and meeting people. So you cut back on staff exponentially and ramp up the profits. Am I not right, Mr Patel?"

"There are advantages. However," replied the other, returning with a visible effort to his earlier manner, "I do believe, sir, the immediate problem is the state of your overdraft... do you think we could discuss now a strategy for reducing it?"

Further debate was fruitless. Bryn found himself, over the next ten minutes, meekly undertaking to review his 'budget' and make whatever savings he could. He was asked if his income was likely to rise. He agreed, optimistically, that that was likely, and Mr Patel placed a note on his file.

The truth was that Bryn's university salary was pretty well set in aspic, with no further increments and only an annual increase which might reflect inflation. If he wanted to improve his circumstances, he would have to look elsewhere. His mind turned to freelance lecturing in the long vacation, the last resort of impecunious academics. And – once again – to his long-gestating monograph.

Chapter 15

He spent the rest of the afternoon in his office at UCL.

He started by looking up Marshall's entry in the departmental copy of *Who's Who:*

> **HALL, Marshall Philip**; QC 1998; *b* 10 March 1955; *s* of Stanley and Iris Hall; *m* 1975, Deborah Edwards (marr. diss. 1998). *Educ:* Handsworth Grammar Sch., Birmingham; Hertford Coll., Oxford (Schol., MA, BCL); Princeton Univ. Called to the Bar, Middle Temple, 1978, Bencher 2004. Visiting Prof. Warwick Univ. 2006-. Mem., Edtl. Bd, Media Law 1998-. Chm., Inquiry into Football Hooliganism, 2008-9. Chm., BMA Cttee on Patient Confidentiality 2009-10. *Publications:* In Whose Opinion? (The Obscene Publications Acts), 1984, 3rd edn 2008; Whither Section 28?, 1991; contribs to legal jls. *Recreations:* food, music, playing the recorder. *Address:* Brunswick Chambers, Brunswick House, Temple, EC4 1DA. *Clubs:* Garrick.

Pretty impressive. The heart-warming story of a working class boy who had won a scholarship to Oxford and taken off like a rocket. A practising barrister in his very early twenties, with an interest in public and private morality. A strictly professional interest, perhaps, since Bryn could not recall Marshall in conversation ever taking a particularly moral stance on anything. He would probably characterize him briefly as a sceptic and a moral agnostic.

The *Who's Who* profile revealed little about the cases Marshall had taken as he had become more successful. Bryn knew that, with his speciality in media law, he had represented the likes of Rupert Murdoch, the Barclay Brothers and Conrad Black in the High Court and won cases for all of them. More recently – and this *was* reflected in the profile – he had begun to cut back on his litigation and had accepted jobs chairing government enquiries or making recommendations to public organizations as to how they should conduct their affairs.

Though he seemed never to have directly dabbled in politics, or accepted any political honour, he had many friends in government. He had, in short, worked himself into a position close to the centre of power. He had achieved this whilst retaining a usefully low public profile: he had in effect 'risen without trace'. He had become one of that small body of wise men upon whom the country's leaders call when they need a notionally independent, intellectual underpinning for what they probably intended to do anyway.

Not for the first – or indeed the last – time, Bryn pondered on the paradox that was Marshall. How distant this mighty *Who's Who* profile was from the person he knew. A man driven by the confident belief that he was smarter than anyone else. Who was able to make a cynical play for his friend's wife. Who – long ago in his youth – had left a deadly hostage to fortune which had returned to haunt him. Well, Bryn thought ruefully, I suppose you can trust me to keep it safe now.

He turned on his computer and put the word *GodWorks* into the search engine. He was instantly offered 151,000 results. He sighed, and started trawling through the first few web pages. Most of the entries related to the American organization; and Jack C Smith's name came up frequently. For the moment though he was more interested in the British connection and anything more it might reveal about Marshall's rôle within it.

Here he noticed another name recurring: someone called Harry Darke. He seemed to be an important financial backer for the organization in the UK. It emerged, for example, that the British *GodWorks* was based in the West Midlands and that its headquarters building was registered in Darke's name. There were other references to him, generally as a background figure and never in the front line. Various other people acted as spokespersons for the organization and provided the *Daily Mail* with its ready quotations on matters of public morality.

He tried Googling in Darke's and Marshall's names together. He hit the bullseye immediately. A couple of keystrokes and he was looking at a list of classmates on a school website. There – side by side – they were. He scrolled down to a photograph of about twenty-five boys, squatting, sitting, standing behind each other in rows as they used to in those days. Marshall sat at the dead centre of the picture with arms folded, the image of the stand-out top boy in the class. Slim, handsome, long black hair, as in Graeme's photograph. Alongside him was a smaller, squatter, round-faced boy, already looking like an adult, whose confident gaze into the camera lens matched the young Marshall's.

Then, without at first knowing quite why, he re-entered just their surnames, omitting the 'e' in 'Darke'. This time, as he scrolled through a seemingly limitless list of irrelevant references, he was not so successful. So he tried again, thoughtfully adding the extra word: 'productions'.

He had struck the mother lode. There were about fifty entries, running back over a number of years. He began to read them through from the top.

Mostly they were stories from the BBC and other news websites. A few were on a website called Melon Farmers which appeared to be a pressure group for the removal of restrictions on pornography. Some of the others were postings by local government authorities about applications for sex shop licences. Marshall's name came up as the legal representative in the various actions referred to. But the most frequent reference was to the company at the centre of all these stories: 'Dark Productions', the same name that had been inked on the back of the photograph which Bryn had two hours previously consigned to a safe custody envelope.

He went to the official Companies House site and clicked on its *WebCHeck* facility. He typed 'Dark Productions' into the search box. The name came up at once and he went through to its details. Incorporated in 1977; its business described gnomically as 'Wholesale other intermediate goods' and 'Other business activities'. Its address was certainly familiar: the street number placed it next door to the *GodWorks* organization.

He returned to the earlier websites. He was struck by a law report about an action from nearly thirty years ago, when Dark Productions challenged a judicial decision against it all the way to the European Court of Human Rights. British magistrates – supported by the British higher courts – had been interpreting the Obscene Publications Acts in such a way that the company was prevented from trading their – so they argued – *inoffensively* adult sex videos. The case was argued before the European Court in Strasbourg on the basis of Article 10 of the European Convention about freedom of speech. The lawyer representing Dark Productions, and its owner Harry Darke, was the young Marshall.

The European Court in its legalistic way did not formally conclude in the appellants' favour. But elements of its judgment were sufficiently critical of the British courts to require some relaxation of the standards applied. From Dark Productions' point of view, this was a most satisfactory outcome. It was clear that the young lawyer had achieved a considerable and lucrative triumph for his client.

A porn empire, then, run by Marshall's oldest friend. Bryn looked for a connection with Graeme. But Googling in his name produced nothing of interest beyond a couple of references in *www.imdb.com* to films in which he had taken minor roles as a young man. There was nothing, for example, to substantiate Bryn's guess that the Marshall/Graeme acquaintance may have originated way back in the 1980s when they were both employed by Harry Darke, one as a lawyer, the other as a director of the very same videos that Marshall was defending.

And what should he make of this man, Darke? At one stage, a merchant in pornography, at another a principal sponsor of the leading moral pressure group in the country. Had he undergone a Damascene conversion? What had happened to the porn empire? So far as Bryn could tell, it had continued to thrive. But it was noticeable that any association of Harry Darke's name with his company had declined sharply over the years. The more recent applications for sex shop licences were all being made on behalf of someone called Dave Devine. It was as if Darke had cleared the decks for the new cause.

He wandered for a little while longer through the references to *GodWorks*' activities. Its main objectives in the UK appeared to be the prohibition of abortion with no permissible exceptions, public recognition of homosexuality as 'anti-family and unChristian', and the restoration of capital punishment. Multiple hits on *www.dailymail.co.uk* confirmed its status as first port of call whenever that paper required a quote about standards on television, in the cinema and even – with some irony – in relation to screen pornography.

The organization's achievements, at least early on when Marshall had been most active on its behalf, had been substantial. In 1988 it had succeeded in passing into British law a prohibition on the "promotion of homosexuality" by local authorities or in schools "as a pretended family relationship". This was a direct consequence of the lobbying of MPs and select members of the House of Lords by friends of *GodWorks*. It had lobbied also for tighter restrictions on television content and this too was achieved, with new legislation introducing further layers of regulation. The fall of Mrs Thatcher had been a setback. And during the period when New Labour was in government, progress had been slow. There were recent signs, however, of a revival in *GodWorks*' fortunes, with encouraging movement particularly on the abortion front.

Bryn turned off the search engine and sat back. He was glad sometimes that he was a professional historian, able to draw consistent themes and stories out of the ball of wool of the securely distant past. The present always seemed to him to be too tangled and complicated. He flicked on his Outlook Express. There were two new emails.

One was from Zelma. Not from her usual address, the one Bryn had been unsuccessfully trying to access, but from a hotmail address in someone else's name. She did not want him to reply. She did not want him to pursue any further correspondence with her at all. She had resigned from her post at the University of Michigan and moved away. He was not to attempt to find her. She was sorry it had ended the way it did. Look out for yourself anyway. It was great while it lasted. I mean that. Zelma.

Pretty final. And yet the tone seemed at odds with the message. If she had really wanted to break off all connection with him, then she hardly needed to tell him that, and in so regretful an email. He was not convinced he had seen her for the last time.

The other message was from a New York publisher called Barton Showalter, forwarded to Bryn by his agent. It was radiant with the manic enthusiasm of the salesman. He had received Bryn's 'property' and it was a world-beater, the most 'challenging take' on the Civil War he had ever read. It was too good to put out as a school book. It needed a higher profile, maybe through airport stores. He was thinking syndication and movie rights. He knew of at least three independent producers, big players, who would want to option it for serious money. Just one thing though. It could do with more about the private lives of the generals and their women.

Bryn emailed back to his agent to say he was already working on an expanded draft (incidentally: how long does an airport book need to be) and he would make sure he included plenty of personal detail. He could feel another visit to the States coming on, perhaps to get into some of those personal archives in the southern universities. This was not the time to stand upon academic dignity. It was an ill wind.

Showalter's email had excited him. But he needed to work on something more immediately productive. He caught up with Ken Burns in the college refectory and quizzed him about the chances of dipping into the freelance long vacation work that occasionally came into the department's office. Ken never pretended that he approved of this. Lecturers after all were paid on a full-time basis and, even in the long vacation, there was an unexpressed assumption that they were using their spare time for research and for preparation for the year ahead. But Ken had to recognize that this was the real world, with mortgages and families to support. If forced to, he could defend the activity on the usual grounds of academic cross-fertilization.

As it happened, he had just received a request from an old colleague who was running a lecture programme for visiting American students from some minor east coast colleges. The old colleague needed someone at short notice to talk about the history of British institutions, including Parliament, the Monarchy, and the Judiciary.

The job was surprisingly easy to set up. Ken's friend had been let down by his usual retired professor, who had accepted a more lucrative invitation to lecture to rich tourists on a luxury liner cruising the Mediterranean. His normal alternative lecturer was unavailable because he was leading a Martin Randall tour of historic Reformation sites in Germany.

The students were due into London in three days' time. When Bryn rang, Ken's friend fell upon him like manna. Hands were rapidly and metaphorically shaken. Could he start next week? The money was pretty good, at roughly one hundred pounds an hour. The subject was not one that Bryn knew much about and he had little time to prepare. But what the hell. That had never been an impediment in the past.

It did not take very long to discover why his predecessors might have sought alternative employment. The American students were bored and alienated before the lectures had even started. Most had enrolled on the course purely in order to get to Europe for a couple of months. For a few, those who arrived in the

157

classroom in pairs, it was the price they had paid for a carnal vacation. Several wore their iPhone earpieces throughout the lectures and one young man at the back of the room had brought in a mini Blu-ray player and a supply of gothic horror films to help him while away these tedious hours.

Bryn's rustiness about the history of the British Monarchy, Parliament and the rest turned out to be no kind of problem at all. His first, fairly well-prepared lecture, delivered from extensive notes about the medieval origins of kingship, produced one contribution in the fifteen minutes he had reserved at the end for questions. It was from the only individual who had appeared to pay attention throughout, a serious-looking young man sitting on his own.

"Does the Queen still live at Camelot?" asked the student.

Bryn studied him for any sign of irony.

"Who can say?" he replied at last.

After that, he limited his preparation to scribbling down about five short phrases. For his talk about the growth of Parliament, for example, he wrote 'Norman Councils. Magna Carta. Oliver Cromwell. Political Parties. Winston Churchill'. And he did not even need to refer to that. He became content to improvize randomly while monitoring his audience for any unusual sign of interest. He began to measure his success by the number of plastic plugs that were on the students' desks rather than in their ears. Then he would riff for a while on whatever element in his discourse might briefly have engaged them. His lecture about the Judiciary never needed to get further than the bloody assizes of Judge Jeffreys in 1685. Even the young man at the back paused his copy of *The Exorcist* and leant forward attentively.

One subject on which he had expected some evidence of animation was current American politics – particularly in this election year. Accordingly, he struggled to find analogies between British and American history: the rise of successful military leaders to political supremacy (Wellington/Eisenhower), or of charismatic young men with little executive experience

(Blair/Obama), or the serial inability of Vice Presidents and Prime Ministers designate alike (Johnson-Ford-Bush Senior/Eden-Douglas Home-Callaghan) to hang onto power. He argued – more to provoke his audience than because he believed his thesis – that in American politics charm and charisma always prevailed over experience, whereas in Britain ability, or the palpable lack of it, was the decisive factor.

He might have been lecturing to himself. The names he recited, even the American ones, seemed for the most part unfamiliar to his audience. They had heard at least of one or other of the candidates currently pursuing the presidential nomination – the former governor of Minnesota, the black lady senator – but were deeply unclear about their policies or experience. Any comments they ventured were couched in open-ended clichés – 'hope', 'opportunity', 'freedom' – or focussed upon the candidates' physical attractiveness. It all seemed rather to prove his point. On the other hand, given his own preoccupation with other and different times, it was probably just as well he went unchallenged.

June and July passed peacefully and the concerns of the earlier part of the year faded back into the distance. Except for one. His suspicions that Marion and Marshall might be having an affair had grown stronger. His walk to the station every morning took him past Marshall's house, set grandly back from the main road. If Marshall's car was parked in the carriage-sweep driveway, then its owner was in town. And he began to notice that Marion's lunch dates coincided with periods when Marshall had returned from his frequent business visits to America. He considered challenging her but decided, unless he had clearer evidence, to keep his thoughts to himself. He was confused too by the uncharacteristic warmth she was showing towards him, which made him more reluctant than ever to provoke a confrontation whose consequences, he recognized, could not be predicted.

He was having coffee one day in the canteen in the Cromwell Road building where he went to lecture his American students. His companion was one of the American professors accompanying them and the conversation had turned to internet security. Bryn had mentioned his exchange with Mr Patel about bank exposure to online fraud, and his new friend capped it with a chilling story about a female colleague back in Maryland, whose computer had become infected with a worm which transmitted back to its originator every key stroke the colleague made.

The motive in this case was not fraud but infatuation. It turned out that a student in another department had secretly fallen in love with her, and was using the information to track her every movement. So, if she went online to book an air flight or order a ticket to the theatre, he would always be there, sometimes sitting in the seat behind her. In the end, she had to take out a court order against him. And buy a new computer.

Bryn found the story peculiarly disturbing. He dropped out of the conversation for a while.

"Are you still with us, bud?" asked the American professor.

"I was just thinking how much more comfortable it is worrying about the past than the present," said Bryn.

"I guess this is a bit of come-down for you, professor," said the American. "So what do you really do when you're not filling time with this bunch of hoodlums?"

He laughed. It was remarkable how easily he got on with his American colleagues. Maybe they tried harder to be friendly. And they always seemed flattered by his professional interest in their country.

He already knew what was coming.

"Actually my specialty," said Bryn, using the American version of the word for the second time this year, "is your Civil War. And currently, when I'm not trying to anaesthetize your students, I'm writing a book about Lee and Jackson and Forrest and all the rest. The Confederate generals."

"Did you know I live in Sharpsburg?" said his new friend.

Of course he did. He had overheard it a few days previously in an exchange between Karl and another colleague, and his ears had pricked up. Sharpsburg was a tiny town in western Maryland

and one of the key locations of the Civil War. A battle was fought there which helped to change the course of American history. And Bryn had not visited it for twenty years or more.

"Do you?" he said innocently.

"When did you last visit the battlefield?"

"Oh, dear me… it must be, ooh, twenty years ago. I expect it has changed a lot since then."

"Maybe not so much. But you gotta come and see. We'd love to have you."

"Oh… that is so kind."

"You promise you'll visit us. Got a diary?" asked Karl.

And so, with American inevitability, it was agreed. Email addresses were exchanged. The first outlines of a new plan of campaign began to form in his mind. One which might involve a professional visit to Maryland and to neighbouring Pennsylvania. And a re-connection, whatever her last message might have said to the contrary, with Zelma.

Chapter 16

When he got home, the house – as he expected – was empty. He went upstairs to his bedroom and sorted through the wardrobe until he arrived at his best lecturing jacket. He had not worn it since he returned from Salt Lake City. He held his breath. But there, in an inside pocket, it was: Zelma's large, unfashionable wind-up watch, now stopped and silent. He turned it over and looked at the numerals engraved on the back.

He went back downstairs to his study and switched on the new PC he had bought with the insurance from the burglary. Most likely the numerals would lead him nowhere at all. Even if they referred to a telephone number, it was by no means certain, after so many years since the engraving, that it still existed in this form.

The computer burst into life and he clicked on Internet Explorer and then Google. He typed in 'american telephone numbers' and a screen-full of options presented themselves to him. He tried the second one (*"411.com* allows you to find people, business listings, phone numbers..."*) and typed the number from Zelma's watch into the search box for 'Reverse Phone'. An address in Maplewood, New Jersey came up and a name: Sarah Weiskopf aged 65. This then must be Zelma's childhood home and the telephone subscriber in all probability her mother. There was something almost chilling about the ease with which he had tracked them down.

As an experiment, he clicked on the 'People Search' facility and typed in 'Zelma Weiskopf'. Just one option came up – for a 'Z Weiskopf' with an address and telephone number in Ann Arbor – almost certainly the address she had recently left. Alongside it was an invitation to 'View ALL records Located for Z Weiskopf'. Another box invited him to 'View web results and profiles for this person'. He clicked on both of them and in each case was informed that he had made an 'HTTP 400 Bad Request' and that the web page could not be accessed.

It gave him some comfort to discover that, at least for the moment, there was a limit to the availability of so much personal information. On second thoughts, he doubted that a more sophisticated web surfer than himself would have found the 'Bad Request' prohibitions to be a great impediment. What a wonderful thing the freedom of the web was, before which even ancient liberties like the right to privacy crumbled to dust.

He printed off the street map for the Maplewood address provided by the site, and folded it into his wallet. Who could say when it might be useful.

There was still no sign of Marion. It was not like her to be out at this time, unless of course… He dialled into his landline for any answerphone messages. She had rung home earlier from school and he listened to her crisply detached, rather too business-like voice.

"Hi, darling. Sorry I won't be home till late. I'm going out with a girlfriend. One of the other teachers, you wouldn't know her, she's new. If I'm not back, there's a Waitrose meal in the freezer. Give it 30 minutes on defrost first."

If only she could be less transparent. He recalled Marshall's Porsche in the driveway as he had walked back home from the station. He remembered thinking it looked in need of a wash. Maybe Marshall's life was just too crowded these days.

Perhaps he should pay him a call. Why not? It would be

natural enough to drop in on him, as if he was on his way home from work. He even had an excuse. At their last recorder group meeting on the night of Graeme's death, Marshall had left his music behind and he had promised Janet to deliver it. A promise promptly forgotten, till now.

So then. An innocent visit. An accidental discovery.

And the moral high ground entirely his.

He retrieved the music from his recorder bag and stuffed it into a plastic carrier. Instead of walking straight down the road, he circled round the back of Marshall's block so that he could approach the house from the same side as the station. When he was within fifty yards of it, he stopped.

The image he had cherished of the impending confrontation was becoming less clear-cut. Icy moral outrage, after all, was not without its downside. What *if* he caught them together? How likely was Marion, after so many years, to be impressed by his improbable machismo? And, just as he had always regarded Zelma – and his other affairs – as no threat to their marriage so long as Marion never found out about them, so might she feel about her liaison with Marshall. However disturbing the thought of them together, it could be a great deal less intolerable than the trauma and break-up that was the predictable consequence of forcing the guilty pair into the sunlight.

He walked on a lot more slowly. As he approached the house, he had still not decided whether he was going to march up to the door and ring the bell, or just pass on by. It was early evening. The lights were on in the front room though the curtains were still undrawn. There were now two cars in the driveway: Marshall's Porsche and an old Rover 75. He could see Marshall within, a glass in his hand. Another man was sitting in an armchair with his back to the window. It was impossible at first to see his face. Marshall himself appeared unusually animated and made a couple of emphatic, sweeping gestures with his free hand.

It seemed unlikely that Marion was here. He waited awhile beneath a plane tree in the street, watching for further developments. Nothing. Marshall continued to move about in the room. The other man's hand reached out from time to time to a side table, for what looked like a highball, or maybe just a coca-cola. Bryn waited long enough to be satisfied there was no-one else in the house. Then he slipped quietly away. As he began to quicken his pace, he took a last look back.

His eye fell on the rear number of the Rover 75. It was a personalized plate of six characters: DEV 1NE. The space between the two elements of the number had been narrowed to the minimum width likely to be acceptable to the licensing authorities. Above the plate was a tattered sticker bearing the legend 'Computer Nerds Rule'.

Devine. As in Dave Devine. The front man and licensee for Dark Productions.

The man rose from the armchair and approached the window. He was tall and floppy-haired and had the whey-faced complexion of a life spent almost wholly indoors. He was wearing circular spectacles with the flesh-coloured plastic frames once associated with the National Health Service. He was talking into a mobile telephone and did not notice him.

Bryn was reminded of a call he needed to make on his own mobile.

At the corner of the next street, he rang Dieter. It took him a while to answer. In the background, Bryn could hear Wagner again. Something more peaceful than the last time. *Parsifal* perhaps.

"Dieter. It's Bryn. Just to let you know. I've put the photograph in a secure place where nobody can get at it except me. And I'm not proposing to do anything with it. I need to know how you feel about that."

There was a very long pause.

"Did you recognize the faces?" Dieter said at last.

"I recognized one. Can you tell me anything about it?"

The pause this time was even longer.

"You know what Graeme did for a living?"

"He directed videos."

"*Porn* videos. You have no need to pussyfoot with me, Bryn. The photo was given to Graeme by the man who took it, who was a colleague. Who died of Aids."

By now Bryn was turning the last corner before his house.

"Is that all you know?" he asked, after a while.

"No."

It was clear enough that Dieter had more to say. But he needed to be coaxed a little like a new lover, before he would – in the crudely appropriate Americanism – put out.

"I know our friend used to work for Harry Darke, when he was very young," Bryn offered. "Is that how it happened? "

"OK. OK. I will tell you… your friend won a big case for Mr Darke and they had a big party. A great deal of *Cristal*, too much for a young man, I'm sure. They played a joke on him and next morning when he woke up, before I think he was fully awake perhaps, the photo was taken."

"Who was the other guy?"

"That I do not know. Graeme was told he was an actor but I do not think he was in the videos. A friend of one of the porno boys perhaps."

"Dieter…"

Bryn paused. It was the question he most needed to ask. But Dieter pre-empted him.

"Was Graeme *using* the photo?" said Dieter abruptly. "I think so. He showed it your friend once, I think, when they were going home after one of your recorder meetings. Then there were gifts. Not so big. Tickets to operas – through Mr Hall's political connections." He sounded distressed. "But Graeme was *not* a blackmailer."

"Why did he want me to have it? What exactly did the Will say?"

He was outside his own home now. He stood by the front wall waiting for Dieter's reply.

"There is nothing in the Will," said Dieter, finally. "I'm sorry. I did not know what to do about it. I did not want the police to have it, just to insult him more. And I have no good memories of policemen. Graeme liked you and trusted you. So I gave it to you for safe-keeping, in case... I do not know what in case. I think perhaps you should destroy it now."

There was no more to be had from Dieter. The conversation ended.

When he walked into the house, Marion was in the kitchen. She had a friend with her, an attractive, younger woman. They were already more than half-way through a bottle of red wine.

"Darling!" exclaimed his wife. "This is Yvonne. I told you about her on the phone. We decided it would be more fun to eat in so I brought her back. I hope you didn't take that meal out of the freezer."

She busied herself with pasta while he entertained the new colleague. It was not an onerous task. Yvonne, who pronounced her name with the accent on the first syllable, was conspicuously an East Londoner, with the liveliness and forthrightness he expected in women from that side of the city. This was her first post as a mathematics teacher and Marion had taken her under her wing since she arrived. She evidently thought the world of her and had spent the day shadowing her. Yvonne wondered whether Bryn appreciated how admired and respected Marion was at the school. He acknowledged that, yes indeed, there were sides to his wife of which he knew barely anything.

"Oh," said Marion, as she put three plates of *carbonara* in front of them, "I completely forgot. Your agent rang. You're to see her in her office at 9 o'clock tomorrow morning. It's very important and I promised you'd be there."

She beamed and turned to Yvonne.

"I think he's got a sale for that book about the generals I was telling you about. Perhaps we'll be rich at last."

He arrived for his appointment, with a couple of CDs of the latest draft of his *oeuvre* in his shoulder bag. The reason for the urgency became rapidly apparent. An email had come in the previous day from Barton Showalter, demanding a meeting with Bryn's agent.

"I'm sorry, darling," she said, "I'm completely tied up with book festivals and Julian's new novel. But I've had a wonderful idea. Why don't you go instead? What he really wants to discuss is your ideas for making the generals book more, well you know, accessible. We're not near the money stage yet and if he does raise that you will of course refer him straight back to me. I'm sure we could get him to pay your fares and overnights."

Showalter's chief concern was to make the book attractive as a film property. He had been talking to the producers of *Gods & Generals* and *Glory* – two successful Civil War feature films of a few years previously, neither of which Bryn's agent had heard of – and was sure they would be very interested in the new project. But they needed to move fast. Civil War stories were hot again, and other writers would be crowding in with similar projects if they did not get there first.

The agent emailed a reply to Showalter. She would send the author over to New York right away. Almost as an afterthought, she asked Bryn when he might be free. He said he would be finished with his American students within the week and then had two or three weeks before he needed to start preparing for the new academic year. Of course he had been hoping to spend some of that time pulling together his ideas about the book. But otherwise there were no problems.

It did not turn out quite as the agent had predicted. Showalter was not at all forthcoming on the matter of the air-fares and Bryn's agent discovered that her own travel budget was, by chance and most regrettably, over-extended. At one time, it seemed as if the project might fail. Then Bryn found that he had still enough air-miles accumulated on his credit card to pay for a return flight to New York – though he would have to fly at an inconvenient time and land at unfashionable Newark rather than Kennedy. Showalter unexpectedly offered to put him up in a New York hotel for two nights and suddenly it all seemed a done deal. He might be able to fit it in with the other plans that had been gestating in his mind, particularly when he calculated that he could also pay for a hire car out of the air-miles and take that trip south-west to the battlefields.

He stocked up with some large scale maps of Pennsylvania and Maryland from Stanfords in Covent Garden, and found a pair of tough walking shoes at the YHA shop, knocked down in price because of some minor scuffing to the leather. He checked the foreign exchange rates at a few banks and outlets around London and wound up as usual buying his dollars from the Eurochange shop on Oxford Street.

On the way home, he picked up a discarded newspaper on the tube. A story on the inside pages headlined *Bank Fraud Scandal* caught his eye. It was a disturbing report about major computer attacks suffered by a number of large UK companies. Though the average loss for the businesses was not much more than a few hundred thousand pounds, some of the biggest companies had been losing in excess of a million a year, much of it spirited away to bank accounts in Eastern Europe and quickly laundered. A body called the National Crime Agency, a separate organization from the police which had responsibility for pursuing 'e-criminals', had concluded that the major players in the online banking fraud were likely to be Russian crime syndicates.

The newspaper, however, speculated that the problem ran rather deeper and that it was too convenient for the NCA and Home Office to blame the new crime wave on nameless foreigners well beyond the reach of British enforcement. In an editorial headlined *Conspiracy of Silence*, the paper referred to evidence of a network of native British hackers against whom the banks had no effective answer, and who were now a threat as much to ordinary members of the public as to business. Their modus operandi was to break into thousands of individual internet bank accounts, siphon off cash through multiple ATM withdrawals and cover their tracks. The banks chose not to reveal this activity in case it undermined confidence in the whole internet banking system.

The editorial argued sensationally that the hackers were encouraging the banks to keep their criminal activity confidential by alerting them as soon as funds had been spirited away –

enabling the banks to repair the damage before smaller account holders noticed any discrepancy. The sums involved, in terms of individual accounts, or even overall compared with the banks' turnover, were not huge. Nonetheless, somebody – somewhere – was making serious money.

It was a terrific story. There was even a Robin Hood quality to it, with the banks and the big companies the only obvious victims and the ordinary citizen protected. By implication, the criminals were not gun-toting gangsters from Moscow but a few bespectacled geeks more interested in the technical accomplishment than the money they generated. It was rumoured that they might be putting their winnings into New Age projects or good causes like War on Want and Amnesty.

The recorder group was due to gather that evening at Bryn and Marion's. There was a lot to discuss. They had missed a meeting because of the summer holidays and Graeme's death. The main topic inevitably was whether the group could continue to survive – even with the attachment of Janet, accepted at the last meeting as an 'occasional' continuo player.

To general surprise, the strongest advocate for continuation turned out to be Marshall. Bill was equivocal, but happy to fall in with the consensus. Janet – and Marion (permitted as the hostess to express a view) – both feared that the friends would drift apart without regular meetings. Marshall argued, with uncharacteristic emotion, that they had been through too much together to let the group go. Their children, he pointed out, had grown up and moved away. They were now – more or less – in the same relationship with each other as when they had first met. The group, he declaimed, with a more flippant flourish as if he had begun to regret his earnestness, kept them all young.

Over dinner, after a brief musical session, there was some speculation about Graeme's death. Neither Bryn nor Marshall said a great deal. Bill, who seemed to know everybody in West London, had met a reporter from the local newspaper at a party and had some interesting information. The reporter had learned from his police contact that the real reason why the case on Graeme had been closed was that they were now convinced that the killer had left the country. He had made a phone call on his mobile from the scene of the murder, to an overseas number. The police had been able to trace the mobile's owner to a hotel in South Kensington, but by then he had been long gone and the trail was cold. Nothing in this, however, had disturbed the official conclusion that Graeme was killed by a chance pick-up – in their view, someone who had been looking to combine business in a foreign country with dubious pleasures. Given the hazardous nature of the sexual activity involved, the police retained an open mind as to whether the death was accidental or not.

When they pulled out their diaries to fix the next meeting, there were the usual difficulties of co-ordinating busy lives. Normally they started with Marshall's diary as the one least likely to be tractable. But this time Bryn was the main obstacle. He admitted sheepishly that he would be in New York 'to meet a man about a movie deal' and got the ribbing (and admiration) he deserved. Then it emerged that his time there would coincide with one of Marshall's regular visits. Bryn caught an exchange of looks between Marion and his friend and a sharp flicker of irritation from his wife. Marshall turned to Bryn.

"Why don't we meet for dinner," he said briskly.

As the two of them entered the date in their diaries, Marion left the table.

THREE

Chapter 17

He was on the road out of Newark Airport towards New York City, and in a savage mood.

The miserable August weather for a start. It was close, sticky and overcast. A recent thunderstorm had left the highway pot-holes awash but done nothing to relieve the enervating humidity. The terrain passing by the vehicle windows was once more the run-down underbelly of America in economic depression. Stained concrete bridges. Overpasses shrouded in faded and artless graffiti. Monstrous advertising hoardings dominating the bleak landscape with a persistent mocking reminder of how other people might live. How ugly and horrid it was.

And then the SuperShuttle experience. This was the real reason why he was so furious. A wiser person, if he could afford it, would have paid for a taxi; or even taken his chances with the public transport system. Bryn's mistake was yet again to have been seduced by the efficiency and immediacy of the internet. How to get from Newark most easily to Manhattan? The Airport's own website, very lucratively no doubt, highlighted on its home page the convenience of the SuperShuttle. All you had to do was input the details of your flight and where you needed to go, pay online with your credit card – and look forward to the vehicle that would gather up you and a few other passengers arriving at that time.

His plane had been early, which was as well since the internet instructions had initially directed him to the wrong section of the airport. When at last he found the right place, there was no vehicle to be seen. Instead, he came upon a disconsolate queue of travellers, with a range of different destinations, none of them New Yorkers, and all sharing the same faltering expectation that something, soon, would turn up. A well-meaning airport official had pointed them to the SuperShuttle help-line, which provided an identical parroted assurance ("Your van will be with you in twenty minutes") every time a caller managed to get through. After an hour of this, the voice switched to a different script ("Your vehicle will be with you in five minutes").

A further three-quarters of an hour later, something *had* arrived. The driver was a depressed, middle-aged black man in jeans and a beat-up bomber jacket ("our driver will be uniformed"), the very image of a demoralized employee, heartily sick and tired of being the only visible target for his passengers' frustration. The vehicle was a tattered van, stuffed to the gunwhales with steaming and resentful clients familiar already with most of the pick-up points around Newark's three terminals. But it was at least going Bryn's way and he and a couple of others from the queue had managed to get on. There were several more stops before finally they left the airport precinct, and plenty more abuse for the driver each time he gave his decreasingly audible assurance that "there's another van right behind".

Bryn reflected morosely, as they travelled down the miserable highway to New York, that the SuperShuttle was – after all – just another metaphor for the American experience. If you could afford it, the life here was great. If you couldn't, you should expect to be treated like the no-account underclass you were. And which he, for a while, had become.

The van worked its way slowly round downtown New York, decanting passengers into hostel-like 'budget' inns off the main thoroughfares, until it reached West 71st Street. There Bryn disembarked, hauled out his luggage, and checked in at the West End Family Hotel.

Or he would have done if the clerk had been able to find the reservation made for him by Barton Showalter.

After some trawling of the hotel database, and a fruitless call to Showalter's office, Bryn asked if in fact the hotel had any spare rooms. He waited while the clerk again checked his records. A group of young back-packers wandered through the lobby. Somewhere in the recesses of the hotel, a woman was screaming at someone else in Spanish.

"Yes we have a few," said the clerk, finally, "but they won't be ready yet."

It was agreed that his bags would be temporarily stowed under the reception desk while he went out for a meal.

He caught a subway train to downtown Manhattan and walked up East 19th Street until he arrived at the *Foxx* Restaurant. It was not entirely unknown to him. He remembered it being hailed as the best new restaurant in America a few years previously and it had been winning awards from champagne houses, finance companies, food magazines and other bodies with an interest in the success of the restaurant business. Why, even television celebrity Graham Norton had singled it out in a newspaper article as his favourite place to eat in the world. He only hoped he would be able to afford his share of the bill.

It was barely 6.30 in the evening and the place was packed. Marshall was already waiting for him at the bar.

"What's wrong with you?" he enquired.

"Nothing's wrong with me," said Bryn. "Why are you asking?"

"You seem to be in a bad mood."

"Nonsense."

The waitress led the way towards a reserved table.

In the familiar modern style, *Foxx* consisted of a long bar where clients could sip cocktails, and beyond that a dining room. The eating area was quite gloomy, and rather like being in a modern art museum, with textured and cambered walls, a few abstract pictures and the odd impenetrable installation. The youthful waiting staff were charming and teasingly androgynous. Their own very good-looking waitress was an exciting clone of the young Sigourney Weaver. Tall, slim, crop-haired, trousers, waistcoat, man's shirt, wonderfully ambiguous. They did not have to look far for the reason for one gay Irishman's enthusiasm. She/he placed a regulation 'amuse-bouche' in front of each of them. It was a tiny timbale containing two or three sips of truffled white bean soup with a split half of a pea floating on the surface. Not very original perhaps, but delicious.

"Where are you staying?" asked Marshall and Bryn described his hotel, or rather his experience of its reception desk and lobby.

"You're not staying there," said his friend, and Bryn could see he was serious. Just as he knew he was going to insist on paying for the meal, and would overwhelm any attempt by Bryn at parity, so it was certain that he would show off his greater experience of New York and browbeat him into some new hotel. The kind of establishment more suited to one of Marshall's business friends. Bryn hated, really hated, being patronized like this. And he *loathed* the foreknowledge of his own acquiescence. He would not put it past Marshall trying to pay the hotel bill as well. But that at least he might be in a position to pre-empt.

"What's wrong with it?" said Bryn.

"It's not the right hotel for you. Leave it to me."

He rang a number on his mobile.

"It's all fixed," he said, clicking the phone shut like a castanet. "I've put you in the Whitney Hotel near the Lincoln Center and they're picking up your luggage. It's on my account so you can't pay anyway. Or you can pay me back, if you like, when you've sold the film rights for your novel."

"Book. It's not fiction."

"Right."

"Thank you. You're very kind. And I wish you wouldn't do it."

Bryn had ordered sweetbreads for his first course, because he had thought it would be interesting to compare them with his memory of the *Cordelia*. They had been quickly pan-fried so that the surface was lightly crispy, though greasy, and the white meat inside soft to the point of dissolution. They came with lightly cooked spinach on the stalk, and a small dollop of mushroom and olive chutney. Less flavour on the plate than Chicago and less well presented. And unexpectedly filling.

His main course, consequently, was already a mistake. He could see now that he had over-ordered, and should in any case have gone for a lighter dish. The generous portion of braised beef was tender and flaky with a rich, heavily reduced sauce. It was accompanied by two huge side dishes, one of chanterelles and one of fava beans. He could not remember having fava beans before and had been intrigued by them ever since the villain in *The Silence of the Lambs* had unforgettably eaten the liver of one of his victims "with some fava beans and a nice Chianti". But these were disappointingly unexotic. As presented at *Foxx*, Hannibal Lector's lip-smacking delicacy was worryingly similar to the humble broad bean. Was this another case of two nations divided by a common language? The other dish, with its reliably French name, was meantime a disaster: a mass of overcooked grey (not golden) funghi; and greasy again.

While he struggled to put down a respectable portion of the mountain before him, Marshall talked on. At first he ranged over mutual concerns. Whether they should persist with Janet in the recorder group. Whether it was wise to consider co-opting another (male) player – as Bryn himself had recently proposed – who was known to all of them and had been a candidate in the past. Whether they could always rely on Bill, who played with other groups and might have to reduce his commitments now that he was running his own company. And how long indeed he, Marshall, would be able to remain a member. It was all beginning to sound like a last quietus; and very different from the up-beat Marshall of a few weeks previously.

And then, he began most uncharacteristically to talk about himself. He had not ordered as much food as Bryn, and had been drinking more freely, and probably for longer. This was not the controlled, and controlling, man he knew. He was not drunk. But a new Marshall had begun to emerge, perceptibly gentler, less arrogant, more attentive, more intimate. The kind of person whom Bryn could easily imagine a woman falling for, late in the evening, over dinner for instance.

"I'm glad we're friends," Marshall said. "And I hope you don't mind my high-handed ways of showing it. I would miss our friendship."

"So would I. I'm not sure we're very well matched. But we get on."

"The truth is… I'm thinking of leaving the UK. Somewhere in France perhaps. Possibly America. Apart from you guys, there's nothing for me now. It's probably time for me to cash in and move on."

"Why on earth should you want to do that?" said Bryn, genuinely bewildered. "At the peak of your career when everything is going so well. There's so much for you to do."

"Mmm. Maybe. But I have an opportunity now. A financial opportunity which may not arise again."

"Is that why you are in New York?"

"Well partly, yes."

Bryn had failed also to resist the cheese and dessert list and had ordered something from both. A plate of three cheeses arrived: *Houligan*, from Connecticut; Sprout Creek's *Toussaint* from Poughkeepsie; and *Malvarosa*, a medium-hard sheep cheese from Valencia in Spain.

Marshall waited until the waitress had left.

He looked up from his wine glass.

"I would be grateful if you didn't mention this conversation to anyone, Bryn."

"Why should I?"

"Well, for example, Jack Smith."

He had not expected this. Marshall was gazing at him with what seemed like genuine concern.

"I'm barely acquainted with Jack Smith. And I don't expect to see him again."

Marshall looked relieved. Bryn briefly recounted his experience at Claridge's and the absence of any further communication. Neither of them referred to the part Marshall had played in setting the meeting up. But then at the end of his little discourse, Bryn asked disingenuously if Marshall's earlier remark meant *he* knew Smith.

"I have known Jack Smith," said his friend, "since the 1980s when he was just a television evangelist."

And he talked, more freely now, about his first visits to New York and Washington in the 80s, to discuss 'on behalf of an English client' how Smith's *GodWorks* organization might be extended to the UK. About his admiration for Smith, whose energy and ambition exceeded that of any man he had met before. He perceived Smith as a man driven to succeed in whatever sphere of activity he set his mind to. And likely to do so. When he first knew him, it was religion and to an extent that had remained Smith's motive force. But over the years, as he had developed political ambitions, he had become more pragmatic.

"He also seems to have made himself very rich," said Bryn, remembering the suite at Claridge's.

Two unsolicited palate-cleansers of sparkling 'homemade' lemonade arrived, followed by Bryn's dessert. A generous pair of fruit sorbets – Muscat Grape and Pear – with a banana ice-cream. He was back in the land of American portions. Only the cheeses had come in French-style small slices. He winced and took up his spoon.

"Phenomenally rich," said Marshall. "You have no idea how rich he is. And that gives him real power. He has built up, without I think anyone particularly noticing, a network of political, media and military contacts. His university is now the main think-tank for evangelical politics. I am sure he has the Presidency in mind. If not for himself, then for someone he might hope to control. Just as Cheney controlled Bush."

"Who could that possibly be?" asked Bryn.

He was used to Marshall boasting about his political connections, but this was beginning to strain his credulity.

"He has such a man," replied Marshall, quite slowly and seriously, "who you may not have heard of. His name is Kendall. He's just finished a single term as a state governor and is the perfect candidate for Smith's people. Politically he comes out of nowhere, so he has hardly any baggage. His face is familiar already to every American voter through television soaps – playing doctors, businessmen, senators, in one series he was the President of the United States. He even has the right overseas credentials or anyway the only overseas credentials that carry weight with Smith's constituency: he's married to an English girl."

"So what would Smith hope to do? Get a cabinet post in his administration?"

"Maybe."

"It sounds to me as if we've been here before."

"Except that they want it to work better this time," said Marshall.

After the dessert, a plate of chocolates arrived with the espressos. Bryn did what he could to do them justice. He allowed Marshall to pay the bill this time without demur, and they shook hands. Feeling somewhat like Mr Creosote, he made his way tenderly out of the restaurant and picked up a taxi to the Whitney Hotel at the door.

The Whitney was a sort of expensive kids' hotel. From the street, it had an unprepossessing slab-like exterior relieved only with what might have passed as a few wittily post-modern art deco and Bauhaus touches. Inside it was a different world. The arriving guest passed from daylight into immediate deep gloom, and was whisked up a narrow escalator to a cavernous lobby. Not much light there either, with three or four counter clerks standing to attention behind the long reception bar, cheekbones eerily thrown into relief by the illumination from their open laptops. Rock music throbbed quietly in the background. Occasionally a well-dressed young executive from a Bret Easton Ellis novel drifted in from a party in one of the adjacent rooms.

Bryn checked in – much cool computer work by his very cool,

182

well-dressed receptionist – and picked his way through the gloom until he recognized the location of the lifts from the little red lights glowing above them. Up twelve floors at warp speed, along a corridor full of dark turnings (would he ever find his way back to mission control) and, with some relief, into his room.

Tiny, but very clean, tidy and chic. Not so much en suite as a bedroom, mini hallway, bath/shower, loo, clothes cupboard, all co-ordinated with remarkable skill into a single space not significantly greater than a walk-in closet. To save on space-eating walls, the partitions between the different elements had been reduced to diaphanous hangings. A little too intimate, he thought, if there were two of you. But after the usual initial process of opening, twiddling and testing all the interesting things in the room, he discovered that the hangings worked like a theatre scrim: if you varied the clever lighting arrangements they became – well, almost – opaque, and some token degree of privacy in the bath/shower/toilet/bedroom areas appeared possible.

But the *sine qua non* of a good hotel room, in Bryn's experience, was the linen and soap arrangements. And here were excellent crisp, new-looking sheets and pillows, big boutique soap, huge fluffy towels; plus perfumed hand tissues, a CD and radio music centre and the usual television set, an internet point, mini-bar and so on and so on. Ten out of ten for everything except space; and perhaps personal odours. The final test was the view. He moved the floaty curtain aside and gazed at the bleak unwindowed flank of a skyscraper. What else should he have expected? This *was* Manhattan.

His bags were neatly stacked by the door. He unpacked a few things for the next twenty-four hours. His suit for the meeting with Showalter next morning. A CD of the latest draft – though he suspected that his revisions and amplifications might not yet be what Showalter wanted. He had also taken the precaution of rescuing his Trevor Pickett attaché case from its UCL glory-hole, with its spare copy of the original draft his agent had sent to Showalter, in case he needed to refer to that.

And Zelma's watch. He looked at it as it lay on the bed. Then he picked it up and carefully dialled the telephone number on the back. He waited while it rang for a minute or more. He was just about to put the receiver down when Zelma answered.

Her tone was veiled and cautious. Not at all the Zelma he was used to.

"Who is that?"

"Bryn. Bryn from London."

"Who? Bryn? Oh my God... how d'you get my number, Bryn?"

"You left your watch behind, do you remember?"

"Right... you know I'm not sure we should be having this conversation, Bryn."

Her voice now sounded cold and distant.

"I just wanted to find out how you were doing."

"I'm fine, Bryn. I'm OK. Say... do you think you could stick it in the post? I was given it when I was a kid and I'm kinda missing it."

"Why don't I bring it over?"

"From London?"

"From New York. I'm here on business."

Then, as an afterthought, to pre-empt an objection: "I've got your address."

"I don't think so."

"Your mother's address."

"Oh... right..."

He waited. Somewhere, in the background, he thought he could hear a dog bark, a low, bass, echoing sound. And then a child's voice reprimanding it.

"OK," said Zelma at last. "Why don't you come round tomorrow? Would two be good for you?"

It would. He tried to extend the conversation further. But –

"I gotta go now," she said briskly. "Let's talk tomorrow, huh?"

And she was gone.

The meal, alcohol and the jetlag put him to sleep almost at once. He awoke early in the morning and dozed unsatisfactorily until he became too restless to stay in bed. He got up, showered, watched CNN, put on his suit, and slipped the CD in the jacket pocket. It occurred to him that he could fill in a little time before it was possible to go down to breakfast by refreshing his memory of the last, hard-copy, draft. He pulled across the attaché case and took out his key.

It would not open. The key slipped easily enough into the two locks but it would not turn. No amount of jiggling and force made any difference. After several minutes of toil, he was obliged to give up when the key itself began to twist out of shape. He cursed the unreliability of fashion and wished, ungratefully, that Marion had given him something less chic and more robust.

On the way down to breakfast, he asked a desk clerk if he knew where he might be able to get the locks unjammed.

"Sure," said the clerk, as though this was a regular enquiry. "Just give me a call when you get back to your room. I'll get the bellboy to come up and open it for you."

After his waffles and syrup and weak American coffee, he called as instructed. A very young man in uniform came to his room and peered closely at the case. He produced a small ring of what looked like skeleton keys, and selected one. The locks clicked open immediately. Bryn thanked him and awkwardly fished out a five-dollar bill which the boy accepted with a brief nod.

The first thing that Bryn noticed when he raised the attaché case lid was that the lining was quite different. And, instead of the folder containing his monograph, there was a single sheet of paper. He twisted it in his hand in puzzlement. It was a letter signed in a scrawl he could not decipher, and headed with a crest and the legend 'from the office of the Governor of Minnesota'. It appeared to be some kind of bread and butter thank-you letter for 'your good works on my behalf'.

And then he noticed another thing. At first it baffled him, and he picked up the whole case and held it for a while at eye-level. He ran his thumb around the inside of it and pushed at the bottom lining. There was not a great deal in it but he was sure that the case was shallower than his own. He picked a little at the edge of the fabric and the whole base moved slightly under his fingers.

He found a plastic corkscrew in the mini-bar, and hooked it round the bottom inside edge of the attaché case, and gently pulled. The floor of the case swung smoothly up towards him. Underneath, in a false compartment not more than half an inch deep, was a plastic folder, not unlike the one into which he had slipped his monograph. He took the folder out and opened it. It contained what appeared to be lists, about a dozen of them, typed out with occasional annotations in the margins in a manuscript hand.

At first they made little sense at all. Then he gradually began to comprehend that there were two types of lists. One came in three columns: surnames, telephone numbers, and sums in dollars generally running to five, six and – rarely – seven figures. The other type of list was headed 'Cherry Grove' and had two columns only, one of names and the other of dates and, in some cases, times. Someone had placed ticks alongside a number of the names with a ballpoint pen and the occasional one word comment: 'pledge', 'delegate' or 'caucus'. A few of these names were starred and he saw that this was because they appeared on both types of lists. Finally, he found at the back of the folder a single sheet which listed about twenty names from the second set of lists. None of these, he noticed, had been either starred or annotated. The single sheet had been enigmatically headed, in ballpoint, "MARK 11".

Although most of the material, so far as Bryn was concerned, was pretty incomprehensible, a few matters nonetheless were beginning to resolve themselves. First, and blazingly obviously, *this* was Jack Smith's case. How apt of Smith to have one made by an English company with the same name, Pickett, as the Confederate general whose charge at Gettysburg was the high-water mark of the South's success in the Civil War. It was not hard to guess that Bryn's own almost identical attaché case lay still forgotten behind a chair in the Claridge's vestibule or – more likely perhaps – had long ago been tidied away to some terminal glory-hole.

There was no doubt, however, that the lists he held in his hand were Jack's and, given the nature of their hiding place, profoundly sensitive and confidential. He slipped all the papers back into their folder and eased up the floor of the case once more. He was struck by the unnatural white shininess of the base of the false compartment itself, and picked at it a little with his fingernail. Sure enough, it too came away and revealed itself as the reverse side of a photographic sheet.

He lifted the sheet out of the case and turned it over. What he saw stunned and bewildered him. It was the old photograph of Marshall and his gay lover. Graeme's photograph, or rather a second generation copy of it. The very same. His mind shot back to the conversation last night. Could this be connected in some way with Marshall's current visit to New York?

But one thing at least seemed now beyond argument. The possession of the attaché case and its contents placed him in serious jeopardy. The thought that they almost certainly had had something to do with his nightmare adventures a few months ago, which all took place in the weeks following the meeting with Smith, was irresistible. As a rational individual, this was still somewhat too rich for him to digest. But he was frightened nonetheless.

He pondered whether his wisest course now would be to destroy the attaché case, the papers and the photograph completely. But he doubted whether that would help to erase the lethal connection he had established with them. And, in spite of everything, that could never be his way. His professional training and instinct pointed always towards protecting the primary material. In London, he might have hurried round to his branch on the Tottenham Court Road and stowed it all away in his security envelope. In New York, he needed to find a different kind of bank. And very quickly.

After testing the case to make sure it could close and open again without a key, he put all the documents back inside and – carrying it self-consciously with him – set off for his meeting with Barton Showalter. It was raining, so he picked up a cab outside the hotel and gave the driver an address some way north on the west side.

Chapter 18

Showalter's office was on the 24th floor of a high-rise office block. For the second time in a year, Bryn was greeted by an American with a cigar wedged in the side of his mouth. But there the comparison lapsed. The man in front of him was rumpled, cheaply suited, and obese; and the cigar came with plastic mouthpiece attached. On the walls there were photographs of actors whom Showalter, presumably, represented. None was recognizable to Bryn. The tables and surfaces in the office were piled with files and scripts and there was no sign of a secretary or any other form of administrative support aside from a large computer and keyboard on a corner table. Showalter offered him coffee in a Dixie cup from a large commercial machine behind his desk and, after a few niceties about the New York summer weather, they settled down to business.

It was a pretty hopeless meeting. For a start, Bryn's mind was otherwise engaged. He fielded Showalter's absurd proposals for amending the book entirely without his customary resentment at authorial interference. In the absence of a draft to write notes on, the jottings he made at the back of his small pocket diary were gnomic and random. He did not respond to Showalter's crude suggestions that they should agree a deal for American rights that would effectively cut out his London agent. It would have been difficult at the end of the session to know what, if anything at all, had been achieved.

Not that this appeared to concern Showalter. He evidently regarded the meeting as a great success and congratulated Bryn yet again, as he ushered him back to the lift, on his great, truly great novel. There was no point in attempting to correct him. Bryn promised to let him have, as soon as he got back to London, a note of the changes he intended to make. Whatever they might be...

Back in downtown Manhattan, he went into a coffee shop on Sixth Avenue opposite the Hilton Hotel and ordered – via Rio de Janeiro and Seattle – a cup of *ipanema bourbon grande*. There was a public telephone in the corner and he dialled Marshall's mobile number. Marshall was not pleased. The warmth of the previous evening seemed to have evaporated and his old, rather testy friend had returned. Like many busy people, he had never developed an ingratiating telephone manner. He addressed the telephone, whoever was at the other end, more or less as if it was the office secretary. And a slightly deaf one at that.

"Something really important has turned up," Bryn began, "and I have to speak to you."

"Not today, Bryn. I have meetings."

"Marshall, it can't wait."

"Why can't it wait, precisely?"

"I've found some documents which I really..." He lowered his voice. "Which really I should not *have*... concerning someone we spoke about last night. And concerning you. I think I should give them to you. As soon as possible."

"We can't talk on the phone," replied Marshall, after a pause. "Can you get to the Waldorf Astoria on Park Avenue by 12 noon? I can only give you a few minutes."

"That's OK. I have to be away by 12.30 anyway."

"I'll meet you in the lobby. Have you got that? At the bar in Peacock Alley."

He had a little time to waste so he decided to walk the few

blocks from the coffee shop. He strolled east along 53rd and south down Park Avenue. Past a remarkable parade of alternating New York ancient and modern – the Museum of Modern Art, High Gothic St Thomas Church, the Seagram Building, the Byzantine temple of St Bartholomew – until it began again to rain. He had now arrived at the architectural climax of his stroll: that art deco confection, with gilded reliefs on its façade and Stars and Stripes fluttering above, which is the Waldorf Astoria Hotel.

He sauntered in and climbed the stairs.

The entrance lobby was a wild pastiche of the British Museum. In the grand space that opened before him hung a chandelier from Versailles (or Versailles, Kentucky). Below were Minoan columns, a Roman mosaic floor of entwined and naked figures, Egyptian funerary urns on stands. A bride passed through on her father's arm, trailing oceans of flowing white silk. Young and perfectly suited men passed to and fro. On a small balcony overlooking the lobby stood the painted Steinway on which Cole Porter, a Waldorf resident for twenty-five years, had composed his songs. Compared with Claridge's, this was Hollywood to Ealing Studios.

Peacock Alley was further on, past the elevators and away to the side. It was dominated by the obligatory long bar, in a richly polished wood and with a regiment of high wooden chairs drawn up alongside it. It was too early for the main drinking crowd, but one familiar man sat alone at the far end, thirty feet away, sipping from a china cup and reading the Financial Times.

Bryn declined his offer of a cocktail and settled instead for the same *Americano* coffee that Marshall was drinking. He observed with a little satisfaction that neither of them seemed to have recovered entirely from the previous evening. He planted the attaché case on the bar and began to open it. Marshall put down his cup and placed a hand softly on the lid.

"Is this yours?" he said, his voice hushed almost to a whisper.

"I thought it was," said Bryn. "There was a mix-up when I was at Claridge's."

"You don't say," said Marshall. "I've only ever seen a case like that once before."

He closed the lid again and led the way to a room behind the bar, out of sight of the main crowd, and set down his saucer and cup at a window table looking out over the street. Bryn followed him with the case.

"How on earth did you get hold of it?" he asked at last.

And Bryn explained about his confusion after Smith had left him in the hotel room. How he had put the case aside until a few days previously, and only that morning opened it for the first time since the meeting with Smith.

"It *is* quite distinctive," said Marshall quietly.

"So it's Jack Smith's?"

"Well I should say so. I suppose you want me to return it to him."

"I think you should look inside first."

Marshall seemed initially reluctant to take his advice. Then he carefully placed the case on his knees and opened it. He did not remove the papers. Instead he studied them for a while, quietly shuffling them under the cover of the raised lid. He arrived at last at the photograph and took it out. He gazed at it, as still as a praying mantis. He said nothing. Finally, he turned the picture over and replaced it, face down, in the case.

"What do you think?" asked Bryn.

"I think you were wise to give them to me."

Marshall's expression as he looked at him was unreadable. And he was speaking so quietly now that Bryn could barely hear him.

"Why do you think Jack Smith never asked for his case back?"

"I have no idea," said Bryn. "I would have returned it immediately and got mine back in return."

"Did it occur to you that he may have concluded you took it deliberately?"

Bryn had been avoiding that conclusion, ever since the first wave of alarm that overtook him in his hotel room that morning. He had hoped that, by passing the case and the papers to Marshall, he might put it all out of his mind. He particularly did not want to think about the trilby-hatted man who, not long after Smith would have discovered his loss, had tried to kill him in London. Or of the two others who, by incredible fortune, had failed to finish him off in Chicago and Utah.

Marshall's unwelcome clarity had set his heart pounding and he began to feel sick.

"You will give this back to him?"

Marshall put the papers back in their plastic folder and gently closed the lid upon them. He gave an almost imperceptible nod.

"I must say," he remarked, "this does explain some probing I got from Smith a while back about what kind of person you were."

"If you get a chance," continued Bryn energetically, "perhaps you could explain the circumstances. It would really help if you could explain that I am not a thief or a blackmailer. Or *any* kind of threat."

"I'll do my best," said Marshall. "Leave it with me."

"You might tell him that I did not read the papers."

He wished he sounded more credible and composed than he felt.

"They would mean nothing to me," he added. "And of course I returned it all to you immediately I knew of the mistake, so he could get them back as soon as possible. Then, hopefully, if there have been any difficulties that will be the end of it."

"I hear what you say, Bryn," said Marshall briefly. "I have to go now."

He stood up and took Bryn's elbow.

"It would be a weight off my mind," said Bryn with feeling.

"I know," replied his friend.

He ushered him to the top of the exit stairs to Park Avenue and they shook hands and parted.

It was still raining, a slow, even drizzle that for most New York pedestrians merited no greater cover than a baseball cap. A few wore the kind of transparent plastic cape that can be rolled up and carried in a coat pocket. Here and there a small black umbrella bobbed by, less frequently than you might expect in London.

The sky was beginning to clear from the north and Bryn decided to wait a few moments under the Waldorf Astoria's stainless steel awning. A few people scurried past in busy haste but the rest – the tourists, he assumed – drifted by as nonchalantly as if they were in Oxford Street. Among the crowd in front of St Bartholomew's, one hundred yards away, floated an umbrella that was larger and brighter than any of the others. It was blue and patterned with black and yellow shields with blue swallow-like birds superimposed upon them. A Cardiff City Bluebirds supporter in New York no less. How extraordinary.

He came down from the Waldorf steps to take a closer look. As he did so, the last of the drizzle eased away and the blue umbrella folded back into the crowd. He glimpsed a hand holding it and a man's profile under a hat and briefly tried to follow him. But the image melted away, and the umbrella was no more to be seen. Bryn walked further up the Avenue, searching for a flicker of azure blue and yellow. Nothing.

He turned back to look for a subway station that might link up with Penn Station. But as he walked back down Park Avenue towards 49th Street, a long Lincoln Limousine with dark tinted windows drew up in front of the Waldorf Astoria. Two burly men in dark glasses jumped out of the front seats and stood either side of the hotel entrance with arms out-stretched. Bryn waited with the expectant crowd for the celebrity they hoped might pass in front of them.

But it was Jack C Smith who emerged from the rear of the limousine. His finger was resting lightly upon a plug in his right ear and he was speaking quietly into a wire that curled down into his top pocket. He stopped on the sidewalk and glanced sharply right and left while Bryn instinctively slipped behind some over-weight American tourists. Smith paced on into the hotel. The two burly retainers followed him, the limousine eased away from the kerbside and the crowd moved on.

After a sensible interval, Bryn went back into the hotel. He waited for a group of four or five German businessmen to walk up the steps and fell in close behind them. The lobby was already busier than before. Clusters of expensively suited men were shaking hands, chatting and moving off towards their non-alcoholic aperitifs and calory-conscious lunches. He took up a position by one of the Minoan columns, where a huge potted fern partly obscured him.

The first thing he noticed was the two burly retainers. Like him, they were trying to make themselves inconspicuous by standing at the edges of the lobby amongst the furniture. He observed that they both had wires similar to Smith's dangling from their ears. One had his head bowed and was whispering into a small device cupped in his hand. The other was watching Smith.

Jack C Smith was standing in the centre of the lobby, talking to Marshall. They appeared to be enjoying each other's company. Indeed they seemed to be the best of friends. Smith clapped his friend cheerily on the shoulder and the pair of them marched off towards one of the dining rooms, while the burly men stayed behind in the lobby. It was at this point that Bryn realized that neither Marshall nor Smith was carrying the Pickett attaché case that he had given Marshall barely fifteen minutes previously.

As soon as the crowd cover permitted, Bryn slipped down the stairs and back again to the street. He made his way, by a less direct subway route than he had intended, to Penn Station. As in Chicago, he cursed the Transit Authority's evident lack of concern about making its railway system comprehensible to non-residents. He lost himself twice within Penn Station itself. He longed once more for the signing clarity of the French Metro or the London Underground. How non-English speakers got around New York remained a mystery. But it was clear enough why so many tourists travelled everywhere in the city, even when shopping, with a paid guide.

The train out to Maplewood, New Jersey, was slow and stopped frequently. It was cleaner and less worn-down than the suburban trains out of Chicago, and Bryn was encouraged to see a conductor moving through the carriages checking tickets. The commuters were all ages and included families and even the occasional man in a business suit. The stations they stopped at were less stripped down and utilitarian, with the odd gesture towards a rural, vaguely English, *Brief Encounter* kind of character. Maplewood station typically was a craggy, gothic building with a large, warm waiting room in which he could imagine the American equivalents of Trevor Howard and Celia Johnson, meeting for their clandestine *bourbon grandes*.

He studied a street map of Maplewood, helpfully framed on one of the walls of the waiting room. He resolved to walk the rest of the way, and it was a good decision. Maplewood was a classic American dream of a dormitory suburb. Gracious and leafy avenues. Houses detached and isolated in their little plots of land. Not so different from Oak Park but maybe with a more eclectic mix of modern styles alongside the familiar weather-boarding and pillared porches. There were few other pedestrians. Two or three cars passed up the shaded, peaceful streets.

Ahead, parked at the kerbside between two trees, was a bright yellow Volkswagen Beetle. His pace slowed. Now that he had almost arrived, he was once again at a loss as to what he hoped to achieve. A mild gloom settled over him.

He recognized well enough what he had done. He had preoccupied himself so comprehensively with the challenge of finding Zelma and persuading her to let him visit – in short the *chase* – that the tangled consequences of meeting her again had gone entirely unexplored. He was mortified to recognize that his underlying motive was a sentimental memory of what had happened last time and an expectation, suppressed till now, of more pleasure to be had. There was no more time left for displacement activity. And he had passed the point where it was realistic to stop, examine, retrench.

Of course he had been in similar situations often enough in his life to know what to do next. So he thrust these unhelpful thoughts aside, and marched purposefully on.

Chapter 19

Zelma's house was smaller than most of the others in the avenue, and in poorer condition. A small flight of steps led up to the front porch.

A blonde, ten-year old girl opened the door.

"Hi," said the child.

She made no attempt to let him in and fixed him with a frank, unfriendly gaze, like a Midwich cuckoo.

"I'm Bryn from England," said Bryn. "I've come to see Zelma."

"Mom!" shouted the child suddenly, without turning.

She continued to stare at Bryn.

Two large brown Rhodesian Ridgebacks came round the corner of the house and snuffled at his legs. He tried to pat one but both backed away and inspected him from a safer distance.

"Mom!!" shouted the girl again.

Then she abruptly disappeared, leaving Bryn to contemplate the half-opened door while the Ridgebacks continued to circle him.

Zelma emerged from inside the house. It was not at all the Zelma he had expected. This one seemed older, with no make-up, and jeans instead of a skirt. She wore a 'U of M alumni' t-shirt, tied in a knot below her unsupported breasts and exposing her untanned stomach. She shouted harshly at the two dogs – "Bobby! Huey!" – and they bounded away around the side of the house. She looked at him in the same coldly appraising way as her daughter had. The little girl appeared alongside her. The two of them gazed at Bryn.

"We just met," said Bryn, indicating the child.

"Go on back in, Angie," she said, and the girl pulled a cross face and withdrew only when her mother placed a hand on her shoulder.

"Why don't you come in, Bryn."

She led him through a dark hallway to a sitting room. While she made a pot of coffee in the small kitchen beyond, the girl stood at the entrance to the room, watching him. Zelma spoke to him briefly from the kitchen.

"Angela lives here with my mother. You were very lucky to find me. I'm only here because her grandma's out west visiting my brother's family. Angie, could you get the cookies from the TV room?"

The girl made no attempt to move. Zelma repeated the instruction and she pulled the same, sour little face as before. She still didn't move. Only when Zelma came in with a tray of coffee and mugs did Angela shift from her on guard position by the door frame. He heard her leave the house by the back door. Zelma sighed quietly and placed the tray on a table in front of him. She left the room briefly and returned with a box of *Mrs Fields* chocolate chip cookies.

"Before I forget," said Bryn, and he produced Zelma's watch from his pocket.

She took it up and examined it.

"I've reset it for Eastern Time," he said.

Zelma said nothing. She removed a small digital watch from her wrist and silently strapped the old one back in its place. The unfamiliar reticence disconcerted him. She busied herself with the coffee pot almost as though he were not there. Only when she passed the mug along the table to him did he manage to catch her eye, and hold it for a moment. Then she frowned and looked away.

"Do you think we owe each other an explanation?" she said at last.

"Do we?" said Bryn, reflexively.

"I think we do… it's not as though you know much about me, Bryn. And I don't think I know much about you. And now I'm not sure how much either of us wants to know."

He was at a loss. He had heard words like these before, when previous lovers had decided to end an affair. But Zelma's delivery was not right. He missed the necessary underlying edge of determination. Or hostility. Maybe, contrary to all expectation, she was just not very good at ending a relationship and was looking to him for once to take the initiative. He wasn't yet ready for that role, though.

"I was worried about you," he said. "I looked you up on the internet to see if I could find out where you were. I didn't get very far. I've picked up a fair amount about your political activities, of course. Which, for the record, I admire. I wish I had the balls. Trashing Rush Limbaugh seems to me an all round admirable thing to do. But I thought something bad might have happened to you. The law or perhaps something worse…"

"I'm not in trouble with the law. I *am* with the present government, which is not yet quite the same. On their 'un-American' lists. Sure. They leak stuff about me and my friends – probably you picked some of that up. They don't bother me. They've always left me alone at Ann Arbor where they can keep an eye on me. That's not the problem, Bryn."

She paused.

"Bryn, I think we need to level. You know a guy called Jack Smith."

There was no mistaking the accusatory tone in her voice and for a while he was unable to respond. He sipped his coffee and tried to collect his thoughts. Easiest to start at the beginning.

"I do know Jack Smith. Slightly. His politics and mine are not the same, of course… I applied for a job at his university – a full professorship – and he interviewed me and it didn't go well. So I didn't get the job. But I accidentally took something of his away with me which seemed to cause a problem between us. I hope that's all sorted now" he ended lamely.

"You're not working for Jack?"

"No!" he laughed involuntarily. "I've never worked for Jack Smith and I don't think I ever could, even if he offered me a job. Definitely *not* my scene."

She was clearly confused.

"In that case, why…"

She paused.

"Do you know what happened to me in Ann Arbor?"

"In the morning? No."

"Didn't you wonder what happened?"

"Of course. I was worried. I thought I found some blood by your car. But I was told you had rung in and you were sick. So I thought perhaps a nose bleed. Then of course you emailed me and told me more or less in terms to fuck off…"

He stopped.

"Why did you ask me just now if I knew Jack Smith?"

"Because it was Smith who beat me up that morning."

Bryn stared at her uncomprehendingly. She took a deep breath and continued.

"I went outside for a smoke and to make a cellphone call. I didn't want to wake you… There were two big fellers waiting in a car and they grabbed me. One of them hit me real hard. It was professional though. They had me in their car in a couple of seconds and took me a few miles west, parked up off the highway and… worked me over."

She was reluctant to go further. Bryn poured her some more coffee and placed an arm tentatively round her shoulder.

"Smith was one of them?"

"No, no. Do you really know *nothing* about this? I meant they were his guys, his heavies. Smith is a fascist bastard who sub-contracts to professionals when he wants something done. He would never be involved."

"Why did they beat you?" he asked.

"Because of you," she replied.

She caught his perplexed and troubled frown and her eyes filled with tears. He drew her closer to him.

"I didn't know what to think," she continued. "They wanted to know when I'd last been in touch with you, what I had on you. I thought at first that they'd picked up on the U of M lecture, seen I was with you, and were warning me off, protecting you as it were. It's not the first time people in our group have been roughed up by Smith."

"I don't understand. Who were they waiting for? You or me?"

"I didn't know. They'd been tracking *my* movements, I'm quite sure of that. I thought at first they might have known you were at the motel with me, but in the end it didn't seem to be so. They probably thought I was there with one of the guys in our group. They started talking about London which made no sense to me, asking whether I had got anything off you. I said that all that happened was that I'd had dinner with you the *previous* day – by that time I was pretty confused and I figured they might have spied on us anyway. And the weird thing was that they then stopped immediately. They seemed shocked. I'm not sure they believed me at first and one guy went off and made a call on his cellphone. Then they just told me to keep clear of you and – very kindly, oh, real gentlemen – dropped me off on the outskirts of town. After that, another quite different guy drove up in my own VW and took me back to my apartment, of course he knew where it was, and told me to get the hell out. I took the hint."

"You are one hell of a brave woman," he said at last, with feeling.

She shivered.

"Braver than I could have been," he said.

He withdrew his arm to pick up his coffee mug. He needed time to take in what she had just told him.

But she put a hand to his face and peered sharply into his eyes, with a fierce concentration that took him quite by surprise. This was disconcertingly different territory from the frigid appraisal he had received at the door. He held her gaze, discomfited by her intensity but perversely unwilling to release himself from it. Her hand slid round and grasped the hair at the back of his head; and she turned his mouth in on hers. He was lost at once. A heedless tide of passion flooded over him and he wrapped himself in her embrace.

"Wait a moment," she said and for another dreadful instant he thought it was all over. She slipped away from him and went to lock the sliding doors into the room. But she had already pulled off her t-shirt and was unbuttoning her jeans as she returned.

They scattered some cushions on the floor. He lowered her onto them. As he did so, he heard a scuffling sound outside, followed by an insistent hammering on the sliding doors. In the distance, the dogs began to bark.

"Go away, Angie," shouted Zelma.

The hammering stopped. She took his head in her hands and pulled him towards her. Outside the door a small voice began calling out: "Mommy... Mommy..."

His legs slid between hers and he kissed her again on the lips. But the hammering started up again, now with a vocal accompaniment, and Zelma's mouth suddenly was no longer under his. She wriggled to the side and raised herself on her elbow and shouted again at her daughter to go away. The daughter began to cry. The dogs had returned back into the house and were now becoming frantic.

It was awful, and hopeless. He struggled for a while to continue. Finally, even Zelma's determination began to fade and he slipped from her embrace. He rolled away to the side, and reached out for his clothes. As he did so, the racket outside subsided.

While Zelma slowly dressed, he could not resist reflecting on how many times in her life previously this scene might have been played out. On what unresolved mix of jealousy, rejection and bewilderment was running through that child's mind. He was fond of Zelma, genuinely fond, he believed. And a part of him felt guilty at letting her down. But this was not a world he could possibly inhabit. He had expected to feel frustrated. But he simply felt hollow. There was no future for them as lovers.

Zelma did not speak for a while.

"I'm sorry," she said at last. "I don't think that's what you wanted."

"I'm sorry too," he said.

"Would you like a drink?"

Sensible girl. She unlocked the doors and went into the kitchen. He became aware of noises in the street outside and was surprised at how late it was. Commuters were already beginning to return to some of the other houses and he could smell an early evening barbecue nearby. Zelma returned with a half-full bottle of *Virginia Gentleman* bourbon and a couple of straight tumblers.

"It's good bourbon," she said. "A friend left it here. A gentleman caller… and I expect I know what you're thinking."

She smiled ruefully.

Bryn examined the label. It was a picture of an eighteenth century grandee in a Southern plantation setting. The whiskey had been distilled in the famous Civil War town of Fredericksburg, Virginia. It was an unusually pale amber, and light and easy on the tongue.

"It *is* good," he said. "A taste of honey and caramel, and cocoa. Sweet."

She frowned.

"I wouldn't know," she said. "It's all alcohol to me. I'm in the Ogden Nash camp. You know: candy is dandy but liquor is quicker."

She left him for a while. When she did not return, he picked up his glass and followed through to the kitchen. The dogs were nose down in their earthenware bowls eating their dinner and paying no attention. At the bottom of the long, unkempt garden, Zelma was attempting to negotiate with her daughter. And perhaps succeeding. At all events, the pair of them shortly started, hand-in-hand, to return to the house. He thought it prudent to withdraw.

Zelma came back into the room alone. She closed the doors but this time did not lock them. A rhythmic thud of rock music started up in the bedroom above them.

"She'll be all right," said Zelma and sat down next to him with a long exhalation of breath. She ran her fingers through her hair and gave him her rueful smile again.

"Mothers and daughters, eh?" said Bryn.

"She's all right," she said again. "I'm just not a very good mother. At all events, she'll see more of me now. I've jacked in my Ann Arbor job."

"Why?"

"Why do you think?"

She filled her tumbler to the brim. The *Virginia Gentleman* was now almost empty and she went to a cupboard in the corner of the room and brought out a fresh bottle of the same brand and placed it next to the first on the table in front of them.

"Same gentleman caller," she said quietly, as if in answer to his question.

She took a long sip and sat back and smiled wanly at him.

"You really don't know much about Jack Smith, do you?" she said.

"Not really, no. Except that he doesn't like me."

"Let me tell you about him then."

So much time passed before she next spoke that he began to assume that she had changed her mind. Maybe whatever memories she wanted to share were still too difficult. He listened to the toneless thud from the ceiling and wondered if he should drink up now, make his apologies and leave Zelma and her daughter to themselves. Then…

"My group have been tracking Jack and his people for a few years," she said. "Nobody seems to know it yet, but he's a major threat. I don't think he paid much mind to *us* either until very recently, when they discovered we had planted a mole in their organization. And now our guy's dead. Oh yeah. Of course we can't be sure that they killed him, the official line is that he fell into the Potomac and drowned. But there have been a few other

203

accidents over the last couple of years which were, let's say, kind of convenient."

"Did you find anything out through the mole?"

"Pretty well how Jack finances himself. Our guy was helping with their IT. Get into the computers and you can find out what's going on. The scale of the operation, the funding, where it's all coming from. A lot of the money's legitimate, from rich guys on their side, evangelical groups. But some of it is hush money from other guys – and corporations – who don't want their laundry washed in public. And then they have stuff on congressmen, even White House people, who make sure the wheels are oiled for them. They have some computer genius of their own – a Brit, by the way – who can get into anybody else's systems, and divert cash, deliver dirt, whatever. There's a big connection with the UK."

"Would that be the *GodWorks* organization?"

"Yeah, yeah. Could be. There's another guy they deal with, comes over from London regularly. I actually thought at one time it might be you."

She laughed.

"That was pretty ridiculous," she said and spluttered on a gulp of liquor.

Bryn kept his thoughts to himself.

"So what's all this about?" he asked. "Is Smith just trying to make himself richer, or what?"

"He wants to be President," she said.

"You're not serious."

"Never more. Not yet though. We think he's playing a long game. He needs a power base in Washington and he's working on that. We think he's got his sights for now on the Vice Presidency."

" 'Not worth a bucket of warm piss' " said Bryn, enunciating now quite carefully.

"Maybe. However, things have moved on a bit since John Nance Garner. We've had five ex-VPs since the War who have become President. Or, if they don't want to wait, they can be like Dick Cheney and run the show anyway and let the front man take the flak. What Smith needs is a weak and acquiescent figurehead while he pulls the levers. You don't think that could happen? You ain't seen nothing yet, baby."

"Evidently," said Bryn. "Can I ask you a question?"

"Sure." She looked at the watch on her wrist.

"Can we reel back to when they picked you up in Ann Arbor? How did they know where you were? If they'd been following us, they would have known I was with you. But you said they were surprised."

"Yeah. I couldn't figure that out either. Then I learnt that one of the things their computer guy does is penetrate credit card accounts. Not just for fraud, that's only a part of it. Also to find out about what people are doing. It's all there in the credit card traffic. They target you and know, the moment you do a transaction, the location and what it was for. So, if it's the Cherry Grove, say, or a – "

"What's the Cherry Grove?"

"A high class bordello in Washington," she said irritably and continued. "So, like if you've paid on your card for something sleazy, I guess they blackmail you. But it also tells them exactly where you are at any time. Which is useful if they want to take someone out. Which in my case is what happened."

"Sorry?"

"Look… what I think now is that they were already into my account when I paid up the tab that night at your Best Western. Remember? Up it came on their screen and they were ready and waiting for me next morning."

"That's terrifying."

"Well it's taught me one thing. Pay in cash if you don't want them to know where you are. And use an ATM somewhere that doesn't tell them anything too useful about your location. Like a really big railway station with crowds and lots of lines to choose from."

He wondered whether it was worth telling Zelma about the adventure with his attaché case, and about its contents. On balance, he thought, perhaps not. It would only confirm what she already knew about the Smith modus operandi. But importantly, the attaché case was something he had put behind him, he hoped for ever. He had to trust Marshall to give Smith the right assurances about him so that there would be no further trouble. And trouble was what might surely get stirred up if he shared these confidences with Zelma and her group.

She glanced at her watch again. It was already quite dark outside. Bryn got to his feet with a little difficulty and grasped her shoulder to prevent himself swaying.

"I've gotta go," he said.

They kissed. She stroked his cheek gently and nodded.

"I think so," she said.

The walk back alone to Maplewood station and the cool early evening air helped to clear his head. He rode the stopping train to New York and the subway back to the Whitney Hotel.

Next morning he checked out around six. There was nothing to pay since Marshall had, predictably and irresistibly, covered his entire account. Even the expensive bottled water he had taken from the mini-bar was already paid for.

He took the C Line to Pennsylvania Station and found an ATM in the main concourse, not far away from a couple of NYPD men, comfortingly armed as usual to the teeth. He took out as much cash as he thought he could possibly need for the rest of his journey – and half as much again just in case – and stowed it all away safely in an inside pocket.

Then, instead of taking a train, he found the Olympia Express Bus Terminal and paid cash for a ticket to Newark Airport. At Newark, though he was obliged to present his credit card before he could hire a car, he was assured that there would be no transaction on it until he returned. In any event, he reasoned, no-one could have any idea where he would be taking the vehicle.

He took Route 78 west through New Jersey and Pennsylvania to Harrisburg, where he turned south down Route 15. Sometime before noon he passed the small town of Gettysburg and fell in with the lengthening line of cars and SUVs motoring south towards the battlefield.

Chapter 20

It was more than twenty years since he had visited the site and he had forgotten how huge it was. And how little had changed since the great conflict, a century and a half ago. The lone highway through the battlefield remained pretty much as it would have been then, with the same simple country name: the 'Emmitsburg Road'. The difference was that it was now surfaced with dusty tarmac instead of traffic-compacted stone and dirt. Around it lay clear, open countryside interrupted at intervals by roadside memorials to outlying skirmishes and dead heroes.

What a contrast, he reflected passionately, to the neglected civil war battlefields of England, tucked into corners of the terrain, half-erased by motorways and development, difficult to find. This battlefield proclaimed itself. You *knew*, as you drove across the landscape, that the wide valley and the low, brooding ridges bordering it to the east and west were sacred to this nation.

A battlefield should in any case feel, or so it seemed to Bryn, like an ancient and mighty cathedral. This was the place to which thousands of men had come, in many cases quite consciously, to meet their Maker. Their monuments lined the way. Their graves lay beneath your feet. Altar-like stones marked a particularly terrible passage of bloodshed where the greatest numbers had fallen to their knees in a terminal communion. Over the centuries that followed, people would come reverentially to pay their respects. For a God-fearing believer, steeped in the battles of the Old Testament, the sense of the hand of the Almighty on this windless valley would surely be irresistible.

The Civil War lasted for four years, from 1861 to 1865. Three-quarters of a million people died, more American lives than all the other wars *combined* that America has been involved in, before or since, to this day.

Gettysburg was the greatest battle of that War. At the height of the battle more than 170,000 men were on the field. There were more casualties than in any other engagement in American history. The Normandy landings in 1944 cost the USA around a tenth of the number of those who were killed or wounded here.

Bryn had sometimes challenged his students to come up with a battle of greater significance not just for America, but for Europe or the world in general. For this was where the Union was saved. If it had been Robert E Lee, commanding the armies of the South, who had won at Gettysburg, the rebels would have advanced upon Philadelphia, cut off Washington and won the war. Palmerston in England and Napoleon III in France would have been obliged to recognize a new, disaffiliated Confederate States of America. North America would have entered the twentieth century as not two but three nations, each markedly weaker than the USA of modern history and each with a correspondingly more modest political and military agenda.

He followed the cars and SUVs to the Visitor Center. It was a brand new complex, and a welcome replacement for the worn and uninspiring museum he remembered from twenty years ago. But the car park was already crowded and vehicles were waiting in lines for spaces. Parties of boisterous school-children were pouring through the main entrance into the building. Families sat in their cars picnicking. He decided to drive on.

He circled back to the north of the Center and joined the road which ran down from the town and along the western side of the battlefield. It was nose to tail with vehicles. As cathedrals

208

went, the battlefield was as secular and crowded as St Paul's in London. Even though the traffic was one-way only, movement was already at snail's pace. Opportunities to park by the roadside and meditate on the surroundings were few and far between. Bryn recalled nostalgically that his previous visit had been much earlier in the season, when he had been able to leave his car by the roadside and just wander about undisturbed and alone.

The road ran south on the crest of Seminary Ridge, following more or less the line along which Lee had drawn up his forces for the main part of the battle. The ridge was crowned by woodland, just as it had been 150 years before, like a traverse curtain running the length of the Confederate line. Only the roadside memorials disturbed the natural simplicity of the scenery.

Gettysburg's valley of death stretched away for a mile or so to the east, serene and unremarkable. On the morning of July 3rd 1863, it would have been as empty of soldiers as it was now. The Union forces were drawn up along the ridge on the other side, awaiting Lee's onslaught. The only feature of consequence between the two armies would have been, then as now, the Emmitsburg Road crossing the valley diagonally from north to south.

The crawling column of tourist traffic arrived at a clearing in the woods. An equestrian statue had been erected here, facing the east: Robert E Lee on his horse, Traveller, standing where he had been throughout that day. Just as Bryn arrived, a car pulled out ahead of him and he slipped thankfully into the parking space it had vacated.

He walked across the road and stood at the edge of the trees looking across the valley to the Union ridge beyond.

This was what it was all about. He felt the back of his neck prickle with pleasure. He sank back into the cocoon of his own private contemplation. The crowds of kids and parents surging around and across the battlefield dissolved into silence. If any part of the ground was hallowed, *this* was. It was at such moments that he felt most at home with himself and with the profession he had chosen. These few square feet were where

America had been won and lost. This was where the great general, until now the unvanquished champion of the war, had committed his fatal, hubristic blunder. He had sent the best of his army out across the valley to total disaster. How extraordinary that the Charge of the Light Brigade was a mere nine years previously. Except that in Lee's case the entire enterprise was carefully planned and intended.

For it was from here that Robert E Lee launched *Pickett's Charge*, so-named through history after the undistinguished general – a Virginian like Lee – whose division had the honour of leading the assault. It was more like a walk than a charge as, with fixed bayonets, 15,000 men crossed the mile wide valley in the face of withering fire from the Union lines. A few heroes made it to the opposite ridge and were cut down. The survivors struggled back to their lines, and the battle was effectively over.

The next day, ironically and appropriately the Fourth of July, Lee retreated back to Virginia, with a third of his army lost. He never attempted to take the war to the north again.

When he had last visited the battlefield, in late winter, Bryn had been able to trace the line of Pickett's attack and walk the whole course from Lee's position to the Union lines – alone. Few visitors came to Gettysburg in the cold months. No shrieking children and crowds then disturbed his private march across the marshy turf, over field trestles and round criss-crossing water-courses, across the Emmitsburg Road and into the teeth of the cannon fire and muskets. He had arrived at the same outcrop of rocks – at the summit of the aptly-named Cemetery Ridge – where the surviving Confederate troops foundered and finally fell back. He had stood and gazed back across the murderous field, alone with the ghosts of the dead and nearly dead, before retracing his steps, as so many did not, back to the sheltering Confederacy woods. Back to Robert E Lee, no longer now on his horse, and bare-headed with hat in hand, moving through the retreating survivors, and repeating over and over again: "I'm so sorry. It is all my fault. Forgive me. I am so sorry". A broken general of a broken army.

It was a mistake to return to Gettysburg in the summer. And to imagine he could revisit the sensations he had experienced as a younger man. He turned away and walked back to his car. He drove on round the battlefield until he picked up the road south to Frederick and then west through Middletown and Boonsboro. By the time he arrived in the little town of Sharpsburg in western Maryland, it was nearly evening.

Sharpsburg had the feel of a Victorian community fallen on hard times. Such industrial wealth as it once had derived from its convenient proximity to the water highways of the Potomac and the Chesapeake and Ohio Canal. As with many other small towns in the later part of the nineteenth century, the democratizing advent of the railway had progressively eroded these special advantages away. It was obvious now that new wealth had all but passed Sharpsburg by. It remained pretty well a one street town. It had a few bars, a few basic places to eat, a few shops. He guessed that it was mostly sustained these days by its adjacency to the site of the most important battle of the civil war before Gettysburg – the field of Antietam.

His first priority, though, was to find the Historic Paul Schwarz House, the home of his professorial friend, Karl, and wife Eva. It stood tight up against the sidewalk on Main Street, a large square house with elaborately detailed cast-iron balconies. According to a small wooden board swinging above the front porch, it had been built in 1804, by an early German settler.

He never ceased to be surprised by the generosity of ordinary Americans. Because he had angled so flagrantly for this invitation, he half-expected to be greeted now with a degree of reticence. From his own perspective, he had taken fairly crude advantage of a very new friendship. But if that was the way Karl had perceived the arrangement, then neither he nor Eva gave any sign of it. Their welcome was total and unreserved. When he had settled in, they informed him that they would be taking him out to a restaurant across the border in West Virginia. They wanted him to enjoy himself. Dinner would be on Karl, and Eva would be driving, so no excuses...

Eva ushered him into what appeared to be the grandest bedroom in the house and left him discreetly to himself. Clearly the special room for guests. As neat and crisp, though nothing like so cramped, as the Whitney Hotel. Here and there, small typed-out notes explained how to turn the television and DVD player on, or how you should dispose of any bathroom waste. The soaps and shampoos were set out in tidy rows, and scrupulously eco-friendly.

Karl knocked contritely on his door.

"Say, Bryn, I almost forgot. Your wife called from England a while back today. She said, would you call her."

He was insistent that Bryn used the house phone in the hall; and only with the greatest difficulty did Bryn manage to insist in return that he be allowed to use his BT card to charge his home account. It was a small moral victory.

Marion was in bed when he rang through. He had quite forgotten the time difference. At first he thought she was cross with him for ringing back so late. But it was more serious than that.

"Bryn, do you know someone called Ed?"

"Is this why you called me?"

"Answer me."

"No of course I don't know anyone called Ed. Why are you asking me this?"

"I spoke to a man on the phone this morning."

She paused, and he heard a long intake of breath.

"He seemed very nice at first," she continued. "American. I guess, a Southern accent. He said he was a friend of yours, called Ed. He said he'd met up with you in New York the other day and needed to get in touch again. I couldn't find Karl and Eva's phone number at first so I gave him their email address. Then he said, where do they live and I couldn't remember. I said Maryland somewhere. He started pushing for the phone number again and got quite cross. I said, I'm *sorry* – I don't have it. Then he asked where were you going later and what car hire company were you using and I said I didn't know and – finally, he got so pushy – I said I really didn't think that was any business of his. And then he abused me, said I must know, called me a bitch, accused me of lying. I put the phone down... I thought you should know."

She was breathing quite fast and he could tell she was close to tears.

"I'm sure you did the right thing," he said, more sympathetically. "Whoever he is, he's not a friend of mine."

"But he knew who you were. Are you sure you don't know someone called Ed? He was so rude."

"I don't know who it was. It might be to do with something that happened a while ago. But that's all sorted now so I honestly don't think there's anything for you to worry about. It sounds as though you've done a really good job getting rid of him."

He sounded more convincing than he felt. He reassured her that, whoever it was, she had not told him anything very useful. If the man did manage to get in touch, he would clear up any misunderstanding there might be and let her know. But his best guess was that nothing further would happen. She seemed to calm down. They exchanged affectionate goodbyes, and he went through to the main sitting room, to which Karl and Eva had politely retired at the start of the conversation. He was relieved to hear that no, nobody had emailed or called for him that day – except of course Marion.

It was already time to go to dinner.

"It will be very German," said Karl.

And so it was.

He had expected a long drive but in fact the state border was only a few miles away and just beyond it was their objective: the Heidelberg Inn, a three storey West Virginian Rhine castle, sitting on a rise overlooking the Potomac River.

Most of the tables were already full. Americans do not eat late in the south. The pretensions of the place, at first glimpse, were alarming. The large menus appeared to be printed on vellum and displayed the evening's recommendations by Chef Friedrich Plumpe ("a native of Germany"). The dishes, which seemed to be a fusion of different European cuisines, were elaborately and lengthily described and the wine list ran to 600 labels and 5000 bottles. Bryn was reminded of Evelyn Waugh's remark to a fellow soldier during the War as they cowered under a relentless German bombardment: 'It's very impressive but like everything German, overdone'. Looking around at the summer dress and chino clad clientele, and the large salads and highball glasses of coca-cola, he feared the worst.

It was not to be. He might have criticized the sheer weight of food on the plate and some blandness of flavour, but this was after all rural America (and the chef was German). He could not criticize the expert efficiency of the cooking or the excellence and freshness of the ingredients. "Shot locally," said Karl cheerfully, as he addressed his giant portion of elk and venison tenderloin with German gnocchi. And the *Englische Suppe*, with which they all finished, was unimpeachably rich, alcoholic and authentic.

By the time they were ready to leave, all the other tables were empty and in a far corner of the room a waiter was discreetly laying for breakfast. Karl, showing unexpected weakness, allowed Bryn at least to pay for the wine. Eva drained her last Perrier and ushered them to the door.

There had been no emails and no telephone calls.

He went out very early next morning. After his experience at Gettysburg, he was determined to avoid the tourist crowds. He drove directly to the Antietam Visitor Center, a few hundred yards north of town. As he turned off the main road towards the Center, a solitary black saloon passed, travelling in the opposite direction towards Sharpsburg.

His plan was to spend the morning on the main part of the battlefield, return for lunch with Karl and Eva, and hope to cover the more outlying elements in the afternoon and evening. The battle itself only lasted a day, and was over by 5.30pm. But it bore comparison with Gettysburg for two reasons. The first was the scale of the carnage. A total of 27,000 men were killed or wounded here, making 17th September 1862 the bloodiest *single* day in American military history. It was not less terrible than the four days of Gettysburg; just shorter.

The other reason was its pivotal rôle in the War. After his defeat of the Federals at Bull Run in August that same year, Lee had decided to move north via Maryland in a foreshadowing of his strategy before Gettysburg. He hoped that Maryland, affiliated to the Union but a slave-owning state, might be persuaded to switch sides. He also hoped, as in 1863, that success in the field might encourage the European nations to recognize the Confederacy.

Unfortunately, the Federals were able to confront him outside Sharpsburg with an army more than twice the size of his, and with superior matériel. He had no choice but to draw up in a defensive position on a ridge above a small river called Antietam Creek. By a mixture of a great general's luck, superior tactics, and the heroism of his ill-equipped troops, he fought the attackers to a draw and the next day withdrew, with no further serious losses, to the south.

For a professional historian, Antietam had another, special, significance. This was the first battle in the annals of war for which there is a photographic record. And it made the worldwide reputation of Mathew Brady, whose team of photographers took pictures of the immediate aftermath of the action at the main sites of conflict. The images were exhibited in New York later that year (as 'The Dead of Antietam'). They opened the eyes of the ordinary public to the carnage and horror of the Civil War, and of war in general.

Bryn was in luck. It was still too early in the morning for more than a handful of tourists. The only sizable group was a party of disabled, mostly middle-aged people whose main concern seemed to be to utilize the excellent toilet facilities in the Visitor Center. Then they promptly remounted their charabanc and disappeared off towards the west.

The Visitor Center had been built right on the Confederate ridge, about a third of the way down Lee's line. He went inside and climbed up a flight of stairs to a belvedere room overlooking the battlefield, where a young uniformed male ranger had just begun to deliver the first lecture of the day. A group of six East Coast tourists stood in the middle, wheeling left and right as he pointed to features of the unfolding conflict in the real-life panorama beyond the floor-to-ceiling windows. He was impressive: clear, succinct and scholarly. Like the young woman at Frank Lloyd Wright's House in Illinois, this fresh-faced southern gentleman knew his stuff.

Bryn left the Center and walked down to the woods from which the first wave of the Federal army had emerged at around 5.30am that 1862 day. There still was the cornfield that changed hands so many times, and the lonely farmhouse standing incongruously to one side of it, whose bewildered residents had awoken to a nightmare beyond their imagining. At 5.30am on that September morning, the corn was a tall, mature crop ready for harvesting. By mid-day the rifle, canister and artillery fire had so razed it that, in the words of the Union general commanding that sector: "every stalk… was cut as closely as could have been done with a knife, and the slain lay in rows precisely as they had stood in their ranks".

He drifted on a quarter of a mile across the tight, crowded little battlefield, to the so-called Bloody Lane. This was a short track barely a hundred metres long. It had been a cart-way that, over succeeding generations, had worn deeper and deeper into the landscape until it provided a perfect natural trench from which Lee's soldiers were able to ambush the Union host advancing across their front. That is, until the sheer weight of Federal numbers finally outflanked them, and the rebels were trapped in their *cul de sac* and shot down mercilessly, like rats in a sewer. Some of Brady's most moving pictures show masses of soldiers huddled here together in death, as if they had been pitched into a mass grave. There was not, on this frantic and terrible day, much scope for white flags and orderly surrender.

The crowds were already beginning to gather, so he went back to his car and drove round to Burnside's Bridge. He had missed this on his previous visit to Antietam, partly because it was to the south of the main battlefield and slightly detached from it.

A Union general called Ambrose Burnside – whose eccentric whiskers are commemorated forever in the reversed version of his surname – had sent more than twelve thousand men forward against a bridge over Antietam Creek defended by four hundred soldiers from the state of Georgia. If he had crossed it that afternoon, he would have rolled up Lee's flank and won the battle. But he did not.

The Georgian riflemen, outnumbered in identical ratio to the defenders of Rorke's Drift (and, Bryn noted for his book, just a hundred more than Leonidas and his Thermopylae Spartans) pinned the Union army down for several hours, picking off Burnside's troops from a bluff overlooking the river. By the time the Federals finally prevailed and streamed across the bridge, the day and the battle was nearing its end. The Georgians had held out long enough for a fresh southern division, arriving from the east, to smash into Burnside's flank and drive him back. Heroes indeed.

It was an exceptionally pretty spot. He could have been in the English countryside, somewhere between the Chilterns and Suffolk. Woodland skirted the rebel side of the river bank. The bridge was a low, stone-built crossing from a Constable painting, just wide enough for a single cart. A solitary ancient tree, the only living survivor of the conflict, stood hard up against the Union side. Beyond and behind it, the ground was grassed and open. A perfect place for a picnic.

He sat down on a wooden bench and made a few professional notes. As he did so, he observed a man in the distance. He might have been a farmer. Perhaps a descendant of the German settlers whose land was devastated so abruptly that September day. He watched the man walk up the far hillside and climb into an open-backed pick-up truck of the type seen all over the American country roads; and drive off over the horizon.

He reluctantly dragged himself away from the idyllic scene, returned to his car and drove back into Sharpsburg.

A police wagon was parked outside Karl and Eva's house and the front door was open.

Eva was sitting in the living room, in a state of shock. A table had been overturned and a pile of Karl's books and papers strewn on the floor. A uniformed officer was there – his notebook lay open on a chair – and he was now sharing a beer with Karl.

"Hi, Bryn," exclaimed Karl, before he could say anything. "Sorry about the mess. This is Officer Schmidt. He's a friend of ours."

"Good to meet you, sir," said the policeman, in a perceptibly German accent.

"Has something happened?" asked Bryn redundantly.

They explained. It appeared that sometime earlier that morning, when Eva was alone in the house, a man had come in through the back door. In communities like this, where everybody knew everybody else, it was not usual to lock back or even front doors. The man had asked Eva if there was anyone else in the house and, without thinking, she had said no.

"That was very stupid," said Eva. "I knew it at once. I should have lied and said my husband was here."

"No need to apologize, Eva," said the policeman.

Then the man had attempted to get past her towards the upstairs rooms and she had screamed – quite loudly and effectively because the man panicked and pushed her away so that she fell to the floor, knocking over the table. Then he rushed out of the house and ran into Karl who was returning from shopping and who tried unsuccessfully to intercept him.

"You shouldna done that, Karl," said Officer Schmidt. "Who knows what the guy might've been packing."

At all events, the man escaped to his car, and drove away north. Karl found Eva in some distress but unharmed and they called the local police.

At this point in their narrative, Officer Schmidt's radio phone buzzed and he took the call. What he heard satisfied him.

"We got the guy," he said. "Paul and Heinz picked him up at the Antietam Visitor Center and they've taken him in for questioning and perhaps a little... you know..." His eyes slid across to Bryn and then back to Karl.

"We'll need an ID," he continued.

It was decided that Eva would stay home and rest awhile, and Karl would do the necessary. Bryn asked if he might come along. "Sure," said Officer Schmidt.

They climbed into the police wagon and drove a hundred yards to the station. A black saloon was parked by the kerb outside. Officer Schmidt took them through to a corridor inside the building. On either side of it was a small room, with a grille on the door. Karl peered through one and nodded. Bryn slipped in behind him and quickly took a look for himself.

A man was sitting on a bench in the tiny cell, gazing at the ground. It was Bryn's old adversary. The same pale-faced, hooded, mirror-lensed man who had tracked him in Chicago and whom he had encountered, smart and shaven, in Salt Lake City airport. This time he wore no glasses, and the side of his face was badly bruised, with one eye swollen and closed. He looked – as Bryn might have observed, had the recognition left him less shaken – the picture of dejection.

He said nothing to the police. Once it was clear that they intended to charge the man with assault and hold him until they could establish his identity – the man had no papers or credit cards with him – his impulse was to leave Sharpsburg immediately. And put space between himself and his nameless nemesis.

Not that he gave any of this very considered thought. He was anxious simply to be somewhere else. A somewhere that had not been part of any schedule or any discussion with any individual, including his own wife. He apologized to his startled hosts, picked up his bags, and drove out of town towards the south.

He had two days to lose before his return flight to England from Newark. He considered trying for an earlier plane but it seemed best simply to disappear until it was time to fly home. The important thing was to keep on the move. Maybe explore a part of the country he was unfamiliar with.

He would lose himself in Virginia.

Chapter 21

If you go down to the woods today,
You'd better not go alone.
It's lovely out in the woods today,
But safer to stay at home.

For a while he had no particular plan. He aimed roughly south, following minor roads through small towns with names that read like a gazetteer from the Old World: Nineveh, Moscow, Gretna, Finchley. He was struck by the numbers of roadside churches and the seemingly limitless range of sects and denominations. The New Life Assembly of God, The Church of the Nazarene, The Church on the Rock, The New Baptist Assembly, The Church of the Covenant, The Calvary Chapel. And by their billboards, as brash, aggressive and direct as the advertising displays he had seen on the Newark-New York Road a few days previously.

"Can't Sleep? Counting Sheep? Talk to the Shepherd."

"Don't Give Up! Moses was once a basket case!"

"Tomorrow's forecast – God reigns and the sun shines!"

"Try Jesus. If you don't like Him, the Devil will take you back."

"You're on Heaven's Most Wanted list."

"Life Stinks. We have a pew for you."

"What part of *Thou Shalt Not* don't you understand?"

Towards evening, he turned north. He was nagged by a profound depression somewhere at the centre of his being. For hours now the driving, the bizarre surrounding landscape, the country music on the car radio, all had helped to displace some very dark thoughts. He stopped at a gas station for food and to fill up. And try and collect himself.

The depression, he unwillingly comprehended, was fear. At first this surprised him. No-one this time had shot at him or threatened him. He had been spooked simply by the arrival of a man who was now safely in jail. But the real shock was the recognition that, after so many months since the events in London and in Utah, he was still being stalked. He knew now, beyond further argument or rationalisation, that someone was determined to kill him. And the fear in his gut was greater than any he had known, worse than Utah and certainly worse than Chicago.

He leaned on the car and began to retch, just as he had six months before on the mountain road amidst the snow. The same involuntary reaction to a presentiment of death. The fear flowed through him, like a black, demoralizing tide. He wondered if he was actually going to cry.

Then a part of him began to marvel at it all. Was *this* what real fear was about? He had so little in his experience to compare it with. Worse than losing a child in a shopping precinct? Worse than a hospital operation? Worse than advancing across the battlefield of Gettysburg against cannon and musket-fire?

There was a passage covering this in a Russian novel, he couldn't remember which: 'Take a soldier and put him in front of a cannon in battle and fire at him and he will still hope, but read the same soldier his death sentence *for certain* and he will go mad...'

He flattered himself. How could he compare his feelings with the fears of the soldiers out of whose experiences he had fashioned a whole career? And yet it helped him to begin to understand the sensation which had so unmanned him. Real fear was a finished narrative, a rabbit trapped in the headlights with nowhere to go. That was *not* his situation.

He pulled out his map of Virginia and unfolded it on the bonnet. And now, as he studied it, his fear began to give way to a fury that he could have been so complacent. He had been given warnings enough – by the succession of near scrapes, by Zelma, by Graeme's death, even by his cousin back in London. He gazed ferociously at the map. He had to force himself to concentrate.

'The Wilderness'.

Two words that suddenly seemed like the perfect invitation. A place that presumably people did not go to unless they wished to be somewhere remote and unvisited. It lay about fifty miles or so north of his present position. He knew about it. It had been a recurring motif in the American Civil War: a dense, barely penetrable, unfarmable wasteland of scrub and small trees into which successive armies had blundered and come to grief. Three major battles had been fought there, forces manoeuvring blindly in the leafy darkness and smoke and the terrible, incinerating brush fires. It was an Armageddon of a place; and just where he now ought to be.

By the time he arrived on the outskirts of the nearest town, Fredericksburg, it was well into the evening. Immediately adjacent to The New Welcome Church of Christ ("You may party in hell but you will be the Barbeque"), he found a motel, more Bates than Best Western, and checked in. The chain-smoking old lady in reception did not, unusually, insist on a credit card imprint from him. She did, however, require him to leave his car keys with her and she popped them in a pigeon hole behind her as security against a dawn flit.

His room was part of a block running parallel to the road. As he slipped his door key into the lock, a couple of streetwalkers shouted at him encouragingly. He acknowledged them with an automatic wave of the hand and a polite nod; and the larger of the two – whose skirt barely cleared her crotch – started to climb over the low roadside wall towards him. He bolted indoors.

The place was as seedy inside as out. When he switched on the main light, a dim fluorescent tube above a wall mirror convulsed into life and the air-conditioning cranked up to a sharp, rattling breeze. The bed was hard, with wrinkled nylon sheets. Apart from the regulation television set in the corner, the only other piece of furniture in the room was a frayed, under-stuffed armchair.

He sat on the bed and munched indifferently on the assortment of pies and cookies he had bought at the gas station. At first he thought the television was in black and white; and then it dawned on him that the last guest in this room had left it tuned to a porn channel showing extremely old videos. He flicked to another, and another. All the channels seemed to be pornography. On each of them, after a minute, the picture froze and a message came up advising the viewer that he would need to use the interactive facility to put in his credit card details, if he wished to view further.

Bryn flicked on and was startled to discover, alongside all the simulated heterosexual humping, a sequence of male-on-male channels, all generically titled: 'Bare in Paradise', 'Bare in the Mountains' and so on. They were no more explicit than the rest and the invitation to pay up before, by implication, the harder stuff might be unveiled arrived on cue as usual. He was about to turn the set off when something in the last frozen frame riveted his attention. Two men were kissing in a dappled, woodland glade. The image had been arrested in mid-movement and was blurred and indistinct. But both faces looked familiar, and one, he felt sure, was Graeme.

He tapped the required credit card details into the handset and the picture jumped into life again. The scenario remained as ungraphic as before – barely a *15*-rated movie in the UK – but he no longer had any doubts. The more passive of the two participants was about twenty-years old, slim, very pretty, with a head of hair like a seventies soccer star but unmistakeably Graeme. He struggled to identify the other man. Also young, slim to the point of emaciated, fresh faced with head close shaven in an unsuccessful attempt to disguise his already advancing baldness. And then it came to him.

It was that same face he had pushed from his thoughts those many months ago and had not expected ever to see again. The face he had glimpsed in Denny's car park in March, climbing into his black SUV. The face in the worshipping crowd on TV a few days later.

He had missed the video's title but a couple of credits came up: 'with Teddy Roosevelt' and 'a Dark Productions film'. He watched it for another five minutes while the activity, clumsily simulated and masked, worked its way unenthusiastically through three or four regulation positions.

He switched the television off and thought about it.

Darke. The bald man. Marshall perhaps. Graeme. Maybe, when he got back to England, he would at last speak to the police and get some of this on the record, if only to alleviate his fears by sharing them. It might be that they had evidence of their own with which his might mesh. Of course there could still be a problem with his flimsy narrative and absence of hard evidence…

He was shaken from this reverie by a fearsome pounding at the door of his room.

"Hey, mister! Are you in thy-er?" shrieked a voice with a richly southern accent.

He peered through the slats in the dirty Venetian window blind. The two ladies he had seen earlier were standing outside, shifting restlessly from foot to foot. He guessed that at the end of an unfruitful day they were making one last bid for a pay-off.

He turned off the light and crept into bed and closed his eyes.

The last sounds he heard were of high heels clicking slowly away into the hot Virginia night.

He awoke shortly after six. The sun had already risen beyond his window and a cloud of dust particles hung in the shafts of gold light spearing through the slats. It was already later than he had intended, so he rolled out of bed and quickly showered, stuffed his safety razor and little shaving cream canister into his pocket for a later opportunity, downed two cups of coffee in the motel office, paid up in cash and retrieved his keys, and left.

He took the old Plank Road to the west. It was an iconic highway. This had been the main nineteenth century route for all traffic out of Fredericksburg and – inevitably – for the armies. There were other roads but they became impassable when the weather was bad, as it frequently was. But this road was laid from end to end with planks so that the essential carts would not be lost in the engulfing Virginia mud, and supplies could always get through. It was both the lifeblood of the western Virginia communities and a reason why so many of the horrors of war were visited upon them.

In the century that followed it became Route 3, a fast, modern, multi-lane highway. For several miles, he drove alone, with the sun casting the long shadow of his car ahead of him. The early morning light was bright and sharp, until he began to approach the forests of the Wilderness. Then, almost imperceptibly, the light grew softer and the sun faded to a reddish disc behind him and he was driving through a ghost-like mist. He had arrived on the battlefield of Chancellorsville.

At the beginning of May 1863, Lee had confronted a Union force once again considerably greater than his own, deployed around a clearing in the Wilderness in which stood the house which was to give the battle its name. Lee divided his own army into two parts and sent the larger contingent under his best general, Thomas 'Stonewall' Jackson, on a long, secret march through the forest and around the back of the Union lines. Meantime, Lee himself remained in their front with a force less than a quarter the size of the Union host, feinting up and down to keep them occupied.

The ruse was stunningly successful. Late in the day, Jackson launched a furious attack upon the unsuspecting Union rear and drove them hurtling back. Only nightfall prevented a complete rout. The forest, the confusion, and some luck, allowed the demoralized Union army finally to withdraw across the nearby Rappahannock River to safety.

As soon as he had replenished his forces and supplies, Lee determined to capitalize on his glorious success by marching north, towards the final victory. That next battle, less than two months later, was to be Gettysburg. Hubris indeed.

Bryn turned off the road and drove down a country lane for a mile or so until he found the small clearing in the forest he had been looking for. There were no other cars, no traffic passing through. In the sun-excluding mist, and under the canopy of trees, all was dark, silent and shadowless. He had come here because, like the valley of Pickett's Charge or the bluff overlooking Burnside's Bridge at Antietam, this was a place where the course of history had trembled for a period in the balance.

One reason why Bryn was not a more successful historian was that he had never entirely reconciled two strands in his nature. The academic within him took a broadly deterministic view of events which he saw as driven by forces, mostly economic, beyond the control of individuals. On the other hand he could not resist the impulse to characterize a story in terms of the failures and achievements of the personalities involved. He had always recognized that his attachment to the American Civil War was essentially romantic. It was a mythic struggle between the Greeks and Trojans, and with heroes whose particular genius really did seem to shape events. If Lee was the wily Ulysses, then Jackson – perhaps the most formidable fighter of the War on either side – was the doomed Achilles.

This tiny clearing was where the two of them met up the night before Jackson's Great March through the Wilderness. It was here that they concocted the ruse which was to determine the outcome of the battle. It was here also that Lee and Jackson, comrades in arms together throughout the War, saw each other for the last time.

Bryn stood transfixed by the silence of the forest. No birds sang. Only the faint and intermittent hum of Route 3 somewhere to the north reminded him that this was the twenty-first century.

But he had a duty to perform. He left the clearing and his car behind and threaded his way down a long, dark, winding, little path, back towards the highway. When he reached it, he waited until the road was for a few seconds empty in both directions and then crossed and plunged deep into the forest on the other side. His memory and sense of direction had not failed him. With a shiver of recognition, he knew that he had arrived at one of the most numinous places of the entire conflict.

During the night following the great flanking march and attack, Jackson had reconnoitred ahead into the forest in preparation for the following day. As he returned, he was mistaken by a panicky troop of his own men for a Union soldier and shot down. His arm had to be amputated and he was taken to a place of safety well away from the battlefield ("He has lost his left arm" was Lee's first comment on hearing of his injuries, "but I have lost my right arm"), but he relapsed and a few days later died of pneumonia.

A small scrub-surrounded stone at Bryn's feet now marked the place where the greatest of the dead Southern heroes fell. Early as it was, someone had already visited the shrine before him. A fresh spray of the four-petalled white flowers of the American Dogwood tree lay across the base of the memorial.

He walked on. It was the medieval forest from Grimm's *Children's Tales*. He had to rely on the occasional glimpse of the watery disc of the sun through the trees to preserve his sense of direction. Even now, as he followed the narrow tourist trails with their occasional signposts, it was easy to imagine the disorientation of the troops picking their way through the undifferentiated wilderness. Easy also to picture the confusion and fearfulness of those waiting Confederate soldiers, in the pitch dark, jumping at shadows and sudden horsemen.

He came upon the line of entrenchments where the Confederates had lain. Shallower than the trenches of the First World War and half-hidden under trees, but no less poignant. This was where the soldiers dozed, even while they had to be on the *qui vive* for an attack at any time from an enemy lying in another set of trenches only twenty yards away. It was a place of ghosts, without question. Who could say how many dead bodies lay beneath his feet just here, in the forest dark crypt? A few under-nourished ground squirrels scrabbled noisily in the undergrowth. No doubt some of their ancestors had been an involuntary supplement for the soldiers' inadequate rations.

The Union lines further on were more impressive. But that was because later in the battle the Confederates drove the original occupiers out and excavated them again and added new defensive breastworks facing to the east. It was possible for a historian to trace the fluctuating course of the battle, over the two days, through the condition and orientation of these entrenchments.

He followed the battle lines and the sun until he emerged at last into a large grassy clearing. He had arrived at Chancellorsville itself. There again, a hundred yards to his right, was Route 3 – the Plank Road. The traffic was beginning to build up and cars were flashing past at seventy or eighty miles an hour. In front of him were the ruins of the Chancellorsville house – not much more than a few outlines of stone. He made another note to remind his students that this clearing was also the setting for the main action described in *The Red Badge of Courage* (and that, if they found the academic commentaries heavy going, at least they should read Stephen Crane's civil war novel – the chief merit of which, from their point of view, would be that it was very short).

The house was a metaphor for what had happened to the South. The wealthy Chancellor family owned this part of Virginia. Its tenant farmers were scattered across the other cultivable clearings in the forest. The house was a fine mansion, described in 1846 as "one of the most celebrated houses in Virginia". Well-dressed southern ladies stood on its balconies in late April 1863 and waved to the troops as they passed by. Then the War came to their doorstep and the life of civilized privilege was suddenly over.

One of the family's daughters later wrote of the day the Confederate army swept back through the clearing. "The woods around the house were a sheet of fire, the air was filled with shot and shell; horses were running, rearing and screaming; the men were amass with confusion, moaning, cursing and praying. They were bringing the wounded out of the house for it was on fire in several places [...] at our last look, our old home was completely enveloped in flames... all was destroyed."

He stood on the low ruined wall of the house, watching the cars flying by and occasionally scribbling down his thoughts in his notebook.

It was time to return the way he had come. He planned now to trace the Great March from its starting point in the clearing where he had left his car, to its pitiless dénouement twelve miles later. Jackson's column had been so narrow and long that, marching at more than two miles an hour, it took six hours to pass any given spot. Bryn, however, intended to motor along it.

He spotted the Visitor Center through a gap in the trees. He guessed it would be unlocked now. It was a long time since all that morning coffee. A couple of vehicles, a family saloon and an open-backed pickup truck, had been drawn up in the car park. The building itself appeared empty but the entrance door was ajar. The toilets were easy to find and, thank heavens, open.

As he stood at one of the sinks washing his hands, the door to a cubicle behind him swung back. He looked briefly up at the mirror. The man who was emerging was still putting his jacket back on. Below his left armpit, visible for barely half a second, was a shoulder holster, and in it a large handgun. The man glanced at Bryn's back and discreetly buttoned up. Then he took up a position alongside him and started also to wash his hands.

The man had not seen Bryn's averted face, but Bryn had recognized *him*. It was the hooded man. The man's face was bruised, and there was a small plaster on his chin as if it had been cut while shaving.

Time suspended itself. He was rigid with fear. His right hand, the only part of Bryn's being which seemed still to have life, crept into the pocket of his jacket and his fingers tightened round, not keys this time, but the ridiculous little shaving foam can. It was the best he could manage.

The man lifted his face to the mirror and caught Bryn's wide-eyed gaze. His own pale blue eyes dilated with shock. But before he could do anything else, Bryn snapped open the little can and ejected a stream of foam, with all his force, into the man's face. It was extraordinary the amount it produced. And how powerfully it discharged. The face disappeared almost instantaneously under a cascading heap of white lather. The man lurched backwards, scrabbling at his eyes. Bryn seized the moment to kick his ankles away, knock him back into the cubicle, and flee.

His uncomplicated intention was to race back to his car and get out of Virginia as fast as he could. But for the first time, his sense of direction failed him. Instead of arriving at the highway, he soon found himself deeper in the forest than he had ever been before. The sky had clouded over and the sun was nowhere to be seen. He could hear the distant hum of the traffic but could no longer work out which direction it was coming from. He stood for a while with his fists tensed, listening for clues. He thought he could hear some tourists talking together somewhere nearby in the forest. He decided to join them.

It was a chimera. He found no tourists. He did, however, find a forest path. Since all paths, he reasoned, ended finally at the Visitor Center, he would – very cautiously – follow it until he could see the buildings again, re-orientate himself and work his way back to the road.

He had been travelling down the path for only a few minutes when something occurred which at first he could not understand. There was a rushing sound, not very loud but close at hand, and a tug at his sleeve. He turned reflexively to see what had grabbed him. There was nothing. Not even a spiky shrub. Then he looked at his coat and saw two holes in the left sleeve, a few inches apart. As the truth began to dawn on him, a tree by his shoulder splintered violently, and he flung himself to the ground.

He had been here before. As in Utah, he was surprised to discover how cool and focussed his thoughts immediately became. The first thing to do was change his location. A few yards to his right was a Civil War trench, not very deep but snaking through some conveniently thick undergrowth. He lifted his head warily and peered around. Not more than fifty yards away, advancing slowly through the trees, his face shaded now by a cowboy hat, was his nemesis again. The handgun hung loosely in his right hand. Attached to it was the long, tin-coloured barrel of a silencer.

Bryn waited until the man passed behind a small thicket. Then he hurled himself forward, crouching as close to the ground as he could at full sprint, and dived into the trench. It was shallower than he had expected, hardly a couple of feet. It was just enough for him to scuttle along, like a cockroach on its belly, through the dense brushwood until he reached a junction of entrenchments.

The incoming trench curved away to the left and was deeper and wider. It might have been one of those dug out at more leisure by the Confederates, after they had thrown the enemy back through the forest. He carried on down it. Even if it took him yet further into the forest until he was utterly lost, it was a safer place to be.

Instead, after another ten minutes or so, he began to hear again the noise of the highway, first as a quiet murmur but increasing, as he wriggled closer, to a low, toneless roar. He peeped over the edge of the breastwork. The sun was beginning to disperse the mist. In the distance light flashed back to him through the trees from the reflecting windows of passing cars. Then he saw something that made him duck back down again, heart in mouth, ears pounding, unable even to breathe.

The man was barely thirty yards away, so close he could have thrown a stone at him. But he seemed unaware of his presence. He was standing in the forest with his back to him, the silenced pistol still dangling by his side, looking left and right.

He did not dare move. Even as he lay there, he was conscious of a certain, pathetic irony in his position. He had managed to crawl all the way back to the site of Stonewall Jackson's fatal shooting. There was no more perfect place for a civil war historian to meet his – unmemorialized – end.

He eased along a couple of yards until he was behind a small bush sprouting from the earthwork. Very, very carefully he raised his head to peer over the edge. The man was moving in the general direction of the road, but still with his back towards him. The trench itself curved on through the trees on a course almost parallel with the one the man was taking. He decided to continue on down it.

As he did so, two things became apparent. The man was scouring the forest in a series of slow, methodical sweeps. In due time it was inevitable that a sweep would take him to Bryn's trench and, like the men in the sunken road at Antietam, he would be trapped, helpless, and shortly dead.

But he had noticed too that the rushing traffic also seemed to have a pattern. He remembered that a mile or so away to the east there was a crossroads where the cars were obliged to stop every few minutes for red lights. There was probably something similar to the west. At all events, the traffic was coming in waves: first from the left, then from the right. And at regular intervals there would be a fifteen seconds period of silence when nothing passed.

He crawled on down the entrenchment. It was already getting more shallow. Before long, and probably about a hundred yards before he reached the road, it was likely to peter out and leave him with no cover at all. To make matters worse, he now suspected the man might have picked up the sounds of his progress. He froze in mid movement. The slow footsteps in the dead leaves were, without question, coming closer.

He no longer dared check what was happening. Any movement might give him away.

There was only one choice left to him.

He waited as a mass of cars and lorries raced through from the east, followed by another from the west. For a while the highway was full of traffic streaming past in both directions. He began his countdown, silently mouthing the falling seconds.

He very slowly drew his feet up beneath him and tensed in the position of a sprinter. It was time. He catapulted from the gully with a wild shout. Out of the side of his eye, he caught the man wheeling on the spot and raising the gun. This time it was close enough for him to hear the pop of the silencer – twice. He hurtled through the brush, side-stepping once again with the forgotten skills of the rugby field, grateful for the larger trees near the road and the cover their trunks provided. The man raced after him, firing with apparently little concern for anyone passing on the road. At every second, Bryn expected a pole-axing pain in his chest or stomach. But nothing came.

Just as he had calculated, the road had become clear and empty for a brief interval, waiting for the next dark mass of vehicles to come hurtling from the west. His lungs were screaming with the pain of his effort; but he forced himself into one final sprint. He shot – arms flailing, barely upright – across the highway. And tripped, tottered, and collapsed into a drainage ditch on the other side.

Behind him there was a terrible screaming of tyres. A motorbike was approaching at high speed, already out of control. It crashed ear-splittingly onto its side and hurtled, wheels first, into his assailant standing in the middle of the road, as if rooted in horror. The man's body was flung high into the air and the biker – separated from his careering bike – rolled over and over until he plunged into brushwood at the side of the road.

Around the scene, cars screeched and swerved to a stop. Three or more collided with each other. A few brave and compassionate souls, only partly protected by the cordon of crashed vehicles, jumped out and ran to the two bodies. The leathered biker, wondrously, seemed barely harmed. Within seconds he was on his feet, groggy but intact. The other man, however, lay still on the tarmac.

Bryn was unable to stand. There were no bones broken. But his frame had transformed into jelly. He clambered on all fours out of the ditch and knelt, quivering, by the roadside. A man, probably a doctor, was ministering to the body in the centre of the road. His efforts were evidently futile, but the doctor continued assiduously to bind a huge pad of what looked like cotton wool to the man's head. The cowboy hat had fallen off and come to rest a few yards from Bryn's ditch. As he forced himself to his feet, he looked across at the dying man. He was tanned and completely bald. Not at all the individual he had expected – though he knew the face well enough.

He walked slowly back to the clearing where he had left his car. The tension and adrenalin was seeping out of him and he had become aware of the pain in his body. His ribs ached where he had flung himself to the ground, and the palms of his hands were raw from scrabbling along the trenches. He was also terribly tired. All he wanted now was to climb back into his vehicle, drive twenty miles away or so, and lie back and sleep.

At first he thought he must have mistaken the clearing. There was no sign anywhere of his car. Perhaps he had misremembered where he had parked it. He walked up and down the road, searching for it. But it was, unequivocally, gone. Stolen, though he thought he had taken every precaution when he left it. He sat down, exhausted, on a wooden bench at the entrance to the clearing and under the explanatory sign. "At this place, General Robert E Lee and General Thomas 'Stonewall' Jackson met for the last time…"

As he brooded on what to do next, a large black car with opaque, tinted windows came slowly and silently down the road towards him. It was a Lincoln Continental Sedan; not at all the kind of vehicle you would expect on a country lane. Two men were visible through the front windscreen. The driver was a crew-cut man, wearing reflective sunglasses and leather gloves. The face of the passenger was obscured by a sun visor. By the time the car had come to a halt alongside his bench, it was too late for Bryn to flee.

The rear window behind the driver slid down with a quiet, electronic hum and an Oxbridge voice from the recesses of the back seat drawled: "Looks like you need a lift."

And then, after a pause: "Old boy."

Chapter 22

It was cousin Marcus.

Bryn was too dazed and confused to ask for explanations. He climbed into the limousine and accepted the small white plastic cup that was passed wordlessly to him. It was Bourbon and rather good. As he sipped from it, the shivering he had experienced half an hour previously surged up through his body again. The cup shook in his hand and a few drops of the whiskey slopped onto the floor of the car. Marcus gently took it back.

"How are you feeling, old boy?" he said.

Bryn nodded and smiled. The shivering abated and he took the cup and sipped some more. He felt better already. He looked at his cousin, dressed as ever in a neat, dark grey suit with the hint of a pin-stripe running through. He was even wearing his Travellers Club tie.

"This is a dream," he said.

Marcus laughed.

"Bit of a nightmare, perhaps," he replied. "But I think you'll find it's over now."

At that point, the man in the front passenger seat turned round towards Bryn and gave a minatory shake of his head.

"Good to get a chance to talk to you. At last..." he said, grimacing.

The southern, probably Texan, accent was as familiar as the pale, bruised face, still with traces of shaving foam around the ears.

For a second, Bryn's instinct was to get out, fast; and his hand was already halfway to the door release when Marcus pressed him firmly back into his seat. The car executed a U-turn at the forest crossroads and began to accelerate towards the high road.

"This is Miles Archer," said Marcus. "And it could be you owe him an apology. His assignment for the last six months has been to take care of you, and he's done a better job than you realize."

"Marcus," said Bryn, deep in the sea of his confusion, "Who *are* you, who is Miles, and what are you all doing here?"

His cousin did not answer. He leaned forward to look up the road, quietly chuckling to himself.

The car had arrived at the turn-off from Route 3. A quarter of a mile away to the west, the traffic was easing its way past the remains of the accident. Two police cars were parked up, roof lamps blazing.

"Straight to Reagan?" queried the driver.

Marcus nodded back into the mirror, and the Lincoln turned east towards Fredericksburg.

"I'm taking you to Ronald Reagan Airport," said Marcus. "We'll be going back together. It's the Foreign Secretary's plane so it will be full of officials. Of whom you will be one. We've got all your baggage in the boot here, so you don't have to worry about anything. The sooner we get you back to Marion the better."

It was Bryn's turn to laugh: half a giggle, half a long, expiring sigh. He was becoming quite light-headed.

"Aren't you going to tell me *anything*, Marcus?" he said.

"Why not? I might tell you everything. Enjoy your whiskey."

He took out his BlackBerry and checked his messages, then switched it off and gazed out of the window for a while.

"First of all, Bryn," he said at last, "you should know – though I really thought you might have guessed it years ago – that I work for the Foreign Office Secret Intelligence Service. What

236

you call MI6. I always have worked for them. Quite early on in my FCO career, shortly after Cambridge and before I was even posted, I was invited to join the SIS on the understanding that – though I might go to the top – I would forfeit the chance of actually getting an ambassadorship. Well, I have got to the top, or thereabouts. My job now is head of operations which means that I am number two or, if you like, 'M'. For Marcus, naturally. All this used to be deadly confidential, which is why I had to pretend that my postings to Moscow, Pretoria and so on were ordinary First Secretary and Counsellor jobs. But these days, it's about transparency and freedom of information.

"All the same," he continued, after a slight pause, "I would ask you to treat everything I am about to say *from here on* in absolute confidence. Otherwise," he concluded mildly, "this conversation ends now."

"Certainly," said Bryn, already reeling from the difficulty of having to recalibrate everything he had ever assumed about his cousin.

"And this friendly guy, Miles, works for the Central Intelligence Agency out of Washington. You should feel flattered to have him on your case. Because of Roosevelt's involvement, the CIA let us have one of their top weapons men. What Miles doesn't know about a *Heckler and Koch PTR91* wouldn't cover a postage stamp."

The man in the front passenger seat smirked into the mirror.

"Perhaps I should start around the point Miles got involved..." Marcus continued.

The Lincoln, without slacking its speed, swung through the intersection with the main Washington to Richmond motorway outside Fredericksburg, and headed north. They must have been travelling at 90 or 100 miles an hour, but there was almost no sensation of speed. Bryn doubted if he had ever experienced a smoother, quieter, or more luxurious ride.

Marcus was still talking.

"I guess it all began when we picked up some information through the CIA that Jack Smith's people had assigned an

237

operative to track down and terminate one of our agents. The CIA *assumed* it was one of our boys."

"You're going too fast," said Bryn. "What is this about Jack Smith?"

"Just bear with me," said Marcus, with a flicker of irritation. "Let's say that the CIA has had an eye on his organization for some time because of his international connections, and – naturally – our people have given what help they can. Only low level surveillance because, well, he has a lot of influence. And everything could change with a new President. But you can't ignore rumours – more than rumours – of unlawful enforcement activities, including on the British patch. I mean terminations."

"You mean, killing people?"

"That is the normal meaning, yes… Smith had a man – an enforcer – who had been working with him from the earliest days. I got word through my CIA oppo in Washington that he had been sent to make a hit in London on a target who had got some explosive information about the organization. That's why they assumed a British agent. It would be about the start of this year…"

He paused.

"Do you remember our lunch together at the Travellers in February?"

Bryn nodded.

"I already knew about the intended hit, and our people had been alerted. But, at that stage, it just didn't make any sense. None of our agents, so far as we knew, fitted the CIA bill and none who *might* have done were in London anyway. And then you told me about those near accidents of yours. The speeding car and the incident at Oxford Circus. Both of them exactly the kind of 'accident' this guy specializes in. I mean, I couldn't take your story *that* seriously. After all, it was only you… But a week or so later, I had one of my regular briefing meetings in Washington and I asked the CIA if their informant had any more intelligence about who Smith was after. They conceded that it was now looking less likely that the target was any of our agents. It was beginning to look like Smith was after some freelance civilian."

He looked across at Bryn.

"I know the next bit will astonish you," he said. "But the fact of the matter is that I became worried. About *you*. I still couldn't see how you could possibly have got involved. But there were some alarming indicators: the 'accidents', you actually meeting Smith, the dangerous connection with Weiskopf. Then you told me you were travelling to the States."

"Ken Burns told you," said Bryn, recalling his irritation at confidentialities so easily exchanged.

"Maybe," said Marcus. "It occurred to me that, once that was known to Smith's people, and it was pretty sure to be – "

"How? How would it be known to them?" interrupted Bryn. Marcus ignored him.

"Once that was known to them, they would pull out of the London operation, which in any case wasn't working out, and go for you on their home turf. If the target really was you, that is. But I just didn't feel I could take a chance, however little sense it made."

"I think I can help you there," said Bryn.

Marcus ignored him again.

"So I asked the CIA if they *might* keep an eye open while you were there. I didn't expect them to do much. And really I had no right. But – without telling me – my CIA friend put a tail on you the moment you arrived in Chicago. And that of course was Miles."

The man in the front grimaced again at them in the mirror.

"So that's why I was detained at O'Hare?" said Bryn.

"Oh, I expect so. The CIA would have tagged your name on the computer. And Miles would have needed a little time to get into position."

The man in front nodded.

"Well then," continued Marcus. "The information we started receiving from Miles did not impress us. First off, frankly, you getting close up with Ms Weiskopf did not help your cause. At all. Her radical friends are not popular with my friends. Miles' boss was inclined to pull him out there and then and leave you to stew in your own left-wing activist juices. And I think he would have done had Smith's people not caught up with her. Miles found her after she had been worked over by them, and suggested she make herself scarce. But she also confirmed to him that they had been asking about you, which was the *first* time we could be certain you were the target. And then of course Miles saved your life. Twice."

"Thank you, Miles," said Bryn, completely bemused by now.

"You really don't know, do you," drawled the Texan, without turning.

"Tell him," said Marcus.

"Should I tell him about Chicago, too?"

"Why not?" said Marcus.

"Righty-ho…" said the Texan. "I guess you never sussed out that Smith's guy was onto you from the moment you touched down. Or anyway, from the first time you used a credit card. All the killer had to do was to track your transactions on his iPhone. He knew you were going to the opera that first night. I just had to be there, shadowing you, but visible so the guy would know you were protected. He probably intended to terminate you during that performance of Cosy Fanny Tooty. So thank you, professor, for making me stand outside the Lyric for a whole evening. He turned up and he saw me all right. And he left.

"Now the big problem," he continued, clearly none too pleased, "was the next night when you decided *suddenly* to go to the Symphony Orchestra concert and went online to book your ticket. So the killer picked that up on his phone and of course rang the Box Office saying he was you and he'd forgotten to print off his ticket details: 'What was the seat number again?' The tough part is we only found out about it later and anyways I was across the road from the hotel waiting for you to come out. Oh by the way, why *didn't* you go to the concert?"

"I overslept," said Bryn. "Jetlag."

"Sure. Anyway, thanks to you, the guy sitting in your seat got it."

"The man that died? In the news?"

"Oh sure. It's like this. You didn't turn up. So a good seat is unoccupied and this other guy, who is a standee, spots it from the balcony and takes it for the second half. Then Smith's man comes in, sees the target in the seat and thinks it's you. And kills him. One unlucky dude."

"In full view of everybody?" Marcus interrupted.

"We don't know for sure yet how he did it. But it looks like he waited until the end, and the usual huge, standing, ovation. Then threaded his way down through the people on their feet in the aisles, applauding, quietly made his hit, and left. We don't know even if the victim felt it. But if he yelled, no-one was paying any attention. Good professional job."

There was something quite disturbing about Marcus and Miles' dispassionate rehearsal of the details of the murder.

"The killer probably used a lethal injection from behind," the other added. "It's his preferred method when he's in a public place. Usually potassium cyanide, the same stuff that Jim Jones killed his followers with in Guyana back in '78. The symptoms are suffocation and heart failure – which means the local police think it's natural causes and don't catch on, if ever, until the hitman is long gone. Good methodology. As you can see, it still works."

He nodded his head in appreciation.

Marcus took over.

"And then of course," he said, "they thought you were dead. When they roughed up Zelma Weiskopf, two or three days later, they thought all they were doing was checking whether you had passed anything on to her previously."

The man in front sniggered.

"Unfortunately," Marcus continued, "she revealed that she had seen you in Ann Arbor *the day before*. Which I guess was a bit of a shock to them. According to our CIA mole in the organization, there was a lot of loud shouting in Smith's office. And Roosevelt was despatched, again, to finish the job off. By then of course you were on your way to Salt Lake City. Where we lost you."

"But we didn't lose the guy following you," said Miles. "Which is why I wound up halfway up a cliffside in Zion Canyon, watching him – *not* you. Then you turn up out of the blue, he pulls out his 9mm PPK – screws on his silencer – and I shoot him. Well, sorry. I winged him, for sure. But he pulled out. Which makes twice I saved your life. No need to thank me, bud."

Bryn had no idea what to say. There was a sneering quality about the man in the front seat, which he detested. He also felt humiliated by their narrative of his incompetence and vulnerability. It was probably best to just sit there and let them enjoy their professional superiority.

"Unfortunately, Miles did not quite manage to terminate the terminator," said Marcus. "And he returned to London – we thought, to finish the business with you, though it turned out he had more than one job in mind. At all events, I thought I'd try and frighten him off. So I set up our lunch at Merryweather's because, if he *was* tracking you, he would see you there with me and appreciate what he was dealing with. And indeed it seems that he did then take counsel, and things went quiet, at least on your front."

A deeply disturbing thought gathered in Bryn's mind.

"What was the killer's other business in London?"

Marcus seemed reluctant at first to answer. Bryn sensed also some discomfort from their Texan companion.

"It's something which, frankly, we don't understand," Marcus said slowly. "There are, let's say, ramifications. But, yes, it was your friend Graeme. You've probably realized – same modus operandi as in Chicago. Not difficult to make it look like suffocation during sex. Sorry about that, Bryn."

"But why *Graeme*? How does he come into this? You're sure it's not that they thought he was me?"

"No, no, no. They knew it was him all right. It wasn't an accident and it wasn't a coincidence. There is a reason why the pair of you, friends, have been targeted, we're clear about that. You do have certain things in common. Even so, we cannot yet say for sure why they killed him and we still don't know why they were after *you*…"

"I think I might be able to explain that," said Bryn quietly.

"Really?" said Marcus. "Well, well. That would be useful."

Bryn told him about the briefcase and its contents and how it all fell into his hands. About the sheets of paper and the lists. He was careful, however, not to refer to the photograph hidden at the bottom of the case. Marshall, for all his shortcomings, was still his friend and he did not feel that the contents of that particular image were any business of Marcus's. Not yet.

Marcus made some notes. He recorded the few names Bryn could recall, the sums of money, the references to pledges. He commented that these discoveries were not inconsistent with other information they had gathered. Then he laid down his pen and gave Bryn his analysis of what had actually happened over the last few months.

It seemed to him obvious now that Smith had – initially – assumed Bryn to be a cheap thief who intended to use the incriminating papers for blackmail or to sell to the highest bidder. It was very likely that, after the earliest attempts to kill him, a decision had been taken to let him alone while they concentrated on finding out who his contacts might be. Eventually – and this would have been by the time Bryn left for Chicago – Smith would have satisfied himself that Bryn was working alone and that the case could be closed with his termination. He would certainly have intended to finish the job in London after the Utah debacle. But, Marcus congratulated himself, the subsequent revelation that Bryn knew *him* must have come as a real shock. It would certainly explain why nothing then happened for a few months.

"So... where are all the papers now?" asked Marcus, with relish. "In the boot?"

"I'm afraid not," said Bryn. "It seemed to me sensible at the time to give them to a mutual friend who could return them to Jack Smith. I thought that would stop the whole business."

Marcus quietly absorbed this hammer blow. He looked quite deflated.

"Who was this man you gave the papers to?" he said at last.

"Marshall. My recorder group friend. I've mentioned him before."

Marcus sighed.

"Why should I imagine you would do otherwise?"

He paused to collect himself.

"Can I just give you one piece of advice? Since I've told you so much already… *in confidence*… I might as well tell you also that your friend Marshall is not exactly unknown to us. In fact he may be quite close to the centre of this whole business. And that," he continued, pre-empting Bryn's attempt at an interruption, "is as much as I will tell you at this stage. May I just suggest… may I suggest that you steer clear of Mister Marshall. For the time being?"

He turned away and gazed silently out of the window.

They were approaching Ronald Reagan National Airport.

There were still a huge number of questions that Bryn would have liked to have put. One in particular.

"Marcus," he said at last. "Who *was* that guy?"

"Who was who?"

"The bald guy."

His cousin continued to gaze miserably out of the window.

"Roosevelt?" he replied. "He's dead, Bryn. You left him in the middle of the road, remember? You did a good job getting away from him. To tell you the truth, I thought – after you had given Miles the slip this morning – that he would be sure to nail you. So: be grateful, and forget about him."

"What was his name, again?"

"We don't know his real name, or very much at all. He was a Vietnam vet which would explain some of his skills. And he start calling himself Edward Roosevelt when he got a veteran's scholarship to study drama. He was an actor and was successful for a while. Then it seems he killed someone in a brawl and needed to get away. So he moved to the UK. He went into porn… which, incidentally, is how he knew your friend Graeme. And that of course is why your friend got into Roosevelt's car so happily that night. For his last ride.

"Anyway, after his porn period, Roosevelt suddenly had an evangelical conversion. One extreme to the other. He started working for Smith's church. Who knows how long the new born-again Roosevelt would have lasted but the fact is Smith found out about his background and persuaded him to do some jobs for him. He probably didn't have much choice. And eventually he became Smith's private hitman. That's about it."

Bryn gave himself a few moments to take this all in. Perhaps there was one other last question, after all.

"Marcus... am I out of it now? Am I *safe*?"

His cousin made a gurgling noise. The gurgles turned into a coughing fit and he reached out for the last of Bryn's cup of Bourbon. After he had cleared his throat, he turned back and looked him full in the face.

"Bryn," he said. "Let's just get you back to England. You'll be safe there, I think I can promise you. Well, *you* will be..."

And he left it at that.

CODA

Chapter 23

The flight did not take off until very late that evening. Apparently the Foreign Secretary had been irresistibly delayed by a late invitation to dinner in Foggy Bottom. The aeroplane itself was from the RAF's Royal Squadron, with seats facing backwards and separate passenger compartments. When the Minister finally arrived, he was accommodated in the rear with a handful of senior officials. Bryn was assigned a place in the middle, with the more junior passengers.

The aircraft was slower than a commercial passenger jet and there was very little for him to do except sleep. He saw nothing of Marcus until briefly before the plane touched down at Northolt Airport. His cousin came through from the rear of the aircraft to let him know that a car was waiting for him. After that, the journey down the A40 was a short one and he was home within twenty minutes of landing.

He had not warned Marion about his early return. Her little car was missing from the driveway and the house was empty. A pile of uncollected mail lay on the hall floor by the front door. It was an unusually large pile, as though it had accumulated over more than a single day. He threw the letters on the kitchen table, switched on his computer and went to make himself a cup of coffee. There was a cafetiere standing in the sink, the coffee grounds already hardening with age. He swilled it through irritably with cold water and upended it on the draining surface.

Because he had been checking his inbox in America whenever he had had a chance, there were not many emails. One, however, leapt out at him immediately. It bore no message and no sign off. It consisted only of its subject heading: *We'll always have Ann Arbor.*

It was not so much the laconic nature of the sentence – terminal and facetious at the same time – that disconcerted him, as the fact that it had been opened. Someone from his office had unhelpfully forwarded it a couple of days previously, along with a few items of UCL intranet correspondence. He wondered how much Marion would have been able to read into it.

Fortunately, the email had originated from the anonymous hotmail address Zelma had used before. He typed in his own, laconic, reply: *Here's looking at you kid.* Then something more fastidious within him rebelled and he deleted the message. After a little more thought, he retyped briefly: *No matter what the future brings.* When he had pressed the send button, he wished he could have managed to be more final, or less cute.

There was a message from Ken Burns asking for a chat about the new year's arrangements when he got back. It was unlikely to be very important, but he decided anyway to pop into UCL to see him the next morning.

There was nothing from his agent. He sent her an email suggesting that, before the book was any further progressed, she should clarify Showalter's intentions in relation to non-UK rights. But he was now pretty well convinced that they would hear no more on this, or on any other subject, from New York.

He sorted through the letters he had thrown on the table. One of them had an American stamp. It was from Dan Buchanan, his Mormon friend from Provo, Utah, and it enclosed an advertisement for a full professorship in American Studies at the rival Western University of Utah in Salt Lake City. Dan's scrawl was as difficult to read as ever. Nevertheless, the plain upshot was that he believed the job to be tailor-made for Bryn, if he wanted it. The main requirement was that he teach courses in American History since the Founding Fathers, but with an emphasis upon military policy and the Civil War. What was more, he should know that the Departmental Chair had – at Dan's invitation – attended his lecture at Brigham Young University in March and been greatly impressed. Bryn might recall him putting a question at the end.

Bryn knew that Dan would not have written in these terms unless he was confident that the job was pretty well his for the asking. And at any other time in his career, he would probably have leapt at it. Now he was full of uncertainty. Maybe he should discuss it with Marion first. Or Marcus.

He folded the letter and the advertisement together and put them in his inside jacket pocket. As he did so, he noticed again the two small holes in his left sleeve. He gazed at them in a trance. They seemed now as distant a souvenir as moon rock. And the ordeal they recalled, a story that had been told to him by someone else.

He started to shiver again.

He needed to go for a walk. He put his jacket back on and wound a scarf round his neck against the cheerless London weather. He walked south, through a couple of Ealing's many parks, until he reached the Common. A Russian circus was camped untidily in the middle of the open green space. Along the Common's western edge stood the stately, grand Victorian mansions, drawn up in line as if facing down change. On its eastern side, the North Circular traffic streamed past, like debris on floodwater.

It was the matinée interval. He stopped and watched as the little family groups – English, Polish, Asian – scattered across the churned-up grass outside the circus tent, sucking on their candy-floss and nibbling their hot-dogs. He remembered doing exactly the same with his own family years ago, when the children were young, before animals were banned and while the circus was still, at least nominally, a home-grown enterprise.

He was reluctant to move on. A wedding cortège came up

the Uxbridge Road from the west, led by a black London taxi with red ribbons flapping across the bonnet. It turned into the forecourt of a motel on the north side of the Common and decanted a young bride and her new, red-turbanned Sikh husband. The arriving guests piled out from their cars. Some hugged and kissed the happy couple. Others took pictures with their mobile phones. Two little girls in white dresses threw what appeared to be rice at the bride and groom. Then the crowd parted while a small group of large, elderly, sari-clad matrons were escorted through by some bare-headed young men in smart business suits. Bryn watched until the last of the happy crowd had disappeared into the motel, and turned homewards.

As he walked up the street past Marshall's house he saw Marion's little car ahead of him, parked by the kerb. He was easing his pace, with half a mind to take a detour to avoid passing it, when the car began to pull away from the pavement. Twenty yards further on, it stopped in the middle of the road. He carried on until he was level with Marshall's house and then, on a whim, turned into the drive. He heard the car start up again and drive away.

He had never intended to visit Marshall. The sitting room curtains, he noticed, were drawn. He could, if he wished, turn round now and walk away up the road.

He paused only for a moment. Then he pressed the bell.

It took Marshall a while to open the door. He frowned, as if irritated by the interruption, seemed at first not to know what to do, then invited him in with a wordless gesture towards the sitting-room.

He was noticeably the worse for wear. Unshaven, sweaty-faced, in his stockinged feet. He also seemed distracted. The television was on in the corner, tuned to a teletext channel with the sound turned off. A bottle of *Virginia Gentleman* stood in the beam of a small table lamp, alongside a jug of ice cubes and two glasses. One was half-full. The other was clean and empty.

"How are you feeling, Bryn?" he said briefly, and sat down beside his glass.

He waved vaguely towards the second one.

Bryn looked around the room. Marshall had lived alone for ten or fifteen years, since his wife had moved out. A Polish housekeeper came in most days of the week to clear up and clean so that invariably, whenever the recorder group visited for one of its monthly sessions, it was as neat and tidy as a photo-shoot for an interior design magazine. Not so now. Some pieces of Louis Vuitton luggage sat in the centre of the room, open but still half packed. A gabardine overcoat had fallen off the settee onto the floor. A number of documents had been scattered around and no attempt made to tidy them up.

Bryn watched him while he nibbled absently at the edge of a thumb-nail. It had always been a joke in the recorder group that Marshall, the most poised and successful of them all, had finger-nails chewed to the quick and beyond. And yet, it occurred to Bryn, he had never before seen him with a hand to his mouth, in all the years they had been friends. Even if he could not hide his ravaged nails and the tensions they signalled, at least the process of demolition had remained private.

"How did things go in New York?" Marshall enquired.

"I was going to ask the same of you," said Bryn.

He helped himself to some of the whiskey. It tasted better than he remembered; perhaps it was a more up-market version.

"I'm getting out," said Marshall shortly. "Tomorrow. Time to move on."

It was at this point that Bryn registered the black Pickett attaché case he had left with Marshall in the Waldorf Astoria. It was lying open beside his chair. *There* were the incriminating documents in their plastic folder – half out of the case, half in it, the plastic glistening in the light of the table lamp.

He gaped at the papers incredulously.

"Marshall, what in Christ's sake…" he gasped, with sudden rising consternation. "What in Christ's sake have you got there?"

He leant forward to pick the folder up but Marshall's hand, still holding the whiskey glass, lurched out to intercept him and Bourbon slopped down Bryn's sleeve. With his other hand, Marshall closed the case and pushed it under his chair.

Bryn was barely articulate with fury and began – something he never did – to shout at the other man.

"Fuck this, Marshall! You were supposed to return... fucking return that and sort... fucking sort things out... for Christ's sake, Marshall!"

The other made rapid ameliorating gestures with both hands. He started pulling out a handkerchief to mop Bryn's sleeve.

"It's OK, Bryn," he said. "It's OK."

"It is *not* OK. It is *so* not."

In his outrage he was beginning to sound like one of his own children.

"Bryn. Bryn. Bryn."

Marshall made another of his calming movements.

"You *are* off the hook. They know *I* have the papers. Not you."

He leaned towards him with his elbows on his knees, his eyes fixed on Bryn's, and the fingers of his free hand fluttering urgently in Bryn's face.

It took a while for Marshall's words to sink in. The storm passed as rapidly as it had arisen.

When Bryn spoke, his voice was almost a whisper.

"What are you telling me? Are you telling me you're blackmailing them, is that what you're doing?" he said.

Marshall suddenly laughed. For the first time in their conversation he looked, for a moment, as if whatever was oppressing him had passed away. He shook his head and smiled at Bryn affectionately.

"No I'm not," he said. "It's for my protection. It's insurance."

"Against what?"

"Ah..."

He paused as if collecting his thoughts.

"You see, when you gave me the papers," he continued, "I knew at once *I* was in trouble. Because if I had still been trusted, I would have known about you taking the attaché case, they would have told me immediately."

He ran a finger around the rim of his whiskey glass. It vibrated softly.

"And then later I got a call from a source of my own. I learned that you had been followed to the Waldorf last week and seen with me. When Smith arrived, he was already being briefed on his ear-piece about our meeting. And he never said a word to me about it."

"Briefed by Roosevelt," said Bryn.

"Yes. There is a background to this. I have been working within the organization – secretly, obviously – on some investment plans of my own for some while now."

He looked at Bryn sadly.

"I dare say I'm not quite the sea-green incorruptible you took me for..."

He paused again before continuing.

"And then – I suppose it was inevitable – I began to suspect that Smith or Darke, it comes to the same thing, were on to me. New York confirmed my suspicions. So now I need to cash in my assets and move on. Not the UK or the States. Somewhere else. I'm flying out tomorrow before they have a chance to come after me."

"Did you know Roosevelt is dead?"

A succession of emotions passed across Marshall's face. Puzzlement at first, then curiosity and respect, resolving finally into incredulity.

Bryn explained about Chancellorsville and his last sight of the body. He was careful not to mention his cousin's involvement, and was grateful that Marshall's normally forensic mind was otherwise engaged, or sufficiently dulled by drink, not to ask a few of the more obvious, and difficult, questions.

There was a very long silence.

"Roosevelt killed Graeme, didn't he?" said Bryn at last.

Marshall nodded.

"Were you involved in it?"

Marshall refilled his glass and breathed deeply.

He had seen him only once or twice in his cups before. The effect had always been to exaggerate his self-confidence and command. But what seemed to be coming through this time was something softer and without arrogance. He seemed anxious to share his thoughts. Nobody had ever in the past claimed a 'close' friendship with Marshall. He had always been too sealed up in his private ivory tower. Now they were almost friends on equal terms. Comrades in arms.

"When I was very young," he started, "I took a brief from a guy I knew at school called Harry Darke."

Bryn nodded his understanding of the reference.

"Darke was in the porn video business and the CPS was trying to close him down. I had a legal strategy that took us finally to the Human Rights Court in Strasbourg where, in effect, we won. There was a party in Birmingham to celebrate. As I say, I was very young. There were a lot of beautiful people and a lot of Louis Roederer *Cristal*, as I recall, which of course I had never drunk in my life.

"Then years later, after a recorder group evening as it happens, I think it was at your house, I was walking home with Graeme when he produced the picture you have seen. I had absolutely no recollection of it, but there it was. Apparently Graeme had been given it by a friend, maybe the original photographer... who had subsequently died of Aids. At first I thought Graeme was being helpful – because he told me that there were only two copies and Harry Darke had the other one...

"The next day, I rang him up and asked for his copy anyway and he wouldn't give it me. He continued to carry it around in his case with his recorder music, and he made sure I knew. At first he used to ask for a bit of financial help when things weren't going so well. Nothing substantial and I just let it go. But over the years he began to raise the ante, as blackmailers do, to fund those expeditions to Bayreuth with his friends. I – far too late – decided enough was enough and called his bluff; and he threatened to expose me to the papers. That was early this year...

"So I spoke to Harry. He was very sympathetic. He said he'd long since destroyed his own copy – of course I know now that he must have given it to Jack Smith – and that he would arrange a little burglary to retrieve Graeme's."

He sat for a moment, circling the ice cubes around his glass. Then he continued.

"What I hadn't anticipated was that Harry would decide to use our friend Roosevelt, because... as you well know... he happened to be in London on other business. Even so, I think the idea was that Roosevelt would put the fear of God into Graeme, have him hand over the photo, and leave it at that. What I now believe happened was that, after Graeme had got into Roosevelt's car with his music case and the photo in it, Roosevelt for some reason rang through to Smith on his mobile and Smith instructed him to terminate him."

He stopped. He remained silent, gazing at the ice cubes in his glass.

"So what happened to Graeme's photo?" asked Bryn eventually.

"Roosevelt destroyed it. That's what I was told."

"Do you think Graeme might have kept another copy?"

"Well I suppose that was the flaw in the plan. But he's dead, anyway."

Bryn said nothing.

"I recognize that I am of course to blame for Graeme's death," said Marshall quietly. "There's no escaping that. I am perhaps not quite as clever as I thought I was.

"Well," he said, draining his glass, "that's all academic now. Where I am going, neither Smith nor Darke nor the tabloids will find me."

"Are you going alone?"

Marshall sighed. He shook his head slowly and deliberately. "There was nothing between us, Bryn."

"I don't believe you."

"I wish you would," he said earnestly. "I am out of here. Marion is no part of that and she would never want to be. She would never leave you. If she ever left London, it would only be with you."

"Is that so?" said Bryn aggressively. "What about the professorship then? Did you not recommend me to Smith because you reckoned she *would* stay here? For you?"

257

"I might have thought that once. I don't now."

"And what about the burglary?"

There was an unfamiliar, small, bullying flame within him which he did not like but which seemed determined to have its say. He didn't even like the direction the interrogation was taking. "What about the burglary, Marshall?" he asked. "What were you doing with her then?"

He was shocked by his own crudity. But his friend, with almost professional grace, answered as if he only heard the first of the two questions.

"I'm sorry about that too. My only purpose was to make sure she was out of the house so that Roosevelt could do the job. You *should* keep your wife better informed, Bryn. She was sure you would be out all day. And I thought I could rely on that."

He shuddered and looked genuinely distressed.

"If you had come back only ten minutes earlier than you did, I'm afraid you would now be dead. Roosevelt didn't find the attaché case – which of course I didn't know he was looking for – but he did get your laptop, which meant that all your contacts, credit cards, everything, was known to Smith. Oh and by the way, if you think that twice-deleting makes you secure, there are people who can retrieve anything from your hard drive, however many times you attempt to erase it."

Bryn thought about this for a moment. It occurred to him that, if Roosevelt and Smith had used his laptop to track his movements, they would also have discovered his email exchanges with Marcus. That might have been the real reason why they had backed off from any further attempt to dispose of him in London.

He remembered the old Rover 75 parked outside Marshall's house earlier in the summer, with its personalized number plate and the torn *Computer Nerds Rule* sticker.

"Would the person retrieving all this stuff be Dave Devine?" he asked.

"Oh yes," said Marshall. He shrugged his shoulders.

"And he's your source? He is your mole within the Darke/Smith organization."

"That's correct," said Marshall.

"Are you sure you should be telling me all this?"

"Oh Bryn," he laughed. "Tomorrow it won't matter anyway."

Bryn got up from his chair. He seemed to have passed through his attack of jealousy. At least his rival would be permanently out of the way.

Marshall put down his glass and rose to his feet. They clasped hands.

"Bryn," he said. "Before you go, I want to give you something."

He cast around uncertainly for a while and then made a little sortie to an antique corner cupboard at the far end of the room. He came back carrying a small rectangular wooden box about a foot or so long, with a tiny lock attached to it. It looked like a coffin for a small, thin dog. Marshall took out a pen and wrote something on it.

"It's a piece of American history," he said. "And I want you to enjoy it."

He thrust the object into Bryn's hands.

They went together to the door. They stood for a while on the step, looking out at the road beyond.

"I'm sorry it took so long to get to know each other properly," said Marshall eventually.

"So am I," said Bryn.

They grasped each other abruptly in a bear-hug and then, with a little mutual embarrassment, broke apart and shook hands again. Marshall was still looking after him as Bryn reached the street.

Chapter 24

Marion's car was in its usual place when he got home. She did not ask him where he had been and he did not mention his visit to Marshall. Nor did she say anything about the email from Zelma. He gave a carefully edited account of his latest American adventures – omitting again Zelma and any reference to the events in Virginia.

They ate their pasta supper largely in silence. Marion elected to go to bed early, and when he finally joined her she was deep in slumber, or affecting to be.

He did not sleep well himself, and rose with the dawn. It occurred to him that he might as well impress Ken Burns by turning up in Gower Street ahead of the scrum, and when Ken was likely to be the only academic at his desk. He left a message for Marion on the kitchen table and set off for the station.

He did not take in the maroon Mercedes until he was nearly upon it. It was parked neatly by the kerb outside Marshall's house. Even then, he gave it only a brief glance as he walked by – sufficient to notice that both front windows were wound down and there was, of all things, a bible on the front passenger seat. But his mind was on his meeting with Ken, and the early morning stream of commuting pedestrians swept him on.

He was another thirty or forty yards down the road before the singularity of what he had seen registered with him and caused him to slow up and look back. A man was leaving Marshall's house, leaning on a stick and limping badly. He wore a trilby hat and an unbuttoned black overcoat and his tanned face was thin and intent. It was a ghost from another world.

Bryn shrank back into a private driveway and ducked behind a parked car. He was grateful for the flow of commuters. As the Mercedes purred past him, he caught a glimpse of a profile he had thought never to see again, concentrated now on the road ahead. Almost at the last second, his presence of mind returned and he pulled the advertisement for the Utah professorship out of his pocket — and scribbled on it the rear plate registration number.

He started back. He sprinted the last thirty or forty yards to the house. The frame alongside the front door lock had been splintered exactly as his own had been back in April. The door was slightly open. He pushed through and went directly to the sitting room.

It was much as he had last seen it, with suitcases partly opened and the whiskey glasses and bottle still on the table – though there were no ice-cubes now in the jug, only water. Marshall was also still there, in the same clothes as the previous evening, except that he was now barefoot and his socks lay neatly side by side on the carpet.

And he was dead. He was sitting back in his chair, with his mouth and eyes slightly open. At the centre of his forehead was a dark red circle within a surrounding pink aureole, like a tiny sunspot. At first, there seemed to be no blood apart from the small, hardening gobbet where the bullet had entered. But when Bryn peered closer, he saw that the fabric of the chair behind Marshall's head was red and wet. And that the shiny patch was spreading slowly outwards.

It was the first time he had ever been close up with a corpse. He had that old shivering urge to throw up, just as on those two occasions before, and he walked away to the end of the room to compose himself.

For a while, whenever he looked back at his friend, the impulse to be sick overtook him again. It was a few moments before he could breath more freely. His heart-beat settled and his mind came back into focus. He looked around the room. Two things he now saw were different. His Pickett attaché case and the papers had disappeared. And – lying serenely and absurdly on the settee, neatly rolled and buttoned – was a Cardiff Bluebirds umbrella.

He picked up the telephone and dialled his cousin. No secretary intercepted the call this time and he was, within a couple of rings, straight through to Marcus.

"Hello Bryn," he said, before he could open his mouth. "Is everything OK?"

He explained the situation as dispassionately as he could, between a few more pauses to drag air into his lungs and recompose himself. When he had finished, Marcus for a while made no reply. He wondered if he was still listening. Then he heard his cousin's voice quite faintly, as if in the middle distance, talking quickly and urgently.

"Marcus?"

The voice came back to him.

"Where are you now?"

"In the sitting room. With his body."

"Stay there. The safest place for you is the place Roosevelt just left. So don't move. There'll be a car outside any moment. I'll be coming over."

"Do you need the address?"

"Of course I know the address."

He put the phone down. He did not have to wait long. Within minutes, he saw through the half-drawn curtains a dark medium-sized saloon drawing up alongside the house. A youngish man in jeans and a leather jacket got out and walked up the drive. He watched him come to a halt just short of the front door. And there he stayed, face on to the road like a sentry. He was talking into a small button in his lapel, but too quietly for Bryn to hear him.

262

He turned back to the body in the chair. It was extraordinary how quickly you got used to death and how banal it began to seem. The bullet hole looked hardly more shocking than a Halloween transfer bought from a joke shop. As he gazed at it, it seemed to transform itself into a small flower, with lighter-coloured petals radiating from the livid centre. Marshall's face was becoming paler, and he noticed that his bare feet were darker and more purple than when he had arrived. The mouth had drifted a bit further open and he had the uncomfortable sensation that Marshall was appraising him from below the half-closed eyelids.

He left the room and opened the front door.

"Please go back inside, sir," said the leather jacket briskly.

"I need some fresh air."

"I believe you may be a target, sir," said the man with a mixture of formal politeness and impatience. "Please go back inside."

"Not on *your* watch, eh?" said Bryn, hoping to relax the atmosphere.

But his sentry was unimpressed.

"And close the door behind you if you don't mind, sir."

He did not return to the sitting room but lingered in the hallway. There was a pile of letters on a side table, a few of them roughly torn open, presumably by Marshall when he had got back from his last trip to New York. He flicked through them idly, more as a diversion from the sitting room than out of any particular curiosity.

The first two letters were clearly bills.

The third had no address, only the single word 'Marshall' on the envelope – in Marion's handwriting. It was still sealed. He turned it over in his hands and held it to his nose. He could not mistake her scent. He began to open it and then stopped. Not now. He slipped it sadly into his jacket pocket. For some later occasion perhaps.

He toyed with the remainder of the pile, trying to summon up interest. There were a couple of travel brochures and letters from *Who's Who* and *Debrett's People of Today* and a fair number of circulars and other unsolicited mail. A single sheet of paper, which had already been removed from its envelope, fell to the floor and he picked it up.

It was from a company in Gibraltar, in reply to a recent telephone enquiry, and the message it conveyed was brief but arresting. The letter informed Marshall that the current value of 'your investment' was 10.54 million euros.

He could see the leather-jacket through the Victorian stained-glass of the front door, still talking quietly into his mouthpiece. He walked around the house to pass the time. He looked into the state-of-the art kitchen, which Marshall never used. A cafetiere was standing in the sink, with two inches of hardening coffee grounds. He picked it up and swilled it clean under the tap. It was a familiar, cheap, supermarket model, not perhaps what Marshall would have chosen. He placed it gently on the marble work surface to drain.

He wandered past the music room, with its loudspeakers the size of fireplaces, towards the stairs and a more private part of the house he had never seen. Halfway up, he slowed to a halt. Through the door to the main bedroom, he could glimpse the foot of a large four-poster, and some clothes on a chair. He contemplated it for a while then retraced his steps, back to the front hall.

Propped against the wall beside the door was the coffin-like box Marshall had given him the previous evening and which he must absent-mindedly have laid down while they made their farewells; and quite forgotten. He sat down on the bottom step of the stairs and turned it over in his hands. It was surprisingly heavy. A paper label had been neatly pasted to it, with Marshall's name printed in small capitals above a scrawled signature: 'Jacksy'. Scribbled across all this was the dedication Marshall had then added the previous evening, in his barely legible hand. "For Bryn. My friend."

The box was secured with a tiny padlock. It would have been a small job to snap it off, but he fished a bunch of keys from his jacket pocket and sorted through them till he found the little skeleton he used for the padlock on his travelling bag. It fitted perfectly and the lock clicked open.

Inside the box, padded in satin, was a bottle of wine. Bryn thought himself something of a wine buff, but he had never seen one quite like this. It was made of an opaque, dark green glass, round-shouldered like a bowling pin and sealed at the top with thick black wax. The glass carried a few slight abrasions and he noticed that the bottle, as he revolved it between his fingers, was imperfectly symmetrical. He might have guessed that it was old even without its inscription. There was no label. Just a brief rubric, etched lightly into the glass: *1784 Lafitte Th:J*

For a moment he wondered whether he had been given something of real value. But then he began to reflect on its provenance, probably as dubious as its two previous owners. A flashy memento of a visit to a winery perhaps. The inscription was the give-away. If it was really meant to celebrate a famous claret, then they should at least have got the spelling right. But the initials on the bottle were a nice touch – a reference, he supposed, to America's third President, with an authentic colon after the first part of his name. He returned the bottle to its box and laid it carefully on the hall table.

The gravel drive crunched and Marcus came through the door, followed by the leather-jacket man.

"Are you OK?" he said.

Bryn nodded. He scrabbled around in his jacket until he found the piece of paper he was looking for. He tore a fragment off and gave it to Marcus.

"When I was passing the house, I saw Roosevelt leaving. This is the number of the car."

Marcus looked at it briefly and pocketed it. Then he went through into the sitting room and returned shortly with Bryn's umbrella.

"I believe this is yours," he said.

"Isn't it evidence?"

"No. Can we sit down somewhere?"

He ushered Bryn through into the kitchen and they perched on a couple of stainless steel bar-stools, Bryn clutching his umbrella.

"I don't want you involved," said Marcus, as if by explanation. "We've picked up Roosevelt at Heathrow. Of course, he didn't have any incriminating papers on him. He had left a rather nice attaché case in the car but the contents had been incinerated. Also, unfortunately, he seems to have been rather busy. Another important British contact died last night, similar modus operandi."

"Who was that?"

"No-one you would know. Fellow called Harry Darke."

"I know him. I know *of* him. He was an associate of Marshall's. Used to run a porn empire before he saw the light."

Marcus seemed briefly impressed.

"Well, then you'll be aware of the connection with Jack Smith. Dangerous man to know. And that's why I want you to take a low profile. *Very* low. The other reason is your relationship with me. It's unlikely we will be able to proceed against Roosevelt. He's never going to tell us anything and it's too political for the police. Plus any court proceedings would want to call you as a witness which would put you back in jeopardy and – more importantly – drag *my* name into it. There are other ways of skinning this cat. So please take your peculiar umbrella and forget everything that happened today."

To Bryn, this was as incredible as it was infuriating.

"What about the body, Marcus?" he said. "We *have* to call the police."

"Perhaps I'm not making myself clear."

There was a new and not particularly pleasant edge to Marcus's soft voice.

"You see the police will get it wrong. They will focus on the last person who admits to having seen the victim alive – especially if he also happens to be the first person to see him dead. And how would you handle the interrogation, Bryn? How would you deal with obvious questions like: might there be a reason why you would want Marshall dead? How well did he know your wife, for example? Did he by any chance know you were having an affair with someone else, a younger model possibly? Questions like that..."

He tailed off, almost apologetically.

Bryn was at a loss for a reply.

"OK," said Marcus, at last. "I will make sure the police stay out of this. And of course if anybody asks, you have never been here. You understand? Your friend died of a heart attack. If you don't believe me, read about it in the papers in a couple of days' time."

"I can't tell lies, Marcus," said Bryn, when he had found his voice. "It's not what I do."

"Oh really?"

His cousin raised an archly theatrical eyebrow. Bryn realized, as doubtless he was meant to realize, that there was very little now that Marcus did *not* know about his adventures.

"Look..." said the other. His tone was more amenable. "I'll keep in touch, you can rely on that. If you have any trouble, let me know *right* away. In return, I'll keep you up to speed on any developments that might concern you. Is that a deal?"

It wasn't much of a deal at all. And Bryn wondered whether he could reliably fulfil his own end of it, without error and absent-mindedness. Yet he knew well enough how glad he would be to put this latest business back in a dark hole with all the rest; where he might – more or less – forget it. From that point of view, Marcus' proposal was not unreasonable.

"OK," he agreed.

When they returned to the hall, the leather-jacketed man was examining the contents of the open wine box.

"Sorry, sir," he said. "Is this yours?"

"No. I think you'll find it belonged to the deceased... I don't want it."

Marcus, as Marshall had done the day before, watched him cross the gravel drive to the road. But this time, after a moment's hesitation, he turned left instead of right and carried on downhill towards his much-delayed meeting with Ken Burns.

Chapter 25

The meeting turned out to be more significant than he had anticipated. Ken was looking for somebody to coordinate his burgeoning project for the exchange of foreign lecturers and students. There would have to be an open competition of some kind, but Bryn – in Ken's opinion (and Ken's opinion, notwithstanding the formal proprieties, was the only one of substance here) – was the man for the job. He would of course move up a salary grade.

Bryn heard all this through in a daze. He had gone straight from Marcus to Ken's office, pretty well on autopilot. It was one thing to conduct himself as though he had never visited Marshall's house that morning, quite another to overlay the experience with a cheerful facsimile of normal behaviour. How other people accomplished it he could not imagine. He kept his gaze unflinchingly on Ken while he rehearsed the reasons why Bryn was the *ideal* candidate, and nodded from time to time to convey attention. But he was preoccupied by that last image of Marshall in his chair. Not that it was an especially clear or graphic image. The details had been rubbed over by shock and he resisted the impulse to clarify them. And yet, hard as he tried to focus on other matters – Ken's bland features, in particular – the image hovered in his mind like the backdrop to a play.

When it was apparent that Ken had finished, he asked for a few days to think about it. He did not mention the rival offer from Utah. But he did remember just in time – as he was leaving the office – to thank Ken for his consideration.

He was intercepted by the faculty secretary. Would he call home immediately, please?

The phone was answered not by Marion but by Janet. He was touched by the delicacy and concern with which she broke the news. Marshall's Polish housekeeper had found his body when she came in that morning. That was all anyone knew at this stage. And no, there was no information either about cause of death – one assumed 'natural causes'. Yes, he would return home immediately.

Marion was in the kitchen, being comforted by Janet. Her eyes were puffy with tears. Janet, perhaps accustomed to loss, had become quite matter-of-fact and business-like. But she seemed surprised – even shocked – by his lack of more than token solicitude for his wife's distress.

He was a little shocked himself. After Janet had gone, he volunteered to cook a meal – an act so unusual that it cheered Marion up more effectively than a conventional act of comfort.

He busied himself with the only dish he knew she would trust him to make successfully, which was what he called *croque-monsieur* and she more prosaically *welsh rarebit*; though his toasted open sandwich of ham, grated parmesan and worcester sauce was probably neither one thing nor the other. He did not ask her, as he worked, how she had learnt of Marshall's death or how she felt about it. She in turn helped things along by asking him instead about his own day, whom he had seen, what he had done.

This was how it always was. The mutual blandness which had long been their normal default position had its advantages of course. It allowed passing difficulties to wither and it helped them avoid unproductive confrontation. They had been fortunate that, for the greater part of their marriage, there had been no really inescapable issues between them. But both had begun to sense that they might now finally have arrived at a watershed in their relationship. They were still fearful of the consequences of acknowledging it, to each other or even themselves. In the end it was Bryn who took the initiative, though the small grenade he lobbed into the conversation was less of an assault upon the issue than a tactical sortie across its flanks.

"I've had two job offers this week," he said.

"Oh!"

She looked surprised. He took the two slices of bread off the grill and started piling the cheese and ham on the untoasted sides.

"Are you going to tell me about them?"

He put the slices to one side and turned round to face her. Whatever he said now would surely determine the future of their marriage.

"Ken asked me today whether I would head up the international operation. It would be additional to my normal duties which as you know are not onerous. And there would be a salary increase. I would have an office of my own in Gower Street and other advantages."

"That's fine, Bryn. If that's really what you want, go for it."

And now he was coming to the point.

"And there's another. I don't know if it's certain. I may be offered a professorship in Salt Lake City."

"I know," she said.

He looked at her uncomprehendingly.

"Dan rang while you were away. He didn't want to send the letter if it would be unwelcome. I said I thought you would probably jump at it."

"Dan said that?"

"Yes."

"And you told him I would take it?"

"Well I wasn't going to give him the answer he was really after," she said sharply.

"Which was what?"

"He wanted me to tell him that I would go along with whatever you did, like a good little woman. But I wasn't going to give him the satisfaction."

270

She looked at him unblinkingly but he could see she was trembling.

He had no idea what to think.

"Does that mean you want me to go?" he asked.

"If that's what you want."

"While you stayed in London."

"If that's what you want."

She had always made it clear that she had no desire to give up that part of her life she had built for herself, her school, her friends. That was why, when they talked early in the year about the Nathan Bedford Forrest job, he had agreed that she would stay in London and he would return as frequently as his duties allowed. At that time of course he had not known that she had another quite different reason for wanting to stay behind.

He turned away to attend to the slices of half-toasted bread.

"Do you want me to stay in London?" she asked, to his back.

He placed the piled-high slices back in the blazing hot grill, and waited to make sure he knew exactly what he wanted to say.

"I think if I go to America alone, that will be the end for us," he said at last.

There was no reply. The cheese was bubbling. He took the slices down and ladled them onto separate plates and brought them round to the table in front of her. He searched around in a drawer for some knives and forks.

It was a terrible moment. The genie was out of the bottle; and he did not regret it. The difficulty of course was that he did not know whether Dan's offer was what he wanted. If he was not careful, he could wind up going to America simply in order to resolve their marriage. It was right that their differences were in the open. But that did not mean that he had to force them to a conclusion.

"If you do not want to come," he added, "I can take the UCL job."

She shook her head.

"I think you should go to America," she replied. "I said so to Dan and I meant it. I think you need a new beginning."

"You make me sound like a pioneer," he said sadly. "Off to the New World I go."

She took his hands in hers and gripped them – so tightly that he grimaced with the pain.

"I think we should both start again," she said. "That is, if you are happy for me to come with you."

Marcus was right of course about the cause of death. The obituaries in the more serious newspapers all referred to a heart attack. The Guardian mentioned in passing a 'long-standing cardiac condition'. The quality of the writers was impressive, including the shadow Home Secretary and a retired Master of the Rolls, who (respectively) regretted the loss to the nation of a potential Attorney General and future Law Lord.

The funeral took place the following week and was a small, private affair in the West Midlands from which all but Marshall's closest relatives were excluded. The family let it be known, however, that a special memorial service was planned at which Marshall's wider circle of friends would have an opportunity to pay their last respects. Arrangements were made for it to be held at St George's Church, Hanover Square, followed by a reception at Marshall's old club, the Garrick.

Meantime, rather more attention – in the tabloids at least – was given to the equally unexpected demise of Harry Darke OBE. Though reported initially as the sad loss of a man who had almost single-handedly fought for traditional public values in television and the cinema, his earlier history soon leaked out. Marcus seemed again to have been successful in recalibrating the cause of death: this time it was reported as a fatal stroke. But he failed to prevent one ex-employee, no longer constrained by fears of retribution, from revealing to the *Sunday Sport* the sordid origins of his boss's fortune.

As the outrage built, the American headquarters of *GodWorks* speedily disowned the UK branch of its organization and severed all links. With the story continuing to unravel, it next emerged that the companies controlled by Darke had fallen into deep financial difficulty. Assets had been siphoned off to various untraceable overseas locations; it was generally assumed that Darke himself was responsible. The *Daily Mail*, for so long one of his most vociferous supporters, ran a front page picture of his shiny, bespectacled face below the banner headline: 'Is this the greatest hypocrite of our time?' But with no living person left to pursue, the editor soon lost interest, the story ran into the sand and the paper's journalists moved on to the next available outrage. Unsurprisingly, no connection was ever made between the simultaneous passing of two men who, as a little research might have revealed, were as closely linked in life as they were in death.

The intervening period was a busy one for Bryn. He still did not know whether he wanted to accept Ken's offer or go for the Salt Lake City job, and the process of keeping both in suspension was quite time-consuming. He was relieved when the college bureaucracy prevented Ken from making the formal offer that would have put him on the spot. The job had to be advertised internally – not, sadly, externally which would have imposed an even longer time scale – and interview dates agreed some weeks in advance.

On the other hand, he was anxious not to disabuse Ken of his keenness for the post, in case he should finally decide that it *was*, after all, what he wanted. Unfortunately Ken was already planning – 'off the record and strictly between ourselves of course' – a number of overseas meetings (with a fair amount of preparatory work) which would require an early commitment from him. In the end he felt obliged to set his students a full schedule of projects and essays for the new term – something they had become comfortably unaccustomed to – so that the pressure of supervision would justify, for the time being, his persistent unavailability.

The Americans, by contrast, were less pressing. Their remoteness and unfamiliarity with British ways, even in this email age, gave him some latitude. They did not ask him to explain himself when he said he had to sort out his present contractual position (no problem really, but it *would* require a little more time…). But the main reason for their lack of urgency was that Bryn's prospective departmental head in Salt Lake City was temporarily distracted by other matters. The convention season was rapidly approaching and he was advising the Mormon candidate for the vice-presidential nomination.

In one of those developments so characteristic of American politics, an east coast newspaper had published a list of Capitol Hill clients of *Cherry Grove*, a Washington establishment variously described as a bordello, cathouse, massage parlor or bunny ranch. Most of the presidential candidates, including the Mormon, were tumbling over each other to express outrage. The current front-runner, the former Governor of Minnesota, had trumped the rest with a fiery and effective speech which revealed an under-appreciated evangelical streak and pledged his administration to clean up Congress and (here he quoted the Gospel of St Mark, Chapter Eleven) "cast the unworthy out of the temple."

The day before the memorial service, Bryn had lunch again with Marcus at the Travellers Club – their first lunch together since they had met at Merryweather's in April. On his way in, Bryn stopped at his bank and retrieved the photograph he had put away in his mother's security envelope. This time fortune smiled upon him and he was able to slip in and out of the building without incurring further advice about his chronically unimproved finances.

It was a Monday and few Travellers had yet made it in from their weekends. Marcus, however, was in exuberant form. He led the way to a table at the far end of the dining room, separated by half the length of the chamber from a small handful of other diners.

The waiter approached with a bottle of champagne in a silver bucket which he placed alongside them on a trestle stand.

"I have already ordered for both of us," said Marcus. "Pâté de foie, main course lobster, plum duff. Hope that's OK."

"Are we celebrating something, Marcus?" asked Bryn.

"Good question. Really good question."

While one waiter placed their starter plates in front of them and another uncorked and distributed the champagne, Marcus moved seamlessly to the latest news of a very old mutual aunt with whom, characteristically, he alone of all her nephews had managed to keep in touch. Bryn reflected that his own last visit to her tiny Oswestry bungalow had been a shameful decade or more previously. His cousin's energy and range of commitment never ceased to astonish and impress and irritate him. And today, even by his own ebullient standards, Marcus was on an exceptional high.

When the waiters had withdrawn, he thrust his champagne flute high into the air. Bryn demurely copied him.

"Congratulations," Marcus beamed, and tipped the wine back down his throat in a single draught.

"Congratulations?"

"Yes. A job well done, which we could *never* have managed without you. Thanks to you – well partly to you – I think I can claim that we are in a more influential position now with our American cousins than we have been for... well... rather a long time. Enjoy your pâté and your shampoo and I'll bring you up to date."

He was quite unbearable. It was as if, now that he had dropped all pretence of being a modestly anonymous foreign office apparatchik, he had no compunction about displaying the arrogant know-all he had always been. Bryn noted in particular that there was no longer any of that fake-deferential business of yielding to Bryn's 'superior intellect'. This was Marcus in his pomp; and Bryn was the groundling to his performance.

"Of course we did not get a great deal out of Roosevelt. He's too professional for that. He was completely clean when we picked him up at Heathrow – not even a gun. But we took all his biometrics – fingerprints, eyes, DNA – and we can make sure he's no longer able to come here or travel anywhere in Europe. We've also passed the data to the CIA. So I think that really is the end of Roosevelt as an effective.

"But the best part of it is what we've learned as a consequence of Harry Darke's death. Killing him was a *big* mistake because it put the fear of God – and I mean that quite literally – into Darke's number two. He could not run into our arms fast enough. He's spilt a lot of really useful information. The Americans are gagging for it. Great situation. Great situation."

He emitted a brazen, self-satisfied guffaw.

"Congratulations," said Bryn, sardonically.

Marcus ignored him.

"Of course I can't tell you anything about *that*."

He flicked his fingers at a waiter for more champagne. A couple of fellow Club members acknowledged him from the far end of the room and he waved cheerily back.

"But I *can* tell you about your friend Marshall," he continued. "Would you believe that he had been secretly siphoning funds out of the *GodWorks* organization, with the help of the sidekick?"

"Dave Devine," said Bryn.

"Yes. Mr David Devine," echoed Marcus. "Very good. Have you met him?"

"Seen him," said Bryn.

"Well then, you probably know about him. Very private guy, no social life, no friends, totally locked into computers, and God of course. Originally, he was recruited to manage the British *GodWorks* database, but then his talents really flowered. Word spread and Darke lent him to the American organization for a period, during which he hacked into the PCs of the politicians and government officials Smith was targeting. But he also seems around that time to have fallen under the spell of your friend Marshall. Because the first thing he did when he got back to the UK was to divert *GodWorks'* own money into a private slush fund, controlled by the pair of them together. Unfortunately he hadn't quite learnt enough then about covering his tracks. A lot of the cash belonged to the American organization and, sometime earlier this year, Smith found out about the slush fund.

"In the meantime, however, Devine had moved onto other things. He had managed to develop a worm, a programme, which actually allowed him to break into *anyone*'s internet bank account and siphon off cash. The technique was never to take out too much at one time. And there was a clever built-in delay before any details could come up on screen; and after that – and this is the best bit – an automatic alert to the *banks* so that they could repair the damage before account-holders noticed. That way client confidence in the online system would not be undermined.

"For Marshall and Devine, this was the really big one. We don't know how much they salted away in various off-shore havens, but it was a lot more than they got out of *GodWorks*. By the autumn they were ready to cash in and disappear.

"Great plan, *bad* timing. Smith had already decided that Marshall at least had to be terminated. You were the complication. Were you and Marshall planning together to blackmail him? It took him till late summer to establish – to his own satisfaction – that no-one except you and Marshall had seen the papers in the attaché case. Then the way was clear to finish both of you off and that's why he sent Roosevelt into Virginia after you. With Marshall next on the hit list. I don't know why he had to kill Darke as well. Maybe to ensure his silence."

"Wow," said Bryn.

Marcus smiled smugly.

"And this you've got from interrogating Dave Devine?"

"Chiefly," said Marcus. "And a deal of other stuff besides about the nature of Smith's organization, and what he holds on a number of Senators and officials. We haven't yet shared that with our friends in Washington. Of course they know in broad terms what we've got, but the devil is in the details. And that's what makes our position so *very* interesting. We're keeping Devine safely under wraps. For his own sake, naturally…

"The way Smith is behaving is very interesting too. He

277

obviously knows we have information on him. And yet he has shown no sign at all, not a glimmer, of concern. He is still maintaining a high political profile. Why is that? Is he not scared that some of the bad stuff will come out? He seems very confident."

"Maybe he doesn't believe the Brits have enough credibility. Or that you won't want to reveal your hand and lose your leverage," Bryn suggested.

"Maybe," said Marcus. "Or maybe he has other fish to fry…"

They had arrived at the plum pudding and Marcus summoned the list of dessert wines. He had barely begun to study it when a new thought seemed to strike him.

"Excuse me," he said, and left the table.

The waiter removed the wine list from Bryn's field of view.

"I expect he has gone to the loo," said Bryn after a while.

"I don't think so, sir," said the waiter.

When Marcus returned, he was carrying a Harrods bag. He placed it in the middle of the table in front of Bryn.

"This is a thank you present," he said in explanation. "That parcel you got from your late friend gave me the idea."

Inside was a wooden wine box not very different from the one Marshall had handed to him a few weeks previously, except that the scrawled dedication this time was from 'Marcus and the boys'. He opened it and there, suspended within a slender framework of wood scaffolding, was a bottle of Chateau Lafite-Rothschild 2001.

"You can drink it now," said Marcus.

"You mean *now*?"

"Well, it's up to you."

The wine waiter was already hovering.

"Well thank you, Marcus," he said. "You really didn't need to go to such trouble."

"Oh, I think so," said his cousin. "You ought to get something out of all this… you could think of it as a special present from Jack Smith, if you like."

He chuckled quietly to himself. Then he made a sign to the waiter.

The plum duffs were whisked away. The Lafite was painstakingly dribbled into a wide-bottomed decanter in front of them, and a chariot of English and continental cheeses trundled into view.

After the waiters had withdrawn, Bryn recalled that he too had a small gift to bestow. He burrowed into the old briefcase he had parked beside his chair and brought it out.

"This is something I probably should have given you before," he said. "It was in the attaché case, along with the other papers I told you about. It's too complicated to explain why I still have a copy. But if it was important to Smith then I guess it might be important to you too."

And he handed to Marcus the envelope he had retrieved from the bank earlier that day. Marcus looked at him in a mix of mild wonderment and boredom, and opened it. He glanced at the picture briefly.

"Marshall," he confirmed. "Taken a long time ago. Wouldn't have guessed he was into that kind of behaviour though." He shrugged his shoulders in a pantomime of indifference and began to slip the photograph back into its envelope.

And then he stiffened. He *froze*.

For two or three seconds, he sat across the table staring at Bryn as if paralysed, his mouth slightly open, one hand still halfway into the envelope. Then his eyes moved slowly downwards to his hand and he withdrew the photograph and placed it carefully on the table in front of him.

When he spoke, his ebullience had entirely faded. His voice was quiet and serious.

"You really should have given this to me a long time ago," he said, still gazing at the picture. "I think it might have prevented most of the unpleasantness of the last nine months."

He returned the picture to its envelope. He looked up at Bryn and smiled thinly.

"Game, set and match. What can I say... thank you, old boy."

Chapter 26

St George's, Hanover Square, is the parish church of Mayfair and has been for nearly three hundred years. In the eighteenth century, the open countryside was barely half a mile away to the north and west, the Serpentine was a sequence of ponds and Hyde Park was the royal hunting ground. The church itself was erected in the grandly unimaginative style of its times, with neo-classical portico and Wren-style bell tower. A Virginian gentleman from pre-revolutionary Williamsburg or Jamestown could have gazed upon it and felt entirely at home.

The memorial service was scheduled for eleven o'clock but Marion and Bryn arrived early. They had thought to spend a little time looking around the building before the congregation arrived, but already there was a small crowd of busy people inside. Portable lights were being discreetly erected beside the pillars, and a sound engineer was running a cable to a small microphone in the chancel. Someone whom they later identified as the shadow Home Secretary was standing in the pulpit rehearsing part of his tribute. Another man was being coached by a middle-aged lady with a clip-board into how to process from his seat in the pews to a side aisle alongside the chancel, and thence into the pulpit, after the shadow minister had finished. They were surprised to recognize the chief executive of the Football Association; but then Bryn recalled that he had been a friend since Marshall had once helped the FA fend off the government by chairing a temporizing enquiry into hooliganism.

It was not a huge church, but airy and grand. There were galleries on three sides, probably intended originally for the wives but now for late arrivals to the memorial service and for the less privileged who had not been given numbered tickets. At the east end, the chancel, with its chequered black-and-white marble floor, was as bare and tidy as a Dutch interior. Beyond it by contrast was a splendidly excessive eighteenth century painting of the Last Supper in an elaborate dark wood frame.

They picked up a copy of the order of service from a table at the back of the nave, and took their ticketed places in one of the red velvet cushioned pews in the body of the church; and waited.

Some time before the time appointed, the organist began to play. It was a quiet, sad little piece by César Franck – so simple that Bryn found himself day-dreaming a version for recorder ensemble. He imagined the winding melody, constantly turning back upon itself as if frightened to lose touch with its beginning, being played in descant unison by Guy and Marshall. The long pedal notes would be perfect for him and Bill on tenor and bass. He could hear Graeme's soprano recorder dotting in the disturbing little off-beats.

Funerals always heightened his emotions. He supposed it was the same for everyone else, but, looking around, wondered for how many of them attendance was more a matter of social duty than sentiment. As on a previous occasion, people tended to come in representative groups, wrapped within their own separateness. There were, so far as he could tell, no Rotarians this time. But he guessed that one bunch of men in dark, rather weathered suits, talking quietly amongst themselves, might be Members of Parliament or civil servants. A smaller group signalled their origins more flagrantly with their pea-green and salmon pink Garrick ties: the only Club garment, as the old joke went, which told you not only where its owner had lunched, but also what he had eaten.

The church was already quite full and seats were being taken in the gallery as well. He caught sight of a man threading his way along the front row a few feet above him. Behind the man, with a hand permanently on his shoulder, was a thick-set, rain-coated individual in whose charge he clearly was. A carer perhaps; or a plain clothes policeman or prison officer possibly?

He did not for a while recognize the first man. And then a memory of someone briefly glimpsed through a window in North Ealing returned to him. It was Dave Devine, the computer genius. The flesh-coloured spectacles, with the little tag of sticking plaster at the junction of frame and plastic arm; a lank forelock drifting over the eyes; a blue tie in a too-large Windsor knot; a fawn corduroy jacket worn quite out of shape. The man took off his glasses and wiped the lenses with a crusty grey handkerchief and then, more surreptitiously, his cheeks.

"Do you know the lady?" whispered Marion.

She inclined her head in the direction of a couple who were about to take their seats on the other side of the aisle. The man was large and – uniquely of anyone in this building – wearing dark, reflective sunglasses. He registered Bryn's interest at once and stared straight back at him. His demeanour – notwithstanding their sanctified location – was palpably threatening. Bryn held his gaze. He had seen men like this in the atrium of the Waldorf Astoria, where such behaviour might have been less inappropriate.

And then he saw that the heavy's companion – a matronly lady dressed throughout in black, with a small toque-like hat from which a fringe of net hung over her forehead – was also looking at him. He had no difficulty recalling her. It was Miss Gloria Teasdale, whom he had last seen in the Royal Suite at Claridge's at the start of the year.

"Miss Teasdale," he said. "What a surprise."

There was something about her manner which suggested that she recognized him but could not remember yet who he was. Instead of enquiring directly, she smiled at him blankly for a moment – possibly hoping he would volunteer the needful

282

information. Meantime, the bodyguard continued to scan the congregation as if he expected a pin-stripe suited terrorist to erupt from one of the pews with a handgun and a Molotov cocktail.

"Mr Smith has been detained by the Convention," she offered vaguely. "Otherwise he would have come himself. Mr Marshall was a very good friend."

And then the penny, or the cent, seemed to drop.

"Aren't you the gentleman who came for the university job?" she said.

"Indeed I am," said Bryn.

"Yes I know who you are," she said, with a sudden flash of hostility.

The bodyguard stepped instinctively alongside her.

"No problem," said Bryn.

And then, before he could stop himself: "We've accepted another post. At a more prestigious American university, I'm afraid."

She sat down abruptly and the bodyguard placed himself next to the aisle. The conversation was at an end.

As the organist changed to a more assertive voluntary and the choir and rector of St George's began to process down the nave to the chancel, Marion turned to Bryn and whispered again in his ear. This time he could not make out what she had said, though he could guess. He nodded and she squeezed his arm. It was a tiny, trivial moment; and one he knew at once he would remember for the rest of his life.

The service was unexpectedly entertaining. The hymns were bracing old Victorian tunes and the small professional choir sang, exquisitely, a couple of Tudor motets. There were five contributions from the pulpit, all warmly affectionate – the memories of friends and colleagues from different stages of Marshall's life. A picture began to emerge of an altogether wittier, more self-deprecating, relaxed, happy, companionable character than the person Bryn recognized. Who, he wondered, had known him best?

Then he found himself harking back to Marcus's remark just before they had parted the previous day and the suggestion that somehow *he* might have prevented the 'unpleasantness' of the past year – including, in that case, Marshall's own death. It was a bleakly troubling thought that had not been far from his mind since. But now, under the influence of this relentless flow of unmediated tribute, he felt the clouds begin to lift a little and some sunlight filter through. He looked at his wife sitting beside him. How very different the memorialized Marshall was from the secret man they had both known. In this, the official version, there would be no mention of his troubled private life; or of the web of theft and embezzlement and projected flight from retribution and taxation.

He mourned his friend, genuinely. But he now perceived that, even as they had sat together on that last evening, Marshall had already, quite lucidly, chosen death rather than flight. He had known – somehow – that Roosevelt was on his way. It would have been clear to that dry, forensic mind that the glowing encomia of the memorial service, which he surely anticipated, could never have outlasted his survival.

The congregation roared at an anecdote from a fellow QC about their days together in pupillage. Bryn glanced again at Marion. She was not laughing and her eyes had filled up. He looked away quickly. He reflected that the pair of them, like Marshall, had the power to choose either of two possible narratives. One, perhaps the more conventional, would require them to examine their bad consciences together, frankly and honestly. He felt her hand reach into his. She was trembling and he squeezed her fingers until she became calm. Like Marshall, he preferred an alternative, less candid but also less damaging, narrative.

After the last laughter had subsided, the rector tactfully wound up proceedings with a formal reminder of the Christian context of the service. The organ played Bach extremely loudly, and the choir and rector led the way out.

The reception was at the Garrick itself, just up the road from

Leicester Square underground station. Rather less than half the congregation had been invited. Apart from the small Ealing contingent, nearly all of them were Garrick Club members or, for a rare treat, their wives. Most went from Hanover Square by taxi; a small handful – like Marion and Bryn – walked. As they passed a street waste bin on Shaftesbury Avenue, Bryn pulled out Marion's last letter to Marshall, which had lain in his pocket unopened since that day, and discreetly dropped it in.

He had never been to the Garrick before. He had always thought of it as the rather dirty and featureless East European building on the way to Covent Garden. But a major clean had revealed an austerely handsome brownstone exterior that would not have been out of place in Boston, Massachusetts. The public entrance was as tightly policed to prevent riff-raff as you might expect of such an exclusive establishment. Bryn and Marion's *bona fides* once established, they were directed up the stairs, away from the main male-only members' area, to the reception in the 'Old Card Room'.

There was a very pleasant spread of canapés and wine. He was sorting a generous selection of mini-blinis, cheese and celeriac tartlets, tiny mushroom frittatas, bite-size fillets of beef, quails' eggs and savoury meat balls onto his plate, when his friend Bill plucked him by the sleeve. He had been dreading this moment.

"Have you brought your tenor?"

"I'm afraid so," replied Bryn gloomily. "I don't suppose you've forgotten your bass?"

"I have not," said Bill. "It's picnic time."

Bryn looked past him to the end of the room, where Janet was arranging two chairs and two music stands. One of Marshall's Garrick friends, a celebrated television actor, cleared his throat stertorously.

"Fellow Members, ladies and gentlemen," he intoned. "There is one more important function to be performed. As I think many of you know, one of Marshall's greatest loves was music. Now I think it's fair to say that his talent – his *forte*, dare I suggest – lay more in appreciation than performance. But he did play the recorder. Indeed, it is a well-kept secret that he had been part of a group from Ealing which has played together for..."

He looked across at Bill and Bryn, busily screwing together the various elements of their instruments.

"Twenty years," said Bryn.

"Twenty-five years," said Bill.

"A long time," said the actor. "And two members of that group are here today to, in a sense, play him out. Please welcome Bill and..."

"Bryn," said Bryn.

The crowd in the room became respectfully silent.

"It's a very short piece," said Bryn, "and you will all know it. It may seem a strange choice for an occasion like this, though in fact we have played it once previously at a funeral. It was the signature theme of our group and the one Marshall would certainly have wanted us to play today. This will also be the last time we shall ever perform it."

Janet had done the arrangement. She had been tempted to include the keyboard, but understood that this time it could only be Bill and Bryn. In ingeniously reducing the five original parts to two, however, she had produced a uniquely difficult version which, though they had managed to practice it a little beforehand, compelled them to play now more carefully and slowly than they ever had before. The jaunty rhythms as a result were transformed into a sad and mysterious threnody. They played as quietly as they could without losing tone or pitch, and the effect was of something distantly remembered. The audience listened with a gratifying attentiveness. Not even the clink of a wineglass.

If you go down to the woods today...

As he played, Bryn began to think not so much about those occasions before when they had played the little tune, but about what might lie in the future. His mind wandered away to the white spires of Salt Lake City and that strange community that was so different and separate from the rest of America. A community where music had unusual priority and where no-one would find the idea of grown men meeting once a month to play together on their plastic recorders in the least bit surprising.

He liked the idea. A new recorder group would be his first American project.

When they reached the end of the piece, there was a polite silence and a ripple of applause. What the Garrick had made of their interlude was anyone's guess. The two performers smiled back gratefully and began to break down and pack away their instruments.

As he was zipping up his music bag, Bryn realized with irritation that one of the members had, throughout their performance and quite blatantly, been watching a television programme on what looked like an iPhone. He peered over his shoulder: it was a news channel transmitting breaking stories. He could be grateful at least that the member's earplug had prevented him sharing the sound track with the rest of their audience.

Marion joined him.

"Would you like to come home?" she whispered.

He kissed her. She held him dangerously close and ran a hand under his jacket. It was an enjoyably HM Bateman moment. All it needed to be complete was a smart tap on the shoulder for behaviour so unbefitting to these august and woman-fearing premises; and ejection swifter than clay pigeons from a target launcher...

After Bryn and Marion had slipped away, Bill – a little the worse for wear – stayed on. His new drinking partner, the man with the mobile news coverage, was happy to share the transmission with him.

Two stories dominated, both – typically enough – from America.

The lead one was about an amazing auction that had just closed in Sotheby's New York, at which a new world record had been set for a single bottle of wine. The record breaker was a fully authenticated 1784 Lafitte (with the unusual but correct eighteenth century spelling of two 't' s). It was the last bottle of its vintage known still to be in existence, and its value was greatly enhanced by the fact that it had once been owned by America's third President, Thomas Jefferson, the greatest vinophile of his day. The gavel had come down for the last time on a winning bid of $250,000. The vendor wished to remain anonymous; and the delighted buyer, a Virginia billionaire, had declared that the precious bottle would never be opened but would remain at the centre of his collection, for ever.

The second item was some live coverage from that week's presidential nominating convention in Los Angeles. But what it lacked, relatively speaking, in headline appeal it more than made up for in significance.

The nominee, the former Governor of Minnesota, could be seen arriving at the podium with his vice-presidential running mate. The polls indicated a landslide victory in two months' time over the candidate for the other main party, a liberal black woman senator. Cameras swooped over the wildly acclaiming crowd while a band played the National Anthem and streamers in the colours of the American flag cascaded from the ceiling. The future President introduced the future Vice President to the nation.

His running mate – a choice that had surprised most of the pundits – was none other than the Congressman for the 7th District of South Carolina, Jack C Smith. The television channel's political commentator, who seemed to share the unpreparedness of his colleagues, was resorting to familiar clichés. Jack Smith was an enigma, *politically untested* and relatively unknown, the man who would be a *heartbeat away* from the presidency. But it was a *winning combination*: the South Carolinan's southern and evangelical appeal and the northern and more mainstream credentials of the Presidential nominee.

The television camera eased back from a close two-shot to a wider framing. As it did so, the two candidates, simultaneously and on cue, raised their outside arms to the massed crowd and the worldwide audience beyond. Bill leaned forward to study the face of the handsome, smiling man standing beside Jack Smith. It was a face still relatively unknown to audiences outside America but destined to become the most famous in the world. Bill wondered what kind of president he would be. A Kennedy or Clinton? A Bush? He searched the confident, beaming face for clues.

Bryn would not catch up with the news for a few days. Nevertheless – and in common with a *few* other privileged onlookers in London – he would not find the enigma of the vice-presidential candidate and the likely rôle of the future president too difficult to penetrate. Because the individual beside whom Jack C Smith now stood was – more than thirty years on but with good looks still intact – none other than the companion of Marshall's youthful indiscretion. It was the other man in the photograph which Bryn, only the day before, had handed to his cousin Marcus.

Lightning Source UK Ltd.
Milton Keynes UK
UKOW02f1809190814

237198UK00001B/23/P